I0685726

COMING HOME TO BYLAND CRESCENT

An absolutely heartbreaking and unputdownable
historical family saga

BILL KITSON

The Cowgill Family Saga Book 3

Originally published as
Retribution

Revised edition 2022
Joffe Books, London
www.joffebooks.com

First published in Great Britain in 2019
as *Retribution*

This paperback edition was first published
in Great Britain in 2022

Cover art by Jarmila Takač

ISBN: 978-1-80405-147-4

For Val
My wife, lover and best friend.
Also my copyeditor, continuity girl, proofreader and agent.
So many reasons to admire her talents.
So many more reasons to love her.

PROLOGUE

In Britain, the post-war social change was dramatic — for many it was traumatic. Gone was the empire that had once seen over half the countries in a world atlas coloured red. It had been replaced with a commonwealth, a vastly different body. Gone at last was the power of the aristocracy, finally blown away by the winds of war. Gone were the Bright Young Things of the twenties and thirties, their brightness either dimmed or snuffed out by the dark clouds of strife, their hopeful youth turned to world-weary acceptance. In post-war Britain the struggle for survival against the tyranny of an evil oppressor had been won — just.

Now, an impoverished and careworn nation faced another, equally daunting challenge, or rather the twin challenges before them. Having survived the war, they now had to survive the peace. Not only that but they had to wrestle with the fight to recover, to accept renewal and social change.

It was the dawn of a new age, although few would have recognized it as such. It would be an age ruled by the common people, their manifesto — the common good of all the people. The rule of the plutocrat had been replaced by that of the proletariat. How permanent that rule would be was questionable.

All over Britain, as the country came off a war footing, men were returning home. The dreadful toll exacted on many towns and cities by enemy bombers meant that a lot of them would have no home to return to. For others, the homecoming would be a bitter one, for quite different reasons. Women who had been alone for up to six years found it difficult to adjust to the presence of someone who had become a virtual stranger. Others had been either unable, or unwilling, to wait and had made other domestic arrangements.

Even when there was no other cause for disharmony, the dreadful acts of war that had been witnessed by some of the returning soldiers had left scars that were both physical and mental. Some of these would take a long time to heal. Others would never heal.

The former combatants returned to a Britain that had changed immeasurably. The British Empire was no more, in truth it had been close to ending when war broke out. Those countries from within it that had spent years fighting for the cause of freedom, saw no purpose in remaining under the domination of a small island off the coast of Europe.

Many British soldiers found it difficult to adjust to a world where their wives had become accustomed to living independently, making their own decisions, following their own instincts. That independence stretched beyond their domestic arrangements. With the majority of the nation's workforce, be it in factories or farms having been co-opted into the task of fighting the enemy, their jobs had been taken up by a formidable army of female volunteers or conscripts.

Not only were they by now accustomed to fending for themselves, but the novelty of earning their own wages rather than having to rely on their partner's housekeeping allowance was a luxury they were extremely reluctant to forego.

This created huge and immediate problems on two fronts. The returning combatants had to become accustomed to the presence of a new breadwinner in the house, but they were also faced with the difficult task of seeking post-war employment. This search was hampered as many of those jobs and skills they had previously regarded as theirs by right were no longer available through mechanisation.

This created a massive pool of unemployment, made worse by the semi-stagnation of British industry, which had to face enormous challenges. Their first task was to convert the production of armaments and similar articles of war to items more suitable for peacetime. This was a slow process.

Some things hadn't changed. Rationing remained, and with it, strict limits on food, on clothing, on petrol and other essentials would stay in place, in some instances for almost a decade after the cessation of hostilities. There were those, who, in the early years of hardship, questioned whether the cause had been worth the effort, but gradually, as facts emerged about the full horrors inflicted by the evil regime they had been fighting, these feelings of discontent subsided.

As with Britain, so many other nations were coming to terms with the difficulties that remained in a post-war society. Twice, within thirty years, the cream of a generation had been called upon to fight, to kill, and in many cases, to pay the ultimate sacrifice. They had been asked to do this to protect a lifestyle they cherished and believed in — only to discover on their return that the way of life they had defended so stoutly had changed beyond recognition.

PART ONE: 1946–1948

"If in some smothering dreams you too could pace
Behind the wagon that we flung him in,
And watch the white eyes writhing in his face,
His hanging face, like a devil's sick of sin:
If you could hear, at every jolt, the blood
Come gargling from the froth-corrupted lungs,
Obscene as cancer, bitter as the cud
Of vile, incurable sores on innocent tongues,
My friend, you would not tell with such high zest
To children ardent for some desperate glory,
The old Lie: Dulce et Decorum est
Pro Patria Mori."

Wilfred Owen (1893–1918)
Excerpt from 'Dulce et Decorum est'

CHAPTER ONE

In Byland Crescent, Sonny Cowgill glanced out of the window of his Scarborough home, his expression as bleak as the weather. Even one whose natural disposition matched his nickname would have found it hard to be cheerful that day. The glorious autumn of 1946 was now only a treasured memory. As Christmas beckoned from a distance, the early November weather was giving menacing indications of the winter ahead.

The house was quiet, so different from his childhood when sounds from the staff echoed throughout the grand house as preparations were made for family visits. Horse drawn cabs would clatter over the cobbles as they delivered their occupants from the station, to be greeted by the butler.

He looked down at his grandson Andrew, sitting at his feet drawing a picture, and smiled. They heard the telephone ringing in the hall.

'Who will it be, Grandpa?'

'I have no idea, but George will tell us.'

As he spoke the sitting room door opened and George, the butler, stepped inside. 'Excuse me, Mr Sonny. There is a telephone call for Mrs Cowgill.'

Andrew was quick to respond. 'Which one?' He giggled at his joke.

'Your mother, Master Andrew,' George replied with a sly wink, while trying to maintain his pose as befitted his position.

'Kitchen!' was the unanimous response.

'Thank you, sirs.' The door closed quietly.

Moments later the door flew open and Jenny Cowgill bounded into the room. 'He's coming home! Andrew, Daddy's coming home!'

Sonny jumped to his feet and watched his daughter-in-law hug her son as another Mrs Cowgill came hurrying through the door to find the cause of the unexpected commotion.

Sonny reached out and took his wife in his arms. 'Rachael, my darling, he's coming home, Mark's coming home.'

It had been the only good piece of news recently. How ironic that their son Mark had gone through the war virtually unscathed, only to be shot on the final day of hostilities. Mark's long sojourn in a succession of military hospitals was almost over. Jenny had been able to visit regularly as he was moved nearer home and had sat patiently with him when he told her of some, but not all, of the sights he had witnessed, the futility of the slaughter. He was more fortunate than some of those returning. He would, in time, return to full health in both body and mind, but best of all he would be home for Christmas.

'Come on, Andrew. Let's go tell your other grandma the news.' They ran from the room, hand in hand, heading for the kitchen where Jenny's mother was the cook.

Rachael smiled at Sonny. 'This is wonderful news.' She gently wiped away her tears and turned to leave but stood for a moment in the doorway. As she watched her husband, Rachael realized for the first time that Sonny was beginning to look every one of his fifty-four years. The war had taken a heavy toll on the whole family.

'I'll make a pot of tea. Well, I will if I can get in the kitchen. Would you like some?' Rachael kept the conversation light, trying not to allow Sonny to maunder. He had been too prone to long abstracted silences lately.

Sonny smiled. 'That would be nice. But I don't think our cook will allow you the pleasure, even if her daughter is married to our son. You know how she protects her domain.' There was a flash, momentarily, of Sonny's old grin. 'No doubt things will improve now we know that Mark's coming home at last.'

Jenny's mother, Joyce Holgate, had taken the job as cook at Byland Crescent in 1921 after she had been widowed in the First World War, bringing her young daughter with her. The previous cook and butler had decided to retire, and, after so many years working alongside each other, surprised the family by getting married.

Now, Joyce was a family member, she and Rachael ran the household together, with the aid of a daily charlady and George the butler. George, as a teenager, had joined the Cowgill family as general factotum when they moved to Scarborough in 1897. He had taken over the role when the previous incumbent had retired. Now, much older, he was a respected member of staff. Sonny allocated a sum for household expenses and left them to it, which neatly avoided him having to become involved in the delicate subject of salaries, which remained a secret between the mothers-in-law. The days of five full-time staff as a necessity were long gone.

The door closed and Sonny's eyes fell on a framed photograph on the windowsill. It depicted a young cricketer, triumphantly holding a silver cup, and Sonny felt that sick, nauseous sensation whenever he thought of his younger son: 'missing, believed killed' during the desperate withdrawal from Crete.

In the latter stages of the Great War, Sonny had also been posted 'missing, believed killed' but had turned up alive four years later. The evidence in Billy's case seemed to argue against history repeating itself. Sometimes, Sonny thought, it might have been less cruel had the report stated that Billy had definitely been killed. That word 'missing' left just a faint sliver of hope, despite all the evidence to the contrary. Throughout the heartbreak the news of Billy's death had brought to both him and Rachael, Sonny had burdened himself with an extra degree of guilt. He often wondered had he not survived, and had he not returned, then Rachael would not have been tormented by the grief that at times now threatened to overwhelm her.

On a brighter note, he reflected that had he not survived, Sonny would not have witnessed the burgeoning romance between his elder son Mark and his childhood sweetheart Jenny. When the world had been preparing for the second global conflict within thirty years, Jenny, had presented Sonny and Rachael with their grandson Andrew, adding to their contentment at the time.

Sonny's gaze shifted to another photograph and with it, his thoughts. He knew that he and his sister Connie were the sole remaining representatives of the older generation of the Cowgill family. Their father Albert had married Hannah Ackroyd in 1878, and became partner in Haigh Ackroyd & Cowgill, the leading wool merchants in Bradford.

His eyes strayed to other photographs on the wall, so many faces. Some were family groups, grandparents, aunts and uncles. In one image, at his mother's side sat his three sisters, one lost to tuberculosis at the age of nine, the other, a nurse killed during the First World War, and big sister Connie. On mother's lap sat Sonny as a baby. His father was shown in another in the rigid, unsmiling, stance required of Victorian England. Only one member of the family was missing, the eldest son James. Sonny sighed, James, his big brother, thrown out by his father because he fell in love with the housemaid — never to be reconciled.

Unknown to the family, James and his wife Alice had settled in Australia, where, with his business acumen he had founded Fisher Springs, which had grown over the years into a multi-faceted company. Through an intermediary James had acquired a foothold in England, buying the biggest rival to his father's company, and later, in the guise of a mystery benefactor, had come to the rescue of Sonny's ailing business, forming Fisher Springs UK. James and his wife had died tragically in 1929, and the family connection died with them. Their children, the new owners of the empire, were in total ignorance of the fact they were dealing with their own kin.

Sonny had scarcely noticed his wife's departure to brew the promised tea, as he stared again at the photograph on the windowsill of Connie, her husband Michael Haigh and their family, all smiling, all content. The snap had been taken in the early days of the war. How quickly things had changed. It was as if 1942 had been earmarked for the destruction of the Haigh family. Both sons had been killed, the elder during Rommel's capture of Tobruk, the younger serving on a destroyer patrolling the Atlantic. The telegram that arrived at the Haigh's home conveyed little but the bare facts, emphasizing the stark brutality of the message, 'Lost with all hands', which left no room for ambiguity or misunderstanding.

It was shocking rather than surprising when Michael Haigh succumbed to a heart attack less than ten weeks later. Sonny was convinced it was heartbreak rather than a heart attack that had killed him. Within six months Connie had lost almost all that was dear to her apart from her eldest child, a daughter now living in America.

Sonny had been impressed by the unexpected core of steel in his gentle sister. Maybe it had been inherited from their father. Instead of moping into a decline, Connie had thrown herself with grim determination into whatever work she could find to aid the war effort.

When she and Michael had moved to live in Baildon, shortly after the end of the First World War, Connie had become infected with the gardening bug. She had an able assistant, a villager known to one and all as Barty. He had been a soldier at one time, but that career had been terminated by the rifle of a skilled Boer. By way of mementos he lacked two fingers on his left hand and had a permanently stiffened left leg. Unfit for active service and lacking any skill or trade, Barty was reduced to any sort of casual or menial labour that would keep body and soul together, enabling him to support his wife and large brood of children.

When he heard that Michael and Connie Haigh had moved into the big house, Barty lost no time in calling to introduce himself and offer his services.

Connie had taken a liking to the old soldier. With the active encouragement of her husband and the unstinting assistance of her new gardener-cum-handyman, the extensive gardens, overgrown and untended for years, first regained their former glory then surpassed it. Nor was she frightened to get her hands dirty. Gone was the notion of the polite Victorian lady gardener. Connie was of the new breed, familiar with hoe, trowel, and spade, ruthlessly waging war on encroaching weeds, heeling in new plants with a stout leather boot.

When every scrap of food became vital in the war years, Connie turned her hobby into a major project to ensure the long-term productivity with even greater contributions from the vegetable garden. With the erection of a greenhouse her effort resulted in year-round production, on a scale many commercial growers could not match. The final piece in the jigsaw came with the addition of a hen house.

When grieving, first for her sons and then her husband, Connie directed her anger and sorrow into ensuring every bit of land available to her was used productively. Dig for Victory, the slogan told the nation, and Connie, with Barty's assistance, dug and hoed, fertilized and weeded, watered, tended and cared for her plants, shrubs and trees, and picked, packed and distributed all she could.

'Sonny,' she had told him, 'we have lost so much, but no more than many households. Now we have to channel every effort into ensuring a better future so our remaining children and all their generation never have to go through this again.'

If Sonny needed proof that Connie was right, he could find it within the ranks of his own family, for it was not only those mourning the dead who had to be considered. Many survivors were little more than that. Crippled, orphaned, childless, homeless, stateless or prisoners, they were survivors in name only.

Sonny's reverie was interrupted as the door opened once more. He looked up to see his wife regarding him, concern in her eyes.

'Ah,' he said, looking at the tray Rachael carried, 'tea at last, I was beginning to think you'd gone to Ceylon for it.'

* * *

Connie Haigh was looking forward to Christmas, visiting Scarborough, and seeing her nephew Mark and his wife again. She had always admired them as a couple, and of course had loved Mark since he was a tiny baby. Watching them grow into childhood sweethearts before they eventually married had been a source of great delight.

She was well aware that Sonny and Rachael had undergone the same torment as she had, the dread every parent faced at the loss of their offspring. The young men marched off to war, so full of great ideals and heroism. Connie had one great solace in her loss, albeit a long distance one. Her daughter Marguerite, who was married to a diplomat, was currently in Washington along with Connie's two grandsons. Her son-in-law's mission was scheduled to keep them in America for a further three years, but Connie had received a letter from Marguerite only a week earlier, in which she expressed her hope that she and the boys would be able to visit Britain once the school summer term had ended. The final sentence had made Connie smile. Marguerite had used the word vacation instead of holiday. How quickly her daughter had picked up the American idiom.

Connie decided she ought to go shopping. In the days of rationing, that was no easy task, simply scraping together sufficient coupons to allow the necessary purchases was an art many housewives had not mastered. Connie, however, with her ample all-year-round supply of produce from her own garden, was able to hoard the precious slips of paper against any visits from family or friends.

Before leaving for the village, she wrapped up warmly against the biting cold, and greeted Barty, her long-time gardener, or, as Sonny referred to him, her accomplice. Connie made him a pot of tea which she placed on a battered tray, knowing Barty would take it down to the potting shed, where, before collecting the eggs from the henhouse, he would sit quietly with a roll-up and his tea, studying racing form in the morning paper. She asked him to bring some potatoes in from the clamp they had built the previous autumn, and also to pick some carrots from the vegetable plot.

The shopping took longer than expected, not because there was too much to do, but because the grocer treated each customer more as a friend, moreover, one he hadn't seen for some time and who he needed to regale with the latest gossip. When Connie eventually got back home, the first thing she noticed was how cold the house was. Walking up the long hill from the village carrying the shopping had warmed her, and the contrast on entering the hallway was noticeable. She dumped her shopping on the table in the breakfast room and went into the sitting room to light the fire she'd laid first thing that morning. She opened the top vent on the Rayburn to allow more draught, before going through to the large kitchen with her purchases.

She was about to start putting these away when she noticed that the vegetables she'd asked Barty to pick hadn't been brought inside. Connie frowned, this was most unlike him. Barty, for all his imperfections, was meticulous when it came to carrying out her requests. He was extremely fond of his employer and would not have let her down if he could help it. Was his memory failing? Connie knew the old soldier was getting on in years. Although she had no idea precisely what his age was, she knew he had been wounded in the Boer War, which must, she reasoned, put him well on the wrong side of seventy.

Connie let herself out of the back door and hurried down the long path leading past the apple trees, the strawberry bed and the vegetable plots to the large greenhouse and beyond it to the potting shed. There was no sign of him in the greenhouse, but Connie could see a wisp of smoke

13

coming out of the flue from the pot-bellied stove in the shed beyond. The stove powered the heating system that enabled Connie to grow vegetables all year round.

She headed for the door, reasoning that Barty must be inside. I bet he's fallen asleep, she thought. Not that it mattered, Connie wasn't the sort to begrudge the old man a nap if he so wished. She opened the door, and saw immediately that the stove was burning brightly, the dancing flames clearly visible through the glass panes facing her. Her concern was more for Barty. The gardener was seated in the old armchair that had once graced Connie's sitting room but was now alongside the workbench. On the counter nearby was the mug of tea she had made him, now cold. The old man was sleeping, his head slightly on one side, resting on the wing of the chair.

'Barty, are you alright?'

There was no answer and Connie was seized with dread, was he ill? 'Barty,' she repeated her cry, advancing cautiously towards the chair and its occupant.

The old man stirred and opened his eyes. He sat up, his face a mixture of bewilderment and shame. 'Sorry, Mrs H,' he muttered. 'I must have nodded off.'

'Barty, you scared the living daylights out of me,' Connie masked her concern with the severity of her tone. 'Are you unwell, or something?'

'Er, no, it's just that this sort of thing seems to be happening more often these days. Must be age, I guess.'

'Did you manage to get the vegetables I wanted before you did your Rip Van Winkle impersonation?'

'Yes, they're in the sack by the door. I'll bring them down to the house.'

Barty stood up and stretched, but as he did so, Connie saw an expression of extreme pain cross the old soldier's face. He swayed, white as a sheet, agony in his eyes as he slumped into Connie's arms. She lowered him to the armchair. She felt for a pulse but knew instinctively that it would be in vain. Sure enough, Barty, the veteran of the Boer War campaign, had at last succumbed.

CHAPTER TWO

Christmas of 1946 was a quiet, muted affair. Delight and relief at the long-awaited safe return of Mark Cowgill was tempered by the terrible losses suffered within the ranks of the family. When it came time to sit down for the Christmas meal, there would be sadness, created by the vacant places at the table, and the inevitable reflection of those that gathered there about the ones who were missing.

Connie was unable to attend due to heavy snow. Although she was always welcome in Byland Crescent for as long as she wished, should the bad weather continue, and without Barty to tend her crops, the risk that she would be unable to return to West Yorkshire was too great.

The Cowgill's youngest daughter, Elizabeth, had been dreadfully upset by her brother Billy's death. But nobody could have foreseen that the event would have driven a wedge between her and her parents, a wound that was apparently unable to be healed. It had resulted in a schism that had torn apart the family.

Frances, the elder of Mark's sisters was another absentee, but in her case the reason was at least more joyful. Frances had sailed earlier that year along with her husband Henry, bound for a new life in his home country of America. Henry, nicknamed 'Hank the Yank' by Sonny, had been an airman stationed in England, and revealed his ambition to his prospective father-in-law to continue his flying career as a pilot of civilian airliners now that the war was over.

'I guess there will be a whole raft of guys like me, so if they won't have me, I guess I'll have to join the old man running the family ranch. How Frances will take to life on a Texas ranch, I've no idea.' Hank looked at Sonny, his expression serious. 'I'd say you folks could have reservations about your daughter being so far away, amongst strangers, but I assure you, sir, I'll take real good care of her. I love her, you see.'

Sonny had clapped him on the shoulder. 'That's good enough for me, Hank. Besides,' he added, straight-faced, 'if you don't, you'll have her mother to answer to.' He lowered his voice. 'And you wouldn't want that, believe me. She has a dreadful temper. I wouldn't put it past her to jump on the next sailing boat and go out there with a sharp knife. I can't imagine she would trust one of the new-fangled transatlantic flights. She's not that brave!'

Hank had looked worried for a second, then shook his head. 'I guess I'll get used to the British sense of humour in time.'

'You could always get Frances to give you lessons,' Sonny suggested. 'It'll help you while away the time of an evening — if you can't think of anything else to do.'

That joke Hank did get immediately. His booming laughter echoed through the Byland Crescent house.

Although Rachael moped for a while after Frances left, the homecoming of Mark in time for the festivities lifted her spirits and helped distract her.

* * *

It came as something of a shock to Mark Cowgill to realize that this would only be the second Christmas in seven years that he would be spending at home. Although he was

16

naturally delighted to be reunited with his beloved Jenny and Andrew, and to be safe in the bosom of his family, those who knew him best were aware that Mark, when he wasn't being diverted by the antics of his young son, was troubled by something. It was small wonder that anyone returning after the horrors Mark and thousands of others had witnessed should be disturbed, or restless, but Mark's family had the feeling his unease was rooted in some more personal, private disquiet.

Some of the reason for his introspection was explained on Christmas morning. Mark and Jenny were the first to rise, a legacy within their subconscious from the time when they had gone on early morning fitness runs together.

'I'd better see if Andrew's awake,' Jenny said. 'You can go put the kettle on.'

'OK, sweetheart,' Mark said, in an appalling attempt at a Humphrey Bogart impersonation. As she passed him, he tapped her on the backside. 'God, I've missed you,' he told her.

Jenny looked back and smiled affectionately. 'I noticed that last night,' she commented, 'and the night before that. And twice on the night you arrived home. Maybe you should check that bed out to see how sturdy it is.'

'That's a good point. This room is where my Uncle James got up to no good with Alice, the housemaid. There's a long history of seducing the servants and their relatives in my family.' He grinned at her. 'Bugger the tea!'

Another half hour passed, before they eventually left their room, hand in hand like the childhood sweethearts they had once been. Outside the door they separated, with a final squeeze of her hand from Mark.

Jenny walked along the Minstrel's gallery towards her son's room and opened the door. Andrew was up and completing the last stage of getting dressed when his mother entered. She wished him Merry Christmas, and then leaned against the door frame, watching with some amusement the frown of concentration on her son's face as the eight-year-old struggled with the complex procedure of tying his shoelaces. Even the allure of the waiting Christmas presents couldn't distract him from this important task.

When it was done, Andrew straightened up and looked across at his mother. 'Is Daddy up yet?' He was still getting used to the novelty of having his father at home. The first few years of his life had been spent almost exclusively in the company of women, with the exception of his grandfather, Sonny, and occasional, all too fleeting visits from his father, the soldier hero.

'Of course he is,' Jenny laughed. 'I hope he's made tea by now.' She held her hand out to the boy. 'Come on, let's go see, shall we? Who knows, there might even be a parcel under the Christmas tree for you from Santa Claus.'

They descended the broad staircase hand in hand, only to pause at the bottom. Andrew's father had made no effort to go into the kitchen. Instead he was standing in the middle of the hall, staring at a painting that had pride of place on the wall alongside the front door.

'What's wrong, Mark?' Jenny asked.

He looked round, a trifle sheepishly. 'Oh, nothing, I was just wool-gathering. I'll explain later, when Mum and Dad are about. It's a little bit weird, actually. Now, who's for tea? And who's keen to look under the tree?'

The tree won out, but Jenny would only allow Andrew to open his stocking hanging on the large mantel shelf of the fireplace. Inside was an apple and orange, together with some chocolate pennies wrapped in foil, a rare treat during rationing, and a chocolate bar, which was even rarer. Jenny was surprised by the chocolate. 'Where on earth did you get that?' she whispered to Mark, examining the bar. 'I've never heard of this company, Hershey.'

'It was in the parcel from America that was waiting for me when I got home,' Mark explained. 'A GI I met in Berlin sent it, as a thank you.'

'Thank you for what?'

'Saving his life. I shot a Nazi who was about to blow his head off.' Jenny gave him a warning look, her eyes signalling their son, who appeared to be occupied. 'Sorry!' Mark muttered. 'We swapped names and addresses, and I told him about Andrew. The guy had been stationed in England before D-Day, so he knew how tough things are over here, and he promised if he got back Stateside, as he put it, he'd send something as soon as he could. He obviously made it home, which is good news.'

Andrew had obviously been listening. 'Daddy, did you kill the nasty?'

Mark laughed at Andrew's mispronunciation. 'Yes, son, and that's a very good description.'

The rest of the family had joined them and when the present-opening ritual was over, Mark asked the adults to join him in the hall, leaving Andrew to play with his new clockwork train set.

Mark stopped again in front of the painting. It was a landscape, which depicted a picnic being taken in front of a ruined abbey. Byland Abbey, after which the crescent was named, was about forty miles away from Scarborough. It was a site all the family knew well, for they had visited it every year until the outbreak of war, when the strictures of petrol rationing brought such pleasure jaunts to an end. Not that Sonny saw it as purely a pleasure trip. To him, it was as much a pilgrimage, for his recollection of the abbey had been instrumental in patching together his fragmented memory and bringing him back home from France after the Great War.

'I wanted you to hear this, because you've all been to the abbey, and you've heard Dad telling the story of what the abbey meant to him, and how it saved his sanity.' Mark looked at the painting. 'I'm not sure what it is about the place, or what hold it has over our family, but I have to tell you that the reason I'm here with you today is because of Byland Abbey.'

His hand went to his shoulder as he continued speaking, a subconscious gesture that went unnoticed by everyone except Jenny, who was aware how much pain the wound still caused him. 'We'd fought our way across the former occupied countries until we reached Germany. By that time we knew it was almost over, merely a matter of time, and mopping up the last pockets of resistance until they surrendered. Whether that made us relax, become over-confident, I don't know. I happen to think not. I believe the only ones left fighting were the diehard fanatics, who became ever more desperate. All I do know is that some of the fiercest close-combat fighting we'd experienced since we landed in Normandy took place amongst the ruins of Berlin.'

He paused to gather his thoughts. 'When I say ruins, I mean exactly that. The damage inflicted on London during the Blitz was no worse than what the RAF and the American Air Force did to Berlin and other German cities. Anyway, I'm digressing. The streets were so filled with rubble and debris from collapsed buildings that our tanks couldn't make headway, and we came under fire from one machine gun nest after another, interspersed with lone snipers hidden in the ruined, burnt-out shells of houses, flats, you name it. Any place they could find cover.

'A kid at the opposite side of the street shot me with a rifle. The force of the bullet knocked me flat. I suppose I was confused because of the pain, but as I was lying on the ground staring across the street, trying to work out where the shot had come from, the outline of the damaged building opposite was exactly like this view of Byland Abbey.'

Mark gestured to the painting. 'I remembered it clearly, and I laid there thinking, what am I doing at Byland Abbey? Be that as it may, it made me focus on that building in particular, and that's why I was able to spot where the sniper was hiding. Fortunately, I got a burst in from my sub-machine gun. The point is, if he hadn't taken shelter in that building, if he'd chosen another one, or if the building he was in hadn't reminded me of the abbey, I'd probably have been killed.' Mark looked at Sonny. 'I think the abbey saved me, much the same as it saved you, Dad.'

Mark obviously had more on his mind, but only Jenny was aware that her husband was keeping something back.

They had grown up together, then became comrades-in-arms, fighting side by side during the Spanish Civil War, before they returned home as husband and wife. Andrew had been conceived in Spain, and it was Jenny's abiding frustration that the constraints of accepted behaviour and the demands of motherhood prevented her from volunteering to fight alongside her husband in the later conflict that had so recently ended. The closeness of their relationship meant that she often knew what Mark was thinking, sometimes before he was even aware of it himself, and conversely, he knew Jenny's mind as well as her lovely body, and knew also that any attempt to dissemble or deceive her would be bound to fail.

* * *

When Rachael Cowgill looked around the table at Christmas dinner and thought about their losses, she had a major turmoil in her mind. In almost all the casualties of war, there was a dreadful certainty. Whether that helped the grieving process or not is open to question. In the case of Billy, there was the uncertainty contained in the phrase 'missing, believed killed'. That phrase haunted his mother. The information received by the military authorities left them little doubt that Private William Albert Cowgill was dead, and to this end they informed his relatives accordingly.

However, the military authorities did not know that Rachael Cowgill, having endured the same torment when her husband had been reported dead, no longer trusted, nor believed in that phrase 'missing, believed killed'. How could they, for they were not the boy's grieving mother. Far from granting finality, the uncertainty contained in that phrase gave Rachael a slender thread of hope.

When she rationalized the situation, Rachael told herself that she was merely deceiving herself, for surely it could not happen again. She couldn't get that lucky, as she had with the miracle of Sonny's reappearance. That was all very well, but her emotions argued that as a mother she would surely feel it in her heart if Billy was truly dead. And if that was so, she would no longer feel the need to cling to that slender thread.

* * *

Rachael and Joyce had done the occasion justice. Sonny had raided the cellars for some of the dwindling stock of wine he had collected before the war. As a result, when Mark and Jenny retired for the night, having put their weary son to bed, both of them were replete, and slightly less than sober.

As they were lying in bed, Jenny challenged Mark about what he was holding back.

Mark smiled affectionately at her. 'I didn't think I could fool you,' he admitted, 'but I didn't want to say anything in front of the others, and today certainly wasn't the right day. The thing is, I've decided I'm not going to stay in the family business, but I don't want to hurt Dad by blurting it out. I'll talk to him when the time is right.'

'Have you decided what it is that you are going to do?'

'I've a sort of idea, but it needs a lot of researching, it will take time. So when I'm fit again I'll go back to work with Dad and Simon at Fisher Springs until I get it all planned out. Oh, and that reminds me, talking about research,' he slipped his arm around her and began caressing the smooth skin of her back. 'I checked the bed this afternoon, and I'm pleased to report that it's really sturdy, so we don't have to worry about that.'

'Oh good, I had visions of us crashing through the ceiling and landing up in the sitting room still locked together.'

'That would have shocked Mum and Dad.'

'I doubt it. I think they know us well enough by now.'

Downstairs, in the sitting room, Sonny was reading a thriller, while Rachael was listening to dance band music. She had tuned their radiogram to an American radio station from somewhere called Schenectady. She had no idea where that was, but she loved the music they played.

There was a momentary flicker in the lighting as the newly installed electric chandelier vibrated slightly. Rachael glanced upwards, then across at Sonny. Noticing that he'd stopped reading, she said, 'They're at it again.'

Sonny glanced at the clock and grinned. 'Started early too. I think Mark's trying to make up for lost time.'

'There will soon be more mouths to feed if they go on at this rate.'

'Ah, I get it. You're getting broody. You fancy being a grandmother all over again.'

'What of it? It will be nice for Andrew to have a baby brother or sister.'

'That's for the future. As of now, how about taking a grandfather to bed and making love to him. We can't let the youngsters have things all their own way.'

'I've no problem with that, as long as you don't mind sleeping with a grandma.'

'Why would I? I've been doing it for years.'

CHAPTER THREE

In common with many similar large properties, the Byland Crescent house was heavily reliant on solid fuel for both heating and cooking. The range cooker in the kitchen and the open fires in the reception rooms and bedrooms consumed large quantities of coal.

Following snow and bitterly cold weather in December, the coal-place was now three parts empty, the whitewashed walls visible, where normally they would be masked by a young mountain of fuel. It was on a Saturday morning in early January 1947 when Rachael Cowgill made what she thought would be a routine call to the coal merchant to order replenishments, that she encountered the first sign of potential trouble.

When answering her, the coal merchant was apologetic, not wishing to risk upsetting one of his best private customers, as he explained that there was little he could do to help. Rachael's request, for twenty sacks of coal, could not be met.

'I'm very sorry, Mrs Cowgill, but two bags is all I can manage to let you have, at least for the time being. I'm waiting for a delivery that should have been in the depot before Christmas, and it still hasn't arrived. What's worse is that nobody seems to be able to tell me when I can expect it. To be honest, the way things are, this new-fangled National Coal Board seems to be a real mess. I wish they'd never nationalized the mines. And the weather, with snow blocking railway lines, isn't helping either.'

All of which was highly informative, but of little use to the Cowgill family who now faced the possibility of being unable to either cook, or to heat the house. She sought out Sonny, who was in the lounge reading the morning paper.

'We've about ten days' supply left in the coal-place, as far as I can judge. Add to that the two bags the coalman promised me, and at best we'll run out within a fortnight unless we can get some elsewhere, but as the coal merchant told me, everyone is going to be in a similar position.'

Sonny considered the problem for a few minutes. 'OK, here's one idea that might make our stock last a bit longer. If you go to town and order some electric fires, we can use them for background heat. That's assuming you can find any in the shops, because lots of people will have the same idea.' He tapped the newspaper. 'According to reports, they may not be of any use if coal supplies to the electricity company run out. Have we still got the oil lamps?'

'Yes, I put them in the cellar after the electricity supply was installed. Why do you ask?'

'It might be an idea to see if we have any oil left. They're already saying they may have to ration power supplies and we could face blackouts.'

'What! As well as food rationing? This is getting ridiculous.'

Sonny tried to calm her. 'It'll be expensive, I know, but that way we can save the coal for the cooker. If you can, get one each for the sitting room and the dining room, plus each of the bedrooms. If we keep from switching them on until just before the room in question is to be occupied, it might not bankrupt us.' Sonny grinned.

Rachael smiled at Sonny's joke. She had a fair idea how much the family was worth, and it would take a long time to make even a dent in their fortune. 'That's all very well,' she told him, 'but that won't do us much good if we can't cook, or get hot water for baths. Both of those rely on the AGA, and that's a very hungry monster.'

'I agree, so what we need to try and do is think up an alternative. One that springs to mind is that if we could get hold of some timber, we might be able to run the AGA on wood. It would be less convenient, but at least we'd be warm, well fed, and not too smelly.'

'You've got old bits of wood in your carpentry workshop, haven't you?' Rachael asked.

Sonny looked shocked. 'That's oak, you can't burn that!'

They discussed the problem with the family over dinner that evening. It was Jenny who came up with a possible solution. 'If we need timber,' she said hesitantly, 'how about approaching one of the large estates, and ask them if they'd be prepared to sell us some. I seem to remember you telling us that you'd been watching men felling trees from the train window when you were travelling to Bradford, didn't you, Dad?'

Jenny had called her father-in-law Dad for a long time, almost as long as either of them could remember. In truth, Sonny was almost as much a father to her as he was to her husband, replacing her own father, who had been killed when Jenny was only a few weeks old.

Sonny thought about what Jenny had said. 'It's worth a try, I suppose. The only trouble is, which estate?'

'Johnny Hotshot!' Mark exclaimed suddenly.

They all stared at him.

'What?' Jenny asked.

'Sorry, I was thinking aloud. I just remembered this guy who was in our unit in France. He had one of those long, hyphenated names nobody could remember. Because he was an expert marksman, everyone referred to him as Johnny Hotshot. It was far easier.'

'Fascinating,' Rachael said, dryly, 'but I fail to see the relevance. Unless of course you plan to write your wartime reminiscences and we can use them as firelighters.'

'Sorry, Mum, I was going on to tell you that Johnny's family owns a big estate near here. I feel sure if I call him and they have some timber to spare he would let us have it on the Old Pals' Act. If he can do that, all we'd have to do is get it here.'

'Why not give him a call now?' Sonny suggested.

Mark shook his head. 'No fear, Dad. I'll leave it until Monday. They'll be shooting over the weekend. I remember Johnny going on and on about how much he missed the pheasant shoots. He said even killing Nazis wasn't half as much fun. Apparently, from what he told me, they never miss an opportunity during the season.'

'Surely, even if Mark's friend can supply some timber and we can get it here, we'd have to leave it to dry out,' Rachael suggested.

'That's a good point, we can't use it when it's full of sap,' Sonny agreed.

'At least let me try, we can but ask. Failing that, I don't know what to suggest.'

'OK, do that, Mark, and we'll keep our fingers crossed,' Sonny told him.

On Monday morning Mark had the phone number ready to hand.

'They say it's better to be born lucky than handsome, Mark, and that certainly seems to be the case with you. Your luck is right in,' Johnny told him in response to his query. 'Our forester cut down a huge plantation last summer, thinning it out, you know, both for the health of the trees, and to give a better rise for the pheasants when the beaters go through it. The plantation was at the head of our best drive, and to be honest, the birds weren't showing as well as we'd like. We've had a lot of important guests here this season and more expected in autumn, so we need the shoot to be at its best.

'As for the timber, we have far more than we'll need for our own use, dried out, and split down. It should be perfect for what you need. We've already supplied all the cottages on the estate and given loads to the local village, so we're beginning to run out of places to offload the stuff. All you need to do is get across here with a wagon and collect it. I'll even lend you four strong lads to help load it.' Johnny Hotshot coughed apologetically. 'Of course, being a Yorkshireman, the next bit is going to hurt, but I'm afraid we'll have to charge for the wood.'

'I was expecting nothing less, Johnny. I appreciate that the aristocracy's on its uppers and you have to scrape every penny together to survive. Let me know how much and I'll bring you the cash.'

'It's all done by measurement, so much a foot I believe, so I can't tell you beforehand. Don't worry, I can trust you — as long as you don't have a rifle in your hand. I know what a rotten shot you are.'

Mark went into the sitting room to report his success. His mother, along with Jenny and her mother Joyce were discussing Mark's Aunt Connie. Rachael looked across as her son entered.

'We were just saying how wiry and thin your aunt looked last time we saw her. Maybe it's us, but with not seeing her day in, day out, it seems more noticeable, somehow. It makes me wonder if she's properly recovered from Michael's death, or the loss of the boys. I know she still has Marguerite and the grandsons, but they're in America, so she must be lonely in that big house. Especially now she's tending the garden single-handedly. Added to which, grieving alone must be hard. When your father was missing, I don't know how I'd have managed, if I hadn't had you to look after.'

'I shouldn't worry, Mum. Aunt Connie's a tough old bird. If you're concerned, why not give her a ring. Anyway, do you want to hear the good news? Good for you, at least — not so good for Jenny.'

'Why me?' his wife demanded.

'Because it's going to involve you doing some hard work for a change.' Mark ducked and avoided the cushion Jenny hurled at him. 'You throw like a wicket-keeper,' he sneered.

'What's the good news?' Rachael intervened to prevent the squabble that was brewing.

Mark told them the outcome of his telephone conversation. 'So it appears I do have my uses after all, when it comes to obtaining fuel supplies at least. All we have to do is hire a wagon which Jenny will help me unload. The trees were felled last summer, so will be dried out ready for use. I'm going to ask Dad to get a special blade for his bench saw. With that fitted, it will make short work of cutting them to size. If he buys a log-splitting axe I'll do the rest, and we should have all the fuel we need.'

'You mean you've actually bought a load of tree trunks?' Rachael asked. 'How big are they? You're not fit enough to lift them.'

'Don't worry, Mum. They're split down. Johnny assured me they wouldn't be too heavy, even for a weedy girl such as Jenny to handle.'

Without a truck or the fuel rations to go with it, Mark had been puzzled how they would get the timber back to Byland Crescent, until his mother came up with a bright idea.

'As the coal merchant has nothing to deliver, his wagon will be standing idle,' she suggested. 'Why don't I ring him and ask if we can borrow it? It's the least he can do seeing he has no coal for us.'

Mark grinned. 'That's it, Mum, play the emotional blackmail card. But tell him we need it before the weather worsens.'

The trick worked, and the coal merchant even volunteered to drive the truck and bring his assistant, for which Mark readily agreed to leave half a dozen lengths of timber on the wagon.

By the time they returned to Byland Crescent, snow had begun to fall again. The men offloaded the timber, which they stacked under a shelter beside Sonny's workshop in the old stables behind the house. Jenny lent a hand with the shorter lengths. By the time the work was done they were all sweating profusely, despite it being a bitterly cold day with a keen east wind blowing off the sea.

'Now all we have to do is reduce them to smaller pieces and stack them in the coal-place,' Mark told her when the wagon had driven away. 'But that can wait for another day. At least we'll be under cover to do that. I don't know about you, but I'm exhausted.'

'Me too, but at least that should mean I'll get a good night's sleep tonight.'

'That's fine by me,' Mark leered, 'but the bath beforehand — that's a totally different matter.'

'Mark! Where on earth do you get all that energy from?'

'You, my darling. You inspire me. I only have to look at you, and my pulse starts to race.'

'I can see I'll have to start wearing a mask.'

'What? And get me even more excited?'

Jenny groaned, but deep down she was pleased. 'I think a bath's a good idea. A nice deep one we can share.'

Mark looked at her suspiciously. Jenny looked innocent — too innocent. 'What's the catch?' he demanded.

'No catch, dearest. But we can't afford to waste hot water, with fuel supplies as they are.'

* * *

The snowstorm that began with tiny pellets as hard as ice was driven by a strong north-easterly wind. Although almost invisible to the naked eye, they stung the cheeks of anyone exposed to them like a thousand tiny needles. All weekend the snow continued without respite, but although the snowflakes got larger and softer, the ferocity of the wind drove them with greater intensity across the exposed Yorkshire moors.

Connie Haigh had been restless throughout the weekend. Trapped indoors by the blizzard, she had ventured no further than the henhouse, to feed the chickens and collect the eggs. She had combined that with a necessary, but no longer pleasurable, visit to the potting shed and greenhouse. Entering the building where her gardener had died was an effort of will that tested Connie's resolve to the limit, but she knew it was a task she had to perform, as much for the sake of Barty's memory as for her own needs. Connie had no choice, leaving the fire to go out was not an option, certainly not in such adverse weather conditions.

She performed the routine tasks exactly as her gardener used to do, and when she had finished on the Saturday afternoon, she closed the door with a sigh of relief. After returning to the house, Connie wondered what else she could do to fill the weekend. Normally, Saturday night would mean a visit to Baildon's only picture house, but the severity of the snowstorm denied her that small pleasure. Even the attraction of Blue Skies, with Fred Astaire and Bing Crosby would have to be foregone in the face of the blizzard. It had already rendered the roads and footpaths in the village all but impassable, cutting the community off from the outside world. Connie had the radio to entertain her, and a book from the library, but as the weather showed no sign of relenting, her sense of isolation and loneliness intensified.

Sunday was a repeat of the previous day. Snow was still falling heavily, and there was little encouragement to attempt anything. For the first time for many years, Connie dismissed the idea of going to church without a second thought. She stayed indoors, and it was almost lunchtime before she got dressed, an even rarer occurrence.

One glance out of the window was enough to tell Connie that the snow, instead of abating, was still as bad as ever, and there were waist-high drifts in places where the wind had driven it hardest. Despite this, Connie knew that she would have to venture out. She delayed the task as long as she could, hoping that the snow might relent. By mid-afternoon she knew she would have to make the effort before the light went.

Apart from feeding the chickens and collecting the eggs, she was concerned that a marauding fox, driven from his usual habitat by the extreme weather, might have got amongst her poultry. Before setting out, Connie wrapped herself in as much clothing as she could and armed herself with a shovel. The garden path was only a hundred yards long, but it took her quarter of an hour to reach the potting shed, clearing the snow as she went. The arduous task soon had her warm enough to consider removing the outermost layer, but she battled on, each gust of wind bringing a fresh reminder of the severity of the snowstorm.

Once inside, Connie rested, busying herself with cleaning the stove out and replenishing the stock of fuel in the hopper which fed it. This automated system, designed by Connie's late husband, had been constructed with the aid of a blacksmith, and enabled the fire to be kept going for two days without constantly needing attention.

Connie activated the hopper, and, as the snow hadn't relented, she gave the hens extra feed. That way she wouldn't need to return until Tuesday, should the weather not ease up. It was on her way back to the house that trouble overcame her.

A patch of ice created when she had cleared snow with the shovel was her undoing. She fell heavily, the tray of eggs she had been carrying being the first casualty. As she went down Connie hit her head against a piece of stone that formed part of the low wall surrounding the strawberry bed, causing her to black out, briefly.

When she began to come round, in her confused state she believed she had taken a tumble on the ice rink. Skating was a pastime she enjoyed with Michael. He'd be waiting for her, Connie thought, probably in the tearoom at the far end of the rink. She rose unsteadily to her feet and set off, her pace little more than a crawl through the deepening drifts. Her confusion and the near whiteout created by the blizzard that had started again while she was unconscious caused her to lose her bearings.

Connie blundered past the house and out onto the avenue, its surface covered completely by snow that was over a foot deep in places. Reaching the end of the side street she turned left into West Lane, her vision coming and going, her gait more of a stagger than a walk. She had only travelled a few yards before she fell again, to lie concealed by a large beech hedge.

* * *

Weather conditions across Yorkshire were so bad that Sonny didn't attempt the train journey to Bradford on the Monday morning. 'There's no guarantee the trains will be running and how far I'd get,' he told Rachael.

'That makes sense,' she agreed, 'if there's anything urgent they'll have to make do with a phone call. I just hope it doesn't become as harsh as the winter of two years ago.'

Sonny attempted to ring the Bradford office, but without success. 'I reckon the lines might be down,' he told the others. 'Either that, or nobody's made it into work.'

'I think we should all stay indoors and keep warm and safe,' Jenny suggested.

'Shouldn't we try the phone again?' Mark asked. 'I ought to check Aunt Connie's all right.'

'You can, if the lines are open,' his father responded, 'but if not, I wouldn't worry. I think your aunt's bright enough to look after herself. However, if you do get through let me know.'

Although Mark succeeded in getting a connection there was no reply from the Baildon house. This didn't concern him at the time.

Later that day Sonny was summoned by the butler who had answered the Byland Crescent phone. 'It's West Riding Police for you, Mr Sonny,' he explained.

Sonny looked at Rachael, a puzzle frown on his face. 'Why should they want me?'

Mark grinned and replied, in his worst Yorkshire accent, 'There'll be trouble at t' mill, Dad.'

Sonny sighed, rolled his eyes at his son, and hurried from the room, leaving the others to laugh at the joke. The conversation was brief, but when he returned, Rachael could tell by his expression that something was terribly wrong.

'Connie's dead,' he told her bluntly. 'Police think she slipped on some ice and fell into a snowdrift. It appears she died of hypothermia.' Sonny shook his head. 'What she was doing out in the road in this weather, I suppose we'll never know.'

* * *

There were few mourners when Connie Haigh, at the age of sixty-six, was laid to rest. The funeral had been delayed to enable her sole remaining child, Marguerite, to attend. She was pragmatic in her attitude, which made things less traumatic for those seeking to provide solace.

'I think it was inevitable, and in one sense almost a blessing,' she told them. 'Losing Eddie and George one after the other, then Dad and, finding poor old Barty as she did, I think everything was becoming too much for her. In her last letter to me she wrote that she felt she had outlived her purpose in life and was simply dragging out time until the end.'

It was a sad reflection on his sister's life, Sonny thought, and was now faced with the unpalatable truth that the last of his generation had gone, and, with the death of his son Billy, his situation was threatening to become similar to that of Connie.

CHAPTER FOUR

It wasn't only in Britain that the return of loved ones was awaited anxiously — in many cases, impatiently. In Australia, one of the most impatient was Isabella Finnegan, who was awaiting the return of Luke Fisher, the boyfriend she had not seen for over eight years. Now twenty-four, Isabella had longed for Luke to consummate their relationship before he left, but Luke would not do that. Now, she wanted the waiting over as quickly as possible so she could marry him, and they could be together as they had hoped, planned and dreamed of in a spate of letters that had crossed the thousands of miles separating them until Luke had been shot down over France and taken prisoner.

All around her, it seemed to Isabella that she was witnessing scenes of joyful and emotional reunion enjoyed by those from the Australian armed forces and their nearest and dearest. In her more paranoid moments, she wondered if these were being staged especially to torment her. Her work as a reporter for Fisher Springs meant that for the past two years she had to endure many happy reunions of homecoming troops for some of her articles. The problem was that Luke's case wasn't quite as straightforward as many of the others.

Technically speaking, Luke wasn't a member of the Australian forces, travelling to England in early 1938 as a private citizen, then volunteering for duty with the RAF. Having been shot down over France he had been held in a prisoner of war camp for two years. Before he could come home, he would have to be repatriated to Britain from Germany, where he would have to be demobilized by the RAF. But before he could be returned to England, he would have to be found. Luke, along with thousands of other prisoners of war, had been made to move from prison camp to prison camp in the face of the advancing Allied armies.

In her desperation, Isabella confided in her father. Patrick Finnegan was managing director of Fisher Springs Pty, one of the most influential private companies in Australia. 'Can't you do anything, Dad? It's taking too long. He should be home, back with us. Back with me!'

'Sorry, Bella, you'll have to be patient, like everyone else. I might know lots of influential people but what can they do?'

Was there, Patrick wondered, some curse over the Fisher family and their alter egos in England, the Cowgill family. With matriarch Hannah Cowgill dead, Patrick and his wife Louise were, with the exception of a London solicitor Ralph French, the only people who knew exactly how close the connection was. The company, founded by James Cowgill, and his wife Alice Fisher, when they arrived in Australia, was now one of the largest conglomerates in the country. James had legally taken the name Fisher when they married, concealing his true identity while he monitored the family businesses in England, and unknown to them, became a major shareholder, helping them in every way he could.

Patrick pondered all that had happened since he went to work for Fisher Springs. James and Alice, along with one of their daughters, had died tragically in 1929, long before their time, leaving Patrick and his wife to raise the Fisher's remaining children along with their own. The Fisher's eldest son Saul had been killed in the First World War and their daughter Dottie had gone through a wretched marriage with a brutal, abusive, and unfaithful husband. Her elder sister, Ellen, a nursing sister in Singapore, had died during the Japanese invasion in 1942. Their sons Phil and Luke had fought irreconcilably until Luke had walked out of the family business and later, Phil had died in a Japanese POW camp. When Patrick added the roll of misfortune he knew had befallen the Cowgill branch of the family in England it certainly looked as if they were the subject of some malign influence.

Of all the clan, only Luke Fisher had survived the war unscathed. There was irony in that too, Patrick thought, as Luke had been a fighter pilot with the RAF, he had been in the most hazardous position of all. Now it seemed Luke was on his way home to his impatient sweetheart, Isabella.

Patrick's spirits lifted as he thought of Isabella, who had always been outspoken. She had left for Melbourne the day before and Patrick grinned at the memory of her parting words. 'Don't expect us home for Christmas. I know Luke's not due back for a few days yet but it'll give me time to do some shopping and get the bed warmed. I don't suppose we'll be going out for a while.'

'Isabella!' Louise had broken her long silence to protest.

'Well, Mother, he's got eight years of waiting to get out of his system,' Bella had continued unabashed. 'I don't suppose he'll be satisfied with a quickie any more than I will. Just because he was too much of a gentleman to indulge himself with a girl one month away from her sixteenth birthday.'

Patrick had shot his daughter a warning glance but to his surprise Louise laughed. 'I suppose we ought to start planning the wedding then.'

'We'll see about that.'

'And soon!' Louise added by way of warning. 'We have a standing in the community and we don't need a scandal.'

* * *

In the event, Luke and Isabella's meeting was different to all she had imagined during the years they had been apart. Luke

37

looked older, she expected that, but he also looked tired, much thinner, and defeated.

They did not make love that first night or for many nights after his return. Instead, they lay together in Luke's bed and Isabella held him close and listened while Luke talked. Eventually his words trailed off, his breathing became even, and when she was sure he was sleeping, Isabella relaxed and fell asleep herself.

She realized, with wisdom beyond her twenty-four years, that he needed this more than sex. Unlike some returning home, who never spoke of their war service, Luke Fisher was of a different breed. He wasn't injured, had not suffered as so many had. But he needed to rid himself of the shadows his ordeal had cast, to expiate the demons of guilt for having survived where so many had perished.

Luke talked for weeks, interspersed with long periods of silence, as he recalled events from the camps. Now, having purged the memories, he was beginning to feel well again. His time in England prior to repatriation where he had been interviewed and demobbed along with countless others, had taken a long time. He had been well fed and found to be medically fit before waiting for a liner to carry him back to Australia. Now, after a long sea journey he was home, back with Bella.

In contrast to Bella's statement, Christmas had been spent with the family and 1948 had dawned, giving fresh hope to everyone. One morning, the caress along Bella's side was as light as a feather, but it woke her. She opened one eye. Sunlight was streaming through the bedroom window. She turned onto her side and Luke's hand that had been resting on her waist, moved to cup her breast. He was propped on one elbow, a smile on his lips, that well remembered glint of mischief in his eyes. Isabella moved her hand, then smiled. Luke, it seemed, was feeling better.

'Now?' he enquired.

'Too bloody right.'

* * *

Luke's return to Australia had presented a problem for one of those closest to him. His sister Dottie felt she had to find somewhere else to live. During his absence, Dottie had acted as housekeeper for his apartment in the city, but although the couple were content for Dottie to remain there, she wanted to be away. Given her own unhappy experience, the prospect of marital harmony was something she was still unwilling to witness. Even when Luke announced that he and Isabella would need to move closer to Fisher Springs's headquarters once they were married, Dottie wasn't tempted to remain.

'Stay here,' Luke offered. 'I'm not going to chuck you out on the street. You'll get your full inheritance from Mom and Dad when you reach thirty-five, not just your allowance. You could buy the apartment then, if you want?'

Apart from the feeling of playing gooseberry to the couple, and in spite of her brother's kind offer, Dottie had come to realize that city dwelling wasn't really for her. All her life had been spent in either a rural or small-town environment, and a large city felt alien, even after several years. She smiled at Luke. 'No thanks, it's a really kind offer, but I think it's time I struck out on my own. I've never really settled to the city, either as a place to live or work. I guess I'm still a small-town girl at heart.'

'What will you do? Where will you go?'

'I think it's time I returned home. Uncle Patrick and Aunt Louise have offered me my old room back. It's time I faced whatever demons are there. I know one or two of Danny's boozing cronies threatened all sorts of dire things when I left him, but that's all in the past. If they try anything, I'll give them what for. I'm no longer the timid little mouse afraid of life.'

'If that's what you want. I may as well sell this place, I have good use for the money. We can rent somewhere to start with,' — he reached out and took hold of Dottie's hand, — 'I had a lot of thinking time before I came home. I've decided to rebuild the homestead.'

'You have? Luke that's wonderful.'

'It was good enough for us when we were young and I think Mom and Dad would like the idea. Besides, it's only half a mile down the road from where you'll be.'

'It won't be the same though. It won't be the place where you saved me and Bella from the fire.'

'Oh yes it will. The original plans Mom and Dad had drawn up will be in an office somewhere. And that's what I'm going to find.'

'Oh, Luke,' was all Dottie could say, as she wiped away the tears at the memory of their parents' death.

* * *

The news of Dottie's impending arrival had been greeted with enthusiasm in the Finnegan household, with one notable exception. Elliot, Patrick and Louise's older son, heard the announcement with dismay, which fortunately went unnoticed. Neither of his parents spotted the tormented expression or Elliot's obvious agitation, otherwise they would have been certain to ask questions. Dottie was loved by those close to her, and there was much sympathy too for the suffering she had undergone at the hands of her brutal husband. There had been hopes of reconciliation after he'd stopped drinking and tried to make amends, but that had been abruptly cut short by his death when fighting against Rommel's forces in the African campaign. In the meantime, Dottie had remained in Melbourne where she had always been known as Miss Fisher.

As soon as he could, Elliot slipped away and went to his room. Once inside he locked the door and went across to his wardrobe where he kept a case containing all his sketches. Elliot was a talented artist for whom his teacher had voiced high hopes. Now, aged twenty-two, he was pondering whether to try to make painting his career, or whether to get another job and maintain it as a hobby.

He flicked through the sheaf of papers until he found the one he was looking for. It had been drawn almost five years earlier. Since completing the sketch, he had kept it locked away in the portfolio, well away from prying eyes. No one else had ever seen it. The drawing was of a young woman lying on a bed. She was naked, her expression one of dreamy, languorous contentment. Had his art teacher or any expert seen the sketch, they would have found it difficult to believe that a drawing containing such overtly sensual implications had been drawn by someone so young. Indeed, they would have insisted that the artist must have been in an intimate physical relationship with the subject of the sketch to have achieved such a detailed knowledge of every curve and line of her body.

The woman portrayed by Elliot was Dottie Fisher. She had been at the house over Christmas the year news came through of her husband's death. The weather had been hot, and she had taken a bath prior to going for an afternoon nap to escape the worst of the heat. Dottie had lain down to cool off, unaware that the catch on her bedroom door was faulty. By chance, a stray breeze had caused it to open wide enough for Elliot to glance inside the room when he passed.

One look was enough. Elliot stopped, spellbound by his first glimpse of a naked woman. Although Dottie was eight years older than Elliot, she had the slender figure of a young girl. In that instant, it was not only the artist in him that was aroused. Had he been older, more experienced, braver even, Elliot would have gone into the room, chanced his luck, hoped that the dreamy expression on her face concealed a desire as ardent as his own.

Instead, having committed the image to his photographic memory, he went to his own room and began the sketch. It took him over an hour to complete, and once it was done, he hid it away. From time to time, when his memory was awakened, he would take the sketch from its place of concealment and stare at it longingly, aware of the hopelessness of his cause.

Now, the news that Dottie would be returning, and would be sleeping only yards away from him, rekindled hope, desire, and mixed with that, trepidation in the young artist.

In the intervening years, Elliot had developed into a strikingly handsome young man. He had also been far less than celibate during that time. Although Elliot didn't actively pursue them, he became the target of a large number of young girls' amorous advances, many of whom he had indulged. Happy to go to bed with them, none of his conquests had attracted him in the same way as the unattainable Dottie. However, during the time of her absence, he had gained valuable experience from his various encounters. No longer would desire falter in the face of a challenge, or the possibility of rejection.

* * *

Patrick Finnegan was sitting on the veranda talking to Luke, while the womenfolk were indoors discussing weddings. 'When you're fully fit again, I want you back at Fisher Springs. You have to take over the running of the group eventually, I can't go on forever. Let's face it, the only reason you left in the first place was because you couldn't work alongside your brother.' Finnegan paused. 'This is going to sound rotten, but the plain fact is, that now Philip's dead, that reason no longer exists. So there should be no barrier to your return. Once you and Bella are settled I'd like to spend more time with Louise. As far as the business is concerned, there have been a lot of changes over the past few years, so I don't expect to hand over to you and walk out of the door five minutes later. You'll need time to get used to the way things are now. However, I think what we've seen so far is nothing compared to the challenges ahead. They'll need a young man at the helm to make the right decisions in response to them.'

Finnegan eyed Luke with affection. 'When your parents were running the businesses with me as your father's second in command, I was impressed by his ability to foresee the way things were moving. I reckon you've inherited something of that ability, and I think you'll need it when you take over. You'll notice I said when, not if. The fact is, apart from my shares and those that have been placed in trust for Phil's daughter, you own the company. If that's not compelling reason enough, I guess you'll need the job before long, to pay the way for a growing family. I can't think it'll be that long once you're married before Isabella tells you she's in the family way, and you certainly don't want to be hanging around at home where you can get volunteered for nappy changing duty.'

Luke smiled. 'You seem to have forgotten about my shares, they made good dividends while I've been away and unable to spend them. But I suppose I would soon get bored living off them.'

'So, how about it? Will you come back to Fisher Springs?'

'I've no problem with that, but there are several things I want to do first. I just need time. One thing I do need from you though is to find out who built the family homestead.'

'That's easy. I have the details here in my study. We used the same architects for our house. Are you saying you intend to build on the land?'

'Not just build, replicate. All the drainage and some services should be salvageable and that will speed things up, especially if I bring in enough builders.' He paused and watched the creek that ran below the property, along to where their family home had once stood half a mile away, stirring memories of that dreadful day. 'I know how much we all loved that house, and I can't think of a better way to remember Mom and Dad.' He turned to Patrick. 'But there are things I need to get out of my system before I can get involved in the business again.'

'OK, Luke, just don't leave it too long.'

CHAPTER FIVE

The spring of 1948 marked Jessica Tunnicliffe's return to Bradford. With her highly successful war service over, she had joyfully accepted scientist Robert Binks's offer of marriage. Before they left their work in London, Jessica had taken Robert on a pilgrimage. Half a mile from her flat was a large crater, one of thousands that pock-marked the city, evidence of the severity of the Blitz. This bomb site had been created in June of 1940, when the onslaught of German bombing was at its height. Over one hundred civilians had been killed that day, most of them inside an air raid shelter that had taken a direct hit. One of the victims had been searching for, and was on his way to visit, Jessica. She laid a small wreath of flowers at the edge of the crater — the closest Jesse Barker ever came to meeting his daughter.

Before being seconded to an undisclosed scientific role for the government, Robert was a director of Spring Chemical Company based in Bradford, a subsidiary of Fisher Springs UK. His future was bound up in the development of new chemical products, and there was now a vacancy for a new managing director to replace Robert's father, now retired. Although Robert was a director, he left the decision making to the others.

Sonny Cowgill and his cousin, Simon Jones, the UK directors of Fisher Springs, thought long and hard about the appointment. A successful track record of managing a team of scientists, planning and working to budgets were all essential for the post. Only one applicant could claim such a record and stood out above all others. With boldness amounting to daring they decided the outstanding candidate should be offered the appointment, subject to the approval of the company's Australian owners. This was freely given.

On their return from honeymoon, Robert drove to the Bradford plant he had not seen for years. He parked in the bay reserved for the managing director.

One of the process workers, passing by, warned Robert, 'I wouldn't leave it there, mate, the new MD starts today.'

Jessica Binks emerged from the passenger seat. 'It's OK,' she told the worker. 'I've given him my permission.'

Her first act, on the day she officially took office, was to call a meeting of departmental heads. Many of them, like Robert, had spent the war working elsewhere. Some had been all but worn out by the twin pressures of demand and the lack of staff to produce their range of products. They would need careful handling, but Jessica felt confident what she had to tell them would set the tone for the company's development.

She looked around the large boardroom table. Her wartime post had been to head up a team of inventors and scientists, many of whose ideas were eccentric, to put it mildly. Handling this bunch of predominantly middle-aged chemists, should, by comparison, be relatively easy. All Jessica had to do was win them over, and once she had them on her side, to channel their activities into her own plans. She was aware that creating a good first impression would be critical to the success of her relationship with them.

'Gentlemen,' she began, 'I can imagine the surprise you must have felt on learning that a woman had been appointed to head the company. As far as I'm aware, but please feel free to correct me if I'm wrong,' she paused, 'I believe I am the

45

first director of this company to wear a skirt — in the office at least.'

There was a ripple of subdued laughter.

'Let me assure you that I am well qualified for the task.' She went on to outline her wartime career. 'I can't tell you any more than that,' she ended, 'because much of what I was engaged in was, and remains, subject to the confines of the Official Secrets Act. However,' she added with a smile, 'my husband, who has returned to the post he held before the war, will be able to provide you with a reference, in the respect of work, at least.'

Encouraged by the smiles that greeted her opening, Jessica continued, 'My brief is to lift the burden of administration from you and those working for you, in order that you can channel all your energy into developing and producing new and existing products to the highest attainable standards. And,' she added, 'expanding our range into hitherto untouched areas within the industry. With that in mind I am able to tell you that I have already received the backing of our parent company to take the first steps to recruit and train additional staff who will be selected for their expertise in a new range of products the company has thus far not touched.'

Jessica saw one or two looks of mild alarm around the table and hastened to reassure her listeners. 'This will not take place at the expense of any of our existing lines, it will be purely incremental. I am referring to the field of pharmaceutical chemistry. As we move close to the second half of this century, the chemical industry, which has grown beyond all recognition over the past two decades, is scheduled to expand at an even faster rate. It is the intention of the group that this company will be at the forefront of that expansion. That really sums up my brief. I can think of no better way to secure our jobs — and our pensions.'

She paused and waited for them to digest this news before continuing, 'I understand your difficulties and undoubted misgivings, and can appreciate that you might think we are trying to run before we can walk, but that is far from being the case. Most of your problems stem from the fact that you have to work with far from adequate staff levels. Am I right?'

There was a chorus of agreement.

'I know that many of the company's best employees were called up to fight, or like my husband, to work on projects connected with the war effort. Sadly, some of them will not be returning.' Jessica paused as those in the room nodded in silent agreement. 'But those that return and are deemed suitable will be taken on as soon as possible. Added to which, as the armed forces reduce their numbers, I foresee a large pool of potential employees for us to pick and choose from. With that in mind, I would be obliged if you can submit reports to me on the numbers required to bring each department up to strength. And by that I mean maximum efficiency level, not simply enough to get by on. Once I have them, the recruitment drive will begin immediately, so I would like those reports on my desk by Friday.

'That's all for now, gentlemen, except to say that there are exciting times ahead, and I look forward to sharing them with you. I will make it my priority over the course of the next couple of days to meet with you individually, to go into your requirements in greater depth. In the meantime, if I haven't already convinced you, and if you still have doubts about working for and reporting to a woman, let me assure you that the way I will run this business will not be affected in any way from my being female.'

As the department heads were leaving, Jessica's husband heard one of them remark to a colleague, 'I'm not so sure about her last statement. From what I could gather, I reckon she's got more balls than most men I know.'

* * *

As Jessica was finishing her speech, on the other side of Bradford, her half-brother Joshua Jones was conducting a far more stressful conversation with his mother and stepfather.

Sadly, the outcome of his meeting with his parents was far less successful.

Josh's mother, Naomi, hated all things German. On the face of it, the reason was simple. A German bomb had killed her daughters Daisy and Emily and left her husband Simon, director of Fisher Springs UK, confined to a wheelchair.

Behind the surface of Naomi's implacable hatred was another, far more complex and even darker motive. Naomi was half-Austrian by birth, a fact that very few people even suspected, and far fewer knew. Her birth, which included a strong Serbian inheritance, had led her to become a fringe member of the secret organization that had planned and carried out the assassination of the Emperor Franz Ferdinand and his wife in Sarajevo, sparking off the First World War. She had fled to England and headed to Bradford in the hope of finding her lover, Jesse Barker, whose child she was carrying. Without success, she later met and married Simon Jones who adopted Joshua. Guilt over her involvement in the earlier events, and the appalling carnage that followed, left Naomi not only confused and angry, but totally incapable of rational thought regarding her erstwhile countrymen.

When Josh announced his intention to marry Astrid, his Austrian girlfriend, the news had come like a red rag to a bull for Naomi. She was unable to see Joshua, now thirty-two years of age, as anything but the multi-lingual university student who at the age of twenty had been recruited by the British Secret Service. Naomi was unaware of the dangers he had faced during the war, dangers that had turned her son into a man, dangers that had altered him beyond recognition.

The first intimation of the extent to which he had changed came in his parting words to her and Simon, shortly before he left the house.

'It is absolutely no use trying to get me to change my mind. I intend to return to Austria, find Astrid, ask her to marry me, and, if she agrees, I will bring her back to England as soon as the paperwork can be arranged. Whether we stay in England or not is another matter entirely. That will happen with or without your blessing. I would have preferred it to have been with, but if that isn't going to happen, so be it. I will be staying at the Midland Hotel for two more days while my travel arrangements are made. If you should change your mind, you can contact me there.'

His mother rounded on him. 'Do you think for one minute I would countenance your liaison with a woman whose countrymen behaved so atrociously? Let me remind you what those murderous thugs did to your own family. Your sisters were killed and your father is confined to a wheelchair suffering constant pain because of them. Nothing you could say will ever persuade me to accept this female into our ranks.'

'Astrid isn't like them at all. She hates them as much as we do, but I can see there is nothing I can say that will cause you to change your mind.'

Seconds later, as Naomi was still fighting with her emotions, she and Simon heard the front door close. Although Josh didn't slam it on his way out, the sound carried an air of finality to the couple.

As he walked the few miles back into the centre of Bradford, Josh reflected bitterly on the outcome of the quarrel. It was tragically ironic that he would never be allowed to reveal the part Astrid had played alongside him in an action that had contributed hugely towards securing victory for Britain.

Prior to the onset of war, when disguised as a German student supposedly on holiday in Austria, Josh had met and fallen in love with Astrid. While there, his objective was to discover what progress the Germans had made in developing a super weapon, one capable of inflicting huge numbers of casualties and causing immense destruction over a wide area.

The weapon was similar to that used to such deadly effect years later by the Americans against Japanese cities. Its designer, a German industrialist, lived near Salzburg. Josh was able to discover that this man was the only person capable of developing the weapon beyond its theoretical stage. With his mission complete, and following a tearful farewell,

Josh had no option but to leave for England, promising to return.

His report was delivered only days before Neville Chamberlain's sombre announcement — war was declared. Despite his pleas, Josh was denied the opportunity to go back for Astrid.

The information he provided included specific details of the weapon's capabilities and made grim reading. One paragraph, however, provided the germ of a possible solution.

The success of developing this weapon lies exclusively with one man. Papers I found in his desk indicate that there is no one available to the Nazis who could take over the project. Remove him, and the work would cease, the whole concept would have to be abandoned, for the foreseeable future at least.

That was when a major operation was devised to dispose of the threat. The plan had been fraught with danger, to put it mildly. Conceived in extreme haste, the odds against it succeeding, indeed the odds against Josh surviving, had been rated very slim by the planners. Some of them had believed that even slim was an overstatement.

Eventually, Josh was smuggled over the border back to Austria, where he took shelter in Astrid's flat. He explained the delay in his return and asked for her help. Her natural dislike of Germans was augmented by horror when Josh explained what the weapon would do. Although it meant betraying her country, possible imprisonment and almost certain execution if caught, Astrid agreed.

'What do I have to do?' she'd asked.

Josh grinned. 'The first bit's easy. I want you to befriend a German officer, preferably a young, good-looking one, and entice him back here to your flat. Then I'm going to take him to the scientist's house. I'll want you to act as lookout for me. That's all there is to it, simple enough — in theory. Let's hope it works, for all our sakes — and hundreds of thousands more as well.'

Three weeks later, Josh headed back to England, his abiding memory that carried him through the remainder of the war and all the hazards he faced, was of Astrid, her courage and devotion to him, and her final words. 'I will wait for you, Josh, as long as this dreadful war lasts and long beyond. If you fail to make it through, I will never love another man. So take care of yourself. And if I should fail to survive, think of me sometimes as you are sitting in your English garden taking tea.'

By the time Josh had reached the safe neutrality of Switzerland, Austrian police were investigating what they considered to be a straightforward case. Called in by a hysterical phone message from the housekeeper, the police arrived at the house to discover the body of the industrialist in his study, his head a pulpy mass where the bullet from his revolver had removed a sizeable percentage of his brain. In the master bedroom, the corpse of the industrialist's pretty wife was naked on the bed. Alongside her, in a similar state of undress, was a captain in the Wehrmacht. Both of them had been shot in the head from point blank range. It didn't take the greatest of sleuths to work out that this was the classic double murder and suicide following the wife's infidelity with a handsome soldier.

Quite how Josh and Astrid achieved the kidnapping of the soldier, transported him to the house and put him in bed with the scientist's wife prior to shooting them and her husband, would never be revealed.

CHAPTER SIX

The day following Josh's row with his parents, Simon Jones arrived at the offices of Fisher Springs's UK subsidiary and consulted with his co-director Sonny Cowgill. Merely getting to and from work was no easy task for Simon. With the aid of his live-in assistant, Simon had to be lifted from the wheel-chair into his car, chauffeured to the office, and wheeled up the specially installed ramp to the ground floor and into the lift. Despite the difficulties involved, Simon, as befitted his role of group finance director, was usually the first to arrive at work.

Simon explained the situation with Josh.

Sonny listened sympathetically. 'It seems that every-where you look there appear to be arguments, divisions, quarrels. I thought people would have had enough after two wars such as we've endured. Have you any idea what you intend to do?'

'Not really, at least no clear idea as yet. I thought I'd go see him without Naomi. See if I can get him to change his mind. If I can't persuade him, I'm going to suggest he goes to Australia.' Simon paused and looked at Sonny. 'What do you think? If I give him a letter of introduction to Patrick Finnegan at head office, do you think they might give Josh a job over there?' He smiled slightly. 'Flagrant nepotism, I know, but if you can't use your influence on behalf of those close to you, what good is it?'

Sonny agreed. 'For my money, having met Patrick Finnegan when they came to England, and him being aware of what a good job you've done on behalf of the group, I think he'd jump at the chance of employing your son. Would you like me to go along with you when you go to visit Josh? If you prefer, I'll write the letter to Patrick for you. That way it doesn't look quite as blatant.'

'Would you mind? I just feel that if Josh sees someone else he knows and trusts it might stop the meeting from descending into another quarrel and a slanging match.' Simon smiled, a little sadly. 'I'm very much afraid that Josh has inherited his mother's quick temper, and he's very touchy about this girlfriend of his, because she's Austrian, I suppose.'

'Does Josh know the truth about Naomi? About her background? Does he know that his mother's half-Austrian?'

When Simon was lying in hospital after the bombing, with no certainty that he would recover, he had told his cousin about Naomi's past, seeking Sonny's promise that he would protect his wife should he not survive. He was the only person he had ever confided in.

'I don't think he knows. If he had, he would have broached the matter of his plans to marry this Astrid girl differently. Added to which, the only people he could have learned it from are Naomi, me, and Mr Smith, the boss of that department Josh worked for during the war. That he knew Naomi's background was how he, shall we say, "encouraged us" into suggesting Josh go and work for him. He did promise never to reveal what he'd found out to anyone, especially Josh.'

'I know you told me it was some sort of government unit he worked for, but has Josh ever told you exactly what he did for them?'

Simon shook his head. 'Not a word, but then you'd hardly expect him to, would you? His only comment was when he came home in 1944, a couple of months or so before D-Day. He told us he got a few dirty looks, mostly from women strangely enough, because he wasn't wearing a uniform, and he was obviously fit enough to be in the forces. I think it rather amused him. As I remember, he said something along the lines of, "If they only knew. I've seen far more danger than most of the blokes wearing those uniforms will ever face", which might have amused Josh no end, but it worried his mother half to death.'

'OK, let's go and see him. I'll write the letter of introduction to Finnegan and, if it's needed, have it with me. It might help.' Sonny grinned. 'Or it might not.'

The visit was successful to a degree, even if the conversation was stilted and awkward, at least to begin with. One thing that came out as Josh spoke to his stepfather, something he hadn't mentioned previously because he'd been unaware of it, was Astrid's reaction to the possibility of coming to live in England.

'I managed to get to speak to Astrid yesterday,' Josh told Simon. 'It wasn't easy, we didn't get very long, it was a terrible connection. She's well enough, although she told me food is extremely scarce and very expensive. She's desperate to get away from Austria.'

He paused for a moment. 'However, she's very concerned that if she lived here, people would be unpleasant to her when they find out her nationality. She believes there will be a lot of bad feeling against anyone or anything German or Austrian. I think she has a point. She knows I'm going back for her and I'll get her away from there as soon as I'm able. Where to, I'm not sure, but we need to make plans for the future.'

'You think she'd be far happier somewhere else?' Simon suggested.

Josh studied his stepfather for a moment. 'OK, out with it, Dad,' he told him. 'What have you got in mind?'

'I wondered if Astrid would be less uneasy about living in, say, Australia?'

'I've no idea, not without asking her. Why?'

Simon outlined his plan.

Josh smiled when he'd finished. 'That's typical of you, always looking out for others. I believe it was the best day of Mum's life when she met you. You've been so good for her, far better than Jesse Barker would have been. I'm afraid my natural father caused nothing but trouble all his life.'

'How much do you know about him?' Simon was wary, knowing the truth, afraid that Josh did too.

'Not much more than the fact that he did his best to ruin my life, and that of my half-sister as well, even without trying to.'

'Your half-sister? I didn't know you had one,' Simon said.

Josh smiled bitterly. 'Neither did I, not until it was too late. But you ought to know, because she's one of your fellow directors.'

His stepfather stared at Josh in astonishment. 'Jessica Binks? You're saying that Jessica is your half-sister?'

'That's right. Jessica and I met and fell in love when I was at university, and then we found out the true nature of our relationship.'

'Well, well, well.' Simon clicked his fingers. 'Of course, that was the year before you went to work for the mysterious Mr Smith. You were as moody as hell, and you said there was a girl at the bottom of it. Poor you, and poor Jessica, if she felt the same way about you as you did about her.'

'Promise me you won't say a word, Dad. She would be mortified if she even suspected I'd told anyone, especially someone as close as you.' He looked across at Sonny, who nodded agreement.

'I'm afraid I already knew,' Sonny said. 'Jesse Barker was looking for his daughter and sought information from Connie and Michael. Connie told me. We kept quiet to avoid any scandal.'

Simon nodded. 'Well, I won't breathe a word to anyone, I promise.' Simon grinned. 'I remember getting into bother with your mother because I told her I'd suggested to you that what you needed was a passionate affair with another woman to get over what was making you so unhappy.'

It was Josh's turn to grin. 'I got that, right enough. The first job I was given by Mr Smith was to go to Spain and cover the Civil War. While I was there, I got involved with a woman called Carmen, who had suffered dreadfully at the hands of the Nationalists. We ended up leading a group of guerrilla fighters based in the mountains. Towards the end, when it was becoming clear that we were going to finish up on the losing side, I was given orders to return to England, so I never even got chance to say goodbye. I often wonder what happened to her. I can't even be sure she survived.' Josh smiled, slightly ironically. 'It seems to be my fate to fall in love with inappropriate women. One turns out to be a close relative, another is damaged beyond measure by what happened to her. And now I'm planning to marry someone who until a year or so ago was on the opposing side during the war. Not a bad track record.'

From out of nowhere, Sonny remembered stories Mark and Jenny had told of their experiences in Spain during the Civil War working with the resistance, of the need for codenames to protect their identities. He stood up and stared at Josh, a look of pure bewilderment on his face. 'La Trompetista!' he exclaimed. 'Good God! That was you. You were La Trompetista!'

Josh turned to stare at his stepfather's cousin, shock registered in his expression. His eyes widened. 'How on earth did you know that?'

Sonny explained what he knew then added, 'And Carmen did survive, that is, up to the point when Mark and Jenny left her. That's all I know.'

'I remember Carmen mentioned an English couple who had joined the band. But I never met them. So that was Mark and Jenny?' Josh shook his head in disbelief. 'What a weird coincidence. At least that's not covered by the Official Secrets Act.'

* * *

When he reached Byland Crescent that evening, Sonny found the family in the lounge and told Mark and Jenny about the identity of their mysterious erstwhile leader during the Spanish Civil War. When they had recovered from the surprise, Jenny said, 'I'm absolutely certain he didn't know about the baby, though.'

'Baby, what baby?' Sonny looked perplexed.

'Carmen gave birth to a little girl. I had to deliver her.'

'You remember, Dad,' Mark chimed in, 'that was why I made those wooden knitting needles you were so rude about.'

'Oh yes.' Sonny smiled. 'So much has happened since then, it quite slipped my mind. But I think Josh ought to know about this, don't you?'

'Carmen believed the baby was recompense for her young daughter who had been murdered by the Nationalists,' Mark told him.

'But Carmen didn't leave Spain, not altogether. When we said goodbye to her, she told us she intended to take Consuela to Ibiza, where her grandmother lived. I have the address upstairs. It's a village called San Juan Bautista,' Jenny said.

'That translates as St John the Baptist,' Mark added.

'Thank you, son, I think I might have worked that out for myself.'

'Carmen felt she would be safer in Ibiza, among her relatives, because there would be less likelihood of anyone betraying her. And also, if anything did happen to her because of her involvement with the guerrillas, there would be people to care for the baby.'

It was at that moment Joyce, accompanied by Andrew, emerged from the kitchen to announce dinner.

Jenny nudged Mark in the ribs. Mark grinned at her.

'Dad, those much-maligned knitting needles are going to get some further use.'

Rachael looked up sharply from her needlework. 'Does that mean what I think?' she asked.

'It means that Jenny's pregnant, if that's what you thought,' Mark confirmed.

Rachael jumped to her feet and hugged them both. 'Oh congratulations, both of you. It's just what this family needs.'

Joyce then took her turn before Sonny chipped in, 'I'm glad too, because I can get a workman to secure the chandelier in the sitting room. It's beginning to work loose from all the vibration.'

He smiled gently as he saw his son and daughter-in-law's expressions, which were of matching crimson.

Andrew looked mystified. 'Daddy, what does pregnant mean?'

Over dinner there was some discussion about whether or not, in view of his changed circumstances, Josh should be told about Carmen. No clear resolution was reached. In the event, it didn't matter, for when Sonny at last made his mind up and rang the hotel next morning, he was informed that Josh had already booked out, headed, as the receptionist believed, for London.

CHAPTER SEVEN

Luke Fisher pulled his car to a halt at the roadside and stared at the scene in dismay. 'What the hell's happened here?' he muttered.

Alongside him, Isabella looked equally sombre. 'It looks like those photos I've seen in American magazines when tornados have struck.'

'Yes, but we don't get tornados around here.'

The land, which should have been filled with neat rows of young vines, ready to put out their harvest of grapes, was little more than a tangled mass of weeds. Here and there, the couple could see twisted remnants of metal piping, the only remaining sign of the automatic watering system Luke had planned for the vineyard when he had bought the land, and his partner Gianni Rocca had imported the plants. Along the perimeter road, more twisted metal marked what had once been the boundary fence which held up the net roof. Most of it was lying on the ground, with only an occasional panel standing in defiant futility against the encroaching wildlife.

'Did it fall, or was it pushed?' Luke gestured to the fence, but in truth both of them knew that the damage owed nothing to natural causes.

'Maybe we should go up to the house and see Mr and Mrs Rocca, and find out what has gone on here,' Isabella suggested.

'We'll do that in a while. I want to have a look inside the fence first.'

'Be careful, Luke, that wire could give you a nasty scratch.'

Smiling at Bella's concern, but mindful of the warning, Luke stepped carefully over the flattened screen and walked across to where he judged the vines had been planted. He could just about make out the line where the soil had been earthed up to protect the roots of the young plants. Here and there he could see the pathetic remnants of what had once been proud, hopeful young vines, eager to furnish their owners with a crop of grapes worthy of making into a quality wine.

Instead, the brown, withered stems with occasional leaf fragments clinging desperately to the stalks were all that remained of a dream, a dream that appeared to be as dead as the plants themselves.

How could Gianni have allowed this to happen? Where was he? And what had happened to destroy the immigrant's vision, the one he had confided to Luke, and the one they had planned to turn into a reality? Surely it was inconceivable that Gianni would have allowed his dream to wither as these plants had withered. Luke's musing was interrupted by the sound of an engine. He looked back towards the dirt road in time to see a car bearing the insignia of the state police pull to a halt behind his own vehicle.

The officer, who looked to be near retiring age, struggled from the vehicle. 'Hey, you, come out of there. You're trespassing.'

That was adding insult to injury. Luke marched back across the land, jumping the fence in his haste to get answers. 'Where are the people who were working this place? Why is it such a mess?' he demanded.

'The Eyeties, you mean? Who knows, and who the hell cares? I did hear the woman and her brood went back to where they came from after the husband was interned. Why do you want to know? Friends of theirs, are you? Because I should warn you, friends of theirs aren't welcome around here.'

'Is that why the place has been vandalized? Did you know about the vandalism? Turn a blind eye to it, perhaps?'

'What vandalism?'

'That fence, for one thing, it didn't simply blow down. Anyone can tell it's been cut through, same with the irrigation system. And those vines didn't just die. They were allowed to, maybe encouraged with something like DDT.'

'Now listen here, Sonny Jim, I wouldn't know anything about that, but if that's what happened, it serves the bastards right.'

'Do you know who was responsible for the damage?'

'Look, around here, I ask the questions.'

'No, you don't.' The interruption came, not from Luke, but from Bella, who had got out of the car and was standing alongside the passenger door. 'When he asks questions, you answer them, and you do it quickly, truthfully and politely. He's spent the last eight years fighting the Germans, risking death every day while you've been sitting on your fat arse playing cops and robbers in your reservist job. And by the look of it, turning a blind eye to the sort of thuggery he's been fighting against.'

Cowed by this unexpected verbal assault, the officer admitted, 'I did arrest a man, but my boss said not to proceed with the case. It was in early forty-two, a couple of months after the attack on Pearl Harbour, and there was a lot of bad feeling around at the time. Still is.'

'I shall want copies of all your paperwork, together with the name of the culprit, plus the name and rank of the officer who blocked the prosecution.'

'What's it got to do with you?'

'It has everything to do with me. Gianni Rocca and his wife are my business partners, and I intend to sue everyone responsible for this mess for every penny they have. If possible, I want them behind bars.'

'Yeah, fat chance of any of that happening. If you're his partner, I'd keep quiet about the fact if you go into town. You won't be welcome there.'

'If that's the case, I think the sooner I get in touch with the local paper, the sooner the better. This whole stinking mess needs exposing.'

'You could try, but I don't think the editor would be interested in publishing it.'

'He will — if he wants to keep his job.'

'Listen, just who do you think you are? That paper belongs to Fisher Springs Group. They won't sack one of their editors and replace him just because some nosy bloke asks them.'

Bella responded, her face red with anger as she snarled, 'I'll tell you who he thinks he is. He's Squadron Leader Luke Fisher, DFC, DSO and bar, and he's the majority shareholder in Fisher Springs Pty. Not only does he own this land, he owns the paper!'

'Oh shit! Luke Fisher? Not the Luke Fisher who . . .'

'Yes,' she resounded, 'that Luke Fisher! And I also happen to be one of their reporters. So I suggest you get your fat arse into gear and start finding us some answers pretty damn quick. On your way there you might want to stop and have a word with the store owner. Get him to order in extra supplies of paper for the dunny, because there will be a lot of people in town shitting themselves by the time we've finished with them.'

The officer listened to her, his expression a mixture of awe and terror. He snatched his helmet from his head and turned to Luke. 'What exactly do you need, Mr Fisher?'

'First, I want to know where Gianni and Angelina Rocca are. Then I'm going to want my land restoring. Someone's going to have to pay for this damage, and it sure as hell isn't going to be me. Once I've seen Gianni, I'll let you know exactly what I have in mind. And if I do decide to restore this property, it might be worth reminding people that a productive vineyard will need a lot of people working in it.'

'If you'd like to follow me back to the station, I can get the information you want.' The officer was looking worried.

Once back in town, the man had started phoning around, enlisting support for Luke's cause, much to Bella's amusement. 'He's got off his fat arse,' she whispered to Luke.

The first to arrive at the police station had been the editor of the local paper, anxious to meet his employer, to create a good impression, and to interview the returning hero. When he left, forty-five minutes later, he was still smarting from the dressing down he received, not from Luke, but from Bella.

When they arrived at the house where they were assured the Rocca family now rented a couple of rooms, Bella stared at it in dismay. 'God, what a dump,' she muttered. 'It gives the word slum a bad name.'

'Never mind the house, let's see how Gianni and Angelina are.'

Although he did his best not to show it, Luke was shocked at how much Gianni and his wife had aged. The explanation wasn't too difficult to seek. It came via a grim tale, told mostly by Angelina.

'They came one day and took Gianni away to an internment camp. They had a sheet of paper with his name on it. After that, whenever I went into town, people would shout things, rude things. Then they refused to serve me in the shop. Most of that I could deal with, but when they started attacking the house, I was afraid for the children, that was when I had to get away. The little one had already been beaten up at school by a group of the other girls.'

'This is what we've been fighting against. It comes hard to realize this sort of thing was going on back home,' Luke said. He looked at Gianni. 'How was it for you in the camp?'

Rocca shrugged. 'OK, I guess. There were a few snide remarks, nothing more. For the most part it was just boring, nothing to do, nowhere to go. I was far more worried about Angelina and the children. And I felt guilty for letting you down. All that money going to waste. No more vineyard, like we hoped and dreamed of.'

Luke stared hard at Gianni, hoping to prompt a positive response. 'Do I have to remind you that both your names are on the contract?'

Gianni looked to his wife who gazed back, wide eyed. He shrugged.

'Is that it?' Bella looked from Gianni to Angelina. 'Are you going to accept defeat so easily? Spend the rest of your life feeling sorry for yourself and moping about what might have been, instead of getting stuck in and doing something about it?'

'What can we do?'

'I realize it will be a wrench tearing yourselves away from all this luxury,' — Bella gestured around the squalid apartment — 'but why not start by going back to the vineyard, fixing up the house there so you've somewhere decent to live. Then you could start planning to get a new perimeter fence erected, and restoring the irrigation system, and finally importing some new plants.'

Gianni looked at Luke, caught between hope and disbelief. 'But what about the land? I thought you said it had been infected.'

Luke smiled. 'I might have exaggerated a bit to put my point across and get the officer to do something about the mess. I've no evidence they used DDT or anything else. I reckon the plants simply died of neglect.'

'So, how about it?' Bella asked. 'Are you up for the challenge, or are you going to let the sick bastards win?'

Gianni started to laugh. 'By God, Luke. I heard you were flying Spitfires. I didn't know you liked them so much you plan to marry one.' His smile faded as he continued, 'All this will take a lot of time — and a lot more money. Are you willing to risk more after what happened to your investment?'

'I can't see any other way to get a return on my original investment,' Luke told him. 'However, more to the point, as Bella said, we can't allow people like that to trample on our dreams.' He paused, before adding, 'Let's just hope we don't declare war on Italy ever again.'

* * *

If Luke and Isabella had been shocked and dismayed by what they learned from Gianni Rocca and his wife, the testimony they heard some weeks later, when they visited a former soldier who had served with Luke's brother Philip, both saddened and angered them.

Their first surprise came from the man's obvious physical frailty. The man was gaunt, almost skeletal, his shrunken frame emphasized by clothing that looked several sizes too large for him. His face was wizened, and his stooping gait, plus the inability to walk far, even with the aid of the stick on which he leaned heavily, made them think they were talking to an elderly man. Learning that he was no older than Luke appalled them. On the sideboard behind the man's chair was a photograph, obviously taken before the war. The contrast between the robust young man depicted in the frame and the broken remnant in the chair was an obscene testament to his obvious mistreatment.

The story the man had to tell, the story Luke had travelled halfway across Australia to hear, backed up the physical proof of his ordeal. He had been reluctant to talk about it at first, but on hearing that Luke had been a POW in Germany, he relented and grudgingly agreed to tell them what he could.

'After the Nips captured us, they took us to work on the railway. It became known as Death Railway,' he began. 'I'd known Phil before, he was in the same unit as me, so we palled on in the hut, helped one another out, that sort of thing. Phil was in the next bunk to me, so we got to know one another quite well. Talking about home mostly and I got to know about Amelia and Clare.' He paused and added, 'The big shock for me and the rest of the blokes came when he told us about you.'

He grinned at Luke. 'I think it took Phil by surprise, how all the hut knew about you, made him feel proud I guess. And you needed something proud to hold onto in that stinking place, I can tell you. There was something about Phil that impressed the others too, a sort of quiet dignity, allied to a don't-mess-with-me attitude. That became evident soon after we got to the railway. Phil had a few run-ins with the guards. Took a few beatings because of it, but if they thought they could break his spirit, they reckoned with the wrong man. All it did was to make him more stubborn.'

He paused and took a sip of water from the glass on the table alongside his chair. 'Their favourite tools for the beatings were their boots, or the butts of their rifles. They weren't above dishing out a few jabs with their bayonets either, and they could be lethal if the cuts went septic. Phil didn't like being bossed about, I reckon he was too used to giving orders to take kindly to being on the receiving end, and that didn't help.

'There was one bloke in particular, a sadistic brute of a captain, who had it in for Phil. This guy was an animal, he'd think nothing of walking up to a prisoner and shooting him between the eyes, just because he looked at him the wrong way.'

He saw their expressions of incredulity. 'Oh, believe me, it's the truth. I saw him do it. Then one day he and Phil confronted one another. Looking back on it afterwards, I suppose it was inevitable, but if we'd foreseen it, we might have tried to keep Phil out of harm's way. It all started when one of the guards shoved one of our men to the ground. The poor bloke was on his last legs, dysentery had taken its toll on him. Phil told the guard where to go and pushed him to one side. The guard fell over, which made some of our boys laugh. The next minute up steps this captain, and starts in on Phil, kicking and punching him until he was almost unconscious, or so everyone thought.

'The next thing, this captain started pissing on Phil. Laughing all the time. When he'd finished, he turned away and started doing his flies up. Before anybody knew it, Phil jumped up, grabbed one of the guards' rifles, and stuck the bayonet into the captain's fat belly. He ripped the bugger open all the way up to his neck. The captain was on his knees, screaming, his guts spilling out on the ground into that pool of piss, dying in agony. And all our blokes were cheering.'

He stopped and took another sip of water, the third since he'd begun talking, Bella noticed. 'I'm not going to tell you what they did to Phil. That wouldn't be fair. It was enough for those who witnessed it to remember, without inflicting it on others. It took him three days to die, and all I will say is that throughout that time, he never screamed, never whimpered. And all we could think was, "I hope he dies soon for his own sake". That'll give you a clue as to the sort of agony he must have been in.

'Two weeks later the camp got a new commander. We'd already heard whispers that the Nips were on the brink of defeat, so it was no surprise that they started being a bit less inhumane. Then the Yanks dropped those two big ones and they surrendered.'

Luke and Bella left soon afterwards, but before they went, Luke made the man a promise. 'When you feel up to thinking about work, get in touch with me. I'll see there's a job for you with Fisher Springs.'

As they were travelling back to the rail station, Luke said, 'You know your dad wants me to take charge of the group as soon as possible? Well, the first thing I shall do is put a ban on all group companies employing anyone of Japanese extraction, or trading with any Japanese company or organization.'

'I can't see a fault with that,' Bella agreed. 'I wonder how much of that story Phil's wife knows?'

'None of it, I hope. And she won't learn any of it from me.'

'Do you know there was a time when I hated and detested Philip because I blamed him for you leaving us? Now, that all seems so petty, I feel ashamed.'

'I think what's happened in the last few years has caused a lot of people to reassess their attitudes to those around them. A sort of re-evaluation process. The things I heard about in Germany and the rumours that were flying around were pretty bad, but by the sound of it, the Japs were just as evil, if not worse. This century isn't half over yet, and I've lost two brothers in two wars. I was a baby, too young to remember Saul. But I quarrelled bitterly with Philip, which will haunt me for the rest of my life. I think the Fisher family has given enough. Hopefully from here on in we can start concentrating on more peaceful matters, like running a business.'

'And raising a family.'

'I take it you won't be content with just the one, then?'

'No way, I enjoy the process too much.'

* * *

Amelia Fisher, although now approaching forty, still looked highly attractive. Bella, watching her talking to Luke, thought, I hope I look that good when I'm her age.

'Phil loved you. You know that, don't you?' Amelia said.

Luke nodded. 'I never doubted that.'

'He was upset that the two of you couldn't get on, and I know he regretted the way you parted company, blamed himself for it. He wrote to you several times to say sorry. Did you get the letters?'

'I did, and I regret to say I didn't open them. I regret even more that we never made up our differences. That guilt is something I'll have to live with.'

Amelia looked at her brother-in-law, assessing the man she was meeting for the first time, comparing the reality to the legend she had heard so much about. He seemed so quiet, composed, self-effacing almost, nothing like the swaggering hero she had imagined. 'Phil mentioned you in the last letter I got from him. He was replying to one I'd sent, telling him about your DFC, which was in all the papers.'

Luke smiled. 'That was probably because Fisher Springs owns a lot of the papers,' he said lightly.

Amelia laughed. 'Possibly so. Would you like me to read what he wrote?'

'Only if it's not too distressing for you.'

Amelia disappeared into another room and returned clutching a folded paper. The passage read out was poignant, particularly in the light of what Luke and Bella had been told about what had happened to Phil. Amelia's voice quavered from time to time with emotion as she began reading.

'"Terrific news about Luke, and how typical of my brother. There he is in the thick of the action, doing great deeds, while the rest of us are sitting on our backsides twiddling our thumbs and waiting for orders that never arrive."'

Amelia paused and looked across at Luke. 'Do you know what happened? Do you know what they did to him in that beastly place?'

She saw the guarded expression on Luke's face and challenged him.

'You do know, don't you? Will you tell me? Please?'

'No, Amelia. Believe me, you wouldn't want to know. I was told some of it, and that was grim enough. All I will say is that Phil was the real hero. He deserved a medal far more than me. He knew that his actions would mean he'd likely be killed, but that didn't stop him.' Luke paused before continuing, 'I talked to one of his mates a few weeks back. He was there. He told me even though Phil was unarmed and surrounded he managed to kill one of the most sadistic brutes guarding them. That man had inflicted unspeakable torture on a lot of prisoners, but after Phil got shut of him, the treatment the other prisoners received improved no end. Reading between the lines, I'd hazard a guess that a lot of Aussies who made it home from the camp, wouldn't have survived but for what Phil did.'

Bella saw the tears glistening in Amelia's eyes, and thought it was high time the subject was changed for a more cheerful one. 'Tell me about Clare,' she suggested. 'How old is she now, seven?'

'Eight,' Amelia smiled. 'It was her birthday last week. She's a really bright girl, always top of her class. She loves reading and music. A lot like her father.'

'Have you everything you need? I know Philip was always good with money, but I can appreciate how expensive it must be, bringing a youngster up,' Luke asked.

Amelia smiled and patted his arm. 'We're fine, but thanks for asking.' She glanced across at Bella. 'Your father has been very kind. He got the company's accountants and lawyers to do all the tax and legal stuff connected with Phil's estate. However, I think he must be getting a bit absent-minded, because he's forgotten to charge their fees.'

'No, that's part of the group's insurance policy, set up by my mother and father,' Luke explained. 'All our executives' legal and financial costs are taken care of in-house. It was designed as part of a package to attract and retain top-class personnel. Very handy it has proved, too, over the years.'

'Enough business talk,' Bella said. 'The reason we're here is to invite you to our wedding.'

With the details sorted and the promise of Clare as a bridesmaid, they walked down the short drive to their car. 'You were gilding the lily a bit about Philip, weren't you?' Bella said.

'Maybe, maybe not. Look at it this way, all Amelia has left of him, all Clare has of her father, are memories. I feel sure Amelia will tell Clare what I said, and it seems only fitting that the child should grow up thinking of her father as a hero, which he undoubtedly was. And to be honest, how much of an exaggeration was it? Unless we'd been there and experienced those hellish conditions, who are we to judge?'

'Put it like that, I suppose you're right. One thing I would suggest, Luke. I know it's too late for you to mend fences with Philip, but I think we should make sure that we invite Amelia and Clare to all family gatherings from now on. Philip was out of the family circle for long enough and if we don't include Amelia and her daughter that could breed resentment.'

Luke looked at her fondly. 'You're dead right. I know only too well how lonely it can be when you're cut off from the rest of your family as I was when Phil and I fell out.'

'Hah! You were too busy shagging your way around the world to be lonely.'

'It did have its compensations, as I remember,' Luke said smugly.

'Well, memories are all you will have from now on. I'll see to that.'

'Ah, but that was before I fell in love with you, my darling.' Luke attempted to placate her.

'Don't worry, I'll see you're kept far too busy at home — and at work. You won't have time for even a sideways glance at anything wearing a skirt,' Bella promised, before adding, 'unless it's a Scotsman wearing a kilt.'

CHAPTER EIGHT

Mark stood with Jenny outside his father's study, knocked on the door, and was invited in.

'Everything OK, Mark? Jenny, are you OK?'

'She's fine, Dad. We, well I, just wanted a word.'

If Mark had been worried that his father would be shocked by his decision not to stay with the company, in the event, it was Mark who was to receive the surprise.

'I'd say you've made your mind up against staying with the firm. Am I right?' Sonny asked. 'So, why don't you tell me what's troubling you? I take it you have some scheme in mind.'

'How did you know?'

Sonny smiled. 'If I can't guess what my son's thinking by now, I'd be a fairly poor father. I can tell from your demeanour at work that you're unsettled. You've been thinking about this for quite some time, you've been distracted, and you've been tormenting yourself about telling me in case I'm offended.'

'And you're not? Offended, I mean.'

Sonny shook his head. 'Of course not, I want whatever's best for you. Any parent would. I might be disappointed, but that's another matter. So come on, tell me what you're going to do? Has it anything to do with woodworking?'

Mark stared at his father in surprise, both at the calm way Sonny had taken the news, and at his suggestion about woodworking. 'No, it hasn't. What made you think that?'

'It was something I remembered when I was trying to work out what you were scheming about. I recalled all those hours you spent in that workshop of mine when you were a boy. I thought you might have inherited my love for carpentry.'

'Oh, I get you now. You're right, I do enjoy messing about with wood, but I'm nowhere near skilful enough to attempt to earn a living from it. Not like you and—' Mark stopped suddenly.

'Not like Billy, you were going to say?'

Jenny saw the sombre expression on her father-in-law's face at the mention of his younger son.

Mark did not want to upset his father so began to explain. 'It all came from a magazine I picked up in 1944, as we were waiting for the go-ahead on D-Day. It had been left in the camp by an American, and I started reading it, out of sheer boredom mostly. I came across an article on the subject of synthetic fibres, written by some professor or other. He reckoned the advances being made will soon have synthetics rivalling natural fibres for the production of clothing. All types of clothing. I know they've already started putting some into carpet yarn, which they say gives it extra strength. My idea is that at present there are very few people processing synthetics in this country, so I might be able to steal a march on the competition. I've been writing letters and got a lot of information I need, and I've made some discreet enquiries in Bradford. It stands to reason they'd have more knowledge with it being a textile area. If I can obtain licences for such things as polyester from the big chemical manufacturers, I might be able to do really well. I've sat at that desk in Bradford until all I can see are words staring back at me. It might be the family business, but it's not for me. Sorry, Dad.'

'When I think about it, ever since you were a baby, the company has been a subsidiary of an Australian conglomerate, no longer our family business as such. Any sentiment involved has long since vanished. Look at it this way. My grandfather was only a weaver, and when my father announced that he wasn't following him into the weaving shed there was nearly a stand-up fight. Likewise, when my older brother James announced that he was going to marry the housemaid, my father threw him out of the house. Those are just two examples of parents making bad decisions. Josh Jones has fought and fallen out with his mother over his decision to marry an Austrian girl. That is yet another example. I love both of you far too much to risk alienating you by being churlish or refusing to back you to the hilt. It's your life, and I can't live it for you.'

Sonny paused then continued, 'You know something?' He looked from Mark to Jenny and back. 'Your mother still refuses to accept that Billy is dead. I tried to persuade her that the evidence was overwhelming, that other members of his unit had seen him get shot, seen his body falling from the mountainside. It was the closest we've ever come to a row.'

Jenny stirred restlessly in her seat, it was possibly the life she was carrying inside her that made her more attuned to a parent's wants and emotional needs. 'Why don't you take her to Crete?' she suggested. 'Not now, I realize that isn't feasible the way things are at present, but perhaps in a few years when things are more settled, and travel becomes easier. Maybe if she saw the place where it happened, she might be able to accept the truth.'

'That's certainly worth thinking about,' Sonny acknowledged, 'but such a journey seems very unlikely for a long time to come.'

Quite how long it would have to wait, none of them realized. Life, as often happens, got in the way. The decision to visit Crete was a painful one, but before they carried out what to them was almost a pilgrimage, Sonny and Rachael had many further challenges to endure together, both with heartache and deeply felt happiness.

* * *

In November, the tension of the preceding months had been replaced by a mood of elation, as the family celebrated the safe delivery of Mark and Jenny's second child, their daughter Susan Constance Cowgill. The new arrival's older brother Andrew, now a sturdy and rapidly growing eleven-year-old, was also delighted by the birth of his sister. His rapture was tempered by the fact that Susan's nursery, which was alongside her parents' bedroom, also adjoined his quarters. It wasn't long before he realized that his minute sibling kept extremely anti-social hours and had the Cowgill propensity towards strong voices, particularly when her demands for nourishment were not met. This was abetted by her seemingly incessant requirement for toilet assistance or to have her digestive process aided.

'How can something that small make so much noise?' he asked Grandma Rachael.

'She's only taking after you, Andrew,' Rachael replied. Seeing the boy's surprise she added, 'Not only you, but your father and your Uncle Billy, God rest him. You all had very loud voices. But you were the worst. You could bawl the house down if you didn't get what you wanted.'

Andrew was shocked into silence by this foul slander. He was beginning to think there was a conspiracy within the family when Grandpa Sonny, who had listened to the exchange added, 'Not only the house, Andrew. When you were christened, we thought the roof of St Mary's Church was going to lift off from the racket you made after the vicar baptised you.'

Andrew slunk away, unimpressed by his grandparents' lack of understanding. How, he wondered, was he supposed to get sufficient sleep to deal with the complexities of algebra at school, when he had to listen to a wailing banshee half the night? Not that Andrew knew what a banshee was, but he did know they howled a lot.

* * *

Before returning to work, Luke married Isabella Finnegan almost a year after his return home. Louise Finnegan, despite her insistence they should marry as soon as possible, found that staging what in Australian terms became 'the wedding of the year' took some arranging. It was fortunate for Luke that she wasn't within hearing when he'd whispered to Bella, 'Why can't we elope? I don't want all this fuss.'

'Let her have her day. You know Mom loves you, and I am her only daughter. She'll only get one chance at this.' With that, Luke had no alternative.

The December wedding at the height of the Australian summer was followed by a reception, a glittering occasion attended by all the Melbourne society and business community. The press took countless photographs of the happy couple, snaps that were syndicated around the globe along with articles including Luke's heroic deeds from his youth and war record. The radiant bride held her new husband's arm and beamed at the camera. Years of waiting were at last over. The bride's mother, wearing the best designer outfit she could find, marked her happiness by using half a dozen handkerchiefs to dry her tears of joy.

As the bride and groom led the way in the opening waltz, Luke murmured in Isabella's ear, 'Do you know, I think we've broken a Fisher family tradition.'

'What's that?' his bride asked suspiciously.

'Well, at least you're not in the family way.'

Isabella Fisher looked at her husband as he twirled her round the grand hall, love glowing in her eyes. 'Hah! That's what you think!'

Two weeks later in Scarborough, Jenny was glancing through a copy of *The Spectator* when she spotted a black and white photograph of a society wedding in Australia, the bride and groom appeared to be standing in brilliant sunshine on a lawn. She read the caption beneath. 'Mark, what do they call the family who owns Fisher Springs?'

'Fisher.' There was a titter from the others in the room.

'I know that! I mean their Christian names.'

'I have no idea. Why?'

'There's a wedding picture here, taken in Melbourne, of someone called Fisher, that's all. I wondered if they might be one of their family.'

'I haven't a clue.'

Sonny, who was passing behind her chair, glanced over her shoulder and took a look. He shrugged his shoulders. 'And neither have I.' He left the room and chuckled to himself at the ridiculous notion that there was a strong resemblance between the groom and his brother James.

* * *

Rachael Cowgill was listless, restricted by the winter weather. Even the antics of Andrew, delighted that he had an unexpected day off school, enabling him to continue his struggle with the jigsaw he had received for Christmas, could not raise a smile. Her gaze, as so often happened, went to the photograph of Billy and she recalled the dark days following the quarrel with her younger son, and the dreadful fallout of that disagreement.

She and Billy had parted on bad terms. Angry words had been spoken on both sides. Rachael had accused Billy of selfishness in lying about his age in order to join up. 'You don't seem to care how much you hurt those around you. I thought I'd lost your father during the last war and now your brother Mark is in action somewhere. Don't you think I've enough to worry about?'

'I've done it because it's my duty, Mother, and there's an end to it. I'm sorry if it upsets you but I have to do what my conscience tells me.'

'Well, I refuse to sit around here while you go gallivanting off wearing your bright new uniform, impressing the girls and playing the hero. So as of now, I shall not allow mention of you in this house and you needn't bother coming home on leave. If I can forget about you, I will no longer have to worry myself silly about whether you're safe or in danger, alive or dead.'

Of course she hadn't meant it. But Rachael was apt to speak first and think better of it later. As soon as Billy left the Byland Crescent house she regretted her angry words, but by then it was too late. As weeks and then months passed without news, she began to hope that time would heal the rift, but time, it seemed wasn't given the chance. That became evident when the War Office telegram arrived. The grief Sonny felt had been concealed, as far as possible. The anguish Rachael felt was undisguised.

The rift between Rachael and Billy had created a ripple effect that caused distress to the remaining members of the family. The brunt of the fallout hurt Billy's younger sisters most of all. Of the two, Frances, being older than Elizabeth, was able to cope better, particularly during the latter stages of the war when she gained the support of her newly acquired boyfriend, the USAF pilot Henry. No such alleviation came Elizabeth's way, which was unfortunate because she of all the family was closest to Billy.

Elizabeth blamed her mother for the quarrel and refused to hear a word of criticism against her brother. She had idolised Billy for as long as she could remember. Billy had always been there for her, whether it was when playing with her toys, encouraging her reading and writing, or merely taking her for walks, playing ball games on the beach or teaching her to swim.

Billy's death came as a devastating blow to Elizabeth, who was just entering the difficult stage of adolescence, her teenage years. Naturally reserved, this traumatic event caused her to retreat further into her shell and for almost three years thereafter she only spoke to her parents when she was addressed directly, never initiating a discussion. Even when she did respond, her replies were kept to an absolute minimum. When home from boarding school she remained in her room reading or enjoying her favourite pastime, the completion of a wide variety of puzzles. Her favourite were the cryptic crosswords which had become so popular during the pre-war years and, from what little evidence her parents could glean, Elizabeth had progressed from solving these to compiling them as well. The angry silence, as Rachael referred to it, showed little sign of abating, confounding Sonny's prediction that, 'she'll soon grow out of it'.

It was late in 1943 when matters came to a head, the trigger being the visit by a stranger to Byland Crescent. The man requested the presence of both Rachael and Sonny and introduced himself by name and by the government department he represented. Having inspected the paperwork he produced to confirm his credentials, Sonny asked what they could do for him.

'I'm here concerning your daughter Elizabeth.' He saw their bewildered and startled expressions and hurried to explain. 'It's all right, she hasn't done anything wrong. I assume that you're aware that Elizabeth has been submitting crosswords to the local paper.' The couple looked puzzled. 'And with her headmaster's encouragement she entered a cryptic crossword competition run by a national newspaper. We are involved in the project because we sponsor it, and our hidden motive is to identify and examine the brightest performers. Our objective is to pick out candidates with the right mindset and skills for a variety of tasks, and the propensity to think laterally, as in solving a cryptic crossword. I'm pleased to tell you that your daughter has out-performed almost all the other participants and as a result she and a few of her rivals have been cherry-picked to join the ranks of an elite group whose contribution to the war effort has already proved pivotal.'

He paused and, in the silence, Rachael spoke for the first time, her tone one of anger. 'All this is news to us. Our daughter doesn't confide in us and although you might think she would prove useful for whatever it is you're involved with, might I point out that she is far too young to be tackling anything such as that. She has her education to complete before she can consider a career of any description.'

'I'm sorry you didn't know of this beforehand, but it is the very nature of the task for such details to remain secret.

Please rest assured that we wouldn't have gone for someone of such a tender age and with such talents as Elizabeth, had it not been absolutely essential. I can only emphasize again that the work she will be asked to undertake is of national importance and vital to the war effort. Furthermore, she will be in a secure and safe location, in the company of a group of other highly talented and motivated young women, so there is very little chance of any harm coming to her.'

'I still can't agree to it.' Rachael was adamant but her defiance crumbled in the face of the official's reply.

'I'm sorry you feel that way, Mrs Cowgill, and although I don't like saying this, I'm afraid you have no choice in the matter. Given the nature of the task, refusal to cooperate is not an option, and the consequences of non-compliance would be extremely serious.'

Once Elizabeth learned of her selection, her parents had to endure another, even more distressing interview, this time with their youngest child. Elizabeth informed them that she would be happy to go and the rider she added was brutally frank. 'I'll be glad to leave this house. I have only bad memories of it. I will be doing something that is useful, but I'm not going because it will help the war effort, or for the good of the country. I'm doing it for Billy.'

Within six months, as she approached her seventeenth birthday, Elizabeth Cowgill had left Byland Crescent for an unknown location 'somewhere in England', and thereafter the only contact Sonny and Rachael had was via the only permitted medium of an annual postcard. The message on it simply stated, 'I'm well.'

They had no way of ascertaining if this was true or not, and were equally ignorant of her whereabouts. If the news brought them any consolation it was not apparent. Once the war ended, they hoped and expected that Elizabeth would return, but this didn't happen. The postcards continued to arrive on an annual basis, with the similar terse message. The only difference was that with the lifting of certain restrictions they now had an approximate idea of Elizabeth's location.

Having deciphered the postmark they identified that the card had been franked by a London post office, from which they assumed that their daughter was living and working somewhere in the capital, but later the frank changed to Bristol, from which they guessed that she had relocated to the West Country.

It was less than twenty-four hours after Rachael had been recalling the visit of the government official when the snow had at last relented, that further bad news seemed to add weight to Rachael's theory of an ill omen surrounding the Cowgill family, and those connected to them.

PART TWO: 1949–1951

"Is my girl happy,
That I thought hard to leave,
And is she tired of weeping
As she lies down at eve?

Ay, she lies down lightly,
She lies not down to weep:
Your girl is well contented.
Be still, my lad, and sleep."

A.E. Housman (1859–1936)
Is my Team ploughing?

CHAPTER NINE

Jessica Binks knew the time had come for them to move premises. When the chemical division was originally established by Haigh Ackroyd & Cowgill, the only suitable building they could find was a disused woollen mill. Over the years this had become too cramped. Now, with plans for expansion being approved, she was in the process of obtaining estimates for a new, purpose-built headquarters that would house all the facets of the company's operations.

She was also concerned for her husband Robert. Conscious of the need for budgetary control, he had been working every hour he could, often late into the evening. Eventually, Jessica overrode his objections. 'This can't go on, Robert. We've been back over nine months and you've rarely had a day off. You can't work twelve hours a day, seven days a week without your health suffering. Apart from that we don't get any time to ourselves. I'm surprised you managed to remember when it was Christmas. I didn't marry you so that I have to pick up your photograph to remind myself what you look like. I'm going to advertise the vacancy for an assistant, someone who is a competent enough chemist to fill in for you without the work suffering.'

'In that case, make it someone with pharmaceutical experience,' Robert replied. He knew his wife better than to attempt to argue with her. Besides which, he acknowledged that she was right. He'd been feeling the strain these last few months and was aware how close he was to the edge of a breakdown.

'OK, I'll get something drafted and have it put in the papers before the weekend.'

Although Jessica needed approval from her fellow directors to recruit new staff members, especially ones who would command larger salaries, her proposal met with no objection from Sonny Cowgill or Simon Jones. Jessica's performance over the period since she joined the group had been so good that they had already sought and received approval from Fisher Springs Pty for Jessica to be elected to the UK board of directors. The approval granted to their request demonstrated an equal level of confidence in their judgement as they had in Jessica's.

It was over a week before she got any feedback from the advertisement. As they drove through the snow to work on the Monday morning she told Robert, 'My first task today will be to interview a man who has applied for the position. If his credentials are right and he seems suitable you could soon have an assistant. Assuming he meets your criteria,' she added. 'Then you might be able to slow down a little.'

Robert yawned. Although he hadn't been into the factory over the weekend that didn't mean he'd been idle. In his briefcase, the notebook containing page after page of closely detailed text was ample evidence of his work rate. 'That is something I'm looking forward to,' he admitted.

Jessica was pleased. It proved her strategy to get Robert to slow down was actually beginning to work. She hoped and prayed that the job applicant wouldn't prove unsuitable. That would be a real let down.

Despite the long-term optimism of Jessica and her fellow directors, demand was sluggish as Britain struggled to shake off years of deprivation. With rationing there was little they could do to improve sales and were concentrating their efforts on improving and extending their product range. The low level of demand meant that overtime was definitely not an option, and thus when the Friday shift finished, the old mill was unoccupied throughout the weekend. Conscious of the need to keep costs in check, there was no need to heat the building when it was not in use. The idea was economically sound, although it failed to take into account the age and condition of the fabric of the mill, and the effect on it from severe weather.

When the caretaker arrived to open up early on Monday morning, he followed the same routine as always. That meant visiting the canteen and filling the urn that would supply mugs of tea for the staff when they arrived. As that was coming to the boil, the caretaker would switch the heating on. It was when he placed a jug under the cold tap prior to filling the urn that the problem became apparent.

Instead of the usual gush of water, the only reaction was a spluttering sound, accompanied by vibration in the pipe and a trickle of water that almost instantly petered out. The caretaker knew at once what had happened. Last winter they had been forced to call in a maintenance engineer, but having seen what the man had done, the caretaker was sure he could get the water running himself. It would be far quicker and would work out much cheaper.

Having made various impolite remarks about the weather, the antiquated building, and Monday mornings, he set off to get the tool he would need. He called to a worker who had just entered the building and advised him of the situation. Now he would have to locate the frozen section of pipe. That should be easy enough, the most likely location would be in the same spot as before, the pipe from the cold-water storage tank in the attic. To confirm his suspicions, the caretaker stopped on the second floor to flush the toilets and was satisfied when the cisterns failed to refill. The attic was only used as storage space for old equipment, historical files, and sacks of fertilizer that would not be required until spring. In addition to being permanently unheated, the space was only lit by natural daylight via a set of skylights set into the roof. These caused any heat to be lost quickly, rendering the area particularly vulnerable in cold weather.

He reached the corner where the cistern was situated and set to work with a blowtorch, just as he had seen the engineer do. After a few seconds he thought he heard a sound that was unconnected to the roar of the flame from his torch and stopped. Was it running water he had heard? Had he freed the blockage so easily? The caretaker decided to give it a bit longer, just to make certain the ice had cleared. He'd heard somewhere that warm water freezes faster than cold and it was definitely below zero up here. No point him having to trail all the way back up and go through the whole rigmarole again because he'd only done half a job first time round. He relit the blow torch and pointed it at the pipe, humming quietly to himself as he worked.

Although the caretaker knew the building well, he was unaware that the cold water supply ran in close proximity to an old gas pipe, one which had been in use to provide lighting in the laboratories below, prior to electricity having been installed. It was for the most part hidden by the cistern, which was directly behind the frozen section, masking it from view. Although the pipe had been capped, it was still full of gas — and still connected to the mains.

The ignition of the escaping gas alone might have damaged the building severely, possibly destroyed it completely. The proximity of the fertilizer sacks with their highly explosive and flammable content made complete devastation an absolute certainty.

Jessica and Robert Binks had arrived only a few minutes after the caretaker began work to free the ice. Shortly after they entered the building along with the first group of process workers, they heard what sounded like a distant gunshot, quickly followed by another and then a third. The reports were deep and bellowing, more like an artillery salvo than small arms fire. Seconds later a huge blast sucked the air from the building and left those in the reception area gasping for breath, half choked by a cloud of dust that had been disturbed by the vortex. The rush of wind was followed by an enormous detonation that rocked the ground beneath their feet, followed by three more.

With the precision of a well-drilled army unit, the staff turned and ran for the door. The continuing series of explosions shook the solid stonework of the building, sending debris and broken glass cascading around them. The final detonation, louder than all those preceding it, was heard by less than half the fleeing workers. Those at the tail end of the race to leave the building were already dead, killed instantly as they were buried underneath several hundred tons of masonry, concrete, timber and the contents of the upper floors as the building imploded on them.

Jessica was lucky. When she and Robert arrived, he headed straight for his office on the first floor. Jessica waited by the front door, having seen the postman walking across the yard. She saw no point in going to her office only to have to wait for her secretary to bring the morning's mail.

The heavy stone lintel over the door undoubtedly saved her life and that of the other workers who had been in the process of entering the building. It gave them just sufficient time to get far enough away to avoid the impact as the front wall collapsed.

She looked back in horror at the scene of devastation that had been the chemical company's headquarters. In that moment she had no thought for the company she headed, only for Robert. She stared in numb shock at the once-proud stone building, which in the space of a few seconds had been transformed into something resembling the aftermath of a war zone.

Jessica screamed his name, her voice lost in the competing sounds of falling masonry and the roar of the flames from the countless fires ignited by the continued gas escape, the exploding fertilizer sacks, and chemicals in the laboratories.

Without a thought to herself, or the danger she might be risking, Jessica raced towards the entrance she had so recently escaped through. She had to go back: had to find Robert.

The man nearest Jessica undoubtedly saved her life. Seeing what she was about to do, he grabbed her round the waist. Despite her furious struggles to free herself, despite her screamed demands for him to let go, he held on, his voice, and the grim message he conveyed, eventually causing her to stop fighting him.

'It's no use. No use, do you hear. Nobody could have lived through that. They're all dead. You'd only get yourself killed. You have to wait here. We all have to wait here.'

He had to repeat the warning several times, but eventually the message got home. She ceased struggling, accepting the inevitable. As the man said, everyone who had been inside the building must surely have perished. Jessica began to weep, then sob, her tears accompanied by a howling keen of anguish.

If Jessica had been lucky to escape the explosion, her husband's survival was little short of a miracle. He had entered his office seconds before the blast and was in the process of opening the blind at the large picture window to let some daylight into the room when the detonation happened. The force of the explosion blew him through the window. The strength of the shock wave created by the explosion was sufficient to propel him clear of almost all the falling masonry that crashed around the remnants of the building.

Although he was not killed by the blast, that wasn't to say that Robert escaped without serious injury. The hundreds of tiny cuts inflicted by the splintering glass from the window were the least of these. The fall had broken both his legs, but by far the worst visible damage was to his right arm, which had been crushed and severed by a falling section of the front wall as Robert lay helpless on the snow-covered cobbled surface of the old mill yard.

It was there that Jessica found him. The man who had prevented her from going back into the doomed building hurried over in response to hearing her shout for help over the roar of the fire and the continuing crash of debris that rained down, for the most part on the interior of the plant. He assessed the situation quickly, noticing at once the blood pumping from the shattered remnant of Robert's arm.

'We need to stop the bleeding,' he called to Jessica.

'A tourniquet.' Jessica was suddenly calm. The chance to do something, anything that might help save Robert's life was all she needed. 'Find me something to put round his arm.'

The man ripped off his tie and held it out. 'Use that.'

The instruction wasn't necessary, for Jessica had already snatched it and was attempting to secure it around her husband's upper arm. Her helper glanced round and spotted a piece of metal. 'Hang on.' He picked up the beaker stand blown from the laboratory by the blast. 'Push that through the knot and twist it as tight as you can. Whatever you do, don't let go until we can get help. I'm off to see if there's anyone else alive in this hell-hole.'

A few yards away from where Jessica was crouched alongside Robert's comatose body the stranger stooped and picked up a notebook from the ground.

As she worked to stop the blood flow, Jessica stared briefly after the man who had helped her. An unlikely looking hero, he'd already saved Jessica's life, and maybe had been instrumental in saving Robert's too. For both those, she would be eternally grateful. In her distress and shock, Jessica failed to notice that her saviour was not dressed in the uniform worn by the plant's production workers, or question the fact that he, unlike all but the scientists and department heads, was wearing a tie. Nor did she wonder how come, when she knew every member of staff, this man was a complete stranger.

* * *

Jenny looked at her father-in-law intently. He seemed distracted, and there was no wonder, considering the traumatic explosion that was making headlines in the *Bradford Telegraph* and *Argus* and newspapers much further afield. 'You must be very worried about what happened at the plant, Dad.'

'Of course I am. Who wouldn't be? Not only because of the tragedy of losing those workers, which is bad enough, but there are other considerations too. Jessica Binks is in a dreadful state. She escaped with cuts and bruises but her husband, one of the company founders, is very seriously injured. There's no guarantee he'll pull through. He's lost one arm and had multiple injuries to both his head and body, many of them severe, so even if he survives, there's no saying what state he'll be in. Apart from the human tragedy, this accident is going to cost us a lot of money when we're particularly vulnerable.'

'Is trade that bad?' Jenny asked.

'Not good,' Sonny admitted. 'People haven't recovered from the deprivations of the war yet. I'm afraid folk have got out of the habit of spending money unless they absolutely need to. On top of all that, when Simon reported to our Australian parent company about the explosion, he got news back equally as bad. It appears they've a problem of their own. The mineral extraction division is involved in some sort of scandal. Apparently pollution has got into the water supply of a large chunk of territory. There have been a few deaths. Investigations are underway and nothing's been proved that Fisher Springs is responsible, but if they are, this could mean they'll have to stump up a huge amount in compensation. Our bad news will draw attention to our overall weak performance when we can least afford to have someone from a long distance away scrutinize our activities.'

'Do you think they might be in trouble, financially?' Mark asked.

Sonny looked at him thoughtfully. 'No, they're far too sound for that, the group diversified and has many strings to their bow. What really annoys me is that we worked like Trojans for years fighting against the Depression, and just when we had things on an even keel the war put a halt to our progress. Now, when we have the chance for another new beginning, all these problems hit us again. Sometimes I wonder if it wouldn't have been simpler to let the company go and start again.'

'If you're so concerned about the possible repercussions from the accident, why not write to the big boss over in Australia?' Mark suggested. 'You know him, don't you? Isn't he the bloke who came to visit us when I was young? He came with his wife and little girl, didn't he? Patrick somebody?'

'Patrick Finnegan, yes he came as representative of Fisher Springs after they bailed out HAC. I'll have to think about it.'

Later that evening Sonny received a telephone call from Simon Jones. The news from Bradford was not good. 'I'm afraid Robert Binks didn't make it, he succumbed to his injuries this afternoon. Jessica rang me an hour ago to tell me. She's in a terrible state, obviously. I'm just trying to compose a telegram to Patrick Finnegan to let him know.'

1949 would be forever associated in Sonny's mind with funerals. Apart from that of Robert Binks, he felt obliged to attend those of all the victims of the explosion at the factory. When he and the other members of the family reflected on these sad events, they were agreed that the most harrowing of them was that of Robert. Although not closely related, the desolation evident in Jessica's face was terrible to see. There were no words of consolation, as Sonny remarked at the time, that would make her feel in the slightest comforted.

CHAPTER TEN

Luke Fisher's return to the family business he had left almost a decade earlier was hardly a triumphant one. It came as a considerable surprise to the department heads when they gathered for the routine management meeting to find Luke seated at the head of the boardroom table with Patrick Finnegan on his right. Some of the long-term staff recognized him, but until he was introduced, several of the newer managers wondered who the young man was. And, specifically, why he was occupying what they saw as the seat of power.

In order to familiarize himself with the way the group had developed in his absence, and to judge the effect of the war years on their operations, Luke had in fact spent most of the previous weekend in the building. He had inspected the entire premises, especially the large double office that had belonged to his parents, currently occupied by Finnegan, but now to be shared again.

As he waited for the meeting to begin, Luke was already starting to feel at home. He had a sense of belonging, a special sensation that this was the place he was destined to be.

When the meeting was over, he and Finnegan walked the short distance back to their office. As he opened the door

Luke said, 'Before we get down to business, there's something you should know, Grandpa.'

Patrick looked puzzled. 'Sorry, Luke, did you say Grandpa?'

Luke grinned. 'Bella's informed me she's expecting. In fact, she told me on our wedding night but asked me to hold on before I made it public knowledge.'

'That's terrific news, wait till I tell Louise.' Patrick was also grinning. 'Now, getting down to business, what do you reckon to this?' Patrick indicated the files he was carrying.

'Things look to be in pretty good shape, at least here,' Luke replied. 'As for the British end, I suppose it's hardly surprising considering the state the country is in. And that explosion at the chemical plant could turn out expensive once they've sorted it all out. What's the story on the pollution problem here?'

'The managing director of the mining company doesn't think we've anything to worry about, but I'm nowhere near as confident. Investigations are still ongoing.'

Luke thought for a moment. 'His report glossed over it, all he said was there had been one or two unexplained deaths and illnesses in the nearest town, which I didn't like the sound of. Added to which, have you read that complaint from the local fishermen?'

'I have, but there's still no reason to believe their accusations have anything to do with our operation.'

'What do you reckon we should do?' Luke asked.

'Nothing, at least not for the time being. One thing for sure, we can't afford to shut the mining operation down while we wait for tests to be concluded, tests that could prove the events have nothing to do with us. You've seen the figures. You know how much that mine is earning for the group. That figure can only increase as demand gets bigger.'

'On the other hand, we could find ourselves facing a hefty bill for damages if it turns out we've caused the problem.'

'Proving that won't be easy, I think we should wait and see. If it all blows over, we've lost nothing. There could be lots of reasons for these illnesses. Even if they are down to pollution, it could be something as simple as toxins seeping from the riverbed, or some farmer dumping waste in the river. You know how careless some of them are.'

Luke had only been back at Fisher Springs for a month when they received more bad news. He had been in the building less than an hour when he and Finnegan had a visitor.

They watched the head of the mining operation enter their office. He looked nervous, with good reason, as it soon transpired. They both listened to the man's report in silence.

'How did this happen?' Finnegan demanded when the man had finished.

'Part carelessness and part ignorance,' he admitted. 'The site manager wasn't aware of the health risks from the ore-washing waste, or so he reckons, despite the training he was given when we took him on. Added to that, his deputy failed to inspect the ore-washing plant as he should have done. Otherwise he would have seen that the waste water was going into the river upstream of the dam that supplies the town's drinking water, rather than downstream, as it should have done.'

'That's garbage,' Luke interrupted, 'the waste water shouldn't go anywhere near the river. It should be piped to an enclosed lagoon and filtered, processed, and tested to make sure it's safe.'

'Perhaps so, but that's for the future,' Finnegan suggested. 'What's the current situation?'

'Three people have died, seven more are in a critical condition in the local hospital, and another twenty are reported to be crook. Added to that, over two hundred cattle have died.' The man lowered his head and bit his lip.

'Strewth, this is going to cost us a bundle,' Finnegan said. 'There will be a huge compensation claim to pay out.'

'I'll see what can be done to minimize that,' the manager said, trying to regain their confidence.

Luke Fisher rounded on him. 'You'll do no such thing. That's not the way we work here. Never has been. My father and mother set up this business, not only for themselves, but to benefit the local community, not make them ill and swindle them out of their rights.'

Finnegan took up from where Luke had left off. 'You close that mining operation down immediately, until the necessary measures are in place to rectify the problem. And I'm not talking about a temporary fix, I mean a permanent solution. Talk to the water people and find out what they need for a proper clean-up job. Then I suggest you go to the town, meet with the officials there. Offer all the medical help needed, including bringing in specialists from Sydney or Melbourne if needs be, whatever the cost, we'll meet it. Tell them that all compensation claims will be met in full.'

'I'll get someone out there immediately.'

Luke leapt to his feet. 'No, you won't,' his voice was sharp with anger. 'You'll go there in person, right now. And you'll stay there until everything you've been told to do is completed. That means you stay in the town. Maybe if you have to drink the water it will focus your mind a bit. I'll join you there tomorrow, to receive your preliminary findings. I'll visit you on a weekly basis after that to make sure everything is being done to my satisfaction. Is that clear?'

They watched the man depart. 'What do you reckon?' Finnegan asked when the door closed behind him.

'I believe that man has just talked himself out of an extremely well-paid job.'

'Pretty much what I was thinking,' Patrick agreed.

* * *

Two weeks later Patrick Finnegan's secretary was standing in the doorway, a look of great distress on her face.

'I'm sorry to interrupt, Mr Finnegan, but it's your wife. I've just taken a phone call to say she's being taken to hospital.' She looked at Luke. 'Your sister said she found Mrs Finnegan unconscious on the kitchen floor. She has a fever, and a high temperature. The ambulance was loading her up and she wants Mr Finnegan to go straight to the hospital.'

Finnegan stared at his secretary, bemused. 'Dottie called you?'

The secretary nodded.

'Go on, Uncle Patrick,' Luke told him, 'You need to be at the hospital.'

After Finnegan left, Luke glanced around, remembering the room from his childhood. Without really knowing why, he walked over to stand alongside Finnegan's desk. There was an old map of the state on the wall. Luke stared at it for a long time, then began tracing the path of the river as it crossed the land. After a few minutes his expression changed to one of incredulity, mixed with anger.

He walked swiftly to the door and called Finnegan's secretary in. 'I want you to get me the local hospital. I need to speak to whoever will be handling Mrs Finnegan's case. Tell them I have information that might help.'

After some delay he was put through. 'You've a patient being admitted, by the name of Mrs Louise Finnegan,' he told the nurse who answered. 'My name's Luke Fisher, I'm her son-in-law. The thing is, I believe you might be wondering what's caused her illness. Well, I think I know. I believe she's suffering from mineral poisoning.'

'What, you mean from pollution, like those people up-state?'

'That's right. I've been examining an old map of the area and there's a stream that goes straight past the Finnegan property. It's a subsidiary of the river where the pollution occurred.' Luke took a deep breath, 'I know for a fact that my mother-in-law likes to take a swim in that creek every morning. And if she accidentally swallowed some water . . .'

* * *

Although Dottie had been made welcome at the Finnegan home, Elliot had barely spoken to her since her return almost a year ago. Dottie racked her brain to think of something she had said or done to offend him. She was saddened by his

97

attitude, for she thought the world of him. She had always had a soft spot for Elliot, quite why she should have preferred him to the other members of the family, or other young men or boys she knew, Dottie wasn't sure. For him to adopt so distant an attitude hurt her.

How long this situation might have continued had Louise not been taken ill was anyone's guess. With Isabella now married, and the Finnegan's younger son Finlay studying in America, apart from Patrick and Louise, only Elliot was living at home. On the day Dottie found Louise, slumped unconscious on the kitchen floor, she had only time to scribble a brief note to Elliot explaining the situation before accompanying Louise to hospital.

Once Patrick had arrived and reached the private room, Dottie was about to leave. 'I'll get a taxi outside,' she told Finnegan, 'and wait at home for news.'

Patrick nodded, too concerned over Louise's condition to take in much of what she said.

Outside, Dottie was about to hail a taxi when Elliot arrived, pulling his tiny car to a halt with a screech of brakes.

'How's Mom?' he asked as he jumped out of the two-seater.

Dottie laid a hand on his arm. 'I honestly can't say, Eli.' She automatically used the nickname he had been given since the day he was christened. 'It's touch and go. They reckon they know the cause, thanks to Luke, which the doctors think might just be enough to save her.' She explained what they had learned. 'Come on, Eli, I'll take you to see her. Your dad's here.' She took his hand as they walked along the corridor. The gesture was one of comfort, but Dottie noticed that Elliot was trembling slightly. She put it down to fear for his mother's safety, just as she ascribed the pinkness of his complexion to the drive in his open-topped car. Seeing his mother lying in the hospital bed, unconscious and helpless, distressed him deeply.

Patrick gently urged Dottie to take him away. 'Look after Eli for me, will you, Dottie? That will be one less thing for me to worry about. I'll be in touch if there's any change or if you need to come back. Luke and Isabella will be here in a while. I'm staying here for as long as it takes.'

Dottie caught the implication of his final words, and the grim suggestion behind the phrase 'if you need to come back' which she acknowledged with a nod.

Once they reached the car park, Dottie asked, 'Do you want me to drive?'

Eli shook his head. 'No, don't worry, I'll be fine.'

He opened the passenger door for her, a courtesy Dottie was unused to. She was further surprised by his driving, which was hardly typical of someone his age. He kept within the speed limit, made no rash moves or attempted to overtake vehicles, but seemed content to follow the other traffic.

'I thought all young men drove like the wind when they've a girl in the car with them,' she teased him in an attempt to take his mind off the upsetting scene they had just left.

He glanced sideways momentarily and smiled at her. His gaze shifted to her legs before he turned his attention back to the road. Dottie noticed this, and was further puzzled by his words, which were delivered with a fondness that was like a caress. 'Only a complete idiot would drive recklessly when he has something as precious on board as I have.'

Dottie coloured slightly, but beyond staring at Elliot curiously for a few seconds, didn't respond. When they reached the house, she asked, 'Do you want me to fix you something to eat?'

'No thanks, I'm not hungry,' he told her as he moved towards the staircase.

Dottie stared after him. His manner was now brusque, curt even. She believed it was another example of the way he had treated her ever since her return. Set against that, was the moment in the car when his attitude had been so different, so tender and caring. If Dottie's disastrous marriage had taught her one thing, it was that the only way to deal with a situation such as this was to confront it head on before it was allowed to fester. She headed upstairs, determined to have it out with him, to clear the air once and for all.

Her feelings for him confused her. She had regarded him as a brother ever since the Fisher children had been taken in by the Finnegans when their parents died. Now that clear-cut definition was blurred by other emotions. She was attracted to him, and why not? He was a good-looking young man, and for the most part she knew him to be kind and considerate, which made his current behaviour even more baffling.

CHAPTER ELEVEN

The weather was hot, and Elliot had removed his shirt. Dottie walked into his room and was suddenly aware that the boy she had known all her life had become a young man with a magnificent physique. He had been seated on the edge of the bed examining a sheet of paper which he stuffed hurriedly under the pillow when she entered.

'What was that you were looking at?' she asked, momentarily distracted from her main objective.

'Nothing,' he muttered, scarlet faced.

'Go on, show me.'

'It's nothing, I told you.'

'Eli, what's wrong? What have I done to upset you? I know you're worried about your mum, but ever since I came back to live here, you've either ignored me or treated me like a piece of dingo dung. Come on, out with it, why are you being so nasty to me?'

'I'm not . . . I mean, I wasn't being nasty. I couldn't be nasty. Not to you of all people.'

Something in the tone of his voice, the obvious sincerity in his words gave Dottie her first clue. 'Eli,' she said gently, 'does it bother you, me being here?'

'No, of course it doesn't bother me. I love you being here.'

Again, she heard that ardent note in his voice. He shuffled uneasily on the bed, and the movement caused the edge of the sheet of paper to come into view from under the pillow. Before he could stop her, Dottie grabbed it and pulled it clear, ignoring his cry of protest. She stared at it, her gaze transfixed by the figure on the paper.

'Eli,' her voice was gentler still, softer than a caress, little more than a whisper. 'When did you draw this?'

'Over four years ago,' he muttered, his face beetroot-red with mortification.

'But this is a drawing of me. When did you . . . ? How did you see me this way? Have you been spying on me?'

'No, I wouldn't do anything so rotten,' he replied vehemently. 'It was a hot day. I walked past your room and the door was open. I didn't look deliberately. But once I'd seen you lying there like that, I had to draw you.'

'You mean you drew this, with all that detail, from nothing more than a quick glance? Everything, even the . . .' She gestured towards the figure, pointing to the intimate parts of her anatomy.

He nodded, numb with apprehension at her reaction.

'Eli, this is absolutely brilliant. I knew you were talented, but I had no idea you were this good. I only wish I was as pretty as you've made me out to be.'

'Don't be silly, Dot. Of course you're pretty.'

Only Eli called her Dot. It was a pet name he'd given her years back. It had been a long time before she noticed that he never called her it when others were around but kept it for when they were alone. She'd gone along with it, enjoying the intimacy of their shared little secret. She took a longer look at the sketch, absorbing the implication of every line, every curve. She lowered the paper and stared at the artist who knew her body better than anyone else. Almost without thinking, she murmured, 'It looks almost as if it was drawn by a lover looking at his mistress.'

He stood up, the movement bringing him close to her, their bodies almost touching, and the expression on his face told Dottie her half-joking remark had been close to the truth. He put his hands out and clasped her arms above the elbow. 'That's exactly what it was, Dot, in my mind at least. And the reason you thought I was being off with you, or avoiding you, is because I was afraid of giving myself away. I was scared you'd think of it as no more than a kid's fantasy. Scared you might tell the others. I couldn't have stood that — people laughing at me because I was acting like an adolescent with a juvenile crush. Because it isn't that. It never was.'

'You've been living with this for all that time?'

He nodded. 'At first I thought it was infatuation. That I'd get over it. I tried, Dot, believe me I tried. I dated other girls, but none of them could hold a candle to you.'

Dottie felt a sudden pang at the phrase 'other girls' and realized with a shock that it was jealousy.

She looked deep into his eyes as he continued, 'Now, I'm past caring. So if you want to tell the whole world and have them all laugh at me, go ahead. It won't alter the way I feel about you, Dot. Nothing will — ever.'

'Eli,' she told him gently, 'I wouldn't do that. Not to you. I think far too much of you to hurt you in any way. But think about it. I'm thirty-one, and you're twenty-three, added to that I've been married and widowed. Married to a man who abused me mentally and physically. All the scars aren't visible, you know.' She touched her head to illustrate the point. 'If your mom and dad were to draw up a list of all the unsuitable qualities they could think of when choosing a girl for you, I'd probably tick all their boxes.'

'Their opinion doesn't count. It's what I feel for you and what I want you to feel for me that counts. That's all that matters to me.'

'Eli, think about this sensibly. With your head not your . . . groin. You've all the rest of your life in front of you and . . .'

'Yes,' he interrupted, 'and I want to spend it with you.' He took a deep breath. 'And don't think it's simply because I want to go to bed with you, which of course I do. It's because

103

you're good, and wholesome, and loving. You're kind and gentle, caring, and because I love looking at you, being near to you. Even the scent of your body excites me. None of the girls I've slept with ever got me half as aroused as you do, even when you're far away. All I have to do is think about you and I'm all of a dither.'

The pang of jealousy returned, sharper than ever. 'Don't mention those girls again — ever,' she snapped.

Elliot stared at her incredulously for a long moment. Then he smiled, a secret smile of promise, triumph, wanton desire, all mixed. Dottie trembled as he pulled her to him, holding her tightly. She moaned slightly as she felt the heat of his arousal through the fabric of his trousers. 'Eli, don't . . . this is wrong . . . we shouldn't . . .'

He reached behind her and unbuttoned her dress, allowing it to fall to the floor. Seconds later, her bra followed. He began caressing her breasts, his touch light and sure, igniting a desire in her such as she had never experienced before, as if in a dream, unable to stop even had she wanted to. Her resistance melted away, and she turned her face upwards for his kiss.

Seconds later, they were lying on the bed, both naked. Elliot rolled her onto her back and knelt alongside her, a slightly anxious look on his face, as if he couldn't quite believe what was happening. 'Are you sure?' he asked.

She didn't speak, merely smiled.

A long time later, as they clasped each other tightly, their sweat mingling, she murmured, 'Those poor girls. They don't know what they're missing.'

'They never will do now. This is all yours from this moment on. And just to prove it,' he rolled her onto her back again, 'I want you to do what my dad asked, by taking care of me.'

* * *

It was a tense few days before the doctors were able to offer Patrick Finnegan the slightest degree of hope that Louise might recover from the illness that had struck her down so swiftly and so completely. His only concern at home was Elliot and Dottie.

It was two days after Louise had been admitted to hospital that Patrick got chance to have a quiet word with his son. He had returned home only to shower, shave, and change his clothing before paying a flying visit to work en route back to the hospital.

'How are you managing here?' he asked. 'Is Dottie looking after you?' He'd noticed that the two seemed rather distant but had dismissed the notion as little more than perhaps a minor disagreement. Now it seemed more than important that the two of them were able to patch up whatever differences they had and get along better.

Elliot looked him straight in the eye. 'Everything's fine, Dad. Don't worry about me. Dottie's been great. She's taking care of everything I need. You concentrate on making sure Mom gets well.'

'I'm staying at the hospital with Mom and will keep in contact with the office from there, but I wanted to make sure you had everything covered here.'

'Look, Dad, just do what you need to. Dottie will give me whatever I ask for.'

'OK, I'll nip back at teatime and collect my things. I'll call you every day until this is over and I can bring Mom home.'

He didn't say 'over one way or the other', simply because Patrick didn't want to think that way.

Elliot watched until his father's car was out of sight, then walked quickly back upstairs to tell Dottie the development. She was sound asleep in her own room. Elliot undressed quietly, hoping not to wake her, but as he slid into bed alongside her, Dottie turned and drew him close. Then, his voice no more than a whisper, he told her of the unexpected development. 'Don't get me wrong,' he ended, 'I want Mom to get better and come home, but at least we'll have a few days alone together. Now,' he added, as he began to caress her, 'I told my dad you'd give me anything I ask for. You wouldn't want to make me into a liar, would you?'

Dottie looked thoughtful. 'I think it would be better not to say anything about us, as things are.'

'Why not? I want everyone to know.'

'Think about it, Eli. Your dad's beside himself with worry. He doesn't need anything else to fret about. There's your mom's illness to begin with. That's bad enough, but then he's got all the worries from work. I spoke to Luke earlier and apart from the pollution problem there's a crisis over in England. The chemical plant there exploded and a load of people were killed.'

Elliot hugged Dottie. 'That's yet another thing about you that I adore, the way you always think of others before yourself. It's going to be hard keeping it from everyone, though, especially if things do turn out bad for Mom.'

Dottie knew what he meant. If the worst did happen, Elliot would need her support. 'I agree, but we must keep it under wraps for now. Luckily, with your dad spending most of the day either at the hospital or at work we'll have plenty of time to be together.'

'There aren't enough hours in the day as far as I'm concerned.' Eli began to caress her again. Dottie looked at him in surprise.

'Don't you ever stop? You're like a machine.'

'Is that a complaint? I'll slow down if you want.'

Dottie's reply was unspoken, but the message was clear. No, she didn't want him to stop.

Later, as they were about to fall asleep, she thought about this new twist in her life. Although there was no doubt the relationship would cause many problems within the family, at last she was certain of the affection she'd been starved of for most of her life. Losing her parents and sister had been the start of it. Now of the seven Fisher children, only two remained. With Luke being away for so long, and her marriage having proved such a disaster, the knowledge that she could turn to Eli and rely on him for that close companion-ship only a lover could bring was a great solace.

* * *

Luke Fisher accepted the additional responsibility thrust upon him by Patrick Finnegan stoically. Concern over his mother-in-law's health prevailed, as did his worry over the knock-on effect on Isabella. Luke's wife's pregnancy was hampered by prolonged bouts of morning sickness, abetted by occasional extreme mood swings. Luke was never sure from one day to the next whether he would return home from work to be greeted by a loving, caring partner, or a virago with a short fuse and an inability to deal with even the smallest occurrence with anything approaching logic.

Nevertheless, Luke reasoned that the only way to approach the heavy responsibility of running the group was to divorce his mind from all the personal issues that threat-ened to distract him. Separating the two was far easier said than done, and in later years, when Luke thought over the events of that time and the decisions he made, he was rue-fully able to admit that most of those judgements had been harmful to the group rather than beneficial. However, as he came to make those choices, he didn't have the clear vision of hindsight to assist him, or the experience of handling such a large and diverse operation.

His abiding memory of that time would be the way the problems piled up, without giving him chance to deal with them. As he remarked later, 'No sooner did I start to think that I was in with a chance of coming to grips with one dis-aster, than another one landed on my desk, gift-wrapped, and labelled to be opened by addressee only.'

When he had first returned to Fisher Springs, the memo he'd dictated to their secretary certainly had emotional over-tones, in that it reflected Luke's burning anger over the death of his brother Philip. 'I want this to go to all department heads, both here in Australia and in all our overseas branches. As of today, they are forbidden from employing anyone of Japanese nationality or origin. Furthermore, all group companies are banned from trading with any company or organization based in Japan, or with a Japanese parent or with strong Japanese connections. The penalty for failing to comply with any aspect of that order will be instant dismissal without salary or benefits.'

The secretary had looked up and smiled slightly. 'I think that should get the message across,' she stated without emotion.

'Is it too strong?'

'No fear, not for me at least, and to be fair, I don't think many Aussies would quibble with it either. I'll get it typed up straightaway.' Something in her tone of voice suggested more than an unbiased opinion.

'My brother was tortured by the bastards,' Luke explained, 'and by the sound of it, I guess you know someone who suffered too.'

'My brother-in-law,' she'd explained. 'He came home, but he's still little more than a walking skeleton, and that's two years down the line. Apart from the physical damage, he suffers the most horrific nightmares. Apparently he wakes the house up, screaming and carrying on. Bastards, you called them? That's polite, I'd say.'

Luke watched her leave, saddened and angered by this further evidence of the cruelty people such as Philip had undergone. Although she wasn't aware of it, the secretary had just assured herself of a job for life.

There was a curious paradox in Luke's next action. Having issued a ban against one former enemy, he set about aiding someone who might have been regarded as representing another one. However, Luke didn't regard Gianni or Angelina Rocca as anything other than Australian, despite their Italian parentage. Added to which, Luke had witnessed his own countrymen's capacity for loutish vandalism in the damage caused to Gianni's vineyard. That afternoon Luke summoned the head of the building and civil engineering division to his office, together with the managing director of the agricultural subsidiary. He told them what was required of them in terms that allowed for no discussion.

The engineer raised the only objection. 'Getting labour on that site could be a problem.'

Luke shook his head. 'No, it won't. Have a word with the local constable. He knows what went on there, and what I intend to do. He'll make sure there are plenty of men available to work on the job — whether they want to or not.'

CHAPTER TWELVE

Before long, with Jessica on compassionate leave, Sonny, together with Simon Jones and Mark, had other matters to worry about that prevented them from dwelling on the grieving process. Although neither of them saw these as a welcome distraction. It began when a cable arrived from Australia.

'It would seem Patrick Finnegan has far more serious problems than what's happening with the businesses. According to the information I've received, he's not at work right now. Louise, his wife is seriously ill. Unfortunately she was one of the victims of the mining pollution, and there's no indication as to whether she will survive. In his absence, the group is being run by a member of the Fisher family. We have no personal connection with him, so we can't exert any influence on business matters. Added to that, we have no way of knowing how he'll react. He certainly won't feel the same towards us as Finnegan would.'

There was a certain irony in the fact that, unknown to Sonny, the man now running Fisher Springs Group Pty was his nephew. Hannah Cowgill, Sonny's mother, could have enlightened him, but following her death, the secret died with her.

A month later, a letter arrived from their parent company in Australia, signed by the new managing director,

Luke Fisher. The contents were brief, not entirely unexpected, but nonetheless unpalatable. Fisher announced the group's intention to close down the UK operation, citing not only the explosion and the compensation they would have to pay, but also the relatively poor returns the subsidiary was producing. This underperformance was the deciding factor.

'I feel a bit annoyed, to put it mildly,' Sonny told Simon. 'Not so much on my part but for the people we employ. Most of them are in their forties or fifties and with unemployment running high they'll find it next to impossible to find work elsewhere.'

'That's as maybe,' Simon replied, 'but I for one don't see what we can do. We have only the textile arm of the business left and that's not sufficient to provide work for the amount of people we're talking about. I don't much fancy risking setting up another chemicals plant.'

'That's a bit unfair,' Mark made his first contribution to the discussion. 'We've all read the report on the cause of the explosion. The chemical division can hardly be blamed for someone being careless enough to try and thaw out a frozen water main alongside a gas pipe.'

'If we did think about setting up again, we'd require more than the textile division, as Simon rightly says. I agree with Mark about the explosion, though. The problem is that with Robert gone we don't have the technical expertise to restart the chemical plant.'

The meeting closed with no firm decision made. Strangely enough, one solution emerged within weeks of their discussion. The first, as Rachael pointed out, was right under Sonny's nose all along, but he'd been too preoccupied to notice. The idea came from a chance remark made by Jenny over dinner one evening. 'If you're going to be short of something to do, Dad,' she told Sonny, 'perhaps you could help Mark with his grand scheme to take over the world.'

'This synthetic fibre plan's still going strong, is it?' Sonny asked.

'It would be if I had money enough to fund it,' Mark replied. 'I've been offered the chance to produce some of the polyesters under licence from the American patent holders, but the money they need plus the plant required puts it out of my league, I'm afraid. It was a good idea, but it'll have to remain that way unless I get eight draws on the football pools next Saturday.'

'I thought the football season was over,' Rachael commented.

'I was speaking metaphorically, Mum. I meant that the sum of money needed is way beyond me.'

Rachael was about to reply but she glanced at Sonny and changed her mind. She'd seen that expression before and guessed that he was mulling over Mark's scheme and trying to work out if it was feasible and how he could help.

The second solution came in an even more expected way. Jessica Binks had now returned to work and was about to leave her temporary office in the Fisher Springs building when she was told she had a visitor awaiting her in reception. She walked into the room and stopped dead. She recognized the man instantly although she'd only seen him once and that had been fleetingly, and in the most harrowing circumstances.

'You,' she gasped, 'you're the man from the explosion, aren't you?'

He smiled. 'That's correct, although it sounds bad the way you put it.'

'I'm sorry, I don't even know your name.' She reached out and shook his hand. 'However, I am immensely grateful to you. I think you probably saved my life that day, and although Robert . . .' She blinked away her tears. 'Robert, my husband died, I know you tried to do your best for him.' She realized she was still holding his hand and promptly let go. 'What can I do for you?'

'My name's David Lyons. And it's about the explosion that I came to see you.'

Jessica shot him a suspicious glance. Was he about to ask for money, she wondered? At the same time the name sounded familiar but she couldn't think why. 'What about it?' she asked.

'I found this among the debris on the day.' Lyons produced a notebook, one corner of the cover torn away, the rest stained with grime. 'But with everything that was going on I stuffed it in my pocket and forgot about it. I found it when I was about to give the coat to the rag-and-bone man. I'm sorry it's taken so long to return it. Firstly, I didn't know where to find you and when I did come here, I was told you were on leave. I've called on more than one occasion as I felt it should be given to you personally as head of the plant. I wouldn't want it getting into the wrong hands. I don't know who the book belongs to but the contents are interesting — extremely interesting, and that's putting it mildly. I've cleaned it up,' he added.

Jessica relaxed and smiled. She held out her hand and took the notebook from him. One glance at the writing on the first page told her that this was one of Robert's books. 'Thank you for bringing me this.' She paused. 'I think you should come through to my office.'

When they were both seated, she asked, 'Why did you say the contents were interesting?'

'The formulae contained in there,' Lyons pointed to the book, 'are unlike anything I've read or seen before.'

'Really, and are you an expert on chemistry, Mr Lyons?' Jessica paused, frowned, and then asked, 'Why is your name familiar? I'm certain we've never met, except for that day.'

'I suppose I am a bit of an expert. The reason you think my name rings a bell is that I was on my way to see you when the blast happened. I had an interview for the job as a laboratory technician, but naturally that has all gone by the wayside now.'

His words brought the memory of the day back. 'Of course, that's why you had a suit and tie on. I'm glad we've got that sorted out. Now, tell me more about these formulae and why you think they're extra special.'

'I spent a few years working in the pharmaceutical industry prior to the war. By the look of what I read in that book

I'd say they were test projects for a new range of medicines. If they work, they might be a real gold mine for the people who develop them, so I'm glad they didn't get destroyed. I brought them here because I guessed you might know the rightful owner.'

'A lot of people would have kept the book and developed the products themselves.'

Lyons looked horrified by Jessica's statement. 'That would have been stealing.'

Jessica thought for a moment. 'If these are as good as you suggest and I decide they're worth developing I'll need someone with technical knowledge to advise me. If you write down your address, I promise I'll give you first refusal of a job.'

'That's extremely fair of you, Mrs Binks.'

She handed him a piece of paper and biro. He scribbled the address on it.

'You'd better put your phone number on it as well,' she suggested, 'in case I need to call you urgently.'

He smiled, but without much humour. 'I don't have a phone. It's only a bedsitter.'

'You're not married, then?'

His expression soured rapidly. 'I got married a couple of months before war was declared, but after I was posted abroad things changed. I returned home after five years fighting for king and country to find her with a twelve-month-old brat. That was when I walked out.'

'Oh, I'm sorry, that must have been awful for you.'

'I used to worship the ground she walked on. Now I worship the ground that's coming to her — all six feet by three feet of it.'

Jessica tried to steer her visitor away from the painful subject of his failed marriage. 'I need to talk to my fellow directors about this, Mr Lyons. But I have a feeling we'll be contacting you in the very near future, even if it's only in the planning stage.'

Jessica shook hands with Lyons. As she watched him leave, she wondered if she was raising his hopes too high.

Convincing the others, especially Simon Jones, might not be as straightforward as she'd made it sound. But then, Jessica was quite adept at getting men to do what she wanted.

* * *

The next board meeting, which took place a month later, began with startling and more positive news. 'There's been a development that I believe we should consider.' As Sonny was speaking, Jessica stared at him. For a second she wondered if her co-director had taken up telepathy, but then her brain cleared.

'That's a weird coincidence,' she said, 'because I was about to say something along those lines. I've also got a proposition for consideration.'

'Ideas must be like buses,' Simon muttered. 'You wait ages for one to come along and then two arrive together.'

Although they smiled at Simon's remark, both Sonny and Jessica were too intent on putting their point forward to be deterred. 'You start, Jessica,' Sonny offered.

She delved into her briefcase and produced the notebook David Lyons had brought her. She explained its origin and how it had come into her possession. 'There is no doubt in my mind that these formulae are Robert's original work, but we need to check them and register them with the patents office before we can even think of developing the products referred to. Even then they will require clinical testing before we have a marketable commodity. Having said that, I think it might prove highly beneficial to go ahead with it. I've taken the trouble to check this man Lyons out and his story is genuine, at least as far as his own background is concerned. I've also shown one of the formulae to a chemistry professor at Leeds University and he vouches for it. I'd like your opinion first, because I'm conscious that my judgement might be faulty at present, but if I am correct, there could be no finer memorial to Robert's life and his work.'

They discussed the matter for some time without making any decision. Simon suggested they should leave it in abeyance until they'd heard Sonny's idea. 'It isn't actually my brainchild. Mark thought this up and has done some preliminary work, to such an extent that he has an offer on the table. His problem is that he can't proceed for lack of capital. Here's what he has in mind . . .'

Sonny outlined Mark's plan to get involved in the fledgling synthetic fibre industry. 'His timing is almost perfect, I think,' Sonny told them, 'because clothes rationing is due to end soon and the nation will be able to replace things they've had to put up with for over ten years. It might get off to a slow start, but that would work to our advantage, if we are to provide Mark with the financial backing he needs. Entering a market where the competition is already established is difficult, but where the competition doesn't exist, a new venture has chance to develop in step with demand.'

'Both your idea and Jessica's are only holding out the promise of jam tomorrow,' Simon pointed out.

'That might be so,' Jessica countered, 'but Sonny's point is valid too. The promise of jam tomorrow is a very short timescale to a nation that hasn't been able to buy jam freely for a decade.'

'The problem isn't that simple. Even if we adopt both these ideas we would have to fund them and if Fisher Springs shut us down, we wouldn't have access to enough financial muscle to tide us over until we can see a return on our investment.'

'That leads me onto my other idea,' Sonny told them.

'Now I know ideas are like buses.'

Sonny ignored him. 'The idea I had was that we invite an outside investor to back the scheme.'

'Where would we find one? The nation is all but broke. It'll take years to recover from the effects of paying for the war. To get someone interested in a chancy project like this would be well-nigh impossible.'

'Actually, I have someone in mind.'

'Who?' Simon and Jessica asked in chorus.

'Fisher Springs. More precisely, Luke Fisher.'

'One minute they're going to close us down, the next you're suggesting they throw good money after bad on what they'll probably see as a fly-by-night pipedream. I think I can guess what their answer will be.'

'Not necessarily, if we approach it right. Let's look at it this way, Fisher Springs are going to have to pay out large sums in compensation money, both here and in Australia. If we sell this to them as a chance to recoup some of those losses, they might just buy it — and that would keep the UK division going. I think it's worth a try, and if it does work, I think we should take Mark onto the board and invite Mr Lyons for a job interview. To my way of thinking those two might just have saved our bacon.'

CHAPTER THIRTEEN

It seemed to Luke that troubles also came in threes. To begin with, there was the pollution issue, followed by the explosion at their English subsidiary and then Louise's grave illness. Before long however, two more pieces of bad news caused him to rethink his arithmetic.

In the absence of Patrick Finnegan, Luke had to receive the auditor's report alone. The accountant's expression when he entered Luke's office was dour. Luke wasn't sure whether this was habitual or because of the report he was about to give. As he began to outline his findings, the man's face got gloomier, in line with the figures he had to deliver. Luke had prepared himself for part of the bad news but the most shocking revelation came as a highly unpleasant surprise.

'I've built in provisions for compensation pay-outs in line with your instructions for both the mining company and the UK subsidiary. However, it is the banking division's performance, or lack of it that concerns me. I'm afraid there has been malpractice somewhere along the line because the figures simply don't add up. I'm talking about a considerable sum. To be precise,' — he shifted his papers and stared at the figures — 'I'm talking about fifty-three thousand pounds unaccounted for, that's the shortfall. Until such time as we can find out where the money has gone we simply couldn't sign off on an annual audit.'

'Strewth! Over fifty thousand, you say? And that can't be simply an accounting error?'

The accountant stared at him, stony-faced. 'We are not in the habit of making errors, especially not of that magnitude.'

'No, sorry, it's just that the amount took me by surprise. Have you any clues or suggestions for finding out where the money has gone?'

'I got our guys to go over everything with a fine toothcomb, but to no avail. My only idea would be to get someone on the inside, but exactly who is the initial problem. And it would have to be someone from outside the group. I don't for one minute think this embezzlement is a one-off situation such as a cashier with their hand in the till. I think this is a carefully thought-out long-term plan to defraud the group of huge sums.'

Long after the auditor had left, Luke sat alone in his office pondering what he'd learned. The file given to him by the accountant lay unopened on his desk. Eventually, Luke stirred restlessly in his chair. He knew what had to be done and knew how it could be achieved, but he'd been wrestling with the problem of who to select for the difficult assignment. Now, courtesy of a brief conversation several weeks ago with Patrick Finnegan, the germ of an idea had been born.

Seeking to confirm whether his recollection of the discussion was correct, Luke called his secretary in. 'A man came to see Patrick with a letter of introduction, from Cowgill in England I think it was. Find out what you can about him and if there's a file for him, bring it to me. Under normal circumstances I'd ask Patrick but, as things are, that's out of the question.'

Luke waited impatiently for her to return. Ten minutes later she was back with a thin blue folder. 'I think this is the man you're after. His name is Jones, Joshua Jones. This is all we have on him.'

The file contained nothing more than the letter Sonny had written, plus, on a separate sheet, personal details, and an address and contact number for Jones. Luke recognized the address as a less than affluent area of town. He wondered whether to talk to Finnegan about the man, then decided against it. He'd meet with Jones himself and form his own judgement about the man's suitability.

Two days later his secretary ushered the candidate into the office. Fisher was immediately impressed by Jones's bearing and attitude, realizing that they were almost the same age. He invited him to be seated and explained why he'd asked him back. 'I know my colleague Mr Finnegan told you we weren't hiring at present but something has come up that might be suitable. First, I need to know more about you. I believe you're the son of Simon Jones, one of our English directors, is that right?'

'Stepson, actually,' Josh corrected him.

The interview proceeded well until Luke touched on two difficult subjects. The first of these was when he asked why Josh had come to Australia. 'My wife is Austrian by birth and she didn't feel comfortable at the idea of living in England. She hated the Nazis, but that might not have mattered to some of the more bigoted folk back home. So we stayed in Portugal, being a neutral country during the war, then came here.'

'She might bump into similar prejudice here,' Luke told him, remembering what he and Isabella had encountered at Rocca's vineyard. 'Now, I notice there's nothing on file about your war record, and yet you're obviously young enough and look fit enough to have served in the forces. You're not a conchie, are you?'

He saw Jones wince at the suggestion that he might have been a conscientious objector, but the reply was hardly enlightening. 'I worked for the British government.'

Luke waited for Jones to amplify this vague statement, but when nothing was forthcoming, was forced to ask, 'What does that mean?'

Josh smiled. 'It means that's all I'm supposed to say.'

'You do realize that makes it very difficult to employ you without some form of reference or indication of what you're good at.'

'You're telling me. I've met the same reaction countless times.'

'And yet you still won't talk about your wartime job?' Even as he was speaking, Luke was assessing whether it was worth asking the question that was on the tip of his tongue. When Jones didn't reply, he decided to risk it. 'Can I take it that the Official Secrets Act forbids you telling anyone what you did? And that your refusal to talk means you were involved in espionage?'

Jones looked at the wall behind Fisher's desk as he replied, 'You could very well be right, but of course I can't even confirm it.' He paused and then added, 'But if you were wrong, I would tell you so.'

Although Josh didn't realize it, his refusal to divulge his wartime occupation, far from lessening his chances of getting a job, actually increased them. Luke pressed home this slight advantage with further well-constructed questions. 'I guess such work would have involved a fair amount of danger and visits to hostile territories, that sort of thing? Please feel free to correct me if you think I'm wrong.'

'I would certainly tell you if you said something that I disagreed with,' Josh replied.

'I guess it's quite likely that your wife and parents don't even know what you did during the war.'

'My wife Astrid knows some of it because she took part in one such operation.'

That was enough for Luke. His reading of Jones told him the man would be close to ideal for the task ahead. 'Tell me, what do you know about the banking industry here in Australia?'

'Next to nothing, I'm afraid.'

'In that case you're going to have to learn a lot about it in a very short space of time, because the job I have in mind for you calls for that area of expertise. The only questions remaining are, do you think you're up for it, and are you up to doing it? You can answer the first one now. The second will only come when you've accepted the job. If you agree, I can tell you why I called you in.'

Within an hour Josh left the Fisher Springs headquarters building. He hurried back to the small apartment he and Astrid had rented, keen to tell her the good news. It came in two parts. The first was that he had just become Fisher Springs's newest employee as a trainee bank manager. The second was that the salary he'd been offered would enable them to move to more comfortable lodgings. He decided to refrain from mentioning the potentially hazardous part of his assignment. That was in line with so many of the jobs he'd undertaken while working for Edrith Pointon, better known as Mr Smith, and was safer kept from Astrid, who would worry unnecessarily.

* * *

Isabella Fisher was concerned about Luke. The responsibility of running the group when crisis followed crisis was a terrible weight for someone with so little experience and without the luxury of other directors to consult or provide advice. In addition to business worries, Luke and Bella were dreadfully anxious as to the outcome of her mother's illness. Bella had to rely on daily phone reports from her father. Given her pregnancy, nobody within the family was prepared to risk harm to either her or the baby by potential exposure to infection from hospital visits.

With little solid news to provide comfort, it was a tense couple of weeks before they learned that Louise's condition had improved, to the extent that the doctors declared her to be off the danger list. By then Patrick Finnegan had all but worn out a pair of shoes, pacing the hospital corridor. He had spent every night there until he received the cautiously worded OK. Only then did he return home to tell Elliot and Dottie the good news. Then he could ring Bella, Luke, and Finlay. Although their younger son had been told that his mother was poorly, Finlay hadn't been burdened with the knowledge of how dangerously close to losing her they'd been.

When he arrived at the house, neither Elliot nor Dottie were about. Patrick called their names and after a few minutes they came downstairs. By then Patrick was in his study dialling Bella's number.

'Mom's out of danger,' he told them as he waited for Bella to answer. After a minute or so he put the phone down and glanced up, smiling reassuringly at the anxious couple. 'The good news is that Mom is going to pull through. The doctors reckon it will be a long while before she's fully recovered, but at least we aren't going to lose her.'

He choked back tears as Elliot and Dottie comforted him.

'I'd better ring Luke. He'll want to know, and he might be able to tell me where Isabella is. After that, I can call Finlay, once I've figured out the time difference between here and Virginia.'

Luke was naturally delighted by the news and told Patrick he'd let Bella know. 'She said she was going shopping, again! That could mean she'll be gone for hours.' He was silent for a second before adding, 'Or until the money I gave her this morning runs out. Then this evening, we're interviewing nannies. Why, I have no idea.'

Patrick chuckled. 'I think you should remember how it was I came to meet Louise. I seem to recall she had a brood of children to care for while their parents were abroad.'

'Ah, yes, I'd forgotten. Louise was our nanny.'

'She certainly was.' He smiled to himself at the memory. 'Right, enough history for now. How are things at work?'

Luke hesitated before telling Patrick the latest development, then realized even the pause was a dead giveaway. 'Pretty grim, to put it mildly,' he said after a while. 'Apart from the trouble you already know about, the auditors have refused to sign off on the bank's figures. They reckon there's a hole in the accounts of more than fifty thousand.'

'Hell's teeth, how did that happen?'

'Search me, they've no idea, but they reckon it's well organized and professional, and that we need to sort it. Otherwise a whole load more could go missing.'

'Any ideas on how to find out what's going on?'

'Actually I have, and I've taken somebody on board to try and uncover the embezzler. He'll need a bit of training, but his credentials are good as far as I can tell.'

Despite his preoccupation with Louise's illness, Patrick was intrigued enough by Luke's final comment to enquire further. 'How do you mean, "as far as I can tell". Surely you can get a reference from his previous employer.'

He heard the laughter in Luke's voice as he replied. 'I don't think it's that easy. The guy I interviewed is Joshua Jones. If you recall, he came with a letter of recommendation from Sonny Cowgill in England and you told him there was nothing doing when he presented it.'

'That's right, it was just after the mining news hit us and I wasn't feeling like recruiting at the time. Besides, there was nothing suitable and he had no CV, no matter what Sonny Cowgill said. I still don't get what you mean by the reference bit though.'

'His previous employer was the British government. He worked for one of their secret service departments from the mid-thirties until the end of the war. He told me they don't provide references.'

'In other words, he's a spy.'

'Retired spy, I reckon, but I think that's a good recommendation for this task, don't you? Besides which, I like the guy. He was as up front as he could be, given that he's bound by the Official Secrets Act.'

'I'll leave that one with you, but it sounds promising. If we can plug that leak it'll be one thing less to fret about. I reckon it'll be a while yet before I get Louise home. In the meantime, I've Elliot and Dottie here. They seem to be getting along better than before. The way they've been at each other's throats since Dottie moved back, I was a bit concerned that he'd have strangled her by now, or that she might have knifed him. But it hasn't happened so far. It gives me hope for leaving them alone a bit longer. As I won't be needed at the hospital full-time, I can put some hours in at work if that'll help.'

'I can't say I'll be sorry to see you, but only if you can spare the time.'

'I'll need to be here when they release Louise, so perhaps it would be better to come in and play catch-up now rather than later. I must go, I've still got to ring Finlay and tell him the good news.'

* * *

Next morning, Patrick had an early breakfast. 'I'm going into the office and then I'll be visiting Mom,' he told the others. 'Dottie, as you seem to have taken over running the house and doing such a good job of it, is there anything you need, money for shopping, that sort of thing?'

'No, I've got plenty of cash left from the housekeeping you gave me. Eli's promised to take me shopping later, so that'll take care of anything we're short of.'

'I don't remember promising to take you shopping,' Eli said when he and Dottie were alone.

'You don't mind, do you?'

'Of course not, it'll make good practice. We're going to have to think about lots of stuff like that soon anyway.'

Dottie stared at her lover for a moment. 'I don't get you.'

'I'm thinking about after we've got our own place.'

'Is that what you want?'

'Damn right it is. We can't go on forever sneaking around from one room to the other, hiding our feelings and pretending we're like brother and sister. I want us to be able to do what we want, when we want, without being frightened of somebody seeing or hearing something that's private.'

'You're not at all worried about people knowing about us, are you?'

'Not a bit of it, like I told you if it was up to me I'd shout it from the rooftops or take advertising space in the group's newspapers.'

Dottie smiled. 'That would make sensational reading.'

* * *

Sonny had spent hour after hour trying to compose a letter to Luke Fisher, seeking his backing, but was conscious something was missing. He'd outlined Mark's proposal for the synthetic fibres processing development but needed more background regarding the pharmaceutical project. He wandered down the corridor to Jessica's office. She looked up as he entered.

'Bloody insurance companies,' she said in exasperation. 'Filling one of their forms in is like trying to find your way through a maze blindfolded.'

'I think they make them that way on purpose. If people aren't desperate enough, they get frustrated and give up on the claim. Pass it to the legal team, we pay them enough. They should have dealt with them in the first place.'

'What did you want? If it's anything that's going to distract me from this it'll be welcome.'

'I need some background on those pharmaceutical products Robert was working on. I'm trying to draft the letter to Australia and it would be better if I can give them some idea as to what these drugs might be capable of doing.'

'I can't help you there — it's much too technical for me. I suppose the best bet would be to ask David Lyons.'

'Can you phone him?'

'No, he's living in a bedsitter and there's no phone. It sounds as if the poor man's down on his luck. His wife deserted him while he was away fighting for his country, and now he can't find work. Leave it with me, I'll call on my way home this evening and see what he can tell me.'

Although Jessica had not been expecting anything luxurious from the address Lyons had given her, she was shocked when she pulled up outside the property he called home. Run down would have been a compliment, even slum was a slight exaggeration. As she made her way up the short path to the front door, she thought that, like many post-war properties, the house could only be improved by demolition. Even the concrete was cracked, as was one of the ground floor windows, another boarded over. The curtains hanging from the upper windows were filthy. Jessica wondered if they had ever been washed since they were hung. On reaching the door she saw three doorbells. Against each was a name. Selecting the bell next to the cheap piece of torn card bearing the name Lyons, Jessica was about to press it when a voice from behind her said, 'Hello, can I help?'

She turned, to find David Lyons standing a couple of yards away. 'Oh, it's you, Mrs Binks. Sorry, I didn't recognize you. I'm a bit out of practice at receiving visitors.'

He looked unkempt. His hair was longer than she remembered and he was in urgent need of a shave. Jessica explained the reason for her visit.

'Why don't you come inside? It isn't much, I'm afraid.' The bedsit was as shabby as the outside of the building. 'Please excuse the furniture. It came with the luxury apartment. I'll take another dekko at the book and tell you what I can.'

As he was studying the pages, Jessica looked round. She was appalled that anyone should have to live in such squalor. Despite the dilapidation, it was obvious that Lyons had done his utmost to keep the place clean. It was at best always going to be a losing battle. Years of neglect by previous tenants had resulted in irreparable damage to what had started out as cheap and poorly made furniture and fittings.

'Have you had any luck with finding a job?' Jessica asked.

'No, I've had a few near misses. I was hoping to get a job with the council as a gardener but it went to someone else. They told me there were over three hundred applicants for one post. It's pretty hopeless.'

Jessica cast another glance round, comparing this horrid little place to the luxury of the large house she and Robert had bought on their return to Bradford.

Lyons's mention of the gardening job gave her an idea. True to form, Jessica acted on instinct. 'I have a big house in Frizinghall,' she told him, 'and now I'm on my own, there's far too much space for me. Added to which I'm out at work every day. How would you feel about a handyman's job? There's a big garden, an orchard and some outbuildings. I'd also like a couple of the rooms redecorated, along with general maintenance. If you feel up to it the job's yours, and there would be board included. I'm not offering it as a permanent solution,' she added.

Lyons looked at her in astonishment. 'You'd do that? Invite a complete stranger into your house? That's either extremely kind or very foolhardy. For all you know I might be an axe murderer.'

'I don't think so, axe murderers don't try and save people's lives,' she said with a smile. 'Besides, part of my job over the past few years involved character assessment and I think I can trust you. One thing, though, I'd want you to get your haircut and shave regularly.'

Lyons grimaced. 'There's nothing I'd like better. The problem has been that dole money isn't elastic. It was a choice between haircut, razor blades, or food. Food won.'

'So, what's your decision?'

'If you mean it, I accept. I'm very grateful.' He reached out to shake Jessica's hand. As he did so, he recalled her gentle touch when they had held hands at the office.

'When do I start?'

'How soon can you be ready? Have you a lot to pack?'

'Not much. It'll take me less than half an hour.'

'Will it be even less if you have help?'

'You mean right now, this evening?'

'Why not? Unless you need to give notice or something?'

'All I'd have to do is return the key, and that will be a real pleasure.'

'In that case let's get on with it.'

CHAPTER FOURTEEN

It was almost a month before Patrick brought Louise home. On the journey from the hospital, Patrick updated her on several titbits of gossip from work and ended by making a surprising comment about what she would find at the house. Louise stared at him in disbelief but before she could challenge Patrick's outrageous statement the car pulled to a halt outside their door.

Although Louise was still frail and had a lot of convalescence time ahead, there was no doubt she was well and truly on the mend. Prior to her return, Dottie had gone through the house like a whirlwind, washing, dusting, vacuuming and tidying, co-opting Elliot as general assistant, in between sending him into the garden to tend to Louise's favourite plants, weeding borders and mowing the lawns. In consequence the house and grounds looked as immaculate as the day Louise had collapsed.

It was a few days before she was well enough to appreciate how good her surroundings were. As Dottie brought her breakfast in bed, a luxury Patrick insisted on, Louise remarked how clean and tidy the house looked. 'That has to be your doing, Dottie. I am more than grateful. How on earth you found time to do all that and look after the garden too I can't imagine.'

'I had a lot of help from Elliot,' Dottie replied.

Louise stared at her. 'Are we talking about my son Elliot, or have you hired in a handyman with the same name?'

'No, Elliot helped with the vacuuming and dusting. He also mowed the lawns and tidied the flower beds. He's hopeless at ironing though.'

'You got him to do all that? How? Was it a spell you cast, or did you hypnotise him?'

'No, I simply asked him.'

'Of course, I forgot, Elliot would do anything for you. I didn't realize he still felt the same way though.' As she was speaking Louise remembered Patrick's incredible notion about the couple.

Dottie's cheeks felt hot as she said, 'I don't know what you mean.'

'Oh, come off it, Dottie, surely you must have realized by now that Elliot's had a crush on you for years. He likes to think it's his secret but I knew all along.' Louise saw Dottie's expression change and gasped. 'Don't tell me you feel the same way about him. You do, don't you?'

'I . . . er . . . it just happened. We didn't realize it until . . . you were so ill and we were dreadfully worried . . . it was to comfort each other at first and then . . .'

'Then what, Dottie?'

'Things just sort of got out of hand. I'm sorry, Aunt Louise. I would never have agreed to come back to live here if I'd known Eli and I would end up falling in love. I should have stayed at Luke's place. Now I suppose you'll want me to leave.'

'We'll see about that. You'd better send my son here. I want a word with him — alone! Before you do, pass me the phone. I need to speak to Patrick. He must be told what's been going on under his roof.'

Dottie did as she was told, her expression one of abject misery. Soon, she felt certain she would be homeless, cast out and separated from Eli. Leaving the Finnegan house wouldn't be the end of the world. Being parted from Eli was more than she could bear.

Louise waited until Dottie closed the door behind her. She got through to Fisher Springs and when Patrick answered, she assured him she was fine. 'That wasn't why I called you. I rang to tell you that I've just been talking to Dottie and you were dead right. Reading between the lines, I'd say they've been at it like rabbits while they've had the house to themselves.'

At the other end of the line, Patrick grinned. Louise's sense of humour was returning. To him, that had to be one of the best bits of news for a long time.

'Now we've to decide what we're going to do about it,' she continued. 'Have you any ideas?'

'There are two ways of handling it, I reckon. We can either throw them out and leave them to fend for themselves or accept the situation, tolerate things as they stand in the hope that it will eventually fizzle out.'

'But that would imply we approve,' she protested.

'I'm not sure I totally disapprove. Elliot isn't like other young men, only out for what he can get. He's not exactly a novice when it comes to liaisons with girls. I've dreaded the thought of some irate father turning up on our doorstep because Elliot's got his daughter pregnant.'

'I seem to remember the same being said about you.'

'Yes, but that was before you got your hooks in me. Perhaps Elliot's heading for trouble, but that's something we can't alter. I'm not in favour of casting them adrift. We've got an example of how badly that can backfire close to home.'

'How do you mean?'

'I'm referring to James and Alice Fisher. When James's father, Albert Cowgill, threw him and Alice out of the house in England back in 1898, they finished up thousands of miles from home and all but cut off from the rest of their family.'

'Patrick! Shush, Luke might hear you.'

'It's OK. I'm alone at the moment. He's gone to talk to one of the managers.'

'Thank goodness, I wouldn't want us to slip-up after all these years. But, although I take your point, Dottie's years

131

older than Elliot and she had a dreadful marriage, so it's far from ideal. That's hardly the sort of background you look for in your son's girlfriend, is it?'

'Not exactly, but remember we did raise her, treat her as one of our own. I still reckon we play along with it and see if it dies the death.'

'Does that mean you're going to condone them misbehaving in this house?'

'They wouldn't be the first. Not exactly in that house, but we used to do it.'

'That was different.'

'I doubt if your folks would have thought so if I'd had the nerve to tell them. Anyway, as you know I leave all the household decisions to you.'

'Oh, thanks a lot, talk about dodging your responsibilities. You're supposed to be the man of the house, remember.'

'OK, in that case, I've made a decision.'

Louise stared at the phone for a second, wondering if it had developed a fault. She couldn't believe she had heard Patrick correctly. 'Did you say that you've actually made a decision about Elliot and Dottie?'

'Yes, I've decided to leave it entirely up to you. Let me know how you go on.' Patrick rang off, but not before he heard the spluttering sound from the other end of the line. He grinned and turned to studying a report that had landed on his desk that morning. It was an estimate of the compensation settlement claims for the mining pollution. That soon wiped the smile off his face.

Back at the Finnegan house, Elliot knocked on his mother's bedroom door. On being told to enter, he marched in, his attitude one of defensive hostility. 'Dottie's told me you know about us, but it isn't going to change anything, with or without your consent,' he told her. 'If you don't approve of us being together, we'll move out and find somewhere else to live.' He paused and glared at his mother.

To his surprise Louise smiled at him. 'I'm not saying I approve or otherwise. You're both adults, old enough to make your own choices, and your own mistakes. I still haven't made my mind up what to do about it yet, but for the time being I'd prefer it if you keep to separate rooms.'

'You mean you're not throwing us out?'

'Not yet. Not unless you give me reason to. I need time to give it consideration first. However, I should warn you Dottie's had a rotten time of it, and the trauma she's suffered has undoubtedly left scars you can't see. And the last thing a woman like her needs is to be hurt again.'

'It's not like that, Mom. I wouldn't hurt her. I really love Dot. In fact, I've loved her for a long time and we're good together, but it goes much deeper than that. If you can't accept that we're a couple I'll understand, but it won't change anything as far as I'm concerned.'

Despite her misgivings, Louise was impressed by Elliot's clear reasoning and determination. 'You'd better get Dottie and then I can have a word with the two of you together. I've had an idea that will need more time to think through. If it works then we'll know for certain if there's a future for the two of you.'

* * *

'I've received a very interesting letter from England.'

Patrick looked at Luke, his thoughts still on developments at home. It took a few seconds for his brain to clear, then he asked, 'Who from?'

'It's from Sonny Cowgill, writing on behalf of the other directors of Fisher Springs UK.'

'What has Sonny got to say? I suppose it's an appeal to keep the company going.'

'It is in a way, but it's a lot more than that. Here, read it for yourself.' Luke passed the letter across the desk.

Finnegan scanned it, his interest caught by the later paragraphs. 'You're right, Luke, it is a lot more than simply an appeal for us to think again. What do you reckon?'

'Obviously we've provoked a strong reaction. There will be a price to pay as far as the compensation following the explosion goes. However, if our brokers' report is correct, the insurance cover will stand part of that. I suppose that's some recompense for the enormous premiums we pay. What I'm particularly attracted by is the synthetic fibres idea that is Mark Cowgill's brainchild. That and the pharmaceutical project could be money spinners, but it's all very much a long-term investment. I reckon we need two things, maybe even three before we commit to anything.'

'And what are those?' Patrick was eager to hear Luke's assessment of the situation. He was not disappointed.

'I think we need lots more information to begin with. Then we need to know how much these projects are likely to cost, and also how much of their own money they are prepared to commit to the scheme. Finally, I think we need somebody from here to go to England and get a hands-on feel of things, and judge for themselves what the people we're being asked to deal with are like. I know you've met the older blokes before, but Jessica Binks is still something of an unknown quantity, as are Mark Cowgill, and this David Lyons who seems to be advising them. I for one would prefer to look them in the eye and get an impression of what makes them tick before making a final decision, even if it gets that far.'

'Why not write back to Sonny and put your feelings to him and ask for more details at the same time?'

'I was wondering about that, and if the letter would be better coming from you?'

Patrick shook his head. 'No, Luke, this is the future of Fisher Springs we're talking about. Ever since your mom and dad died I've been nothing more than a caretaker for the business. I reckon I've got it in fairly good shape, apart from recent developments, but my day is about over and it will be up to you and others of your generation to carry the group forward into the second half of the century. I'm happy to stick around and give you the benefit of my experience for as long as I can be useful, but that's about all I see my remit as from here on in. On top of that there's the business with your sister and my older son to deal with. I'm still awaiting Louise's decision on that.'

'Sorry, Patrick, you've lost me. What's this about Dottie and Elliot?'

Patrick smiled. 'So you didn't know. Apparently, my son has become romantically involved with your sister.'

'Hang on though. Dottie's a good bit older than him.'

'Yes, but she's not exactly elderly. And she's a strikingly good-looking young woman. I'm not saying I approve of the relationship, but Elliot isn't the sort to enter into something of this sort lightly. I'm waiting for Louise to phone back and tell me what she intends to do about it.'

'I can see this becoming a nightmare unless it's handled right. I don't envy you that. It's a real warning for someone on the verge of parenthood.'

'I shouldn't worry too much about it, Luke, I feel sure that when the time comes Bella will ensure your children behave themselves, if only out of fear for their lives.'

Luke chuckled before replying. 'I'd offer to help, but Dottie's love life isn't exactly the sort of subject I can discuss with her.'

'Don't worry, I think that conversation is taking place at the moment.'

It was over an hour later before Louise rang Patrick.

'Well,' he said, 'have you kicked them out or just kicked their backsides?' He grinned across the office at Luke.

Louise's answer surprised him. 'Neither. I've given them my opinion and told them I want to talk it through with you first. They've gone away like prisoners waiting to hear what their sentence will be. The reason I haven't done anything final is that I've got a plan in mind, but it needs your backing and input. Here's what I've thought up . . .'

Louise's scheme was a clever one, no doubting that, Patrick thought. Her idea was for Elliot to be given a job at Fisher Springs but to be sent to work at one of their branches far away from home. He would be away for long periods and that would give time for the affair to fizzle out. If they still felt the same about one another after such a separation then she and Patrick would have to accept the situation.

'I'll need to think about it and talk it through with Luke.' It was after he'd put the phone down that Patrick recalled his conversation with Luke about developments in England. Perhaps in the future Elliot could go, ostensibly to act as liaison should the schemes Sonny had outlined come to anything. First of all, though, Luke would have to find out how feasible the plan was and meet those concerned. With a new baby due any time now, the immediate future looked as if it was going to be extremely busy for Luke Fisher. Patrick thought he might be better off deferring the retirement plans he'd hinted at recently. After all, he didn't really want to quit yet, just when things were getting interesting.

Any thoughts Patrick had about pitching the idea to Luke were put on hold soon after his and Louise's telephone conversation.

Luke's phone rang and he jumped to his feet, his face strained with worry. 'Crikey, yes, yes, I'm coming. Don't push!' He slammed the phone down and turned to his father-in-law, dread written on his face. 'I'm off home. It's Bella. She's in labour.'

'I thought she wasn't due for two weeks.' Patrick said as Luke headed for the door.

'It was supposed to be. Tell Louise,' he called back. With that Luke ran from the building.

Patrick picked up the phone, wondering how many more grey hairs Luke's announcement would add to his increasing collection. One thing for certain, it looked like indefinite postponement for his retirement plans.

CHAPTER FIFTEEN

At the newly built homestead, built in record time, then lovingly and sympathetically furnished by Bella, it seemed that having signalled its intention to enter the world Luke and Isabella's first child now had second thoughts. This indecision manifested itself in another false alarm before eventually, almost a week later, the baby finally made a grand appearance. By the time he arrived, Luke had become a nervous wreck, panicking every time the office phone rang.

The baby's mother, intensely weary and heartily sick of the unending discomfort, had developed a dislike for the reluctant infant. This attitude changed immediately, when she was presented with the source of her troubles. She stared adoringly at the tiny bundle in her arms and then looked at her husband. 'Isn't he beautiful?'

Luke glanced down at the infant, whose screwed up features, bright red complexion and single wisp of hair didn't strike him as representing any degree of beauty. 'Do you think so? He looks ugly to me. Are you sure he's OK? He looks odd.'

'Don't be ridiculous, Mr Fisher,' the interruption came from the midwife. 'All babies look like that for the first few hours after they're born. He's a handsome young man. He must get his looks from his mother,' she ended tartly before flouncing out of the room.

'Oh dear, I think you've upset her,' Bella said.

'Never mind her. What shall we call this little trouble-maker? Have you made your mind up yet?'

'Yes, I think we should call him Luke, after his father, and James, after yours.'

'Are you sure? Shouldn't it be James Luke? Otherwise it will never be clear who you're talking to. But wouldn't you like your dad in there too?'

'I'm sure he'll understand. He and your father were mates as well as colleagues and I reckon he'll approve. Besides which we need to reserve some family names to use for the others.'

'Others? You still think we should have more?'

'Yes, I do,' Bella sighed wearily, 'but not for a while.'

* * *

It was surprising that such a small event as the birth of a baby could cause so many things in life to change, Luke thought. He mentioned the fact to Patrick when he returned to work. 'I'm glad to be back. That nanny's a stickler!'

'This is only the start of it,' Patrick told him. 'You have to face facts, Luke, your life won't be your own from now on.' He paused for a moment then corrected that remark, 'Come to think of it your life wasn't your own from the moment Bella got her claws into you, although having said that, you don't look too bad on it!'

When they eventually got round to discussing business, Luke was surprised to discover how much had happened in the relatively short time he'd been away. To begin with, Patrick gave him details of the long-awaited report from the officials investigating the explosion in England. 'They're putting it down to negligence on behalf of the caretaker, plus that of the plumbing contractor who, several years back, capped off an open gas pipe instead of sealing it at the main.

One of the survivors reported the caretaker intended to try and free a frozen water pipe with a blowtorch. Unfortunately, the caretaker died in the blast and the contractor was killed during the war. That means neither of them can be held accountable, but it also means that Springs Chemicals is exempt from blame. We'll still be paying compensation, but at least our insurance can't be invalidated.'

'That might well be true, but it won't bring much consolation to the families of those who died. I'd like us to look into some form of trust to assist them, as we've done with the victims of the mining pollution.'

'OK, I'll see what can be done. Now, I have some more positive news for you. I took a phone call intended for you, it was from Gianni Rocca. He rang to say that he and Angelina are now settled back in their house, it's been fixed-up. He's also confident that the vineyard will be productive again. He's already taken on two workers to help with the planting of vines to replace those that perished, said it was more from neglect than vandalism. He's confident the soil hasn't been contaminated.'

'That's good, and I think I should ring the editor of the local paper and tell him to put an article in, thanking everyone for their cooperation and looking forward to the vineyard providing future employment. It might help make Gianni and Angelina more welcome in town and hold out an incentive for the folk to continue to support them.'

'I'd also like a word about something that's both business and personal,' Patrick said. 'It's an idea Louise and I have been mulling over.'

Luke's expression was wary as he wondered what was coming next. He listened as Patrick outlined the plan for Elliot to join Fisher Springs as a trainee and be sent to an outpost of the group's trading empire. 'This isn't simply a plan to split him and Dottie up,' he emphasized, 'more a test of the relationship. If they can withstand the separation, then we'll know it's more than the two of them giving way to their physical needs.'

Luke grinned. 'That was politely put,' he commented. 'I can see the advantages in the idea. I'd be happy for Elliot to work here and I agree that it's important to see if this thing with Dottie will last. I'm concerned for her more than him. She's been through so much that I don't want to see her hurt again. Not that I think Elliot would harm her in the same way as that bastard Molloy did, I'm thinking more of the emotional scars if he was to let her down. Have you suggested this to him?'

'No, I haven't done anything apart from making one or two comments about it being high time he got a job.'

'How did he react to that?'

'He wants to try and find something, but he's not sure what.'

'Sell the idea to him. Tell him we need to fill vacancies left by the war. It will also help you disguise your hidden motive. Go for it, and let's get him on board. Anything else to report?'

'A couple of other things. First off, the guy you took on to investigate the wrongdoing at the bank has completed his training and has been assigned to his first branch. He's reporting directly to either me or you but he says it could take time before he discovers the branch responsible. The other news is that I had a cable from Sonny Cowgill. They're preparing a detailed business plan for a restructuring in Britain to include more in-depth information and research on the new projects. There again, that could also take time. They have all they need for the synthetics side, it's the pharmaceutical element that's going to slow things down.'

'It'll be interesting to see how it stacks up. If there's mileage in it, I still think we need to send someone over there.'

When Luke returned home that evening, Bella was feeding their son. After she'd completed the process, she handed the baby into the care of the nanny. At Bella's request, the nanny had agreed she would become a mother's help, widening her duties to be of more assistance within the large house.

As had become their custom, Luke told Bella what had happened at work that day. Bella enjoyed these chats as they made her feel more involved to be acting as his confidante. He mentioned the problem of getting someone to check out the English subsidiary's development plan.

'Things seem to be settling down so I suppose we ought to address the England proposition,' Luke told her. 'It's either a great opportunity or the makings of a financial disaster. Once they've ironed out all the details, we need someone to go over there and check it out, but I can't for the life of me think who to send. I'd ask your father, but that's not possible the way things are, and there's nobody else I trust enough for such an important task.'

Bella thought this over for a few minutes before responding. Her answer, which provided the perfect solution, came as a shock to Luke. But then Bella had always been able to surprise him. 'Why send anyone? Obviously, somebody has to go, but why not you?'

'Whoever goes will have to be away for a few months. I can't leave you and the little one. That wouldn't be fair.'

'I wasn't suggesting you leave us behind. Let's face it, Luke, we've never had a honeymoon or even taken a holiday together. As soon as you returned after the war we were pitched straight into things and you had to get to grips with the business. I think we've earned ourselves a break, and a good part of the time away will be occupied with work. Besides, I can show you round, I have been to England before, you know.'

Luke looked puzzled. 'When did you go?'

'I have to admit I was only two years old, so I might be a bit hazy on the details. One thing I do remember though, Mom told me by the time they set off home she was expecting Elliot. Perhaps we could make history repeat itself?'

Luke laughed. 'We'll see about that!' He studied her for a moment. 'I'd never thought of going, I have to admit. One thing, though, how are you about boats? We'd be on the ocean for around four weeks.'

Bella looked at her husband before shaking her head sorrowfully. 'And to think that you spent most of your war in the cockpit of a fighter plane! I wasn't talking about sailing to England. Haven't you heard of the Kangaroo Route?'

'The what?'

'It's a new service run by Qantas Airlines. There are regular flights to England stopping off at Singapore and Cairo and some other places. It only takes four days,' Bella paused before adding a none too subtle dig, 'I'm surprised you haven't read about it. There was an article on the subject in one of your newspapers a few weeks ago.'

'Just because we own them doesn't mean I read them. I'll have to look through the back numbers,' Luke replied. 'It could be an option. But what about the baby? Won't it be an ordeal for him — and for you?'

Bella raised her eyebrows and said, pointedly, 'Why me? If we go, Nanny's coming! Besides, it's about time you did your share. You haven't even learned how to change his nappies yet.' She smiled. 'Why not run the idea past Dad. I think it will make a terrific adventure. We could do all sorts of things while we're away. Perhaps we could visit the place where you were stationed in the RAF, and come back the other way, taking in America. I seem to recall the article mentioning there was another route that went the opposite way. If we did that, maybe we could call in on my brother Finlay.'

It was clear that Bella was keen on the idea and Luke didn't even attempt to dissuade her. He felt he owed her a treat of this magnitude at the very least. She had waited loyally for him, patiently writing cheerful letters to keep his spirits up, particularly after he was captured by the Germans. Since his return she had shown the depth of her love in so many ways.

'OK, I'll talk to your father. But if you insist on coming, I think we should wait until Master James is old enough to travel. If Patrick's happy to retake the helm while we're away, I'll find out the details. I'd need to know where we'd stopover and what accommodation we'd require and so forth. This could take some planning.'

Luke was surprised how readily Patrick agreed with his daughter's idea. It made sense, as Patrick remarked on hearing the suggestion, 'If somebody is going to make the final decision about the venture it needs to be the man who will oversee the development and have regular contact with the people. I've already met Sonny Cowgill and Simon Jones, but like me it won't be long before they're looking to give way to a new generation. You ought to be able to put faces to the younger names you'll be dealing with and meeting them will be the ideal way of judging their suitability. You're a fair judge of character and you'll soon spot if one of them doesn't ring true.'

'I'd better start doing some research, then, and try to decide when will be the best time to go. It will be good to give Bella positive news about it, seeing the idea was hers.'

'If you're planning to take young James with you, then I suggest you wait until it's summer in England. You've been, so you know what the English weather is like.' As he was speaking, Patrick was subconsciously rubbing his hands together and shivered at the memory.

* * *

Some weeks later, Sonny Cowgill's in-depth assessment of the project involving Fisher Springs UK subsidiary arrived. Luke was particularly drawn to the final statement of the report in which Sonny declared his conviction of the merits of the proposal. From nowhere a phrase popular in America came to Luke's mind. He mentioned this to Patrick. 'If Cowgill and the others are so keen on the idea, I reckon it might be worth challenging them to put their money where their mouth is.'

Patrick smiled, Luke was really getting to grips with the business ethic, much as his father had done. 'I know that Cowgill is well off, and I know for a fact that Jessica Binks is very wealthy.'

'How do you know that?'

'Because, when her mother died, she inherited some share certificates, thought to be useless at the time. Well, they were. That is until they struck gold, literally! I know because I was asked by her guardian for my opinion at the time.'

'Really? I don't suppose you had any?'

Patrick smiled, raised his eyebrows, and returned to the main topic of conversation. 'As I was saying, there's no doubt having a vested interest will make them try extra hard to ensure the scheme is successful. That's another thing you could put to them while you're there.'

'It might mean releasing some of Fisher Springs's majority shareholding but I reckon it could be worth it in the long run.'

CHAPTER SIXTEEN

In Scarborough, baby Susan, now a healthy one-year-old, had a more established routine. Things settled down to such a degree that Andrew felt much more tolerant of the infant, even to the extent that he consented to act as escort when his mother took the baby out in her pram for fresh air. One of Andrew's favourite walks was along Foreshore Road towards the quayside. There, if he was lucky, he could watch the cranes offloading the ships or the fishing fleet returning. The previous year he had watched in amazement as a gigantic bluefin tuna, known in Britain as tunny, had been landed to cheers from the waiting crowd. The sport was akin to big game hunting and attracted many aristocrats and stars from the stage and screen. The harbour would often contain a sailing vessel belonging to one of the rich and famous.

It was on one such walk that Jenny recounted the story of the early morning runs she used to take along the route with Andrew's father. 'We were quite young. Your dad needed the exercise to recover and get strong because he'd been very poorly, and I went with him and your grandpa for company.'

'Did you and Grandma Joyce always live together with Dad and Grandpa Sonny and Grandma Rachael?'

'Not always, but as far back as I can remember. Your dad and I were great friends when we were children and then when we grew up we fell in love and got married. Then you were born.' Jenny stopped short of telling Andrew that he was already on the way when she and Mark had tied the knot. That was something the boy didn't need to know.

'And when I was born did I have Susan's nursery?'

'You did, but only just. You could just as easily have been born in a cabin in the middle of a forest had things turned out differently.'

Jenny glanced at her son and saw the last remark puzzled him. 'I was expecting you when we came back from Spain.'

'Did you go on holiday there?' It sounded like quite an adventure, but nowhere near as great a one as his mother now revealed.

Jenny laughed. 'It was hardly a holiday, Andrew. We went to Spain to fight in the Civil War. We spent the last winter there in a cabin in the mountains and that was when we decided to have you.'

'You were a soldier, like Dad? He fought in the war.'

'Not really soldiers, more like guerrilla fighters. Those aren't like regular troops. We didn't have uniforms or garrisons. We went there because we believed the cause we wanted to defend was just, and that meant fighting against the fascists, just like the whole country did against the Nazis in the war.'

'Did you have guns and kill people?'

'Sadly, yes, we had to kill them because otherwise they would have killed us and you wouldn't have been born.'

'Oh, I see, and was there a lot of blood? When you killed the Nasties, I mean?'

Jenny smiled to herself, Andrew still hadn't mastered the word. 'Don't let's talk about fighting. There were some good things came out of our going to Spain. We made some great friends. One of them in particular became like a sister to me. She was the leader of our resistance group and was really nice. She was also very beautiful. Her name was Carmen and she had a little baby. I helped her deliver the baby, like the midwife did when Susan was born. And like when you were born too, but of course you won't remember that. Her daughter was called Consuela, and the last time we saw them she was still a tiny baby.'

'Do they still live in Spain?'

'I don't know, Andrew. They were going to the place where Carmen was born to shelter after the Civil War ended. It was a tiny village called San Juan Bautista on a small island off the Spanish mainland called Eivissa. However, we don't know if they got there safely, or what happened to them after that. We did give Carmen our address, but we haven't heard from her. We dare not write to her, because for all we know she might still be a fugitive and we might inadvertently betray her.'

Andrew didn't understand all that, but he did realize that his mother was talking to herself as much as telling him the story. He had one question he must ask though. 'Mum, what does inadvertently mean?'

She began to laugh, which puzzled him, but then quite a few things that grown-ups did baffled Andrew. She was still smiling when she explained, 'Inadvertently means when something happens that you don't intend, Andrew. Like an accident.'

Andrew thought for a moment. 'Mummy, if I promise not to inadvertently drown myself, do you think I could have a fishing rod for Christmas?'

* * *

David Lyons had been Jessica's lodger for five months. During that time she had been impressed by his work ethic. Nothing was too menial a task for him, nor was he afraid to tackle jobs that were less than pleasant, such as attending to a blocked sewer pipe. She was surprised to discover that he was willing to undertake any household chore, from laundry to cooking, ironing to vacuuming and many more beside.

If her intention had been to test him out, and his acceptance of the role as handyman was to impress her by his flexibility and willingness to turn his hand to any job, he passed the test with flying colours. Jessica found it enjoyable to be able to return from work and find a cooked meal awaiting her. It was largely thanks to David's presence that Jessica's pain at the loss of Robert began to lessen slightly.

There was one ache that couldn't be remedied easily though. Jessica's physical needs were as strong as ever and she soon began to feel the need to satisfy those urges. When the chance to do so came along however, it was in a surprising, almost accidental manner.

The office had closed for the Christmas break when things changed. Jessica had endured a tough week and was in need of a rest. They had exchanged small gifts and David had prepared a delicious dinner. After it was over she sat with him listening to the radio. They had both enjoyed a couple of glasses of wine, and that proved sufficient to loosen their inhibitions.

After an hour or so, Jessica stood up and walked across to the radiogram. She switched the set off and turned to find David watching her. His expression wasn't easy to read, so Jessica said, 'I need an early night. I hope you don't mind.'

He continued to stare at her, until she asked, 'Is something wrong?'

'No, I was just admiring your figure. Sorry, I shouldn't have said that.'

'Why not? No woman minds a compliment of that sort.'

'I just wish things had been different. I find you so attractive that I wish we'd met when you weren't grieving, and I wasn't employed by you. I'd have liked to get to know you better.'

Jessica walked slowly across the room and stood in front of him, aware of the old familiar feeing of excited anticipation. Her voice remained calm as she said, 'I suppose it must have been difficult for you being in the same house if you feel that way.'

He laughed. 'You can say that again. The hours I've lain awake thinking of you, wanting you, but knowing it was useless. I'm sorry, I didn't mean to burden you with this. I think it would be better if I find somewhere else to live.'

'I disagree. I can think of a far better way to deal with your problem. As an employer I know the importance of keeping your workers happy.'

She reached out and took David's hand, guiding it towards the buttons of her blouse as she leaned forward and began to unfasten the buttons of his trousers. She drew him to his feet and achieved her objective.

Without speaking but in complete agreement they separated, tearing at each other's clothes in the haste of their desire. They embraced, both quivering with delighted anticipation as their bodies touched. Slowly and with infinite care Jessica sank to the floor, drawing David with her. She attempted a joke, but her voice quivered with unslaked lust as she spoke. 'As your employer, I expect your very best performance.'

His tone was equally husky as he replied, 'If I fail, it will be my fault for wanting you too much. You inspire me.'

He laid her gently down on the carpet and began kissing her.

'Now, David, please. I can't wait any longer.'

'Certainly, ma'am.'

When at last they lay recovering, Jessica said, 'I think we should go to bed now. It will be far more comfortable.'

'I . . . are you sure?'

'Why wouldn't I be?'

'I thought you were simply being kind.'

'Now, don't be silly, David. I did it because I wanted to, because I wanted you. It wasn't a Christmas present. Now I'd like us to go to bed and do it all over again. That, by the way, is an order. As your employer I was happy with your performance but I need to ensure you continue to provide the same level of satisfaction.'

'I'm sure that won't be a problem.'

When David awoke next morning Jessica was lying alongside him, her head resting on her hand as she raised herself on one elbow. 'Good morning,' she smiled and gave him a light kiss. 'That was some night,' she added.

'You can say that again. I don't think I've ever been with a woman who could arouse me so often in such a short space of time.'

'And I was beginning to believe that part of my life was over. I thought after Robert died that side of things died with him, but I guess nature wasn't ready to give up on me. That or my psyche, I suppose.'

'What do you mean by that?'

Jessica's expression darkened as she remembered the past. 'Put it this way, David, let's keep this strictly physical. Don't start to develop feelings for me. When people get too close to me bad things happen to them.'

'I've no objection to keeping it as a straightforward sexual relationship, but why did you say that about bad things?'

'Ever since I was a kid, death and misfortune follow when I get involved with someone.'

'Like your husband, you mean?'

'Robert was just the latest example. It goes back to when I was fourteen. My mother stabbed her lover to death because she caught him with me.'

'You mean he was raping you?' David looked horrified.

'Oh no, nothing like that. I was ready for it, and enjoying every minute until she walked in.'

'What happened?'

'She hanged herself before the police went to arrest her for murder.'

'That's dreadful. I'm surprised it didn't put you off men for life.'

'That's the strange thing, it had the complete opposite effect. I was taken to live with my mother's first husband and his family. There was no one else,' she added by way of explanation. 'But I got thrown out of their house for having sex with both their sons. Later the boys were killed during the war.'

'Yes, but surely that had nothing to do with what happened with you.'

'No, but the worst is still to come. After I left their place, I met a gorgeous man and fell in love with him. He felt the same about me, and we became lovers. It went on for some time and everything was wonderful until I visited him at his home and saw a photo of his father. That was when I realized he was my half-brother.'

'Oh, good Lord.'

'I ended it immediately, obviously, but then discovered I was expecting his child. I had an abortion, even that went wrong. I'd ruined my chances of ever having children.' Jessica paused and then added, 'It's a very sad tale, I'm afraid, but now you know the worst of me. I'm sorry if I've shocked you. Most men I know would be disgusted by what I've just told you.'

If she'd expected her revelations to put a dampener on David's ardour, she was very much mistaken. 'Then those men are idiots. Being here with you makes me feel privileged beyond measure. Making love together takes me to raptures I never dreamed were possible and leaves me wanting more. And if anything bad does happen to me, I won't care, because it will be worth it rather than miss the delight of being with you, holding you in my arms and feeling your divine body against mine.'

It was a long while later when Jessica eventually climbed out of bed. 'I'm going for a bath,' she told him. 'I need a long soak after last night — and this morning.'

She settled back in the bathtub, enjoying the hot water as she pondered the events of the past few hours. David had revealed a nature as passionate as hers, and together they had indulged their needs in a way that fitted them perfectly. On reflection, Jessica realized with some surprise that David was a more accomplished lover than any man she had previously been with. And despite the warning she had given him about getting involved with her, he'd been undeterred. Whatever the future of their relationship held in store, the ride was going to be a lot of fun.

CHAPTER SEVENTEEN

Paul Sugden was born and reared within Bradford city boundaries, but he hadn't been anywhere near home since before the war until he alighted at Shipley from a train bound for Bradford Forster Square station. His demob suit hung from his shoulders, the collar of the shirt gaped loosely round his neck. Having served with distinction in Crete, North Africa and Italy he had been captured by German troops and spent the last two years of the war being transferred from a series of prisoner of war camps. In the last of these, he had intervened when another prisoner was being beaten. His pre-war hobby of boxing enabled him to deal the torturer several resounding blows, the last of which broke the German officer's nose before Paul was overpowered. The German's revenge was terrible and Paul was transferred to a concentration camp. There he had been stripped of all evidence of his identity and service clothing, to become yet another potential victim of what the Nazi regime, euphemistically referred to as 'the final solution'.

Luckily for Paul, only days before he was scheduled to be bundled along with many others into the gas chamber, Russian troops arrived with different ideas.

His life was saved, but it took many months before he was able to establish his nationality, and then his identity, to the satisfaction of his new Russian captors, again being moved from place to place. Later he encountered the bureaucracy surrounding the victorious Allied armies, who had to deal with thousands of similar claims. Eventually, early in 1949 he'd arrived back in England, but his troubles didn't end there. The near starvation of the camps and the subsequent meagre rations allotted to DPs, the slang used for displaced persons, had left Paul susceptible to infection. Landing in Britain during a bitterly cold, damp winter was hardly ideal, and when he contracted influenza, this soon developed into pneumonia. Once again Paul had to fight to survive, this time from a hidden enemy within his own body. Following several months convalescence, although a shadow of himself, Paul eventually recovered.

Resettlement of soldiers after demobilization was a key concern, and Paul was asked what skills he had to equip him for return to civilian life. 'I'm a chartered accountant,' he told his inquisitor. 'But I need to go home. My mother is ill, and I need to visit her before I can think about work. I'm not sure how things are.'

'Does she know you're back in England?'

'No, I doubt whether she knows I'm alive. I haven't been able to contact her.'

'Then how do you know she's ill?'

'As soon as I was well enough, I wrote home, but got no reply. I managed to contact our next-door neighbour and she's written back to say my mother was taken into hospital several weeks ago. She said it was serious.'

'In that case we'd better expedite matters. Come back first thing in the morning. By then I'll have everything ready for your discharge, including your gratuity, civilian clothing etcetera, plus a travel warrant.' The man glanced at Paul's file. 'You need to head for Bradford, correct?'

That had been just over twenty-four hours earlier. On leaving the train, Paul walked to the hospital in Saltaire, where he enquired about Mrs Doris Sugden.

'Are you a relative?' The receptionist asked.

'I'm her son.'

'Please take a seat and I'll get someone to come out in a moment.'

Paul did as he was asked, a trifle puzzled that he hadn't been directed to a ward. A few minutes later a staff nurse with an air of bristling efficiency marched down the corridor. 'Mr Sugden?' she asked, in a tone resembling that of a drill sergeant.

Paul stood up.

'You're Doris Sugden's son, correct?'

'That's right. Can I see her?'

'I'm afraid not. I take it you're here to collect her belongings and arrange for an undertaker.'

Paul swayed, he grasped the back of the chair he'd been sitting on for support. 'Is my mother . . . ?' He couldn't bring himself to finish the question.

The nurse's attitude changed instantly. 'I'm terribly sorry, Mr Sugden, I thought you knew. Your mother was brought in nearly three months ago, after suffering a severe stroke. Yesterday morning she had a second, and later died in her sleep.'

Paul sank back into the chair, his body racked with tears. In a flash the nurse sat alongside him, her hand on his, comforting as best she could someone who was inconsolable. An hour later, the formalities over, Paul walked from the hospital, clutching a paper carrier bag alongside his small suitcase. He had survived the war, returned home, but his life was emptier now than ever before. He was completely alone in the world. He walked the few streets to the small terraced house where he'd been born, and from where he had left to fight the Germans. It had been during his first month in North Africa that he'd received the news that his father had died.

He reached the house and was immediately faced with another problem — he had no key. He knew the bag with his mother's possessions didn't contain one. He was still trying to work out what to do next, when a voice behind him caused him to wheel around abruptly.

'Paul, is that you?'

As he turned, he saw their next-door neighbour Bessie Fletcher standing only a few feet away.

'It is you, Paul.' She hesitated. 'Oh, Paul, have you been told?'

Paul nodded.

'I'm so sorry. The police came round this morning to check on the house and told me she'd passed away. I was going to write to you.'

He gestured to the door. 'I didn't know where else to go, but I can't get in. There's no key in Mum's things.'

'No, I have her key. I locked up and made sure the house was all right after she was taken into hospital. At least, Sally and I did. We cleared away all the food and other stuff like milk that would have gone off. You remember my Sally, don't you?'

'Yes, I do.' Paul was exaggerating. He'd forgotten all about Bessie and Tom Fletcher's daughter until Bessie mentioned her name. 'I'd better get the key and let myself in.'

'Look, you must be tired out, why don't you come in and sit a while. I'll make you a nice cup of tea. There's no food in your house. Are you hungry? When did you last have something to eat?'

Paul shrugged. 'I had a sandwich at the station this morning.'

'A sandwich, that's not very filling. Let's see what we can find for you. Come along, you look as though you need a good feed. You don't want to be sitting next door all alone, not after the news you've just had.'

Without further ado, Bessie took him by the elbow and guided him towards her house. There were no front gardens to these dwellings which were designed with simplicity and cost saving in mind. They had been built during the previous century as workers' cottages by the order of Titus Salt, the Quaker mill-owner and philanthropist, after whom the village was named.

Paul was greeted by Bessie's husband Tom, who immediately announced that he was leaving for work. 'My week on night shift at what used to be HAC,' he explained to the newcomer.

Neither he nor Paul saw anything ironic in the fact that Tom lived in a cottage built for workers of one mill, only to be employed by a different company. After the front door closed behind her husband, Bessie told Paul to take a seat at the table. 'I'll put the kettle on, then see what there is in the pantry.'

As he did as he was told, he heard the light patter of footsteps coming down the stairs, and the door into the kitchen opened. Paul got to his feet awkwardly as a young woman appeared.

'Hello,' she greeted him, her expression one of mild surprise, then she smiled. 'Sorry, it's Paul, isn't it? I didn't recognize you at first. I'm so sorry to have heard about your mother. Mum told me when I came home from work.'

'You must be Sally,' he replied. 'You look a lot different to what I remember.'

He didn't say that he barely remembered what she'd looked like, but he was certain in his own mind that she hadn't been anywhere near as good-looking then as she was now. If she had been, he would never have forgotten her.

'Your mum kindly invited me in for a cup of tea,' he explained. 'I went to the hospital and they told me about my mother, so I came home, but I don't have a key. That's when your mum found me.'

'It can hardly have been the homecoming you were expecting,' Sally said. 'In fact, we didn't think you were coming home at all. Everyone believed you were dead. We knew that you'd been taken prisoner, but after that, when your mother didn't hear anything else she assumed the worst. She didn't give up hoping, though, even when the War Office said they'd made enquiries but couldn't find you and were unable to do anything more.'

Paul remembered the ordeal he'd been through and almost without thinking said, 'Sometimes I think it would have been better if I had died.'

Sally's retort was sharp, angry almost. 'Don't ever say that. Don't even begin to think that way. Remember all the men who weren't lucky enough to make it home. It's your duty to live a full life. You owe it to the ones who didn't return.'

'I suppose you're right, but it's been difficult to think of it in that light, still is I suppose.'

'Well, you must. Anyway, enough of that, I'll have to leave now. I'm off to night school.'

'Really, what are you studying?'

'Accountancy, I hope to take the exams in a couple of years. You're not the only one who can add up!' With that, and a quick wave to her mother, Sally left.

Bessie came to his side bearing a teapot and some cutlery. 'There's a portion of shepherd's pie left over, so I've popped it in the oven to warm through for you. Now, how do you like your tea?'

Conversation was strained at first, but after Bessie refilled his cup it got easier.

'I didn't know Sally was aiming to become an accountant,' he said, trying to find a topic to discuss.

'Yes, her dad encouraged her to go for it. She works as a clerk in the accounts department at the mill and has always had a good head for figures, and it helps take her mind off things.'

She saw Paul's puzzled expression. 'I keep forgetting you've been away so long. Sally was engaged to a nice young man from Shipley, but he was killed during the Normandy landings. Sally was very upset, as you can imagine, we thought she wouldn't get over it, but then Tom saw this accountancy course advertised in the T & A and encouraged her to give it a try, give her something else to think about.'

It was when Bessie talked about such familiar things, like referring to the local paper, the *Telegraph and Argus*, as the T & A that Paul felt he truly was home, but with each revelation came glimpses into other tragedies that mirrored his own. He thought of Sally's deep blue eyes and fair complexion, her hair the shade of ripening corn.

'I must talk to Sally sometime. I was fully qualified when I was called up, and in a good position, but I'd need a refresher before I can consider returning to work. I'd be keen to know if there's any room on her course, even though I'd be joining it midway.'

'I'll mention it to her. I'm sure she would feel happier if there was somebody she knew in the room with her.'

* * *

Like so many returning soldiers before him, Paul Sugden found adjustment to civilian life difficult. In the early days after arriving home, his time was taken up in dealing with the arrangements for his mother's funeral, then the legal and bureaucratic formalities involved in his inheritance of her estate. The rent was up to date, thanks to Bessie, and he discovered with some sadness, that apart from the furniture, his mother had slightly over a hundred pounds in a savings account with Yorkshire Penny Bank. Not much for a life that had spanned almost seventy years, involving working in the mill and later as a married woman and mother.

His bank account had lain untouched during the war years and the situation left Paul in a more advantageous position than a lot of his former comrades-in-arms. However, Paul found himself at a loose end. He was distracted to a slight degree by learning how to live as a single civilian. Things such as signing on for the dole were completely novel to him. Apart from finding employment, his other intention was to regain his fitness. This he began to achieve by visiting the boxing club of his pre-war days and building up his strength.

He was equally unused to domesticity, in the shape of household chores. In these he leaned heavily on Bessie Fletcher and to a lesser degree, her daughter Sally. Eventually he got round to asking Sally the question he had been meaning to put when he learned what her intended profession was to be. 'Do you know if there's any chance of me joining that evening class you're attending? I mentioned it to your mum a while back, but she might have forgotten.'

'No, she did ask me, and I talked to the tutor about it. He promised to give me a decision but I haven't heard anything. Why don't you come with me and you can ask for yourself?'

'Where is it held?'

'Bolton Royd, just off Manningham Lane. It's easy to get to on the trolleybus and then a short walk.'

'That sounds like a good idea. What time?'

'We should be there before seven o'clock, which means grabbing a quick tea and then catching the six thirty trolley.'

'Shall I call for you?'

'Hang on, I've a better idea.'

They were standing outside their respective back doors, talking over the dividing wall. Sally disappeared inside and returned seconds later. 'Why don't you come for tea first then we can go straight from ours?'

'OK, that's a date then, see you tomorrow.'

As he closed the door and returned to the kitchen, Paul reflected on his final statement. It was a date, sort of, although not a proper one. He'd very little experience with girls. He liked Sally, and she was definitely very attractive. Despite that, he was reluctant to try and take their friendship to another level, conscious of his own lack of eligibility, as someone without a job and prospects. Even more daunting to his hopes was the knowledge that even if Sally had the slightest interest in him, she would be forever comparing him with her dead fiancé. Paul's war record was nothing to be ashamed of, but certainly didn't compare, at least in his mind, with that of someone who had made the ultimate sacrifice.

Next evening, he attended the course with Sally. After introducing him to the tutor she explained the reason for Paul's presence.

The tutor's reply began with an apology, 'I'm sorry, I completely forgot that Miss Fletcher asked about you. I'm not exactly sure that I can give you what you need. It's all been fairly basic stuff until now. We start on the more advanced topics next week. But if you're already qualified, I assume you're a member of the Institute of Chartered Accountants of England and Wales?' Paul nodded. 'Then perhaps you ought to be considering the refresher courses they are running for returning servicemen.'

'Thank you for the information,' he glanced at Sally, realizing he would not benefit from her company should he go elsewhere, 'but if it's all the same to you, I'd like to join your group. There are bound to be things I'm out of date with.'

'You're quite right, for one thing, there's the Companies Act. It was amended in nineteen forty-seven, and again in forty-eight.'

'Really?'

The tutor nodded. 'Yes, so if that's what you want to do, fill in a registration form this evening and give it to me, I'll pass it to the office. There is a fee, but they'll reduce the amount for the weeks you've missed.'

Sure enough, there was little in the tutorial that Paul didn't already know, so he was able to relax and spent some of his time watching Sally. Her expression was one of deep concentration as she listened and made notes. After it was over, as they waited for the trolleybus back to Saltaire, she commented on the fact that Paul hadn't written anything down.

'There are several reasons for that. For one thing I already knew what he was talking about. For another, I usually keep it up here.' He tapped his temple as he spoke, before adding, 'and most important of all, I didn't think to bring a notebook with me.'

Sally giggled, a refreshing sound, Paul thought. 'That would make it difficult,' she agreed.

'I have to thank you. I'm not certain he would have accepted me had I turned up on spec.'

'That's not a problem. It's going to be nice having someone to go with, especially in winter. I'm a bit wary of returning home in the dark, and I don't like asking Dad to turn out when he's done a full day's work.'

'I'd have been happy to escort you even if I hadn't been in the same class,' Paul told her. 'And if you want me to take you anywhere else, I'd happily oblige. I don't have much to fill my time.'

When they were walking towards their homes, Sally asked, 'Do you like going to the pictures?'

'I suppose so, I haven't had much chance since I was a boy.'

'There's a film showing on Saturday night I'd like to see and if you were interested, we could go together. It's called *The Third Man* and it's supposed to be very good. You must have heard the theme tune on the radio.'

'Yes, I believe I have. I'd love to go with you, Sally.'

There was a slight emphasis on the word 'you' that Paul hadn't quite intended. He hoped Sally hadn't noticed it. She glanced sideways at him, but apart from the briefest hint of a smile, made no comment. When they reached their front doors, Paul turned to say goodnight. He was wondering whether to shake hands when Sally reached forward and kissed him lightly on the cheek. 'Until Saturday, then,' she told him. 'Goodnight, Paul.'

He went inside. He could still feel the touch of her lips against his cheek. Saturday seemed a long time away. Would the trip to the pictures qualify as a real date, he wondered?

* * *

The film was as good as Sally had predicted, and as they returned home Paul told her how much he'd enjoyed himself. 'Would you like to go again next week?' he asked, almost terrified by his recklessness. What if she said no? What if she hadn't enjoyed it as much as he had? He risked a glance at her and was slightly relieved to see her smiling.

'That would be nice,' she replied, 'unless you'd prefer to go dancing.'

Their Saturday evenings soon fell into a routine. One week they would watch a film, the following Saturday they would go ballroom dancing. Paul soon preferred the latter option, because it gave him chance to hold Sally in his arms.

During their outings, be it to the accountancy classes or on social occasions, Sally learned more about Paul. Much of what she discovered had to be dragged from him reluctantly. Each time they returned from a visit to the pictures, or to the dance hall, or to their evening classes, Sally would kiss him lightly before saying goodnight. He soon became confused. Was she merely being polite, or going with him because she had no one else to accompany her? The idea that she might find him attractive never occurred to him.

CHAPTER EIGHTEEN

It was months after Luke and Patrick instigated the investigation of the banking division fraud that Josh Jones stood in the office at Fisher Springs to report his findings.

'Please, take a seat, Joshua.'

Before he began to explain he said, 'Please, call me Josh.' Then added with a smile, 'Nobody but my mother calls me Joshua, and only when I've misbehaved.' He sighed and shook his head. 'I'm afraid I have some disturbing news for you. As you know, I've visited every branch to check them out, and by my reckoning there are at least three people involved. There might be more, but I can't be certain at this stage.'

'How are they doing it, and more to the point how can we stop them?' Patrick asked.

'That depends on whether you want publicity or not. If you were to involve the police, there will have to be a court case. The evidence is available and there can be no denying what's been going on, or who's responsible.'

'What we need to know first, Josh, is how they're managing to embezzle such large sums without being found out sooner?'

Luke's question brought a smile to Josh's face as he replied, 'I've unearthed two frauds, but there may be more.

One of them came about by me snooping around, the other was almost accidental.'

'Go on then, let us in on the secret.'

'The one I discovered more or less by chance involves boxes and parcels, and the problem you have is that this part of the fraud hasn't been uncovered yet.'

Luke frowned — the term was new to him.

Patrick, whose background was in banking explained, 'That's the term used for safety deposit boxes. How are they manipulating them?'

'Not sure. I was on the banking floor when a customer came in and asked to view his safety deposit box. As he was doing so, I looked round the vault and realized that the number of boxes and the list in the ledger didn't match. My guess is that they've created extra box numbers on paper and are somehow working the system. However, that's a problem for future investigation. It doesn't explain the deficit on the company accounts.'

Josh shook his head. 'It's quite simple really. The loss is via interest charges on both current and deposit accounts, including overdrafts. As you know the managers still write the statements for customers. That is an outmoded practice that you might want to look into. When I suspected something of the sort was happening, that was when I asked you for some cash. I got my wife to open an account with it and left it untouched. It's a savings account that accrues interest, and when I checked the statements, none of the figures credited matched the interest rate. Having established the method, I managed to gain access to the upper floor of the building, which is only used for storage. Up there I found a safe which contained a set of duplicate ledgers. They were in two sections, one for customers with credit balances, and the other for clients with overdrafts. They're mostly business accounts with large sums involved but also include some private individuals. The figures in the hidden ledgers don't match those ledgers in the safe in the manager's office.'

'Surely clients would have noticed if they were being overcharged or not receiving the interest due to them?' Patrick enquired.

Josh shrugged. 'Would you? The beauty of this scheme was that the difference was minimal, a few coppers each month, nothing too flagrant. However, when you multiply those small figures by the number of accounts held at a large branch and then multiply it by twelve to get an annual figure, it becomes far more significant a sum.'

'That's damned cunning,' Finnegan remarked.

Luke was more interested in how Josh had made the discoveries. 'How did you gain access to the place where they hid the ledgers and get into the safes? Don't tell me they were left open.'

'Hardly,' Josh laughed, 'the method I used is commonly known as burglary plus safe-breaking — one of my rather useful skills.'

'What do you suggest we do?'

'Raid the premises, seize both sets of ledgers, and dismiss the manager. When he realizes the game is up, he won't dare challenge your decision to fire him. You could threaten him with prosecution if he doesn't return the cash, or what's left of it. After that, I'd write to all the customers who have been affected by the swindle and apologize for a series of clerical errors, then credit them with the difference. As I said it won't be much in each case but it will be a useful goodwill gesture. As for the shortfall the bank has suffered, I think you'll simply have to write that off.'

'What about the safety deposit boxes? If there's theft involved, that sum could be huge.' Patrick showed his concern.

'Perhaps nowhere near as much as you fear,' Josh replied. 'Think of the reason that people secrete assets in those boxes. I agree that in some cases it's for security, but most of the time it's to prevent the taxman getting his hands on their money. If they were to kick up a fuss, they'd risk the revenue getting wind of it and asking some very nasty questions.'

'We need to know details of the guilty parties and evidence to back up our suspicions before we act. Will you draft a written report and end it with suggestions as to how we proceed from here?' Luke asked.

Later that afternoon, Jones handed them typewritten dossiers containing all the information they'd requested and his theory as to the fraud involving the safety deposit boxes.

'Who typed this?' Luke wanted to know.

'I did, because I thought the fewer people who saw it, the better the chance of it remaining secret and the less likelihood of the criminals being tipped off, either accidentally or deliberately.'

Having received and read his report, Patrick and Luke thanked Josh. As he was leaving, under the impression that his work for the group was over, Patrick detained him. 'Luke and I are agreed that if you're interested, we'd like you to stay on and work for Fisher Springs full-time. In the meantime, we need you back in the branch to finish uncovering this other fraud with the boxes.'

'Patrick's right,' Luke agreed, 'we need people with talent, and you fit the bill.' He grinned as he added, 'For one thing, I'm forever leaving my desk keys at home and with you around I can always have it opened.'

'I'm pleased that you think I'm worth keeping on,' Josh replied, 'but could I ask for a few days' leave before I continue?'

Luke enquired as to the reason and when Josh explained, he and Patrick were more than happy to agree. After Jones left the office, Luke commented, 'I reckon that simply confirms that he's right for us in a roundabout sort of way.'

'Too true. Now, how are your plans for the expedition going?' Patrick asked.

'I've been giving it some thought, and with all that's going on here I've decided to wait a bit longer. Bella will be disappointed of course, but I want this banking business settled first. I'm writing to the UK to say they should continue as they are for now, rescinding my instruction to close the company. Then I'll tell them I intend to visit next year. That way, they can have all the information ready with regards to these new ideas about pharmaceuticals and this synthetics business and possible premises or building sites. Give them time to get everything outlined before I go. The decision making will then be much easier.'

PART THREE: 1951–1955

"All Kings, and all their favourites,
All glory of honours, beauties, wits,
The sun itself, which makes time, as they pass,
Is elder by a year now than it was
When thou and I first one another saw:
All other things to their destruction draw,
Only our love hath no decay;
This, no to-morrow hath, nor yesterday;
Running it never runs from us away,
But truly keeps his first, last, everlasting day."

John Donne (1572–1631)
Excerpt from The Anniversary

CHAPTER NINETEEN

News of an impending visit by Luke Fisher, the head of their
parent company, had brought business matters in Bradford
to a head. As they were discussing the scheme they had to put
before Luke, Simon Jones dropped his bombshell. 'I think
it's time I retired and passed the baton to someone younger
and fitter — someone fitter, certainly.'

'What does that mean?' Sonny was shocked.

'I've been struggling more and more with the pain from
my injuries, it's been getting worse over the last year or so.
I'm afraid the way things are going I'll not be strong enough
to come to work regularly for much longer. In the interim,
I plan to oversee the accounts department on a more part-
time basis until you can find a replacement. When you do,
I'll ensure they know the ropes.'

They had to accept Simon's decision as inevitable, but
his going would leave a big hole in the management structure.
Having determined there was no one suitable from within
the ranks as they were not chartered accountants, Sonny and
Jessica decided to consult with Luke Fisher during his visit
before beginning the search for a new finance director.

Their Australian visitors were due to arrive in May and
requests had been passed that they wished to visit all the sites

under Fisher Springs's ownership. Sonny told his co-directors that when they did meet, apart from supplying information, they should have an agenda of any of their concerns. 'That way they don't leave us in the dark.'

* * *

Josh had resolved the bank issue. Half a dozen bank officials involved in the embezzlement scheme were sacked. A couple of them tried to threaten the directors with court action, but Josh put a stop to that by showing them the evidence he held and gave them the option of going quietly or ending up in jail. After further investigation, he even managed to get some of the items from the bogus safety deposit boxes returned. Once he'd got that dealt with, Josh had been put in charge of clearing up the aftermath of the pollution disaster. Luke and Patrick decided he was a born trouble-shooter, something they were a bit short on.

As the date set for Luke and Isabella's departure approached, Patrick spent more time pondering the problem of Elliot and Dottie's continuing relationship. Elliot had settled in well at Fisher Springs and was already beginning to impress some of the divisional managers with his grasp of different aspects of what had become so diverse a company.

Patrick's concern was how to make the separation of the lovers more effective. Although working in different territories, Elliot still managed to visit home when he could, thus defeating his parents' intentions entirely. Patrick recalled hearing Luke's parents telling him about their early days together and how circumstances had forced them to leave England and start a new life together in Australia. The pain of separation from their family and all that was familiar had been softened by them having each other to share the burden.

More recently Luke had been parted from Isabella, with only sporadic letters over the years to keep their love for each other alive. If they had been able to carry their feelings over such a long time, then surely Dottie and Elliot would be able to manage a twelve-month separation. One thought led to another as he considered the recent conversations he'd had with Luke. If the UK development went ahead, perhaps in the future they could send Elliot to England to act as liaison, under the guidance of Sonny Cowgill, and to gain valuable experience. All things considered there was a lot to resolve and he needed to get all parties to agree his scheme before moving it forward.

* * *

'What do you think of Yorkshire so far?' Luke watched Bella across the table as he asked the question.

She was preoccupied, eating one of the delicacies that the cafe in Harrogate was becoming famous for, while watching for the nanny to return with James from a stroll in Valley Gardens. She considered her answer. 'The countryside is beautiful, the people are genuine and friendly, the food is OK given the rationing problem you explained, but the weather is so cold.'

Luke smiled. 'It takes a while, but eventually you acclimatise. Of course we won't be here that long. What about the folks we've met so far?'

'That's a bit hard. Mr Cowgill and Mr Jones are good businessmen, I guess. I bet Mrs Binks is too, but I wouldn't trust her five minutes alone with you.'

'That's hardly fair. She lost her husband in that explosion.'

'I know, and that's a terrible shame, but I don't reckon it'll be long before she's on the lookout for someone else to warm the sheets for her, if she hasn't found somebody already.'

Luke knew it was useless to pretend to be shocked. Isabella's bluntness was part of her appeal in his eyes. 'Are you up for this trip to Scarborough?'

'Too right, and I'm glad we're going on the train. Your driving's bad enough on Australian roads. I dread to think what it would be like on these narrow twisting lanes. I suppose that's one of the advantages of being a pilot, there are far fewer obstacles for you to crash into.'

The following day they arrived at Scarborough station, where they were met by Sonny Cowgill, who had volunteered to act as taxi driver with the aid of his roomy Bentley. Petrol rationing was over and he was delighted to be of service. After the couple had registered at the Grand Hotel and left the nanny to deal with their trunks when they were delivered, Sonny transported them the short distance to Byland Crescent, where the remaining members of the household were waiting to greet them. Sonny performed the introductions, beginning with Rachael, then Mark and Jenny, ending with Andrew and Susan.

Luke reciprocated by presenting Isabella and James.

Rachael immediately hugged Bella. 'My goodness, look at you. You won't remember me, you were too young. But you very nearly got left here with us.'

Sonny laughed. 'Ah, yes I remember. Louise wanted to kidnap Billy.' His laughter died as he saw his wife's expression change.

'Yes,' was all she said, as she ushered the visitors into the lounge.

Almost immediately, Bella and Jenny began comparing notes about the pros and cons of raising infants in England and Australia. Later, as they were moving into the dining room, Jenny told Mark that she wanted to move to Australia. 'The weather's much warmer and they don't have rationing like we do.'

'There's some news on that,' Rachael informed her. 'Apparently Joyce has made treacle sponge today. Syrup and chocolate biscuits aren't rationed anymore, and there's jelly for the children.'

'The weather might be better over there, but that's still no excuse to move continent, their cricket team will go downhill now that Bradman's announced his retirement,' Mark countered.

'Ooh, that's fighting talk,' Bella remarked, as she placed her son in Susan's highchair, the owner was seated at the table, boosted by a cushion on a chair.

Mark grinned. 'Only because he's been a pain in our side for too long.' He turned and whispered to her, 'Dad saw him bat at Headingley before the war when he got three hundred in one day. Whatever you do, don't mention it though, otherwise he won't shut up for hours. Sometimes I think he'd describe every shot if he was allowed to.'

'What are your plans after you've finished the business side of things?' Sonny asked Luke.

'We're going to fly back via America. I don't want to be away any longer than necessary, because there's so much going on back home and it's asking a lot to saddle Patrick with it all. But this trip combines the new project with a belated honeymoon. I owe Bella more than I could ever repay, so this is just a little way of saying thank you. Her letters kept me going while I was in POW camp. Luckily she knew I was alive, unlike what happened to you. That must have been terrible for you, Rachael.'

'Yes, the only saving grace was that Mark was too young to understand. Anyway, it was worth it when Sonny did come home.'

After they had eaten lunch, as Andrew was playing on the rug with Susan and James, Luke told Sonny about the dilemma facing Patrick and Louise regarding their older son. 'Elliot has started work in the company as a management trainee and is showing a lot of promise. The problem his parents have is that he seems to have fallen for an older woman and they're not sure how strong that relationship is.'

'Do they think she's unsuitable?' Sonny asked.

'If they did, they wouldn't say as much, certainly not to Luke,' Bella intervened. 'The woman he's talking about is Luke's younger sister.'

'That does make it complicated. What are they planning to do about it?'

'That was something we were going to ask you about, but first we had to be sure this new project was worth pursuing. It looked OK from your report but we needed to check it out more thoroughly.'

'What you mean is you wanted to look us in the eye and find out if we were the sort of people you wanted to invest the future in,' Sonny suggested.

The idea embarrassed Luke, but not so Bella. She laughed aloud. 'That's what I like about Yorkshire people, they say what they think. You're dead right, Mr Cowgill.'

'Sonny, please,' he told her. 'Yes, I think we have that in common with Australians.'

Luke continued, 'I think Mark's idea is a winner, and although we can't be nearly as certain about the pharmaceutical products, I reckon they're worth the gamble.' He paused, deciding how to phrase the next bit. 'When Patrick and I discussed it, we thought it best if we were to offer you the chance to invest in the new venture as well as Fisher Springs. That would mean setting up a new company that would operate independently, and be quite separate, from Fisher Springs.'

'What you really mean is that if we believe in this venture, we should put some of our capital into it,' Sonny replied. 'I think that's a fair enough attitude. How much were you thinking of? And what sort of share of the new company would that give us?'

Bella chuckled. 'So much for Luke trying to be subtle, you've rumbled him straightaway.'

Luke responded, somewhat chastened at being exposed so easily. 'I think that's up for discussion, depending on what sort of funds you have available.' He changed the subject slightly. 'I reckon the bigger problem you have in the near future will be finding a replacement for Simon Jones.'

'That's true, he will be a hard act to follow,' Sonny agreed. 'But we're going to concentrate our efforts on someone much younger who we can rely on to help carry the company forward. You, Mark and the others need back-up from someone of your own age rather than being lumbered with someone older, who would be set in their ways.'

'That's sound thinking, I reckon.' Luke was getting more and more confident about his British partners. Everything he'd seen and heard so far confirmed what Patrick had told him about them.

Their weekend in the resort included a trip by the men to North Marine Road, the home of Scarborough Cricket Club, where they spent an agreeable afternoon watching the local side doing battle with their opponents. This was a convenient ruse to avoid having to trail around the shops on the expedition planned by Rachael and Jenny to show Bella the town.

That evening, the visitors entertained their hosts to dinner in the hotel and as they were getting changed beforehand, Luke asked Bella how the day had gone. 'I learned a heck of a lot,' she told him, 'and it wasn't until I saw the lack of goods on display in some of the shops that I realized just how severe the rationing problem is here.'

'It's surprising how long it's taking for things to get back to normal,' Luke agreed. 'But how about your companions?'

'I learned a lot about them too, but I'll tell you about that later. We haven't time this evening.'

It was only when they were on the train back to Harrogate that Bella was able to tell Luke what she had discovered about the Cowgill family. After Luke remarked on how much he'd enjoyed the weekend, she asked, 'You like them, don't you?'

'How could you tell?'

'I know your mind as well as you do, sometimes better. While you were busy watching square cuts, cover drives and spin bowling I found out a lot by chatting to Rachael and Jenny. Apparently, during the war Jenny worked for the Red Cross at the local hospital, and her mother Joyce helped to run a canteen for the Women's Voluntary Service. To be fair, Rachael didn't tell me much, she stayed home and looked after Andrew, but she did tell me how she and Sonny met, and about Mark. Did you know that apart from Mark's war service he also fought in Spain during the Civil War, along with Jenny?'

'Really, she went with him? That was brave of her.'

'She and Mark are devoted to one another. They've been pals since they were little. Rachael told me she and Joyce were certain from when Mark and Jenny were kids that they'd become a couple.'

'What else did you discover? What about when Rachael and Sonny met?'

'Actually, Rachael met Sonny long before he met her. She was a nursing sister during the war in a place called Chichester, when Sonny was brought in severely wounded. From what I can gather, he was unconscious and almost at death's door but Rachael gradually nursed him back to health, and in the process they fell in love. To this day she's immensely proud of him and hugely protective, which is why she must have gone through agonies during the past few years, much like I did.'

Luke frowned, bewildered by that remark. 'I thought Sonny was too old to fight in the Second World War.'

'He was, but in addition to that he had what is called a reserved occupation.'

'So what was it that Sonny did that got Rachael so het up?'

'When war broke out the Ministry of Supply was formed and part of that was a unit called the Wool Control. Their job was to control and allocate supplies of wool coming into this country from anywhere in the world. They had to judge whether the wool could be used for uniforms or suiting, or whether it was for knitwear or carpets.'

'That sounds logical, but where did Sonny fit into that?'

'He was the first man approached to become an appraiser. He and his colleagues had to check every bale of wool and assess what quality it was, then it could be sent to the right sort of mill. The ships bringing the wool here didn't carry any documentation, so that meant visiting the docks before the cargo was unloaded. All the Wool Control knew was that a ship with cargo on board was scheduled to arrive at a certain port on a specific date. After that it was up to the appraisers. Sometimes there would be thousands of bales of wool on board. Some of that I learned from Rachael, but the rest was what Jenny told me. She said that Sonny was in Southampton when the bonded warehouse close by was bombed. He had complained that for days after all he could smell was burning brandy and rancid butter. That wasn't the worst, he was also in the East End of London working in the docks during the Blitz.'

'Now that would have been really dangerous.'

'Yes, but Jenny told me all Sonny said was that the most danger he was in was from empty machine gun shells raining down from the dogfights going on overhead. I made Jenny laugh, but I don't think Rachael was too amused.'

'Why, what did you say?'

'I told her that for all we knew it might have been you firing those machine guns. I then told Rachael about us and how I'd had to wait such long years for you to come home before we could get together. Rachael hugged me then and said it was obviously worth the wait.'

'Too bloody right it was. You know what, Bella, the more I learn about the Cowgill family the greater my respect for them becomes. The good thing is that they now seem to have got over all the traumas, because the whole family seem really happy and content.'

For once, Bella disagreed. 'That's not quite so, Luke. When we were at the house, I was watching Rachael when someone mentioned the war and her face changed immediately. Remember how she reacted when Sonny mentioned Billy? I noticed she was looking at a photo on the windowsill. I didn't like to ask, but my guess is that it was of Mark's younger brother, the one who was killed in Crete.'

She saw Luke's surprised expression. 'Didn't you know about that? Dad got a long, very sad letter from Sonny Cowgill about it. It didn't arrive until late in the war. We thought it was because the post was delayed but when he read it, Dad realized it had taken Mr Cowgill that long to bring himself to write it.'

'That must have been when I was cooped up in Germany. I wonder why he wrote to your father.'

'I think they got on really well when he came here with Mom, you know, both just married, young families, that sort of thing. Good mates. I deliberately left the fact out of the letters I wrote you. I tried to keep all the news positive. Billy was a good few years younger than Mark. He lied about his age in order to join up, and that made Rachael angry, so much so that she tore him off a strip. He walked out of the house and she never saw him again.'

'That is terribly sad. I remember your dad telling me about Sonny being missing for a long time after the end of the first war. It's obvious their family has suffered in much the same way as ours, but then I guess everyone could tell horror stories after the events of the last thirty odd years. For so many countries to lose the best of two generations in succession is almost like a curse.'

'We must guard against that happening again.'

'That's not as easy as it sounds, Bella.'

'In that case the only way is to make provision by increasing the population.'

'That sounds almost like a promise.'

'That's what it's supposed to be.'

'Do you really want another one like this rascal who misbehaves constantly?' Luke indicated the pushchair where their son was lying fast asleep.

'Not just one, Luke. I reckon we should go for a few more.'

'That's up to you. I only contribute at the beginning. You have all the pain and discomfort. However, if you don't mind that I'm happy to oblige.'

'It's worth it, Luke. I think the pain is a small price to pay for the result.' She looked up from James to his father and grinned. 'Besides, you aren't the only one who enjoys the process.'

Later in the journey, Bella asked Luke about his plans for the following week. 'Before we left, Sonny said he was going to get everyone together on Monday and talk through the ideas I've put to them. I said I'd keep well clear and go to Bradford on Tuesday to meet up with the others. By then they'll have made their decision and can give me some idea of what contribution they're prepared to make, if any. I'd like them on board because I believe in the project and, more important, I believe in the people. I don't know why but they almost feel like family. It's quite weird, because sometimes when I'm looking at Sonny and talking with him it's almost like being in the same room as my dad. More to the point, though, I reckon this development is one my mom and dad would have approved of.'

'If that's the case, would you like me to tag along to give a second opinion? Two pairs of eyes are better than one when it comes to watching the expressions on people's faces if there's a roomful.'

'That's OK, but what about Sonny Jim here?' He turned and glanced at the nanny who was sitting some distance away reading a book. 'Didn't you say Nanny could have some time off?'

'We'll take him along with us. After all, you do own the company, sort of, or a big chunk of it, at least.'

CHAPTER TWENTY

The weekend arrangement between Paul Sugden and Sally had been ongoing for some time. It was almost summer before things changed. As they were returning from the cinema, Sally stopped Paul near the entrance to their street. They were a fair distance from the nearest streetlamp, under the shadow of a large elm tree. She took Paul's hand, guiding him towards the stone wall where the light failed to penetrate. She gripped his lapels, pulling him towards her and then kissed him. No polite peck on the cheek, this, but a full-blooded lip encounter. Paul was momentarily stunned, but then returned her kiss with enthusiasm.

After a while they separated, during which Sally said, 'I've been waiting for you to do that for ages, but then I realized you're too much of a gentleman, so I had to do it for you. And now, I'm going to do it again.' She took his hand. 'But we'd be much more comfortable on your sofa.'

Next door, Bessie Fletcher glanced at the clock as Tom came in from the kitchen. 'Our Sally's late,' she remarked. 'Paul's usually brought her home before now.'

'Aye, well Paul did bring her home a while back, but they went in next door. I was coming back from the privy when I heard them.'

'If he's already brought her home, what on earth are they doing?'

Tom looked at his wife. 'What do you think they're doing, Bessie?'

'Oh, I never thought . . .'

'Anyone could see the lad's daft about our Sally, and I've long been convinced she was keen on him.'

'You don't mind, do you?' Bessie studied Tom's face, unsure of his reaction to this new situation.

'Why would I mind? Paul seems a nice enough lad, honest and reliable. I just wish he'd be able to find a job. And our Sally deserves some happiness. She's been grieving far too long. I'll give them five more minutes before I knock on the wall.'

Next door, Sally looked at Paul with affection. 'It's nearly eleven o'clock, so I must go soon, Paul. Mum and Dad will be wondering where I am.'

'I wish you didn't have to go.'

Sally leaned forward and began kissing him again. As they embraced, she whispered, 'I've wanted this for a while now. When we started going out together I realized that all I'd been doing before was going through the motions of living. There was no enjoyment, no excitement left. It was as if I'd become an automaton, guided by a strict routine of working, eating and sleeping. Then you came along and suddenly all the fun returned.'

As he watched her leave, Paul's grin stretched from ear to ear, but only because it could reach no further.

She opened her own front door quietly, conscious that her parents would probably have gone to bed. She tiptoed in and had just reached the foot of the stairs when the sitting room door opened.

'That must have been a long film you went to see?'

'Dad, I'm sorry. I was next door with Paul.'

'I heard your voices when I was outside. I knew where you were.'

'We were just talking.'

'I should bloody well hope so. I don't want my daughter to get a reputation.'

'You don't understand, Dad. I love him.'

'Well in that case you'd better tell your mother. Save her from fretting.'

* * *

It was less than a month later when Paul heard a knock on the door and hurried to answer it, to find Tom Fletcher standing outside. Paul had a momentary vision of him as the angry parent about to take vengeance on him, accusing him of deflowering his daughter.

'I was on the shop floor at work today when Mr Sonny came, and I overheard him talking to the boss, saying that Mr Simon is planning to retire. He's our accountant. He's had a lot of problems, poor bloke — he was crippled when a wall fell on him during an air raid. Anyway, that's beside the point. I thought it would be a good idea if you were to go to the office on Manor Row and put your case forward. Mr Sonny's easy to talk to and it won't do you any harm to talk about what happened to you during the war, either. They've all had people they've lost, and that might help your cause.'

'They won't think I'm being a bit pushy, will they?'

'No, put it this way, my mother always used to say, "if you don't ask, you don't get", so give it a try.'

'I'm very grateful, Mr Fletcher. I thought you'd come because of Sally.'

'You thought I was going to complain, did you? No, lad, as long as you don't hurt her, our Sally's had her heart broken once.'

'I promise I will do everything I possibly can to avoid hurting her. In fact,' Paul lowered his voice to a whisper, 'don't breathe a word to Sally, but I'm only waiting until I've got a job, any sort of a job, and then I intend to ask her to marry me. With your permission of course,' he added.

'That makes it even more important that you go after that post first chance you get. Put your name forward before anyone else beats you to it.'

'I'll be there first thing on Monday morning, and thanks again, Mr Fletcher.'

'If you're going to be my son-in-law, you'd better call me Tom.'

'Sally hasn't said she'll marry me yet.'

Fletcher smiled. 'I wouldn't worry too much about that, lad.'

Although Paul attempted to follow up on the lead on the Monday morning, he was unsuccessful. The receptionist at Fisher Springs told him that the directors were in an important board meeting and would not be seeing callers at all that day. 'There is a visitor here from our Australian parent company so they might be tied up all week. Can anyone else help you?'

'No thanks, I'll try again later.'

* * *

On Tuesday morning Luke and Isabella had arrived, as arranged, at the Fisher Springs UK head office shortly after nine thirty. They went into the boardroom where they began discussions with Sonny, Jessica, and Simon Jones. Mark and David Lyons were invited in case technical information was required by Luke.

The question of the British directors investing in the new venture, to be provisionally named FS Developments until a more suitable title could be found, was never an issue, as Luke soon found out. Their enthusiasm in the potential of both the synthetic textile and pharmaceutical schemes added to Luke's confidence.

When the meeting was about to conclude, with mutual agreement on both sides, Luke raised one more point. 'During the initial stages of setting up the new company, I'd like someone from head office to work alongside you for a while. He won't be here to snoop or to interfere, but rather to learn from you, and I'm asking you to agree — as a favour.'

Luke glanced at Bella, and encouraged by her smile, continued, choosing his words very carefully. 'The young man I have in mind is a management trainee. I want him to see how you run things here. You can be as tough as you want on him,' he smiled faintly, 'and, if he complains tell him it's on my orders. He's Bella's brother, my brother-in-law,' Luke explained.

Sonny glanced sideways at Bella, who nodded her agreement. He turned to Luke. 'There's bound to be plenty to do when these developments kick in, so an extra pair of hands will be useful.'

With their approval secured, Luke asked them to cable Patrick, the text to read, simply, 'Tell Elliot to pack.'

Following a long day of discussion, arrangements were made for the tour of all the company owned sites, to commence the next day, starting with the woollen mill.

'I think I'll come along. I've never seen such an operation. It could be interesting,' Bella announced. 'I understand it's only a short distance from the city centre so I shall bring the pushchair and walk to the shops when you move on to the next premises. I promised Nanny she could have time off,' she added by way of explanation.

Before leaving, Luke had a private meeting with Simon Jones. The discussion didn't take long, but Sonny noticed how thoughtful Simon had become afterwards, and wondered what the conversation had been about.

The next morning, Bella was astounded at the noise generated in the mill and had to be content to stand in the upstairs office with James in her arms, looking at the plant through a large glass window showing all she needed to see from above. She watched as the others walked round and specifics were pointed out and explained to Luke.

Sometime later they returned to the office for refreshments.

'That was interesting,' Luke told her. 'I'll give you the main points later.'

Further discussion was interrupted by baby James, who expressed his displeasure at being cooped up on such a fine day in an extremely vocal fashion while trying to wriggle to the floor. 'I think I'd better take him outside,' Bella told the others. 'He's getting fractious. A breath of fresh air might make him sleepy and quieten him down.'

As she left reception with James settled in his pushchair, she had difficulty opening the door. This was eased by Paul Sugden, who was about to enter. Seeing her struggle, he held the door wide open for her. She thanked him for his courtesy.

Paul noticed her accent but made no comment. Five minutes later he went back outside, his disappointment at his second failure to gain an interview noticeable. As he was walking across the small courtyard, a truck stacked high with bales came round the corner. The load looked a trifle precarious, but Paul thought no more about it until he saw one of them start to move. A swift glance showed him that the young woman, now pushing the infant, was right in the path of the falling bale. Without a second's thought, Paul dived towards them and thrust mother and baby out of harm's way with a rugby tackle that would have been applauded at Odsal Stadium, a couple of miles away. He too rolled clear and sat up, only to receive a blast of withering invective from the mother.

'What the hell do you think you were doing, you bloody drongo? You could have injured me and the ankle biter. I suppose you think . . .' Bella's voice tailed off as she saw the huge bale of wool that had almost crushed her and James. She soon recovered and pointed to the bale. 'Crikey Moses, where the hell did that come from?'

Paul got to his feet. 'Off that wagon,' he said, as he reached out to help her up.

The incident had been seen by the warehouse manager, who had signalled to and halted the truck. The driver, oblivious of the near disaster his shifting load had caused, was being harangued by the manager, the language a mixture of broad Yorkshire and Anglo Saxon.

'Sorry, fella, I owe you a big apology. But for you we could have got it in the neck from that thing. I'm glad you came along when you did.'

Bella began to tremble with shock.

Paul was brushing the dust from his suit. 'It was lucky I didn't get the interview I was trying for, otherwise I'd have been inside, not out here.'

Bella stared at him for a moment, then picked up James from the pushchair. She held him tight in her arms as she asked, 'Who were you supposed to be seeing?'

'Mr Cowgill for choice, but any of the directors if I could.'

'Why did you want to see them?'

Paul explained briefly.

When he'd finished, Bella asked him, 'What's your name?'

'Paul Sugden.'

'Well, you'd better come along with me, Mr Paul Sugden. I think your luck is about to change, big style.'

Bella's return to the office caused everyone to turn and look at her slightly dishevelled appearance. Nobody noticed the young man standing diffidently behind her until she took a couple of paces into the room. It was then that Jessica Binks said, 'Excuse me, this is a private meeting. Kindly report downstairs at reception and ask for whoever you're here to visit.'

Bella held up her free hand. 'Sorry, he's with me.' She beckoned Sugden forward and he stepped reluctantly into the room. 'You'll be receiving a report from your warehouse-man about a bale of wool that fell off a wagon,' she told them. 'It would almost certainly have killed both me and James, had it not been for Mr Sugden's prompt and very courageous action. He was here to see you, Mr Cowgill. He went to Manor Row on Monday but was turned away. He's looking for a job and I suggest you listen to him.' With that she sat down and held baby James even tighter.

The focus of everyone's attention was on Bella and the baby. Eventually, when they were satisfied that she and James had suffered no lasting ill effects from the incident, Luke approached Sugden. 'I don't know how to begin thanking you,' he said. 'I dread to think what would have happened but for your quick thinking. My wife said you were here about a job. Would you tell us more, please?'

'My girlfriend's father heard that your accountant, Mr Jones might be about to retire and he thought it might be worth asking if there was a vacancy in your team.'

'Where did he hear that?' Sonny asked.

'He works here and I believe he overheard a conversation you had last week.'

'Are you a trained accountant?'

'Yes, sir. I'm a fully qualified chartered accountant, I have my papers here.' He reached to the inside pocket of his jacket and produced his documents which he handed to Sonny.

'Why are you looking for work?' Sonny asked.

'I was a soldier, and finding a suitable position is proving very difficult. Although I am prepared to take any work I can find.'

'Then why haven't you returned to your previous employer? You've had plenty of opportunity, surely?' Jessica demanded.

'I'm afraid that isn't possible.' He saw the doubt on their faces and explained, 'The firm I worked for no longer exists. It was in Darley Street, where there's now a crater.'

Paul knew that unless he went into some detail the directors might consider him lazy, and only interested in a sinecure. Although he didn't like talking about his ordeal, he explained why his release from the army had been delayed.

'Your family must have been glad to see you home,' Bella suggested.

The shock they obviously felt at his mistreatment increased markedly at Paul's reply. 'No, ma'am. My father died during the war. My mother died twenty-four hours before I reached home. She didn't know I'd survived. They were my only family.'

The tale was bleak enough to horrify them. For Luke Fisher, in particular, the parallel between Paul's suffering, and what he'd been told of his brother's ordeal at the hands of the Japanese, was especially poignant.

After they'd finished questioning him, Sonny asked Paul if he'd mind waiting outside while they talked things over. 'If you go down to reception and ask the girl there to look after you and provide you with a cup of tea, we'll give you a call when we're ready.'

Paul was about to leave the room when Luke stopped him. 'You said your girlfriend's father mentioned the possible vacancy. I guess that means he likes you. If that's so, how come you're not married?'

'I'm waiting until I have a job before I ask her. It wouldn't be fair asking Sally to marry me without prospects and the means of supporting her.'

Once he was out of earshot they were free to discuss him in candid terms.

'I appreciate that you might feel indebted to him because of what happened this morning, but we can't go handing out a responsible job like Simon's to someone out of charity,' Jessica said.

'That's true, but I wasn't thinking along those lines,' Sonny responded. 'I was interested by his answer to Luke's last question. I think he might make a good fist of the job if he receives some guidance early on. We already know that he's prudent and careful.'

'How do you make that out?'

'Because he's prepared to wait before asking his girl-friend to marry him. If he's as careful with the company's money as he is with his own, he'll do for me.'

Jessica was about to raise further objections, but then she remembered how similar circumstances had led to David Lyons's contribution to the group — and to the upward change in her life. She smiled to herself as she thought of her lover and decided not to put any further objections in Sugden's way.

'He's had a rough deal, but it hasn't made him bitter, which says a lot,' Mark pointed out. 'But we've no idea how competent he might be. I agree with both Sonny and Jessica, but which way we go is a tricky one to answer. I think it would be best to speak to Simon first.'

It was Luke who settled the issue. When he'd listened to the others make their points, he suggested, 'How about we take him on, but on the strict understanding that he's a probationer, and that if he's not deemed satisfactory at the end of say, six months, we have the option to let him go? That way he can receive guidance from Simon and if it doesn't work out we'll at least have given him a chance.'

The idea met with all round approval, and after a phone call to Simon and some further discussion about the terms, Paul was sent for and told the good news. As he was about to leave, his face alight with hope and anticipation, Luke Fisher stopped him. 'I pushed for you to get this, not purely because of today, although I'll be forever grateful to you over that, but because I think you're the right calibre. Don't let me down. Now get off home and propose to your girl.'

After Paul left the building, and they were discussing the recent events, Luke watched out of the window as their newest recruit strode across the yard, head erect. There goes a happy man, Luke thought. He turned and told Sonny quietly, 'Just to be on the safe side, I think it would be sensible to get a private investigator to do a background check on Sugden. I know they say "never look a gift horse in the mouth" but I think we ought to protect our interests, don't you? Even if he's all he appears to be, there's still a question mark over him. He might be as honest as the day's long and determined to try his best, but he's no good to us if he's careless or hopeless at the job.'

'You're not having second thoughts, are you?'

'By no means, just playing safe. I don't doubt him, but we need to be certain he isn't just a smooth-talking confidence trickster. Now, let's get on. Luckily the little troublemaker over there seems to have settled down so Bella doesn't have to leave us yet.'

* * *

Once Luke had satisfied himself that the business end of the trip was in hand, and the visits to the company's sites were complete, he told his fellow directors that although he would have liked to have spent more time with them, pressure back in Australia forbade that. 'We're leaving in a couple of days. Much as we'd like to stay longer, as things are that's not possible. It's a shame because I'd have liked to have traced my family roots. I'm fairly sure they came from around here. My father's accent for one thing leads me to that conclusion. He spoke a lot like you and your dad,' he told Mark.

'Maybe in a few years we might get chance for a longer visit,' Bella added, 'it would have been nice to have got to know Jenny better. In the meantime, we've a family to raise as well as a business to run.'

Having said their farewells, Luke and Bella headed to London ready for the return leg of their journey, which would take them via the westward route to America before heading home. As they boarded the train in Leeds, rain began to fall, and the greater part of their travel to the capital was completed in a heavy drizzle.

'At least we won't miss the weather,' Bella said.

'It's easy to forget how lucky we are in that respect,' Luke agreed, 'having been here before, I know this sort of rain can last for days on end.'

'It's a shame it's putting a dampener on the end of the visit, though. Anyway, what do you reckon to our British colleagues?'

'I think they've got some good ideas and sound business sense. I hope it works out for them,' he grinned, 'and for us too.'

CHAPTER TWENTY-ONE

Back in Australia, Patrick Finnegan phoned his wife. 'Louise, I've had a telegram.' He laughed as he relayed the terse message. 'It's all systems go for Elliot's trip to England. I think we should tell him and Dottie about it tonight. The sooner it's out in the open the better, because it wouldn't be fair to spring it on them at the last minute and not give them chance to spend some time together before they're separated for so long.'

'It sounds as if Luke's trip was successful.'

'The cable doesn't say, but the fact that he wants Elliot to go to England makes it seem that way.'

That evening after dinner, Patrick and Louise took Elliot and Dottie into Patrick's study, where they told the lovers what they had in mind. 'You've been to all the sites here and have picked up a lot, but the UK element needs learning. We also feel you need a longer separation in order to prove to us that your feelings for one another are genuine. Elliot's secondment to Fisher Springs's English division is the ideal opportunity to put that into practice. It won't be easy, but others around you have had to put up with worse.'

Louise looked at Dottie as she added, 'Your brother and Bella for example. They had to wait years before they got together, and during that time she had to live with the constant worry that he might not survive the war. You won't have that worry, and if you still feel the same about one another when he returns, then you will have our blessing.'

When he and Dottie were alone, Elliot said, 'I don't see there's much else we can do. I need this job to be able to support us and give you the life you deserve.'

Dottie stared at him, tears in her eyes. 'No, you don't, Eli. A few more years and I'll have all the money we need.'

'No,' Elliot was adamant. 'It's a husband's role to provide for his family and that's what I intend to do. Besides, your inheritance won't last forever. So I guess we'll have to play along with it. I'll miss you every minute I'm away, but if it means we're able to be together with our folks' blessing, then I guess it'll be worthwhile.'

'Did you suspect they were going to spring something like this on us?'

'Not exactly, although there's been a rumour doing the rounds at work that someone might be sent to England on a long-term basis. I had no idea Dad and Luke had earmarked me for the job, though.'

'It seems so unfair. Why can't they simply accept that we're a couple and leave it at that?'

'Let them think what they want. It's you and me that matter, Dot, and hang the rest of them. In twelve months from now we'll be able to afford a place of our own and then we can shut the door on the world and do what we want, when we want.'

* * *

It was two months after their departure from England that Luke and Bella returned to Australia. Once they had dropped their luggage off at home, their first port of call, quite naturally, was on Bella's parents. After Patrick and Louise had admired James and remarked on the amount the infant had grown, Bella was able to impart news of her brother Finlay, studying in Virginia. Louise was particularly interested in her son's relationship with a farmer's daughter, which Bella told her seemed to make both parties more than happy.

'We'll have some photos for you once we've got the films developed,' Luke added, 'Bella was snapping away furiously throughout the trip. And she's right, Finlay's girlfriend is really pretty.'

'Or to put it another way, every time Luke saw her, he began to drool,' Bella countered waspishly.

Luke grinned sheepishly and hastened to change the subject. 'Finlay has an idea for the company. Between studies, he's working on the farm which grows tobacco, and he reckons he could establish it here when he comes home.'

'We'll have to see about that,' Patrick replied.

Luke agreed. 'And when we were in the UK, I also talked to Josh Jones's father, Simon. It was the day before Bella and little James nearly got killed. I thought it only fair that his parents should know the truth about Astrid's past.'

'Hang on, what's this about Bella and James?' Louise asked, alarmed and shocked.

'I'll let Bella explain, I wasn't there.'

Patrick and Louise were naturally appalled at the narrow escape their daughter and grandson had experienced and expressed their gratitude for the stranger who had saved them.

'You might get to hear a whole lot more about him, Dad,' Bella told Patrick. 'He'd got turned away after he'd gone to the offices to try for an interview. That's why he was onsite, otherwise I might not be here talking to you now. When I heard his situation, I made him go back inside and tell the guys his story.'

Luke took up the tale. 'His name's Paul Sugden and he was looking for an accountancy job, so we've agreed to him serving a six-month probationary period working alongside Simon Jones and, if he passes the test, he will be offered a full-time post. Apart from his bravery that day I was quite impressed with him. He's got a quiet air of confidence about him allied to natural caution that seems just right for that job.'

They were interrupted at that point when Dottie entered the room, clearly delighted by the wanderers' return. She hugged Luke and Bella before scooping up her infant nephew who was desperately toddling away in a bid for freedom.

'You must come by more often,' Patrick said wryly before the discussion went ahead. 'That's the first smile we've had out of her since we said Elliot's going to England.'

Dottie blushed but refused to rise to the bait, wisely preferring to concentrate her attention on baby James. The rest of the afternoon and evening was spent discussing family matters, and it was agreed that Luke would return to Fisher Springs's offices the following week. Before leaving, however, Luke mentioned that he had given the green light to the new venture, in which their British counterparts would hold a fifty per cent shareholding.

'We're moving into unknown territory on both counts, which is quite risky, but I'm confident they'll make a go of it. I agreed that as things move forward, Mark Cowgill, and possibly David Lyons, should be co-opted onto the board. It will give them their rightful place and with the founding of the new divisions they need to be involved.'

When Luke returned to the office, the main item on his agenda was to brief Elliot as to developments in England, and what he expected him to do during his time there. 'You'll be reporting to the UK board and also to me. I need chapter and verse in monthly reports. I want you to learn as much as you can about how the entire operation works. One other point, I'd like you to pay special attention to how their new man in the accounting section performs. His name is Paul Sugden and he'll be working alongside Simon Jones, the finance director, but I've a special reason for wanting to know if he's doing OK or not.'

All too soon the date scheduled for Elliot's departure arrived. In the days before he went, he and Dottie spent as much time together as possible, culminating with a weekend in Sydney, before she watched, as best she could through her tears, as his plane took off on the first leg of his mission. She remembered their final night together, where the desperation of their imminent parting had lent a special urgency and added passion to their lovemaking.

* * *

Having achieved their objective by securing the continued backing of their parent company and approval for their diversification into man-made fibres and pharmaceuticals, Sonny, Jessica, Mark, and Simon held an impromptu meeting at which Simon seemed more cheerful than of late. The reason for this became apparent when he explained the details of his private conversation with Luke Fisher and a newspaper cutting Luke had given him. 'He told me they'd used Josh for an important assignment. It proved so successful that they've offered him a full-time post. However, Luke also revealed that Josh's wife Astrid has been awarded a medal by the British government for her services during the war.'

Jessica smiled to herself. She knew only too well of Josh's activities during the war.

'Apparently, Josh asked for a break before he took up his new position. By the time he returned, it was all over the news. Although the reason wasn't made public knowledge, we think she must have been involved in some part with Josh's work. Perhaps this will enable Naomi to come to terms with Astrid's nationality. Who knows, we might even be fortunate to achieve reconciliation between Josh and his mother, and possibly for Naomi to accept Astrid as her daughter-in-law.'

'How did Naomi react?' Sonny asked.

'I haven't told her yet.'

'But how did the government know where they were?' Mark asked, as he looked at the press cutting.

Jessica was quick to reply, 'I think we have to assume that Josh's former employers will be fully aware of any move he makes.'

When Simon arrived back at their home that evening and his chauffeur had decanted him safely into the house, he was geared up, ready to reveal the startling news that Luke Fisher had imparted, but Naomi was out.

It was a while before she arrived and began by apologizing for her absence. 'I went into town to do some shopping and somewhere between Busby's and Brown & Muff's I lost track of the time.'

'Two department stores in one day?' Simon teased her. 'I suppose that means I'm a ruined man and will have to go singing on the streets.'

'I didn't spend that much money,' Naomi protested before noticing the smile on his face. She was glad, because he'd been suffering some very depressed moods lately, and although he wouldn't admit the fact, she guessed he was at times in more pain than he was prepared to admit.

'As a penance for your spendthrift ways I think you should make us both a nice cup of tea to go with those cream cakes you bought, probably to bribe me with.'

'How do you know I brought cream cakes?'

Simon laughed and pointed towards the kitchen table, visible through the open door of the lounge. 'The box with the name of Silvio's Bakery on it is a kind of giveaway. And when you've made the tea, I'll tell you some news. I think you'll be pleased.'

Once they'd consumed the cakes, Simon wiped the remnants of jam and cream from around his mouth, took a sip of tea, and launched into his story. 'As you know, we've had Luke Fisher, the overall boss of Fisher Springs visiting us over the past few weeks.'

'How did it turn out? I know you've been worried about the future.'

'I don't think I've much cause to be concerned. Fisher's a really nice chap, an astute businessman and as keen as mustard. Before they left, Fisher took me to one side and we had a private conversation.'

'What was it about? Was it your plan to take life easier and retire?'

'Not exactly,' he paused. 'It was about Josh. Well, about Josh and Astrid to be precise.'

Naomi frowned at the name of her errant son and despised daughter-in-law. 'How come Mr Fisher talked to you about them? Does he know them?'

'Josh went to Australia, and before he left, Sonny Cowgill wrote a letter of introduction for him to Patrick Finnegan. After a while they offered him a job. Apparently he's been working undercover to expose a massive embezzlement that hit their banking division. It had already cost the group thousands of pounds. Fisher was so impressed with Josh's work that he's been offered a full-time post within the group.'

'That's good to hear, but it doesn't make things any easier, I'm afraid.'

'No, but the next part of the news will, I'm certain. Before Luke came here, Josh asked for a few days' leave of absence. He wanted to accompany Astrid when she was awarded a medal for her services to the British government during the war. Naturally, Josh wasn't allowed to say exactly what that service involved, but Fisher knows of the difficulties you and I had with Astrid's nationality and he thought we should be aware of the truth. All Josh would reveal was that what she helped him achieve might have altered the course of the war.'

As he was speaking, he passed the press cutting to her. The photo it contained showed a beautiful young woman, holding a medal and smiling at the camera.

Naomi was in tears by now. 'Why on earth didn't Josh tell us? He could at least have given us a hint.'

'For one thing I don't believe we gave him much of a chance, added to which he's as stubborn as you are once he gets upset. I also think he was only able to reveal the sparse details he told Fisher once the news of the medal became public knowledge.'

'I wish we knew where he is so I could write to them and apologize. I suppose it's my wretched past coming home with a vengeance yet again.'

'Luke thought that might be your reaction, so he also supplied this.' Simon took a folded slip of paper from his pocket. Naomi snatched it from him and stared at the address for a long silent moment. She smiled, a watery, tearful expression of happiness and relief combined.

'I'll write to them this evening after dinner.'

'No, you won't,' Simon corrected her. 'We'll do it together, the same as we always do things.'

CHAPTER TWENTY-TWO

Given the renewed optimism generated by the successful outcome of their negotiations with Luke Fisher, the weeks and
months following his visit proved hectic for all the executives
in the UK arm of the group. Maintaining the head office of
Fisher Springs UK in the Manor Row building, they began
setting up the new companies, which by mutual agreement
bore the names FS Pharmaceuticals and FS Textiles respec-
tively. Although nothing had been confirmed, Luke had
intimated that if the enterprise proved successful, he would
give serious consideration to replicating their operation in
Australia, and if that was to take place he would need the
expert guidance provided by those with prior experience.

Locating suitable premises was a task assigned to Jessica
Binks and Mark Cowgill. In this they were assisted by David
Lyons. This led to an interesting conversation between Mark
and his father as they returned to Scarborough, following a
tiring day factory hunting.

'I don't know if you've noticed,' Mark said, 'but
I happened to see Jessica and David before we set off for
Huddersfield today and, unless I'm very much mistaken,
they're a bit more than simply business colleagues. Actually,
I'd suggest they are a lot more than just good friends.'

Sonny whistled with surprise. 'I have heard one or two rumours about her, but I wasn't sure whether or not to believe them. Your Aunt Connie and Uncle Michael did have some problems with their boys and Jessica when they were all in their teens.'

'If they involve an active love life, then I think you probably should believe the rumours.'

Within weeks, the arrival of Elliot Finnegan gave them an extra pair of hands. 'First off, we'd like you to help set up the new companies,' Sonny told him. 'There are two reasons for that. One is that these might prove to be the English trading arm's most profitable operations in the future, so it would be wise to familiarize yourself with the way they're being set up. Also, if they do prove to be as successful as we anticipate, your brother-in-law might want to replicate their activities down under, so your prior-knowledge of what's involved will be invaluable.'

Elsewhere within the group, Simon Jones was keeping a careful eye on his newest staff member, and within a month of Paul Sugden having started work in the accounts department, Simon was able to give a positive initial report on him to his fellow directors at their regular board meeting. 'Sugden gets on with his work in a quiet, unobtrusive manner, but I can already see that he's efficient, hardworking and nobody's fool. I set him several challenging tasks to see how he measured up and he completed them with ease and much earlier than I expected. To make doubly sure, I inserted several traps to see if he'd accept the figures that he'd been given without question. He not only avoided them but also worked out my hidden agenda.'

Simon smiled ruefully as Jessica asked him to explain. 'When Paul handed the completed work back to me, he attached a note to it that read, "I hope that I have spotted all the little ruses you employed to test me and that I passed muster". I think it's safe to allow him to become familiar with the heavier end of my department's work, and if he proves as competent handling those tasks I believe we should go ahead and employ him on a full-time basis.'

'In what capacity?' Jessica asked.

'As my assistant to begin with, then when I'm happy that he's capable and knowledgeable enough to step up to the mark, to promote him as my replacement, that should be nothing more than a formality. At that point I believe we should also make his promotion contingent on him buying a small number of shares in the group. One of the best ways of ensuring the highest level of performance out of executives is to keep them aware that they are in essence working for themselves. That has always been Fisher Springs's business ethic and I fully support it and believe we should adopt the same policy as the group moves forward. Likewise, I think we should consider making a similar offer to David Lyons.'

'That might pose a problem if they haven't the cash to pay for a tranche of shares,' Sonny pointed out.

'I thought of that too,' Simon replied, 'and I think we should offer them the shares with the back-up of an interest-free loan. That way, once they've paid the loan off, we have their total commitment.'

'What do you think, Jessica?' Mark asked slyly. 'You're the one who is most closely involved with David. How do you rate his performance?'

Jessica glanced sharply at Mark and blushed slightly as she saw the wicked twinkle in his eyes. With characteristic boldness she stared him down as she replied, 'I'd rate him as highly satisfactory in every way.'

With Sonny and Simon studying their agenda, she saw Mark still watching her and quickly stuck her tongue out, a gesture that almost made him laugh out loud. He managed to convert this into a cough and the meeting proceeded without further digressions.

When she reached home that evening, Jessica reported on the day's events. David was interested and a little concerned by the news that at least one other person seemed to know their secret. 'Are you certain he suspects that we're lovers, or was it simply an innocent remark you took the wrong way?'

'Judging by the look on Mark's face I certainly don't believe it was innocent. That means we've given ourselves away.'

'Does it concern you if others know about us?'

'Speaking for myself, I don't give a damn who knows. I'm certainly not bothered if our colleagues become aware that we're an item. They're decent people, who won't be critical if they know we've turned to one another for mutual comfort.'

'Speaking of mutual comfort,' — David began to unfasten her blouse buttons, then her skirt — 'I could do with some right now.'

'You mean right now, in the kitchen.' She laughed tremulously as her excitement grew.

'Why not, you look good enough to eat?'

* * *

By spring of 1952 both of the new Fisher Springs UK ventures were up and running and when the newly appointed group finance director, Paul Sugden presented the annual reports they would show small profits. There had been much midnight oil burned in both premises as the executives strived to get their companies in a position to justify the capital investment and faith shown in the risky departures from the traditional sources of revenue.

The midnight oil had been more in evidence in the synthetic fibres division, where Mark Cowgill headed up the manufacture, processing, and sales of the new textiles. Clothes rationing had ended in 1949 but many of the older group customers had initially rebelled against using the products, preferring to opt for the more traditional materials they knew they could trust. Gradually however, with the advantage of lower prices which would appeal to the economically minded Yorkshire spinners and weavers, the more adventurous users were converted.

With a rapidly growing market available and a range of products that had no competitors, the pharmaceutical division made even quicker headway. Their progress had been enhanced by the innovation of the National Health Service established by the post-war labour government of Clement Attlee. It was in July of 1948 that Aneurin Bevan, the Health Secretary, opened the first hospital to operate the new organization, with promises of affordable healthcare for all.

By 1951, when the country returned a Conservative government under the leadership of Winston Churchill, the NHS was too well established for those who opposed it to reverse the process. At FS Pharmaceuticals the managing director, Jessica Binks examined the sales figures with quiet satisfaction, before calling her production director in for a meeting. 'The results are beginning to justify all the hard work, so I see no need for us to spend every hour of the day here. Apart from anything else, you're needed at home.'

David Lyons smiled at his boss and lover affectionately. 'You've no idea how much that excites me,' he replied.

It wasn't only in Bradford that the success of the new companies was greeted with satisfaction. In the Australian head office of Fisher Springs Pty, Luke Fisher reflected on how yet another of the group's gambles was beginning to pay dividends, albeit so far only small ones. Encouraged by the news, he turned his attention to another prospective development that he had recently been presented with and called in the group's new ventures manager for consultation.

He watched his brother-in-law enter the office, reflecting with some pleasure how Elliot had progressed from the eager but inexperienced novice who had been sent to England to learn the business. It wasn't only in the business sense that Elliot had matured rapidly. His relationship with Luke's sister had also withstood their separation and was now a happy marriage. Although Dottie was older than her husband, the love between them seemed as strong as ever, the evidence of which being the son she had recently delivered.

After Elliot had reported on the progress of Luke's scheme to extend their chain of filling stations and diners, he listened carefully as Luke mentioned the idea that had come to him as he was reading an article in one of the morning papers.

'This sort of thing should be right up your street, Elliot,' Luke told him with a grin, 'especially with your arty-farty background.'

Ignoring the insult, Elliot considered Luke's proposition. 'You want me to investigate the possibility of opening a television station, work out costs and so forth, is that right? It could prove very expensive.'

Luke waved the warning aside, while being pleased by Elliot's caution. 'I'm not too concerned about that. Income from the media division is quite strong. The radio and newspaper advertising revenues are climbing slowly but surely, and it isn't as if we're talking about opening up for broadcasting this time tomorrow.'

'That's a relief. You sounded so keen I thought you might be going to tell me you wanted the station to be on air in the morning.'

'I wouldn't put you under that much pressure, tomorrow afternoon will be soon enough.' It was only the wicked twinkle in Luke's eyes that told Elliot he was being teased.

Once the meeting was over, Luke picked up the phone and dialled home. It was a while before Bella answered the call, from which he deduced that she might have been busy attending to their four-month-old daughter, Robyn Louise.

When he suggested this, however, Bella gave a scornful laugh. 'She isn't the problem. It's your father's namesake who is proving a handful. He's been wreaking havoc, behaving like a little sod ever since you left for work. I'll be glad when he can start kindergarten.'

Luke smiled, obviously Bella was on top form, judging by the insults. 'No, you won't, you'll miss him like crazy! Besides, he's only developing his growing strength of character.'

'Growing stubbornness more like, something else he seems to have inherited from you.'

'I suppose with such a bad example so firmly in mind you're not going to be interested in us having any more children.'

'Don't talk baloney, Luke, of course I want more.'

'Oh good, in that case I'll make sure and leave work early today.'

'Yes, darling, please do that.' Bella's altered tone made Luke immediately suspicious, and as she continued his suspicion rapidly became a certainly. Her tone changed to seductive whisper as she added, 'I can't wait for you to come home, beloved, so that we can be together and you'll be able to give me what I really want. It'll be such a pleasant change to have a night off and let you bath the kids and put them to bed.'

'I'll happily let Nanny do that, and afterwards perhaps we can continue the discussion.'

His only response was the dialling tone. Luke smiled contentedly and returned to study the report that his secretary had placed on his desk earlier that day.

The report, compiled by Josh Jones, was the final instalment of the grimmest chapter in the group's trading history, an event that had taken years to resolve. It contained the settlement agreements reached with victims and their families affected by the poison that had leaked from Fisher Springs's mineral extraction site into watercourses, causing widespread illness and, sadly, several fatalities.

The bill for compensation, added to the cost of the lengthy and painstaking clean-up operation, was immense, but that didn't concern Luke overmuch as he read the report. He was glad that the document drew a line under the whole sorry business.

Luke smiled slightly as he skim-read the list of the victims or their relatives. When he'd entrusted the negotiation of the settlements to Jones, Luke had insisted that Louise Finnegan should be included. Although Jones had acceded to the instruction, both Louise and her husband Patrick had protested that it was unnecessary.

Luke had contradicted them, pointing out that if the list was published, the presence of Louise's name would show that the group was treating all victims with equal fairness. In the end, with Bella's support, he won the day. His final comment, that if they felt uneasy accepting the money they could always donate it to charity, clinched the argument.

Luke's other main concern was over the report's complier. Josh had proved to be a highly valuable asset in the time since joining the group, despite having a difficult personal problem to contend with. Luckily, from what little Luke had gleaned, that now seemed to have been resolved, so the remaining question was with regard to Josh's future at Fisher Springs.

With Patrick Finnegan now in semi-retirement and nobody thus far stepping forward to fill Luke's brother Phillip's shoes, there were at least two senior executive roles lying vacant. The need to promote at least one member of staff to board level was not only essential but urgent. Luke wondered how Patrick would react to his two-pronged suggestion, which he was about to put forward at the following day's board meeting.

Looking forward to and planning his strategy for the meeting, Luke intended to point out that their English subsidiary and joint venture had tackled a similar problem head on and achieved what promised to be a satisfactory outcome. His hope was that their example would tip the balance in his favour.

Prior to that, his priority was to clear his desk of any remaining work with as much speed as he could muster so that he was free to leave early. That way he could take Bella up on her implicit offer.

However, Luke's main concern was over the declining health of his mother-in-law. Louise had been waging a long-running battle with the after-effects of being poisoned, and for the most part had appeared to be coping reasonably well. Of late, the family had noticed small indications that her health was beginning to fail. Although Louise didn't complain, Luke was certain that at times she appeared to be in pain, and that thought put him in two minds. On the one hand he would not want Louise to continue suffering when there was no possibility of a reprieve, but on the other he knew what a dreadful loss it would be to the entire family. Not only would they have to endure the grieving process, but they would have to support Patrick in his distress.

In the event, any speculation about family matters and the outcome of the next day's board meeting had to be put on hold, when Luke's secretary asked if he was free to speak to Josh Jones.

As soon as Josh entered his office, Luke noticed that he appeared to be in some distress. The reason became clear once he explained why he had sought the interview. 'I need to request leave of absence,' Josh began. 'I've just received a telegram from my mother. My stepdad is very ill. I must go to see him, to be there for my mother.'

'I'm sorry to hear that, Josh, I like and respect Simon enormously. You must go. Take as long as you need, and don't worry about things here, your future is safe with us.'

CHAPTER TWENTY-THREE

If Josh and Astrid were worried about how Naomi would take to her daughter-in-law, those concerns eased within minutes of their arrival. After hugging her son, an embrace that lasted for a long time, Naomi released him and turned to greet Astrid. Seeing the uncertainty in the younger woman's eyes and the fear of rejection in her expression, melted any resistance Naomi might have felt towards her. She reached out and wrapped Astrid in as close an embrace as the one she had bestowed on Josh. As they hugged, Naomi whispered, 'I am sorry for the wrong I did you, and for the distress I caused to both of you. Please come through to the lounge, you must be tired after your journey.'

'How is he?' Josh was anxious about Simon.

'He's quite comfortable. He was in the Duke of York, not that the Infirmary isn't good, but they're coping with the aftermath of the polio epidemic and I felt he would be just a name in a bed. But he insisted on coming home — to wait for you.' She bit her lip, forced a smile, and said, 'He's sleeping at the moment.' She headed for the kitchen. 'I'll make you some tea while we wait for him to wake. And I need to speak to you first.'

When she returned, Naomi spoke directly to Astrid. 'Now that I am aware of the truth, or as much of it as you

209

are permitted to tell me, I hope you can find it in your heart to forgive me.'

'Of course I do,' Astrid responded, 'but more than that I understand how upsetting it must have been to learn that Josh was about to marry someone whose nationality suggested only those who had caused you such loss and so much pain. Being aware of the dreadful danger he was constantly in made it a terrible time, until I knew he was safe and that he still wanted me. I never doubted my love for Josh, but during all those years apart I sometimes wondered if he'd been using me and had moved on. It is a horrible feeling to believe that you are all alone in the world and that with every sunrise you wonder if there will be a knock on the door today and you will be dragged away to be tortured and killed.'

The willingness with which Astrid accepted Naomi's apology and the fellow feeling generated by her words were all the proof Naomi needed that Josh had chosen well by marrying Astrid.

Although neither Josh nor Astrid knew the facts, Naomi also remembered all too vividly a time when she too had been alone, pregnant, and terrified that there would come a knock on her door and that she would be unmasked as a member of the terrorist group whose actions had led to the outbreak of the First World War.

How similar must Astrid have felt during the long years of the latter conflict? Separated from the man she loved, not knowing if he was alive or dead, alone in what she classed as enemy territory, every day a nightmare that might signal the end for her. In those few sentences the two women had exchanged there was forgiveness, acceptance, mutual understanding, and respect.

If Josh's return to England had been difficult for Naomi and Astrid, his arrival presented a different sort of problem for Mark and Jenny Cowgill. They discussed this over dinner in Byland Crescent with Mark's parents and Jenny's mother Joyce. They had visited Simon in hospital and were aware that Josh had been sent for.

'What do you think we should do about it, Dad?' Jenny's question came immediately Sonny made the announcement that Josh and Astrid had arrived in the country.

Sonny, Rachael and Joyce looked puzzled until Mark clarified the question by adding, 'What Jenny means is, do you think we ought to tell Josh we know about his child in Spain? If we meet up with him, and from what you've just told us that sounds very likely, he's almost certain to ask us about Carmen and if she got away to safety now that he knows we were with her at the end of the Spanish Civil War.'

'Oh Hell, I hadn't thought of that,' Sonny responded, only to be on the receiving end of a fierce glare for swearing in front of his grandchildren. 'What do you suggest, Rachael?' Sonny asked, attempting to redeem himself — without noticeable success.

If Rachael's attitude to her husband's misdeed softened in the slightest it was by no means evident in the fixed stare she gave him. After a few moments' silence, however, they realized that she had merely been weighing up the pros and cons of the dilemma Mark and Jenny faced.

'Speaking as a mother,' Rachael said eventually, 'and as a grandmother, my natural instinct would be to tell him about the child. It was a baby girl, wasn't it?'

Mark and Jenny nodded. 'She named the baby Consuela Genoveva,' Mark added with a touch of pride. 'Consuela being Spanish for consolation and Genoveva being their equivalent of Jennifer.'

'Be that as it may,' Rachael continued, 'I think in this case it would be the wrong course of action to tell Josh. He has made a new life for himself in another country. In doing so, and by choosing to marry the woman he loves in defiance of his family, he has demonstrated forcibly that he is quite prepared to leave the past behind and abandon all former ties rather than be separated from Astrid. I believe we should respect that decision. By all means, if he asks, tell him that Carmen escaped to safety. That will ease any pangs of conscience he might still have over abandoning her, which might surface when he meets up with you. However, informing him of the baby would do no good and might even prove hurtful to his relationship with his new wife.'

'I agree with Rachael,' Joyce interposed her view. 'Even if you told him about the child and he went dashing off to Spain to try and find her it might prove to be all in vain, so why risk upsetting the applecart on what might be a fruitless exercise with no certainty of success.'

'Why do you think it might prove fruitless?' Mark asked.

'I guess what Joyce means is that sadly there is no certainty that either of them survived,' Rachael told them. 'In addition to the countless ailments that could put a young baby's life at risk there is the uncertain situation in Spain to take into account. Simply because Carmen and her baby escaped from the mainland there is no guarantee that Franco's troops or secret police didn't catch up with them and wreak revenge for Carmen's actions during the Civil War. Let me ask you this, Jenny,' she turned to her daughter-in-law. 'Given that you and Carmen were so close, and as you told us she has your name and address, wouldn't it have been natural to have heard from her by now, all these years later, if all had been well?'

'I think you're right, Mum,' Mark agreed, as Jenny absorbed this fact.

'She usually is,' Sonny added with a rueful smile.

'OK.' Jenny accepted the inevitable. 'If and when we meet up with Josh, we merely tell him that Carmen escaped, we don't tell him where to and we definitely don't tell him about Consuela.'

* * *

At approximately the same time as the family in Byland Crescent were discussing Josh's past, his future was being debated in the head office of Fisher Springs. Luke Fisher began to put forward his proposal to his sole listener and fellow director, Patrick Finnegan. 'I've been mulling over the best way forward once you take full retirement. You've borne the responsibility for the group more or less constantly for over twenty years, steering it through some appallingly difficult times and if anyone deserves a rest, you do. I would miss you terribly but it would be churlish of me to try and stand in your way. My intention is to ensure that, in future, nobody is placed in such a difficult position as you were.'

'What exactly do you have in mind?'

'I have a two-fold way of dealing with the situation. First of all, I propose that we make two appointments to the main board. Secondly, I think we should promote at least one manager from each operating division to become a director of that company and also to join a panel I want to set up. It will act as a sort of executive committee, operating at one rank below main board level. My idea is that they should meet regularly, ideally once a month. In those gatherings, they should discuss group progress, talk over new ideas, examine new ventures, and put forward recommendations to the directors. What do you think?'

Patrick didn't take long to decide. 'I think it's an excellent plan. I admit there were times when I found the responsibility for the group extremely onerous and would have loved to have had someone to share the burden with me. This was particularly true in the early days, where all I had to rely on was the experience I'd gained from working alongside your father and mother. It was remarkable the way their skills complemented one another so that they blended to form a perfect team. They both had very keen business acumen. In addition, your mother was blessed with a natural talent for managing people so that she got the best out of them, a skill that is sadly all too rare. Your father's foresight, his uncanny knowledge of what direction markets were going to move in and his perception of how world events were shaping up and the effect they would have on the global economy was visionary.

'That was an impossible act to follow for one man and would have been hard enough for a team of ten. Your plan to gather together the best brains, and most success-hungry executives as possible, represents the best chance of equalling or even surpassing the success your parents achieved. There's also your own bit of talent to throw into the mix,' he added with a cheeky grin. 'That being the case, who do you have in mind for promotion onto the main board?'

'The first candidate I've been considering is Joshua Jones. He's already achieved a lot. By successfully uncovering the fraud and embezzlement in the banking division he saved the group a heck of a lot of money, possibly running into millions. Added to that, the message his action sent out throughout the group should prevent others trying anything dodgy in the banking or other sectors. The way he handled the aftermath of that pollution disaster was most impressive and he seems to have done it with extreme tact towards the sensitivities of the victims and their relatives. I've seen a few letters from the survivors in which they speak of how he made the process a whole lot easier for them. Overall, I think that what Josh lacks in business knowledge and experience he more than makes up for in his man-management ability. I believe if we make him a main board director, with prime responsibility for personnel, that will send a positive message to the troops in the field. It's high time we addressed the problem now that the group payroll has got so big.'

Finnegan took some while considering Luke's suggestion before giving his response. 'OK, I agree your first nominee, who else are you considering?'

Luke smiled slightly before he answered. 'It's a young man you know as well as me, if not better — your older son, Elliot.'

If Patrick had been surprised by Luke's choice of Josh Jones as a candidate for group directorship, he was shocked beyond measure by his second selection. There was a long silence before he said, 'Elliot? Do you really believe that Elliot is capable of handling such a big responsibility?'

'I certainly do, and for a number of reasons. You must remember that since you went into semi-retirement you've not been in touch with the day-to-day running of the group as before, so some of this might come as a surprise to you. The first reason is his track record, which speaks volumes for his steadfast and determined attitude, plus his sense of duty. He's been handed some testing assignments, all of which he's completed with a high degree of success, especially after we sent him to England. Admittedly you had a hidden agenda in selecting him for the task of liaising with our UK counterparts, but he succeeded at both levels. The way he stood up to the separation from Dottie was a good enough recommendation. But his term in England proved pivotal in the development of our relations with the new generation of executives there and the recovery of that trading arm after their tragic setbacks. Sonny Cowgill reported that Elliot had been a great help. Since his return, Elliot has fulfilled his new role exceptionally well, handling several acquisitions and the development of a couple of new ventures very skilfully. Yes, I'd say that Elliot is well ready for this promotion,' Luke paused, and added with a grin, 'despite his dubious parentage.'

Patrick had recovered from his surprise and, after several moments' consideration, agreed to both Luke's candidates. 'I told you several years ago that the future of the group is in your hands, so you have to be totally confident about the team surrounding you. If your choice is to have Josh and Elliot alongside you, I'm happy to go along with your decision.'

'I'm not planning to announce the appointments yet. I'd prefer to wait until Jones returns from England. By the way things sound, I'm afraid Simon is in a pretty bad way.'

'That's extremely sad. We owe Simon more than we could ever hope to repay.'

'I agree, much as the debt we owe you, Patrick. Simon held things together in England like you did here.'

CHAPTER TWENTY-FOUR

Before Naomi would allow Josh and Astrid to visit Simon, she asked them to wait while she checked on him. 'I'd better see if he's awake yet.'

Noticing her husband's distress, Astrid put her hand on his arm as she asked him if he was OK.

'Yes, I suppose so. It's just difficult coming to terms with things as they are now. I realize I ought to have expected it, but as I remember him, Simon was always full of life and energy.'

Naomi returned and told them that Simon was awake and looking forward to seeing them both. They followed her along the hallway to the ground floor bedroom. Although Simon greeted them cheerfully enough, Josh was shocked to see how much he had deteriorated since their last meeting four years earlier. After a few minutes' light conversation Simon asked Naomi and Astrid if they wouldn't mind leaving the room as he needed to speak to Josh alone.

Once they'd gone, Simon asked Josh to check that the door was closed properly. It wasn't, so Josh rectified this before Simon beckoned him back to the bedside. 'You might think that was accidental, but I know otherwise. It's all part of your mother's paranoia. I thought she'd got over it years ago, but since my condition worsened it's returned in full measure.'

'What has she got to be paranoid about?'

'It's to do with the secret she has been carrying for nigh on forty years, a secret she would be mortified to have revealed. Have you ever stopped to consider why you're so talented a linguist, or why your mother was able to teach such an obscure tongue as Serbo-Croatian?'

Josh shook his head, clearly bewildered by the question.

'What I'm about to tell you,' Simon continued, 'is a closely guarded secret. The only people who know it are your mother and me, Sonny Cowgill and Edrith Pointon, your Mr Smith.'

Josh blinked with surprise at the mention of his former boss and spymaster. He was unaware that Simon knew Pointon, or his identity. Simon smiled at his astonishment and said, 'I know Pointon. I met him when you were at university. He came to persuade us to help him recruit you into the intelligence service. It was during our meeting that Pointon revealed his knowledge of your mother's troubled past. What do you know about the Black Hand, or as they were sometimes known, the Unification of Death?'

Josh recoiled slightly. 'Weren't they the Serbian Nationalists who were responsible for the assassinations that led to the outbreak of the First World War?'

'That's correct.'

Josh laughed, but without much evidence of humour. 'Don't tell me Mum was a member of that group.' His laughter died suddenly as Simon nodded.

'Yes, she was, and her role was to ensure the group was supplied with weapons. That entailed liaising with the arms dealer who supplied the terrorists. That man was your father, Jesse Barker.'

Josh looked horror struck.

'After the assassination of the archduke and archduchess in Sarajevo, your mother left Vienna where she'd been living and fled to England, hoping to be reunited with her lover, father of the child she was carrying — you. That was one reason, the main one was from fear of capture. That fear has been with her ever since.' He paused for a few seconds, the strain obviously telling on him.

Josh helped him take a sip of water before Simon recovered sufficiently to continue. 'She'd secured false papers under the identity of Naomi Fleming, which she used on her escape route. She arrived in England just as war broke out. Her real name is Hildegard Cabrinova-Schwartz. It was much later, long after the war ended that we met and she told me the full story. That altered nothing as far as I was concerned, because meeting her was the best day of my life. The reason I'm telling you this now is because I need you to be in possession of the full facts, so that you can ensure nothing bad happens when I'm not here to protect her. I realize it will be difficult with you being so far away, but you will have a staunch ally in Sonny Cowgill. I told him about your mother after I was injured by the bomb, because you were abroad somewhere and there was no certainty that I'd pull through. I had to be sure that there was someone to protect her. She always doubted the assurances given by Edrith Pointon that she was safe.'

'I promise I'll do that, Dad. Despite everything you've told me, she's still my mum. I know you said meeting her was the best day of your life, but I reckon it's true the other way round because I think you're the best thing that could have happened to her. And I've always considered you to be my dad even though there's no direct blood link.'

That night, in the privacy of their room, once they were alone and certain of not being overheard, Josh told Astrid in whispered tones what Simon had revealed. 'I suppose that explains why my mother was so opposed to our marriage, because she associates Germany and Austria with all the evils that have befallen her and those around her. But it leaves me with a huge dilemma. How can I hope to care for my mother as Dad asked when she's in England, and must remain here, and we'll be thousands of miles away?'

Astrid put her arms around him and pulled him close, as she thought about the quandary they faced. This was likely to be a make-or-break point in their marriage, and as huge a test of their love as those they had previously endured. If they could overcome this challenge, it would bind them together for life. Astrid knew that this was what she wanted and was prepared to make sacrifices to achieve it. Josh had already demonstrated the lengths he would go to in order for them to be together, now it was her turn. Now she had to put aside her reservations to satisfy his needs.

'I have an idea, Josh. At some point you must return to Australia and explain the problem to Mr Fisher. Then, if no solution can be found there, we should remain in England. While you are gone, I will stay with your mother and help look after her. She will need our support once your father is no longer with us, and if I can help her it might make things easier between us.'

'You would do that? You're prepared to face the hostility of strangers that might be directed at you simply because of where you were born?'

'I no longer care about the hurtful things other people might say or try to do to me. All I care about is you, Josh.' She held him as he drifted off to sleep, rejoicing that he had turned to her in his hour of need. She felt that the bond between them had been cemented to a point where it could not be broken.

Three nights later Astrid held him close again, as he wept silent tears of grief over the death of his stepfather.

She marvelled at the depth of feeling Josh held for the man who was not a blood relative. When he attempted to apologize Astrid would have none of it. 'You needed to express your sorrow. I quite understand that, and I'm glad I was here when you needed me.'

* * *

If Naomi was surprised by the number of people who gathered to pay their respects at Simon's funeral, she was by no

219

means the only one to be moved by the huge attendance. Although modest and self-effacing, Simon's down-to-earth and genuine character won him a lot of friends and few, if any, enemies.

The whole contingent from Byland Crescent travelled across from Scarborough to Bradford, necessitating two cars to convey the family members from the station. Seeing two of their number he particularly wanted to talk to, Josh bided his time until the opportunity arose during the funeral tea that followed the service and interment. Having received Mark and Jenny's condolences, Josh said, 'I'm really glad you were able to attend today. I still find it remarkable that we were so close together in Spain all those years ago and yet neither of us knew the other was there.'

'I agree,' Mark concurred, 'it was strange, and it came as quite a shock when we found out. If anything had happened to either of us during the war we might never have learned the truth.'

'There is one question I must ask you, though. It's regarding the woman who was the leader of your small group, the woman we referred to as Carmen.' As he mentioned her name Josh saw Mark's knowing smile, but despite this he continued, albeit a trifle nervously, 'I don't know how much Carmen told you about events before she joined the movement, but she underwent a terrible ordeal in which her husband and child were murdered in the cruellest, most sadistic way. Being aware of that, and how much she had suffered, I was concerned to know if she managed to get away to safety after the group disbanded. One of my men made inquiries in Valencia and discovered she was trying to get to Ibiza.'

'She told me all about the dreadful things that had happened,' Jenny responded, 'and she also told me how you comforted her afterwards. That was extremely noble of you, Josh, but then again she wasn't exactly hideous, was she?' Jenny saw Josh's face redden with embarrassment that his cousins knew the truth and noticed the nervous glance he cast over his shoulder.

She smiled slightly and told him not to worry. 'Astrid isn't within earshot, and besides we wouldn't dream of telling her about things that belong in the past. As to your question, as far as we're aware Carmen did get away, but we can't swear to it, because we lost touch once we reached Valencia and we embarked for the voyage home. We hope she made it, but we've no idea where she ended up.'

Mark was watching Josh carefully and noted the relief on his cousin's face. He guessed that although Josh was married, and by all appearances happily so, the dying embers of his affair with Carmen still smouldered.

Later, as they were returning to Scarborough, Jenny remarked that they had got away lightly, managing to avoid any of the searching questions Josh might have been expected to ask. 'That was down to you, Jen,' Mark replied, 'distracting Josh by inferring that we knew he'd been sleeping with Carmen and then mentioning Astrid in the same sentence was pure genius. It got him so worried that we might unintentionally let something slip about the affair that he failed to notice that we were only telling him what we wanted him to hear.'

In the same year as they said farewell to Simon Jones, his family, together with the rest of the nation, was in mourning following the death of King George VI in February 1952. His quiet, modest demeanour hid the resolve that enabled him to rise above the constitutional crisis resulting from his brother's abdication, and later to guide the country, leading by example during the dark days of the Second World War. With his passing, the nation could look forward to their second female monarch within a century as Elizabeth II acceded to the throne.

By the time the new queen was crowned the following year, life had changed for several members of the Cowgill and Fisher families and those close to them. For some the changes were radical, the effects dramatic and long-lasting.

CHAPTER TWENTY-FIVE

'I think you ought to consider retiring.'

Sonny Cowgill stared at Rachael, his surprise apparent. Although they had been married for more than thirty-four years, she still had the capacity to shock him. 'Why would I want to do that? I'm only sixty-one and there's still a lot to achieve within the group.'

'That's as maybe, but there's a new generation who are more than capable of tackling those things you've got in mind. I want more time with my husband before he becomes a doddery old man who has to get his teeth from the bathroom before he can give me a love bite. We got married so we could be together not so that we only saw each other first thing in the morning and for a couple of hours each night. Let me remind you that you fell asleep in front of the television twice last week and three times the week before. That's a sure sign you need to consider taking it easy.'

Sonny grinned at her remark about the doddery old man, but protested, 'It's more a sure sign that there's very little worth watching on the television. You bullied me into getting it for the Queen's Coronation and as far as I'm concerned there's been very little else worth watching. However, I'll take your other comments into account and consider going part-time. It was good enough for my father. I'll also ensure you get more than your share of love bites while I've still got some teeth to do it with. After that I'll keep a spare plate in the bedside drawer for when you get desperate.'

The more that Sonny thought about Rachael's suggestion, the better sense it made. He'd been born in the final decade of the previous century, had lived through two of the most cataclysmic conflicts in history so perhaps it was time for him to allow the next generation to take over the reins.

Among other considerations, one that had bothered him for some time was the new direction in which the group was heading. Although their Australian counterparts held a fifty per cent stake in the English operation, and although they still traded under the title Fisher Springs UK Ltd, the other half of the shares was split between the three departmental heads that formed the board of directors. Originally that division had been a four-way allocation, but following Simon Jones's death, Sonny, Mark, and Jessica had purchased his shareholding from his widow Naomi.

The transaction had been negotiated by Naomi's son Josh, the intention being to provide a lump sum that his mother could draw on in emergencies. The amount Naomi received from the deal, when added to the generous pension that was part of all the Fisher Springs executive packages, would set her up in comfort for life.

It was tragically ironic therefore, that the whole process had proved to be a futile exercise. Little under a year after attending Simon Jones's funeral, the family gathered for another sombre occasion. Naomi had been struck down by a stroke, the severity of which had rendered her all but paralyzed and deprived her of the ability to speak. Less than a month following the first attack a second stroke proved fatal.

Although deeply distressed by his mother's passing, Josh confided in Sonny that in one way the end had come as a merciful release. 'Mum had only been going through the motions of living after Dad left us, even before she became ill. From then on it got worse, and to be fair, I'm not sure whether she was interested in continuing without him.'

About the only small ray of sunshine that had emerged from the sad succession of events, had been the way Josh's wife Astrid stepped up to the mark when the occasion demanded. With Josh torn between his filial duty in England and his new position as a director of the Australian section of Fisher Springs, Astrid had remained by Naomi's side, becoming her companion and, later, her carer. This, for a woman comparatively recently married had been a noble self-sacrifice, but now that their remaining ties to England had been severed, she and Josh had embarked on a second honeymoon, before resuming their married life back in Australia.

These and other thoughts crossed Sonny's mind in the days following Rachael's radical suggestion and a week later he came up with a plan that he divulged to her, before revealing it to his colleagues and later to the Australian board.

'I'm happy to go along with your idea for the most part,' he told Rachael. 'I'll give up the post of managing director, which will free me from the day-to-day involvement with the running of the business but stay on as chairman, at least for the time being, in order to ensure continuity. That will mean I only have to travel to the West Riding for board meetings, which are once a month, and I can even skip them if there is nothing pressing to discuss.'

'That's all very well,' Rachael countered. She too had been having second thoughts about her suggestion. 'What I want to know is how you propose to fill in all the additional leisure time that you'll have?'

Sonny had prepared for that question. A visit to a novelty and joke shop in Scarborough the previous weekend had provided him with what he needed. He produced a small box from his pocket and with a flourish presented it to her. Rachael opened it and stared in surprise at the set of mechanical false teeth Sonny had bought. After recovering from the shock, Rachael threatened to hurl the box and its contents at him, but Sonny protested that he was merely following her advice. 'Of course, that's all for the future,' he leered suggestively at her as he spoke, 'in the meantime I've still got all mine, as I'll demonstrate later.'

* * *

Sonny duly announced his intention of semi-retirement at the next board meeting. If his decision to cease daily involvement in group activities didn't come as a total surprise, his comments regarding the future direction of the business were shocking enough to render his fellow directors speechless.

'I think the time has come when I'm not needed here anywhere near as often and I can foresee circumstances in which to some extent my presence would be counter-productive. I'm happy to continue the role of chairman, overseeing the overall activities and development of the businesses as before, but solely in that capacity. Therefore, I have decided to relinquish the position of managing director and will be writing to Luke Fisher to convey that message after today's meeting. Before I do step aside, however, wearing my managing director's hat for the final time, I would urge you to give serious consideration to a suggestion that has been occupying my mind more frequently of late. Given the ever-changing state of world trading conditions and the increased competition both from our rivals overseas, those more locally and even internally within the group, I believe it is time to shift our operational emphasis.'

He grinned at his son before continuing. 'I think we should consider divesting ourselves of a considerable portion, if not all, of the wool processing businesses, and also reducing the sales force in the merchanting division. Time after time our salesmen have reported losing orders to a competitor within our own ranks, namely the synthetic fibres company. I am not saying this by way of criticism, but as market trends shift and the historic aversion to man-made products lessens, the reliance on the traditional materials such as wool and cotton will subside even further. Those salesmen made redundant by this move could easily be re-trained and redeployed within the synthetics operation, thus potentially boosting revenue there.

'Nylon and polyester, rayon and other filaments are all considerably cheaper to produce than wool and are less susceptible to natural factors that affect prices. As more and more people get to become familiar with these new products, I believe we should stay ahead of the game. Looking at our most recent financial figures, kindly produced for me by Paul,' — Sonny smiled gratefully in Sugden's direction — 'I can tell you that the artificial fibres and pharmaceutical goods now provide more than eighty per cent of the UK trading operation revenue, while accounting for less than half of the overheads. This is a complete reversal of the situation from only a few years ago and I am convinced that those are the areas where we should be concentrating our energy and resources. That is my recommendation. It is now up to you to either accept or reject it. As the saying goes, the ball is in your court.'

Back in Byland Crescent that evening, as they were finishing dinner, Mark protested that his father hadn't given him prior warning of his intentions.

Sonny had been anticipating this question and had his response ready. 'That wouldn't have been fair to Jessica, Paul, or David. I was watching their faces for their reaction as I spoke and I think they were relieved that you looked as surprised as them. It will be important in future for you to have a strong rapport with your co-directors. Being aware that you were being treated differently, favoured because of our relationship, would have been the worst possible start.'

'I suppose you're right, Dad,' Mark admitted, 'and I can tell you they all came to see me this afternoon, not as a gang but one by one and asked if I'd known about it in advance. It certainly made it much easier to tell them that I'd been as shocked by it as them. One thing that wasn't discussed, though, is the question of who should replace you as MD. Have you any thoughts on the matter?'

'I have, and unless I'm very much mistaken they're the same thoughts as you've already had.'

'Jessica Binks?'

'That's who I'd choose — to begin with at least. Perhaps later on you might see the need to change that, but I'm looking well ahead, and even then it might not be either necessary or advisable.'

'What about you, Dad?' Jenny asked. 'While you were talking, I was wondering how you plan to spend all that extra leisure time you'll suddenly have available to you.'

Sonny gave Rachael a sly sideways glance and grinned at the horrified expression on her face. 'I've talked it through at length with Mark's mum and I believe she has her own ideas on that subject, but I'll leave it to her to share them with you if she feels willing to. For my part I'm keen to spend more time in my workshop polishing up my woodworking skills.'

The chorus of groans at Sonny's dreadful pun effectively ended the debate, much to Rachael's relief.

* * *

In Australia, Sonny's decision to relinquish his position met with unqualified approval. The timing of the arrival of the letter was ideal for Luke to present it at the next board meeting. In addition to his co-directors Josh Jones and Elliot Finnegan, Luke had also requested the presence of Patrick at the meeting.

'In a sense, Sonny is only mimicking what Patrick has done here,' Luke said after reading the letter. 'And I for one wouldn't begrudge him the retirement and the chance to take life a little easier. I think he's earned it over and over again.'

There were no opinions to the contrary and the board signified their unanimous approval immediately.

That evening, Luke also discussed Sonny's decision with Bella. 'Cowgill's opted to follow your dad's example by retiring from the day-to-day running of the English businesses. Although he'll still be chairman, that leaves Mark Cowgill,

Paul Sugden, the guy who saved you from that falling bale of wool, Jessica Binks, and David Lyons, the pharmaceutical expert, in control. I reckon that's a strong board to match ours and so do the others, so we've given it the green light.'

'You're only comfortable with it because of the money they're earning the group,' Bella teased him.

'There is that, certainly,' Luke admitted, 'but it's also to do with the personalities involved. Take Mark Cowgill, for instance. I know I once said that Sonny was a lot like my dad in many ways but I also think Mark and I are a bit alike.'

Bella considered this for a while. 'You're about the same age, that's for sure, and you both had distinguished war records, plus he's making such a success of a completely new venture, that's very much like your partnership with Gianni and Angelina in the vineyard.'

That was true, and the venture that Luke had started with the Italian couple before the war was beginning to pay handsome dividends, both in terms of revenue and the accolades their wines were beginning to earn.

'There's another similarity you haven't mentioned,' Luke told her. 'We both chose fine, strong-minded women as our partners. Jenny Cowgill might not be as outspoken as you, and I suspect that's probably only down to her upbringing, but from what we learned about her when we visited England, I'd say she was just as determined and as passionate a champion of Mark as you are of me, albeit in a quieter way.'

'Quieter? Are you saying that I'm noisy?'

At that point their younger son, Saul Patrick, let out an ear-splitting howl of disapproval. The six-month-old was protesting because his evening meal had been interrupted. 'I reckon so,' Luke grinned, 'and that little bundle seems to have inherited your lungs and vocal cords.'

Later, Bella told Luke that she intended to take up cycling. She made this announcement as they were eating dinner and the surprise caused Luke to stop, his fork in mid-air as he stared at her. He wondered briefly if he had developed a hearing problem. Dismissing that theory, he glanced down at his plate. The dish they were eating was coq au vin, and Luke wondered if all the wine had made its way into the casserole, or if Bella had helped herself to some of it.

'You're going to do what?'

'I've bought a bike and I'm going to use it to get fit. It's all arranged with Dottie. She's bought one as well.'

'Was that your idea or hers?'

'Both, really. I mentioned wanting to get my figure back and Dottie said she'd been thinking on the same lines of keeping fit for Elliot's sake. Not that she has much to worry about on that score by the sound of things. Judging by the way she talked about him I'd say they were still as besotted by one another as they were when they first got together. She said he's as attentive as ever.' Bella grinned as she added, 'I think she was putting it politely. I'm coming to the opinion that there must be something in either the air or water round here that acts as a drug to heighten men's libido.'

Luke grinned. 'If that's true and it is in the water, I'll get the pharmaceutical guy from England to come over and test it. Then we can set up a bottling plant and sell the stuff — we'll make a fortune. I'll follow that by setting up a factory to manufacture contraceptives and that should earn us even more money.'

Their dinner was over, the children sound asleep, and the nanny was in her quarters. As they cleared the dishes and washed up, a chore they had performed together ever since their marriage, Luke said, 'Speaking of masculine virility, do you fancy having an early night?'

'I wasn't setting you a test, Luke. You have nothing to prove in that department.'

His disappointment was evident as he said, 'I take it the answer's no?'

'I didn't say that, did I?'

CHAPTER TWENTY-SIX

It was three months later when a board meeting of Fisher Springs UK, held in the group head office in Manor Row, Bradford, duly ratified Jessica Binks as managing director in succession to Sonny Cowgill.

The outgoing MD congratulated his colleagues, expressing confidence in the wisdom of their decision. 'I think Jessica will do a great job. I am sure she's the right person to lead the group — and she's far better-looking than the other candidates.'

Proof that the post she had accepted was no sinecure and that she was the right choice for the job became evident in the first meeting of 1954. The sparking point was a proposal put forward on behalf of senior staff members of the pharmaceutical division and presented, albeit with great reluctance, by David Lyons.

'Three of our senior executives have compiled a business development plan for consideration by the board. In other circumstances I would have refused to put this forward, but their feelings are so strong that they threatened to resign unless we listen to their proposal.'

'Why would the contents be so controversial?' Mark Cowgill asked.

'Because the main thrust of their argument is the suggestion that in order to maximise the potential of the company, we should consider opening a chemical processing plant.'

Lyons's statement was greeted with stunned silence as the directors wrestled with the enormity of the proposal. Recalling the disaster that had befallen their previous chemical manufacturing plant, and the loss of life that included Jessica's husband among the victims, caused an instant reaction: to turn the idea down flat.

Jessica was the first to comment. 'Why wasn't I informed of this beforehand?' she demanded furiously. 'As head of the division, and group managing director, I ought to have been consulted prior to having this obscene suggestion sprung on us. What were you hoping for, some sort of fait accompli with the kudos going to you?'

'Nothing of the sort,' Lyons responded. 'I'm disappointed that you believe me capable of acting in such an underhand and devious manner. The men only came to see me and presented this proposal an hour and a half ago, and you've been tied up with interviews ever since. I did warn them that you would be unhappy, to put it mildly, but they were extremely insistent.'

The only director not to voice outright opposition to the idea was Paul Sugden, who had not been involved with the business when the tragic accident occurred. He bided his time, waiting until the others had spoken before he put forward his idea, which was little more than a filibuster.

'I can easily understand how upsetting this must be for everyone involved, but I believe we ought not to allow our emotions to rule company policy. Before we reject this report out of hand, which, if what David says is correct, would involve the loss of three experienced and valuable members of staff, I recommend that we ought to take a copy of this report each, study all the ramifications of the proposal and attempt to come to a more rational decision with potential for a solution that is to the benefit of the business.'

There was some further discussion, from which nothing constructive emerged until Jessica made the final, telling comment. 'I agree with Paul, although it grieves me deeply to even contemplate adopting a scheme such as this. However, my feelings, and also your feelings are secondary to the need for the company to progress. There are others who must be consulted, others not in this room or even in this country.' She looked at Mark. 'The people I'm thinking of are your father, and the directors of our Australian partners. Their input will be crucial before we can decide how to proceed — one way, or the other.'

* * *

The week had started quietly for Luke Fisher, but by Tuesday afternoon that all changed with dreadful brutality. He was in the middle of a meeting with Elliot Finnegan, discussing the pros and cons of extending the group's media presence by investing in the newly arrived television product now becoming widely available.

Their conversation was rudely interrupted by Luke's secretary who burst into the office unannounced with the gait of an athlete completing a hundred-yard sprint.

'Mr Finnegan, your wife's been on the phone. She's at your parents' house.' The woman paused, unable to think of a way to deliver the unpalatable message. 'She found your father trying to revive your mother.' She swallowed before adding, 'I'm terribly sorry, they think she's . . .' She didn't need to utter the last word, the horrified expression on both men's faces told her they understood.

'Get off home, Eli.' Luke switched his gaze to the secretary. 'Ask Jones to come here immediately. I'll brief him and then set off. How I'm going to break the news to Bella I've no idea.'

By the time Josh arrived, Elliot had already departed and Luke was waiting by his desk, car keys in hand.

Once Josh had received instructions, he watched Luke leave and then called the secretary in. 'It looks as if we're facing a bit of a management crisis. Mr Fisher's asked me to run the show, so I'm going to need all the help I can get. For the moment, keep this to yourself, I don't want news of Mrs Finnegan's death to get leaked to the media. The family and close friends have to be informed properly rather than reading it in the paper. I think it would be sensible to call a meeting of the department heads and the executive panel, schedule it for early tomorrow morning. I'll be chairing that meeting and I'll warn everyone concerned that if word gets out before we're ready to release the obituary, heads will roll. One other thing, will you cable the UK office, Mrs Finnegan knew some of the Cowgill family personally.'

'OK, Mr Jones, anything else?'

Josh gave a half-smile, half grimace before replying. 'When you get a spare few minutes you might say a quick prayer for me.'

* * *

Jessica was still smarting over what she regarded as David's duplicity in the way he had handled, or in her perception mishandled, the report from the scientific officers. When she arrived home that evening, she was surprised to find the front door to the house locked. David usually left the office before she did, a stratagem to avoid their cohabitation being discovered by their colleagues. Having gained entry, she called out David's name but received no reply. She went into the kitchen, only to find the ingredients he'd put out ready for preparing their evening meal still untouched. She went into every room in the house but could find no sign of him, no indication that he'd been home.

Baffled by his absence and with her anger now tinged with mild concern, Jessica paced up and down the sitting room trying to figure out where he might have vanished to. When she eventually heard the front door being opened, she hurried into the hallway to confront him. 'Where have you been? I was worried about you,' she demanded, her voice sharp with annoyance.

233

David stared at her for a moment before replying. 'I went for a pint,' he replied, his tone as curt as hers.

'You didn't think to inform me beforehand? That would have been the right thing to do.'

'I left a message with the girl on reception. Didn't you get it?'

'She left before I did. I was on the phone to Sonny so I didn't get to speak to her. There was a cable from Australia. Patrick Finnegan's wife Louise has died. Perhaps if you hadn't been out boozing with your cronies and paid more attention to work you would have known that.'

David's response was heavily sarcastic. 'My word, how quickly your opinions of people change. Only last week you described my work as invaluable. Now, suddenly I've turned into a bone-idle alcoholic. You've been so busy venting your spleen that you didn't stop to wonder if there might have been a valid reason for me changing my routine out of the blue to go boozing, as you so elegantly described it.'

Jessica demonstrated that she wasn't about to be out-done in sarcasm. 'Well, if by any remote chance there is a valid reason for your behaviour, I'd be fascinated to hear it.'

David wasn't finished yet, not by a long chalk. 'I'm not really certain why I'm bothering to tell you this because you've already given sufficient signs that I'll be wasting my breath, but as I've nothing better to do at the moment I might as well explain why I've suddenly lapsed into alcoholism. When I left the board meeting, I was concerned at the way the proposal those men sent in had upset you. So I took them for a drink with a view to trying to persuade them either to retract the plan or modify it. I tried to explain that what they were proposing was highly contentious, that it had proved extremely distressing and to ask them if they would reconsider because their plan was deeply upsetting.'

'I'm a big girl, I don't need protecting,' she told him sharply, but modified her tone slightly as she added, 'but thanks for trying.'

'You do need protecting in this instance, mostly from yourself. Because you're doing exactly what Paul Sugden warned us against, letting our emotions cloud our business sense and marring our better judgement.'

Jessica sighed, as if wearied by the argument. 'Let's just leave it for now, shall we. I'm going to take a bath.'

David nodded. 'And I'm going into the kitchen to start fixing dinner.'

There was little conversation during their evening meal and the silence continued as they listened to the radio before retiring to bed. Instead of their usual custom of sitting together on the sofa they each chose an armchair, their mind occupied more with their own thoughts than the entertainment provided by the BBC.

A further sign of the constraint between them came at bedtime when David, instead of following Jessica into her bedroom turned and headed for the smaller chamber he'd occupied before they became lovers. It was a simple gesture, but it brought Jessica to her senses and made her realize just how much her petty anger had upset him.

She put her hand on his arm to detain him and said, 'Please, David, don't go there. Don't leave me alone. Whatever happened at work should stay at work. I need you beside me tonight. I need you to comfort me and hold me.'

David knew instinctively that this was the closest to an apology he was going to get. He had either to accept it or their relationship was doomed, and that he wasn't prepared to risk. He took Jessica's hand, smiled slightly, and followed her into the bedroom they shared. They undressed in silence and it was only when Jessica was lying alongside him that she began to cry. David put his arm around her, pulling her into a close embrace as he waited, providing the comfort he knew she needed far more than the passion they had shared on previous occasions. Gradually her weeping lessened, her breathing eased and she fell asleep.

Next morning, although nothing was said, and to an observer it would have seemed as if nothing untoward had happened between them, they both recognized that in some indefinable way their relationship had changed. Knowing that the tacit commitment he had made by giving Jessica the comfort she needed, David was content to let the subject of their disagreement remain untouched and it was Jessica who raised the topic.

'You didn't tell me the outcome,' she said, a trifle hesitantly.

David had been concentrating on the items he would need for the recipe he was planning for their evening meal and asked, 'What outcome?'

'When you went for a drink with those men: did you have any success?'

'Not really, although they did stress that their intention was, and always had been, to create a totally clean, sterile, safe, and controlled environment. The safety element was their overriding concern, which was why they suggested that a new, purpose-built plant with secure storage areas, and rigidly supervised production zones separated into a cellular construction was what they were aiming for.'

'I suppose that's something that might be worth considering,' Jessica said slowly and, David thought, more than a trifle reluctantly. 'I think I'm going to postpone the meeting I had for this morning and spend a few hours reading that report in depth and once I've done that I think you and I should get our heads together and pool our ideas.'

'How do you think the news from Australia will affect things?'

Jessica shrugged. 'I'm not certain it will make much difference in a business sense, although it's extremely sad for the family. Patrick Finnegan had all but retired and had even relinquished his directorship of the group companies.'

CHAPTER TWENTY-SEVEN

In Byland Crescent the news relayed by Jessica Binks that
Louise Finnegan had passed away was greeted with shock
and a deep sense of sadness. With the exception of Mark
and Jenny's children everyone in the household remembered
Louise from the time, thirty years earlier, when she and
Patrick had visited England along with their infant daughter
Isabella. They had come to Yorkshire for Patrick to liaise
with the newly formed English wing of the Fisher Springs
Group. During that visit he had stayed in Byland Crescent
and the occasion had left the residents with a series of mental
images that portrayed Louise as a happy, contented young
wife and mother, glowing with health and happiness. Those
pictures contrasted with stark brutality to the grim tidings
of her death.

'Mrs Finnegan can't have been that old, can she, Dad?'
Jenny asked.

Sonny pondered the question for a couple of seconds
before replying. 'I think from memory she was about the
same age as me, perhaps a year or two younger, but I can't
be certain. She wasn't ancient, that's for sure. However, I
do know that she had been far from well for some while
now. I wasn't told the nature of the problem, but I got the

impression it was serious, something to do with the poisoning. It can't have been easy for them all.'

He saw Jenny's puzzled frown and explained, 'She was one of the victims of the poison that escaped when the group's mineral extraction division caused pollution to spread into the rivers. Although she was one of the luckier ones who survived, she almost didn't make it. The incident must have left its mark, perhaps weakened her resistance, we may never know. Whatever the cause, this is shocking news for her family and for Luke Fisher's, because they are intermarried twice. Worst of all, I dread to think what this might do to Patrick.'

Speculation on the effect that losing his wife might have on Patrick Finnegan strengthened Sonny's resolve to carry out the scheme he had been mulling over for some time. Now that Jessica had assumed control over the business empire, he was free to carry out his plan. The day after the news arrived from Australia Sonny left the house as soon as breakfast was over and headed towards town, his stride quick and purposeful.

Twenty minutes later he was seated in the offices of a travel agency that had recently opened. When he revealed his proposed itinerary and asked them to begin the task of researching options for his twin destinations, the travel agent hid a smile of delight and relief. Opening a business such as this had been a long-held ambition, but the risks involved were many and varied. If this deal went through the commission earned from the agency's new client would meet their overhead expenses for at least three months, perhaps longer.

Before Sonny could put forward his ideas to Rachael, however, his nascent scheme got put on the back burner, being overtaken by events that threatened the alliance between the Australian and British sections of the Fisher Springs Group. In common with many such disputes, the wrangle over the future began with a series of small, seemingly unconnected occurrences.

* * *

As the next board meeting approached, the English directors viewed the inevitable main topic with some unease. Caught between the rock of Jessica's seemingly inflexible opposition, and the hard place of the pharmaceutical division's executives' threat to resign, the directors gathered in the Manor Row boardroom with no clear idea as to how to resolve the issue. As it transpired, only two of them had constructive suggestions to put forward and, in opening the meeting, the group chairman Sonny Cowgill invited one of those two to express her opinion. At least one of Jessica's colleagues winced at the thought of how she might express those views. Forthright was about the most euphemistic way they could think of describing her expression of her opinion.

Sonny was obviously mindful of that possibility in the way he phrased his request. 'Jessica, would you care to give us your views on this report? Without swearing please,' he added with a slight smile.

Jessica took up the challenge. She held her head erect, the posture a possible attempt to hide her tears as she dwelt first on the accident that had killed her husband. However, when she moved on, her reaction to Sonny's request surprised all but one of those seated behind the elongated oval table. But David Lyons had been the recipient of Jessica's thoughts throughout the previous four weeks.

'I believe it would be imprudent of us not to give this report our serious consideration. I appreciate that even if we do decide to undertake the planned development there will be many pitfalls, but I don't believe we should allow thought of those to deter us or cause us to prejudge the issue.'

Mark Cowgill expressed his surprise at Jessica's positive attitude and asked what led her to that point of view.

Jessica nodded, as if anticipating such a question, and replied instantly. 'If the group is to maintain its recent progress and retain its position as market leader, we have to entertain new ideas, explore new products and ways of making the future of the businesses we control secure and profitable. These proposals include the option to construct a brand new, purpose-built manufacturing module that will enable our pharmaceutical division to both complement their existing products in alternative formats, but also allow their sales representatives the luxury of a vastly extended range of goods to offer their clients.'

Jessica glanced down at the open file on the table in front of her before continuing, 'Although no specific mention is made in the proposal of a storage and warehousing facility, should we agree to proceed with the scheme such a building would be necessary. My stipulation concerning this building is, that like the manufacturing centre, the storage depot should be a new construction, and that it should be a safe distance from the production area, and finally, wherever possible it should be robotic.'

Sonny asked for an explanation of Jessica's last remark.

'I mean that, where practical, the process of moving and storing chemicals, or loading the finished article onto vans or trucks, should be completed with as few personnel as possible. I have two reasons for thinking this way. The first is the obvious safety concern in view of past events, but also the use of loading and stacking devices makes the operation smoother and quicker, and therefore less costly. With the cost element in mind there is one advantage of machines over men. Once you have recouped the original outlay, the machines do not demand a salary every Friday.'

'Have you considered the potential problems should we go ahead with this scheme?' Sonny asked.

'I have, and I've made a list of all the snags I could think up.' Jessica rummaged in her file and produced a sheaf of papers, one of which she passed to each of her colleagues. 'I'm aware that the list might be far from complete so if we decide to investigate this proposal in more depth, I'd be grateful for any other thoughts on the implicit dangers that might arise. That way we might be able to eliminate them beforehand. Finally, I'd just like to say that although I was dead set against this project in the first instance, that is no longer the case. I now believe we should go ahead and implement this addition to the company, because I can think of no finer memorial to my husband and his life's work than the successful completion of this ground-breaking plan.'

Once the directors got over their surprise at Jessica's positive endorsement of the proposed venture they discussed the project at great length, during which many of the problems that might occur were brought up and counter measures to negate them suggested.

One potential snag that they thought might prove pivotal was the question of obtaining insurance cover for the new buildings both during and after construction, which, as Sonny told his colleagues might prove prohibitive in one of two ways. 'Given our poor track record, as they would undoubtedly see it, I think they might either set the premiums at a level that would prove prohibitive or decline to cover the project entirely.'

It was decided to leave further discussion on the topic until the following meeting, and in the meantime Paul Sugden was charged with investigating the potential availability and cost of insurance cover and premiums.

After the meeting ended, Sonny asked Jessica to remain seated. Once the others had left the room he told her, 'That was a very courageous thing you did today. I didn't have any doubt regarding your capability for the role of managing director, but if I had entertained any reservations they would have been blown away by your approach to such a contentious issue as the one we've been discussing. The way you set aside your personal issues for the benefit of the business clearly demonstrates that you are the correct choice to lead the group into the future.'

* * *

When the board reconvened a month later it was with little expectation of good news from Paul Sugden's report on his quest to find an insurer willing to underwrite the proposed new chemical plant.

His opening words tended to confirm their worst fears, but by the end of his report they realized that they had seriously underestimated the modest young man who had assumed the mantle worn so well by Simon Jones. The person who seemed well set to become a worthy successor to their much-missed former finance director. The report also demonstrated Sugden's capacity for original thinking and his ability to shock them by providing an innovative solution to their problem.

'I enlisted the assistance of the insurance broker we have used for many years, although I think perhaps assistance is the wrong word. The chap I spoke to more or less implied that we were mad to entertain such an idea. Especially after what happened to the previous plant, and that no reputable insurer would even consider underwriting the project. He proved his point by failing to get a single quotation for us and is no doubt congratulating himself that he's talked us out of what he considers to be a waste of money. Given his less than helpful attitude I would recommend that we should consider moving our whole portfolio to another broker.'

'How practical is that? Would it prove more expensive than it's worth?' Sonny asked. The final part of his question was a test, but if Paul spotted it, the challenge failed to daunt him.

'There is plenty of choice available. Insurance brokers are fairly thick on the ground these days. Obviously we wouldn't move if the cover was less than satisfactory, or the premiums were too costly, but I think we should at least give the competitors chance to quote. As for it being a costly exercise, if they want the business they should be prepared to work for it. In any case, if the other part of my report becomes a practical proposition, the question would be purely hypothetical.'

'I think you're going to have to explain in some detail, Paul,' Jessica said. 'That last comment had me confused for one.'

Glancing round the table, Paul saw that his other colleagues looked equally baffled. 'Having failed to get a satisfactory response from the broker, I made direct contact with some of the better-known insurance companies, and in certain circumstances the broker was proved correct. Several of them refused to consider a quote for the business and one of them even hung up on me. Of those who did quote' — Paul grinned — 'one of them mentioned a figure that was so exorbitant that I put the phone down on him. During my conversation with another well-known company their executive quoted a figure so huge that I told him I wanted insurance cover, not to buy their business.'

Paul waited for the chuckles to die down before explaining, 'The reason I'm telling you this isn't to repeat the joke, but as I was saying those words, I had an idea that I'd like to run past you.'

The directors listened to Sugden's idea, which was on the revolutionary side of ground-breaking. There was a long silence after he finished speaking before Sonny responded, his voice reflecting the incredulity shared by the rest of the board. 'Let me get this straight, you're proposing that we should set up our own in-house insurance company, is that correct?'

'My thoughts were that we either set up one from scratch or look at taking over an existing business. I'm not suggesting we put a bid in for one of the industry giants — that might be well beyond our means. But there are plenty of smaller, well-run companies that we might be able to pick up at a reasonable cost. As things stand, the group is cash-rich, thanks to the progress made by our two principal divisions. Even if we don't adopt this scheme, I would be advising looking into other acquisitions to broaden our sphere of operations. That is the policy our Australian partners have adopted with great success and I see no reason why it can't work here.'

He paused to allow the full ramifications of his suggestion to sink in. When there was no adverse reaction he continued, 'Having given this a lot of thought I actually believe the latter to be our best option. If we buy a company with an existing portfolio it will provide us with a good source of revenue, which is why it would be crucial to pick the right outfit. In doing so, we would have to consider not only the capital cost, but also the need to set aside a reserve to cover underwriting, especially in the event of an unforeseen calamity.'

'Can you explain that in a little more detail?' Jessica asked.

'We would need to ensure that there were sufficient reserves to cope with a batch of claims from unexpected sources such as the effects of extreme weather, and that the client list was a suitable one. Part of that amount could already be in place, but we might deem it advisable to top up that figure. I'd be looking for a company specializing in corporate insurance. If we then got the sales staff involved, offering our clients the insurance services, we could counterbalance the cost of our own project.' He grinned slightly as he added, 'We might even attract our competitors to insure with us, and that would be very satisfying, as they'd be footing the bill for our own cover.'

There was some discussion, little of it being negative, and eventually the board gave Sugden more time to investigate the potential and come up with some estimate of what his scheme would cost.

Later, as Mark was discussing the meeting with his father, Sonny told him that Paul's suggestion was satisfying for its own sake, even if the scheme didn't come to fruition. 'It's yet more evidence of the outstanding ability in our boardroom. Jessica is proving to be a more than capable leader, David came up trumps with the pharmaceutical division, and you've made a success of the artificial fibres operation. And now Paul has shown great flair and a capacity for innovative thinking. All in all that is reason for great confidence as to the group's future. Not bad when we were close to being shut down only a few years back.'

* * *

It was early evening when Paul Sugden arrived home. Home for Paul was still the small terraced house in Saltaire which he now shared with his wife Sally.

Sally had qualified as a certified accountant working for a practice in Shipley and, as usual, she had arrived home before him. Although she enjoyed her work, she took greater pride in everything Paul had achieved. If his career hadn't been exactly a rags-to-riches story, in her mind it was pretty close to it. As they were eating their evening meal she questioned him about the board meeting, being especially keen to discover what the directors thought of his proposal for the group to form their own in-house insurance provider.

'They didn't turn it down flat,' Paul told her. 'Now that the new chemical plant project has been accepted in principle, they've asked me to investigate the practicality of forming our own company, starting from scratch in effect, or buying an established company with an existing clientele base.'

They finished the meal, having discussed the pros and cons of the alternatives when Sally changed the subject. 'Paul, I've been thinking we ought to consider moving into a slightly bigger house. Somewhere reasonably nearby though, so we can still be close to Mum and Dad.'

'Why would we do that? Aren't you happy here? Does it make you uncomfortable being right next door to them?'

'Of course, I'm happy here, but this house is a bit on the small size, don't you agree?'

'We've got a separate lounge and dining kitchen plus a spare bedroom, surely that's enough for our needs?'

'It might not be if we were to have twins. If one's a boy and the other's a girl they'd need their own room eventually so we might as well anticipate that happening.'

'The likelihood of us having twins is very . . .' Paul's voice trailed off as he noticed Sally's expression which was on the smug side of complacent. 'Does that mean you're . . . ?'

'Yes, Paul darling, it means that we're going to have at least one baby. Who knows, it might be twins, or even triplets — but certainly one.'

When Paul arrived at work the following morning, he was impatient to let his colleagues know the exciting news and, in the process, mentioned Sally's idea of a house move. 'We'll need something with more room but still be close to Saltaire and Sally's folks.'

Mark Cowgill congratulated him and after David and Jessica had added their good wishes asked, 'Is Baildon near enough for you? I might know of a possible candidate.'

'Baildon would be close to ideal. What have you in mind?'

'My late aunt and uncle used to live on Cecil Avenue, off West Lane at the top of the village. My cousin Marguerite inherited it, and she and her husband live there when he's not working abroad. He's a diplomat or something. Anyway, I heard Mum and Dad talking the other day and I'm sure Dad said something about Marguerite moving down south to be near her husband's family. If that's right, the house in Baildon might be up for sale.'

CHAPTER TWENTY-EIGHT

In Byland Crescent, Jenny and Rachael now ran the household. Jenny's mother Joyce had died in her sleep less than six months earlier, and although Jenny grieved for her, she was supported and comforted in her loss by the warmth of those around her. Once the family had recovered from the shock of this sudden unhappy event it was felt that for the moment there was no need to look elsewhere to fill the gap in the ranks of those who took care of the home.

One cause of concern that troubled Jenny in particular was the health of their ageing and long-serving butler, George Mills. Now of a venerable age which he coyly refused to divulge, George was beginning to behave oddly, at least in Jenny's opinion. He had become both secretive and forgetful, worrying signs of potential lessening of his mental faculties that might be allied to his advancing years.

Other signs were less noticeable, being misinterpreted initially as carelessness on the part of others within the house. On a few occasions during the preceding months, Jenny, Rachael, and to a lesser extent Sonny and Mark, had been puzzled by the disappearance of odd items, some of them of no discernible value, only for them to reappear when questions were asked. The root of the problem only began to emerge purely by chance, first as nothing more than a vague suspicion, one morning when Rachael happened to be crossing the hallway when the post dropped through the letterbox. Forestalling George, who had adopted the habit of hovering in the vicinity to collect the mail, Rachael glanced through the small bundle of envelopes. Apart from routine items such as household bills there was a letter from her daughter Frances.

As Rachael began reading, she was puzzled by Frances's complaint that her two previous letters had gone unanswered. Rachael was a meticulous correspondent and would certainly not have ignored nor failed to reply to a letter from her daughter. However, she knew for a fact that she had not received any communication from Frances for several months, and in fact had commented on this to Sonny only the previous morning over breakfast.

Rachael discussed Frances's implicit criticism later that morning as she and Jenny were taking morning coffee, a ritual Jenny had introduced. She and Mark had become habitual caffeine addicts while in Spain during the Spanish Civil War. It had taken Jenny some time to wean George away from his instinctive distrust of the alien substance and even longer for him to master the art of preparing it to drinkable standards. Now that he had become successful, Jenny was able to relax in the knowledge that the product would be fit for human consumption. As the butler delivered the tray of coffee and biscuits, and enquired if Mr Sonny would be joining them, Rachael was well into her recital of the strange comment in Frances's letter. She broke off to answer the butler's question. 'I don't think so, George. He's ensconced in his workshop, striving to become a latter-day Chippendale, Hepplewhite, or Sheraton.'

As the butler left the room, Jenny noticed that he had failed to close the door, merely leaving it slightly ajar. It was a pleasant, warm morning so as this didn't seem important, she made no comment, either then or when Rachael had finished her tale.

Jenny pondered the possible causes for the letters going astray. 'Perhaps it's an error in a Texan sorting office,' she suggested with a faint smile.

'How do you mean?'

'Maybe the sorter got confused and misdirected the letters to another town called Scarborough. For all we know it could have finished up in Canada or Australia. I do know there's a Scarborough in Ontario and another in Southern Australia somewhere. I remember at school our Geography teacher explaining that they were probably named by colonists who had emigrated from this area. That led onto him describing how convicted felons were shipped to America until they gained independence and later they were transported to Australia. It was without doubt the most interesting lesson he ever conducted.'

Reverting to their coffee table conversation, the only other topic concerned Jenny's oldest child, Andrew Michael Cowgill. It was a casual statement from Rachael about the deficiencies of one of her teachers that led Jenny to remark, 'I don't think much has changed. It comes to something when a schoolmaster is forced to admit that one of his pupils knows almost more about a given subject than his teacher does.'

'When did that happen?'

'The last time we went to school to discuss his progress and exam results. The linguistics teacher admitted that Andrew's command of the Romance languages was greater than his. I think that might be partly down to us giving him extra tuition in Spanish following our time there. When we wanted to be private with him, we resorted to Spanish, which blocked other people from our conversation.'

'Andrew obviously did well in his exams, so why didn't you tell everyone?'

'He begged us not to because he said it would embarrass him too much. We wanted to, but I guess that's down to parental pride. The comment that made us really happy was when the teacher revealed that Andrew had achieved one hundred per cent in his Spanish and Italian oral exams, which had never happened to earlier pupils. It was so unusual that his master said the only way Andrew could improve would be by visiting Spain and Italy, where he could extend his vocabulary and perhaps hone his pronunciation skills even further.'

'That's all well and good,' Rachael replied, trying unsuccessfully to disguise her pride in her grandson's achievements, 'but has he given any thought to what he wants to do in life? Will he utilize his language skills, do you think?'

'I very much doubt it, and that would be a waste of his talent. At the moment all he seems interested in is either electrical or mechanical devices. He's forever dismantling and reassembling things. Where he got that ability from I've no idea because I don't know any other family members who have those skills.'

'Perhaps you have to look further back than the current generations,' Rachael replied. 'It could be that it's a genetic inheritance via my side of the family. My father was a talented engineer. He ran a highly successful business in Sheffield. Admittedly the machines on the market today are vastly different to those at the turn of the century, but I feel sure many of the principles are similar.'

From there, they discussed the merits and shortcomings of teachers in general, but long afterwards, Jenny pondered the mystery of the missing letters from Frances. It was only then that she recalled their butler's expression as he'd delivered their tray of coffee and biscuits. She was puzzled, as it appeared to be one of guilt and mild alarm combined, which she was intrigued by, but failed to understand the cause.

After some deliberation Jenny wondered if there was any possibility that this might in some way be linked to earlier instances of items going missing. Although there was insufficient evidence for her to make her suspicions public, Jenny resolved to conduct a discreet surveillance operation.

* * *

During her observation, Jenny had seen a number of actions that gave cause for concern, and with a great degree of reluctance she presented her findings to her mother-in-law. 'What do you make of it all?' Jenny asked. 'It's not exactly normal behaviour, is it? Do you think George is going funny because I can't think of a logical explanation? If that's the case, what should we do about it?'

Rachael's background in the nursing profession enabled her to provide valuable insight into the butler's strange behaviour. 'It sounds to me very much as if what you've seen means that George is suffering from a form of senile dementia. That can be a very distressing condition, not only for the sufferer but for those close to him or her. Contending with it means being on the alert for any number of potentially dangerous situations that their confusion can lay them liable to. As to how we tackle this will require careful thought and absolute discretion. Before we do anything at all we should speak to Sonny and Mark to make them aware of what we suspect is going on.'

Although Jenny had observed George eavesdropping on the family as part of his strange behaviour, they were quite safe while holding this conversation openly. As they talked, they were strolling past the lake towards the glen in Peasholm Park.

PART FOUR: 1956–1959

"Indeed let us be frank about it—
most of our people have never had it so good.
Go around the country, go to the industrial towns, go to the farms
and you will see a state of prosperity such as we have never had in my
lifetime—
nor indeed in the history of this country."

Harold MacMillan, British Prime Minister, 20 July 1957

CHAPTER TWENTY-NINE

It was nearly three months after Louise Finnegan's funeral that Luke Fisher eventually returned to work. Although neither he nor his colleagues could have guessed it, the return was destined to be short-lived.

As he prepared to get to grips with work and steeled himself to answer the plethora of well-meant but probing questions about Patrick and the other members of Louise's family he was certain he would have to answer, Luke's first meeting was with Josh Jones.

When Jones entered his office, Luke noticed he appeared to be slightly anxious. Was that because he was concerned about how Luke would view his handling of affairs, he wondered. He thought it better to set that part of the record straight immediately.

'First off, I want to thank you, Josh. Although I phoned for regular updates it isn't the same as being here and it's only now I've returned that I can see what a terrific job you've done and the immense amount of work you've got through. Above all, stepping up to the plate as you've done has been a real Godsend. It's important for you to know how much I appreciate it, and that I can rely on you if things go pear-shaped again, heaven forbid.'

'I'm glad you think so, but it isn't just down to me. I had a lot of help —everyone was keen to pitch in and take a share of the load. The senior executive committee members were invaluable. And what your secretary doesn't know isn't worth knowing. Plus, the systems and controls you've put in place with the information distribution channels make things dead easy to follow.'

Jones continued, changing the subject by asking how things were with Patrick and the family. Luke noticed that Jones still appeared a trifle anxious. Having dealt with one possible cause, Luke wondered what the reason for the worried look was, and whether to ask outright.

For the meantime, however, he replied to Jones's query, 'Patrick's gone to pieces. He sits there for hour after hour on the veranda where he and Louise spent so much time. He's like a waxwork figure, simply staring ahead, never moving, or responding if anyone says or does anything near him. Then, after a while he starts to cry. That's the really heartbreaking part. Tears roll down his face then fall onto the shirt he's wearing. You can almost tell by the size of the wet patch how long he's been crying. Most days he's out there, whatever the weather, until darkness.

'The only person who seems able to get through to him is Dottie. Because we're all so worried about Patrick, we've come up with a sort of plan that we hope will work. It's a short-term thing to begin with but if it meets with any success it'll probably become full-time. The idea is for Elliot and Dottie plus their kids to move back to the Finnegan house. When they're on site they can make certain Patrick gets properly looked after. That's one of the reasons I've told Elliot to take another month off. He'll be there to help Dottie and to mind the children mostly, because Patrick will become Dottie's responsibility. The other thought is that having the kids running around making lots of noise might lift him from this deep depression.'

'How about at your place? How's Bella coping with this?'

'About as well as can be expected, I reckon. You've been in that position, Josh, not once but twice, so I don't have to tell you how tough things can get. Luckily, Bella doesn't have much time to sit around moping, not with our three little monsters to contend with. Not that Bella's the moping type — she's far more of the swearing type.'

Luke was determined to discover the cause of Josh's apparent disquiet and as no reason had been forthcoming, decided to force the issue. 'OK, Josh, what's so bad in that paperwork you're clutching that it's giving you the heebie-jeebies?'

'It's a report from England. It came in on Friday of last week. I'm glad you're back at work because part of it has got me completely stumped. They've dreamed up a scheme that's either total madness or pure genius and for the life of me I can't work out which. I can't decide what to do about it.' Jones smiled briefly and added, 'so I thought I'd dump the responsibility on you.'

Luke shrugged. 'That's why I'm sitting in this chair, I guess. Harry Truman, the US president, had a sign made for his desk in the Oval Office that read, "The buck stops here", so why not bung that bulky folder over and let's see what the problem is. Why is it so big, by the way?'

'The directors thought it advisable to put a load of back-up statistics into the section which covers their plan, plus a report from three of their top chemists.' Jones handed the dossier to Luke. 'Shall I ask your secretary to brew a cup of tea while you're reading? It could take a while to go through that lot.'

'No thanks, I'm fine, but you go ahead and have one if you want.'

Jones watched Luke reading the contents of the thick wad of paperwork Sonny and his colleagues had compiled. Although he read it in silence, Josh knew immediately he'd reached the controversial section by the changing expression on his face. It moved from a dispassionate one as he absorbed the quarter's trading results, which Josh knew were excellent, to incredulity and finally, as he absorbed the full meaning of the proposal, to one that was dark with anger.

After a while he looked up and gave his reaction, which he delivered in what was almost a snarl. 'I'd say your first guess was nearest the mark. This is total madness. What the hell are they thinking of, even giving it the time and trouble to write this garbage?'

Luke didn't bother with the remaining section of the report but returned it unread to Jones, almost tossing it contemptuously across the desk in his fury. 'Tell them there's no way we're going to countenance that crazy scheme. Don't waste time on a letter. Cable them right now.'

* * *

Back in England, the directors gathered for an unscheduled meeting to discuss their Australian counterpart's outright rejection of the expansion scheme. The plan, with its two-pronged approach to the knotty problem of their troubled history involving a chemical plant, had taken much thought and effort and the tone of the dismissal left them annoyed and dismayed.

The directors felt that they had been placed in an invidious position between two equally intractable forces. On the one hand, their leading scientific executives were on the point of resigning if their ideas weren't adopted, and on the other, the fifty per cent shareholder held diametrically opposite views.

Towards the end of the meeting, with no solution available, Jessica asked her colleagues if she could have a word with Sonny in private. When the directors had left the room, she turned to the group chairman and asked, 'How much spare cash do you have available?'

Sonny blinked with surprise, but he told her, 'I've enough to buy a round in the Pig and Whistle on Friday night, why do you ask?'

'I had an idea that might work, if you and I pool our resources. Besides what we've already invested, I've got a large

257

amount sitting in various bank deposit accounts and building societies and I thought if we combine forces we might have sufficient to buy Luke Fisher out. It would mean having to put the development plan on hold or at least slowing it down but we'll be able to go ahead free from interference.'

It took six weeks, several discussions, and financial enquiries made regarding the situation before they came to a decision. Eventually they cabled their Australian counterparts with an offer to purchase their fifty percent holding in the United Kingdom operation. The tone of the cable was as curt as the one they'd received declining to participate in the development plan.

It was late afternoon, shortly before the offices were due to close for the day. Luke Fisher was reading through a letter he'd dictated to his secretary prior to signing it. He picked up his pen and was about to start writing when Josh entered his office.

'I think you'd better read this, because it seems as if you've stirred up a hornet's nest back in England.' He thrust the cable into Luke's hand. 'It sounds as if you've provoked Sonny and the rest of the board to the extent that they're proposing drastic action, and I for one don't blame them.'

Luke's eyes widened with surprise as he read the contents of the telegram. After a few moments he looked across at Jones, his eyes burning with anger. 'You just said you could understand why they've done this and that you don't blame them. Would you care to explain that remark, because it sounds to me like disloyalty?'

'It isn't disloyal to criticise someone you're fairly certain has made a big mistake and seems ready to commit an even bigger error, or to point out the hypocrisy of their stance on a particular subject.' Josh stared back at Luke, his eyes unwavering even in the face of Fisher's obvious hostility.

'Why do you believe I've made such a big mistake? I thought I was making a judgement based on the appalling track record of our English colleagues with regard to the previous chemical works they operated.'

'That's only half the story, as you would have discovered if you'd taken the trouble to read the report through to its conclusion. Making your mind up without the facts is irresponsible in my book. Let me ask you this, was it the fact that they're considering investing in a new chemical facility that worried you, or the cost and type of insurance cover they'd be able to get?'

'It was both, but the insurance element was what worried me most. Even if they did find a company willing to underwrite the venture, I reckon the cost would be astronomical. The exclusion clauses plus the excess they'd write into the policy would make it impractical.'

'So by not reading through to the end of the report you weren't aware that they'd not only anticipated the problem, but that they'd made provision for dealing with such an eventuality. After thinking it through, I consider it to be a ground-breaking piece of imaginative thinking.'

'What sort of provision?'

'They've identified a small insurance company that's well grounded, fits their needs, and has a good existing portfolio. The company they've picked has a lot of experience handling similar ventures and our English board intend to make a takeover bid for it. Their disappointment in your refusal to back them has caused them to re-evaluate the relationship and want to terminate the connection. That's understandable and I have to confess I share their disappointment.'

'That's enough, Jones. You'd better leave now, before one of us says something we'll both regret.'

'Very well, but what do you want me to do about that?' Josh gestured to the cable.

'Leave it, I'll decide what my answer will be and let you know tomorrow.'

That evening he told Bella about the conversation and the reasons for his disagreement with Jones plus the English board's offer to buy the shares back. When he'd finished, he asked for her opinion.

'I think you over-reacted, big time.' Her comment made him wince as did her follow-up remark. 'You did something rash without checking the full facts, which is most unlike you, so don't blame Jones for that — or Sonny Cowgill for that matter.'

'There's something else,' Luke admitted. 'Jones had the nerve to call me a hypocrite because of my reaction to the proposal. I've no idea why. Can you think of a reason?'

'I certainly can, and it's a measure of your crook thinking that you missed the obvious. I wouldn't call it nerve on Jones's part, I'd say it took real balls to face you with it and to point to your error.'

Luke shook his head. 'I'm obviously dense because I don't see it, so you'd better explain.'

'You didn't shut down the mines permanently because of the pollution incident, did you?'

'No, I made damned sure nothing like that could ever happen again. And I kept them running so that they could contribute some profit to offset the huge amount of compensation we'd had to shell out. Are you saying I made a mistake?'

'No, quite the opposite.' Bella stared at him. 'You just don't see it, do you?'

Luke looked even more confused.

'What's the difference between what you did and what they're proposing to do? The only one I can see is that they've been smart enough to cover themselves in case anything does go wrong. Refusing their plan to do almost exactly what you did is where the hypocrisy lies, Luke.'

He stared at her for several moments before he spoke, his tone reflecting none of the anger he'd used previously. 'You know, Bella, I'm damned glad you threw yourself at me. I don't know what I'd do without you to guide me.'

'You'd muddle through — just not half as well.'

Later, as they were preparing to go to bed, Luke said, 'Bella, I've had a great idea.'

She groaned in mock despair as she replied. 'In that case I won't bother putting my nightie on yet.'

Luke chuckled. 'Actually, that wasn't the idea, but I'm happy to accept the offer.'

A good while later as they were snuggled together, Bella asked, 'What was it?'

'What was what?'

'The great idea you were about to tell me about before something else came up?'

Luke explained, and sleep was deferred for a while as they talked it through. Finally, he amplified his earlier comment, 'Bella, you're my inspiration.'

The next morning, he was in the group's offices before any of the staff arrived. He went into Jones's office, abstracted the file containing the UK branch report, and went to his desk to study it. After he'd finished, he paused for a moment, trying to picture the expression on Jones's face when he told him the new plan.

When Luke's secretary arrived, she was surprised to see the connecting door open and her boss already seated at his desk. He called her in and asked her to get Jones to come through the moment he got to work.

He saw the apprehensive expression on Jones's face and hurriedly reassured him. 'You were dead right, Josh, and I apologize for my bad-tempered stupidity. I'm also aware that if it hadn't been for your steadfast refusal to accept my misguided thinking, I could have made a monumental error that might have cost us a huge amount in lost revenue. Here's what I want you to do. In the first instance I want you to cable the English board and tell them those shares are not for sale and that after further consideration we're now behind their scheme one hundred per cent. Furthermore, we're prepared to make new money available to back up our commitment, both for the chemical plant and the insurance company buyout. When you've sent that cable, I want you to contact the head of the banking division here and tell him what's required by way of an interest-free loan to the UK operation, and finally,' Luke paused, 'using the UK template, I want you to go out and buy me an insurance company.'

Luke smiled ruefully at Josh's open-mouthed astonishment. 'The idea Sonny and the guys in England came up with is little short of genius. This group has spent thousand upon thousand, year after year, on insurance premiums. I can't believe I was too dense to see this before, but why should we continue handing profit to an outsider when we can operate our own company and reap the benefits of our investment? We'd not only keep our premium payments within the group, but with proper management we'll be able to attract other firms and individuals and thereby gain valuable extra revenue.'

Before he left Luke's office, Josh asked, 'Did you notice whose idea the insurance company scheme was?'

'No, I assumed it was either Sonny or Jessica who thought it up.'

Josh shook his head. 'It was neither of them. The plan was all down to Paul Sugden's innovative thinking. So, if Paul hadn't been there the day that bale of wool fell off the lorry, not only would you have lost your wife and son, but our counterparts in England would have been denied the services of a first-rate executive. Talk about fate lending a hand, I think this is a prime example of cause and effect.'

CHAPTER THIRTY

To say that this sudden about face from the Australian section of the group took their English counterparts by surprise would be the understatement of the year, probably of the decade. It wasn't only Luke Fisher's endorsement of the plan, which would have been pleasing enough in itself, but the offer that complemented the acceptance of it, whereby the funding for the development and construction of the chemical plant would be made available. In addition, the warm congratulatory tone of the section referring to the proposed purchase of an insurance company gave the directors confidence to press ahead.

In the cable outlining their change of attitude, Josh had acted on Luke's carefully outlined instructions by expressing gratitude for the idea, which he described as a stroke of genius, from which the Australian arm intended to pursue a similar policy once they had identified a suitable target, failing which, they would set up their own. The final statement gave added inspiration and food for thought.

At a hastily convened board meeting, Jessica read aloud from the telegram. "'Looking to the future, we intend to ensure that sufficient funds are set aside from the group's normal trading operation. These will be held in reserve and used to finance suitable investment opportunities, in particular those that enhance the diversity of the group's operations. This policy will apply in equal measure to both the Australian and United Kingdom sectors.'"

'I'd say that has to be one of the biggest re-thinks of all time,' Mark commented. 'And the best part is that it demonstrates their confidence in us in two ways, both by their adoption of an in-house insurance unit and the making available of funds for further expansion.'

'There is one item that hasn't been considered, although that is hardly surprising as it has been side-lined while we concentrated on other aspects of the business,' Sonny told them.

He saw his son's puzzled frown, an expression that was mirrored by the expressions of the other directors.

'I'm talking about my idea for the winding down of the wool processing operations, it appears to have been overlooked.'

'Actually, I have been thinking about that, Dad,' Mark contradicted him, 'and I'm against the idea.' Seeing his father's look of surprise, he explained. 'I've been mulling it over since you mentioned the possibility of shutting those mills and I reckon we'd be daft to do it. The synthetic fibres operation continues to expand and we'll soon need additional premises, both as production units and as warehousing facilities. In addition to the sites, we have workers who are used to handling textiles. Their talents would be much easier to adapt to the new products rather than making them unemployed, to then train up new employees that we don't know and who would have to be overseen more closely. I suggest we cease wool processing, and all we'd have to do is replace the machinery, most of which is fairly long in the tooth anyway.'

As the other directors discussed Mark's suggestion, it gave Sonny greater confidence in their abilities which would enable him to proceed with the plan that had been in his mind for some while. Meanwhile, he had another equally important problem to deal with in Byland Crescent.

When the board broke for lunch, Sonny spoke to Mark and asked him to pass his apologies for an early departure to the others. He left the Manor Row offices, heading for the station in time to catch an earlier train to Scarborough.

The first to notice Sonny's absence was Jessica, who asked Mark where he was. 'I wanted to ask his advice about one or two of the employees at the scouring plant, if we go ahead and adopt your idea.'

'He's had to go home. I don't envy him the job he's got to do when he gets there.'

'Why, is there something wrong? Is somebody ill?

'Not exactly ill. It's George, the butler my grandmother employed. He's getting on in years and from what I can gather he seems to be going a bit senile, acting strangely, and they're trying to persuade him that it's time for him to consider retiring, but doing so without offending him or causing him distress. That isn't going to be an easy or pleasant task.'

'Not a nice job, I agree, especially as he must have been with you a fair number of years.'

'As long as I can remember, that's certain. Over time, things might have changed dramatically, but to George it must all seem much as it was when he was a lad. Apparently there used to be a cook, two housemaids, my grandmother's personal maid, a butler and George, who was general factotum — whatever one of those is?' He shrugged his shoulders. 'Nowadays we don't need all those people, and to be fair I think we'd manage OK without George, but how he'll react I've no idea. I don't know how they're planning to broach the subject to him but sadly it seems as if it will be for the best, even if George can't see it that way.'

'Well, that's a relief. I thought for a moment there might be a problem with Andrew. But of course, then it would be you that had left early.'

Mark laughed. 'No, my son's perfectly safe. He's not been posted abroad, well, not yet.'

'How's he doing?' Paul wanted to know.

'Better than he was when the letter from the War Office first arrived.' Mark shook his head at the memory. The letter received early in the year requested Andrew Michael Cowgill report for a medical prior to his enlistment in the ranks of the British Army. It was clear from the terminology used that the request was in fact a non-negotiable command where National Service was concerned.

* * *

Before calling George into the drawing room, Rachael, who had been charged with the task of making discreet enquiries about the butler's personal circumstances, both past and present, told Sonny and Jenny what she had discovered.

When handing her this unenviable task, Sonny had told her, 'I never knew much about George except that he is from a local family and I believe they were fishermen. I did hear that he was considered to be a disgrace because every time he went to sea he got a massive attack of seasickness, but that might be nothing more than a rumour. I also believe he had sisters, but whether they're still around I can't be sure.'

Rachael began her account by informing them that George hadn't intended to remain single all his life. 'It's a really sad story. George had a childhood sweetheart, a girl called Rosie, and they planned to marry as soon as they were old enough and he had a job that would support them. However, while he was away serving in the forces during the First World War, she contracted diphtheria and died.' Rachael paused and gulped slightly, the emotion threatening to overcome her. 'It was on her seventeenth birthday that she passed away. According to what I was told, from that moment on George had no interest in girls. He told his younger sister that he believed that his heart died along with Rosie.'

'That is terribly sad,' Jenny agreed, 'but how did you find all this out? Surely George didn't tell you? He wouldn't reveal that sort of thing, would he?'

'No, of course not, but I did a bit of detective work. When it was George's day off, I followed him down to the Old Town where he went into one of the fishermen's cottages at the lower end of Paradise. A day later, I called at the cottage and discovered that he has two younger sisters. They still live in the old family home, although one of them is a spinster and the other is a widow.'

'Paradise, isn't that the hill that runs all the way up to St Mary's Church?' Sonny asked.

'That's right, and George goes there to visit his sisters every week on his day off. I had quite a long chat with them and found out what I've just told you and more besides.'

'I didn't realize I'd married a relative of Sherlock Holmes,' Sonny remarked. 'How did you discover all this? Did you interrogate them, give them the third degree?'

Rachael smiled fleetingly. 'Hardly,' she replied, 'we simply chatted over a cup of tea, and they promised not to reveal to George that I'd been to see them. What was really intriguing is that George had mentioned to them on several occasions that he felt it was time he retired, and that the work was getting too much for him. But he won't do so because he would never dream of letting us down.'

Jenny commented, 'That would make it simpler to persuade him to retire. But that's only the start of the problem. Where would he go? And if he was left alone with no way of passing the time, I think it would be very bad for him.'

'That's where my conversation with his sisters came in very useful. They told me that they'd noticed a time or two that George was becoming very forgetful and also behaving a bit oddly. They feel sure he'd be better off in familiar surroundings. And as they have plenty of room in their house, if between us all we can persuade him, they'd like him to go live with them. I told them we would ensure that they would not be financially worse off if that was to happen.' She looked at Sonny as she spoke and saw him nod agreement.

'Absolutely right, we must ensure he does not suffer financially,' Sonny said. 'I'd be happy to make a monthly allowance, sufficient for his and his sister's needs. We have to consider that there might come a time where he needs medical or other care and I don't want him to be worried. The problem, as I see it, is how we should approach him, and how we could persuade him without causing offence.'

'I thought of that as well,' Rachael told them, 'which is why I invited his sisters to come for tea this afternoon. If his sisters add their voices to ours, that might convince him. I haven't told George,' — Rachael glanced towards the clock on the mantelshelf — 'but they should be arriving in around twenty minutes time. That way we can sit down and have a heart to heart with them.' She smiled at her daughter-in-law. 'And if you wouldn't mind, Jenny, I'd like to ask you to take on the role of butler on this occasion.'

Although they had been concerned that George would react badly to the suggestion of his retirement, in the event his response to the proposal was far more positive than they had feared. There were several surprises, but fortunately none of them were unpleasant.

It was George who received the first shock, when he answered the door to find his sisters standing outside. On asking why they were there, he was told, 'We've been invited by Mrs Cowgill senior to take afternoon tea with her and the family.'

The next surprise came after he ushered his siblings into the drawing room. It came from Sonny, who commanded George to sit down alongside the two ladies, while at the same time nodding to his daughter-in-law, who immediately stood up and left the room.

During her absence, Rachael began to explain the reason for the gathering. 'I invited your sisters here today because they, like us, are concerned for your welfare, George. I went to see them because I felt that the work you do is getting a bit much for you and might be taking a toll on your health, which is unfair. They told me that you had commented along the same lines, and that you were concerned that you were no longer able to give your best.'

Rachael paused, and as she looked at the butler, noticed the wary expression on his face. She continued, anxious to allay any fears he might have. 'Once I knew that you were feeling the strain, I talked it over with the rest of the family, and we've put together a plan that we hope will make your life easier. You have been a loyal and valued friend to our family, serving four generations with tact, discretion and a high degree of skill, for which we are immensely grateful. The proposal I am about to put forward, together with the information Mr Sonny will provide, has been discussed in depth both in this house and with your family. The single objective in all of this is to achieve whatever is best for you.

'One thing that has changed dramatically over the years since you came to work here as a teenager is the way this house operates, changes that could not have been envisaged ten, twenty or thirty years ago. The advent of modern household appliances and laundry services has simplified the management of even such a big house as this greatly and has also lessened the requirement for a large number of full-time staff. The number of family members, both resident and visiting, has dwindled markedly. Taking all these factors into consideration we thought it only fair that we should put together an arrangement that would ensure you were able to spend a considerable number of years in comfortable retirement, without having always to consider the needs of others before your own.

'I appreciate that you might be concerned that the loss of your regular income might prove detrimental but I don't think you should worry about that. Although I leave financial matters to my husband, he has assured me that he has arranged a suitable retirement package which he will shortly explain to you before you decide what you want to do.'

Rachael paused again, both to allow George to digest what she had already told him and also to lend emphasis to the next part of her statement. To heighten his attention to her last words on the subject she leaned forward and placed her hand on his arm, looking him in the eye as she spoke. 'Let me make one thing clear before I hand over to Mr Sonny. I want you to know that you will always be welcome in this house, George, because to us you have become a loyal and trusted member of our family.'

There was an interruption at that point, as Jenny opened the sitting room door before guiding the well-laden tea trolley into the room, a task usually performed by their butler. 'I hope I'm doing this right, George. If not, I'll look to you to give me some training and guidance. Even then I believe I'm going to need a lot of practice.'

Determined to ensure the occasion was more a social gathering, Rachael had asked Jenny to ensure that George was included by passing him a cup of tea and inviting him to take his pick from the array of sandwiches and cakes that were on offer.

Conversation during what Sonny referred to later as 'the tea interval' was light, designed to put George and his sisters at their ease, and to a lesser extent to remove or reduce any discomfort they might have felt in such unfamiliar surroundings.

The tactic seemed to have worked, for when Sonny began to outline his proposals some half hour later, he noticed that George was paying rapt attention to everything he said. Any remaining doubts he might have entertained were blown away by the breadth and content of the financial package Sonny put forward.

'In the first instance there would be a lump sum payment of one hundred pounds.' Sonny paused before adding, 'Following that there will be a weekly occupational pension of ten pounds two shillings and sixpence. That amount will be adjusted in line with any rise in the cost-of-living index, which I have asked our finance director Paul Sugden to monitor annually. You have lived here with lesser pay, on an all found basis, and I think it is only fair that you should not suffer by comparison when you incur expenses you are not used to.'

Sonny waited for a moment, allowing George to digest the information, before continuing. 'In addition to that settlement I also propose to set aside a further lump sum which would be available to call on in respect of any medical expenses you might incur for treatment that is not within the remit of the National Health Service.'

Rachael listened, along with the rest of his audience as Sonny concluded the meeting.

'I don't expect you to come to a decision immediately, George. I think it would be sensible to discuss the terms and other matters regarding the future with your sisters before you let us know your feelings on the matter.' He smiled as he added, 'I believe that they have some ideas of their own to put to you regarding your accommodation. But to reiterate what my wife said, you will always be welcome in this house, which has become as much your home as ours.'

Later, when Sonny and Rachael were preparing to go to bed, she tackled him about the financial settlement he'd proposed for George. 'That was extremely generous,' she told him. 'I must admit that I didn't expect it to be nearly as much as you offered him, and by the look on their faces neither did he or his sisters.'

'I don't think it was excessive. There comes a point when it's impossible to put a true value on someone's service. Apart from his wartime service, George has been with our family almost sixty years, through thick and thin, sharing the high and low points. He has celebrated our triumphs and mourned with us when tragedy hit us. I was determined to demonstrate that fact, and also to make it appealing enough for George to accept, secure in the knowledge that neither he nor his family need ever worry about money. Above all, if he feels happy to accept this settlement it will mean that all those years of devoted service and support are free from the contamination that would come from his gradually declining health and any bizarre behaviour he might begin to display because of it.'

Once they were in bed, Rachael reached across and embraced him. 'You're a good man, Sonny Cowgill. I'm so glad I allowed you to seduce me all those years ago. You could do it again if you wish,' she paused and whispered, 'I'd even allow you to give me a love bite as you've still got all your teeth.'

CHAPTER THIRTY-ONE

George didn't take long to make a decision about his retirement. Or perhaps, Sonny thought, George's sisters had made it for him. He asked if it would be acceptable to remain with the family until after Christmas, a time he always enjoyed at Byland Crescent. One thing George was keen to discover was if the Cowgill family would be looking to recruit a younger replacement for the post.

'I don't think so, George, not for the time being.' Sonny thought about it for a second. 'To be fair I'm not sure we're going to need anyone. Before long, I am hoping to do some travelling which will take my wife and I abroad for long periods, so with Master Andrew already away doing his National Service and almost ready to fly the nest, apart from my son, his wife, and Miss Susan, the house will be empty for much of the time. Besides, it wouldn't be fair on anyone who got the job, because we'd be forever comparing them unfavourably to you. Once you've had gold, George, it's not easy to settle for brass.'

When Sonny reported the conversation to Rachael, he decided the time was right to mention their possible travel plans. He thought it would be better to sound her out on these first rather than present her with a fait accompli. He waited until Jenny, Mark and Andrew had taken Susan to feed the ducks in the park before broaching the subject. He began by reiterating the remarks he'd made to George about the family being less reliant on Byland Crescent as a base and followed this by suggesting that he and Rachael should take advantage of this opportunity to do some travelling.

Rachael blinked with surprise as she stared at her husband. She could usually tell what Sonny was thinking and gauge his mood by his facial expression but she'd had no prior inkling of what he was planning, so the idea came as a total shock.

'Travelling?' she asked, playing for time to absorb the news. 'Can it be that now you're no longer a Captain of Industry,' she invested the title with ironic capitals, 'you've suddenly acquired a new-found wanderlust, or has the urge to visit foreign climes always been a latent ambition that you've kept secret, even from me?'

Sonny smiled a trifle ruefully, but only briefly, because part of what he was about to suggest was too delicate and serious a subject to be treated humorously. 'I thought it would be nice to visit Frances and Hank the Yank in Texas.'

Rachael smiled at the reference to their son-in-law Henry. Once his career as an American Air Force bomber pilot ended, Henry had returned home taking his bride along with him. His hopes, matching the dreams of many returning fliers to become a commercial pilot, had been dashed, and he now managed the family ranch in Texas.

Rachael was still considering Sonny's idea when he came up with a further suggestion, one that wiped the smile from her face instantly.

'Before then, I wondered if we should go to Crete. I think we ought to find the place where Billy died and make sure there is a grave, somewhere he can rest in peace. Only then can you perhaps be free from the doubt and guilt that have been tormenting you all these years. If it hasn't been possible to provide a fitting place for him, we could perhaps ensure there will be one. What do you think?'

There was a long silence. Rachael thought long and hard about Sonny's proposal before giving it her cautious approval, but consideration of the project was as far as their preparations reached. As they were consulting the travel agent, who by now had all but given up hope that the business would come his way, they received news that caused the plan to be put on hold yet again.

This came via the BBC as they listened to the bulletins reporting the rapidly worsening situation in the Middle East. Colonel Nasser's Egypt was in conflict with the recently formed state of Israel over the disputed territory flanking the Sinai Desert. Sonny began to fear that their journey might be a casualty of the imminent and threatened hostilities, his fears worsening when French and British policy makers came down on the side of Israel. Aware that Egypt was becoming allied to Russia, the Anglo-French governments withdrew their financial support for the vital Aswan Dam project.

These misgivings escalated when Nasser retaliated by nationalizing the Suez Canal and announcing that the Strait of Tiran would be prohibited for Israeli shipping.

The threat of closure now hung over the Suez Canal itself, the vital artery linking the Mediterranean Sea, and from there the North Atlantic with the Red Sea, the Northern Indian Ocean and beyond to Asia and the Far East.

If this route became blocked off, commercial and passenger traffic would be forced to take the far longer, more time-consuming route. With this in mind, British and French forces invaded Egypt, their intention being to topple the Nasser government. At the same time Israeli troops invaded the Sinai Peninsula.

What had seemed initially nothing more than a minor skirmish was in danger of escalating into a full-blown war. At fractionally over five hundred miles, the relative proximity of Crete to Port Said, the northern terminus of the Suez Canal, was enough to deter Sonny from taking Rachael into such a potential danger area. Naturally, Rachael, by now enthusiastic about the planned trip, resisted his ruling, but to little avail.

* * *

It wasn't until early December of 1956 that a chance discovery shed light on a mystery surrounding their retired butler and shed further light on his declining health. Jenny had made a foray into the cellar, her mission being to secrete a number of parcels bearing festive Christmas wrappings. She needed a place that was safe from prying eyes and, even more important, away from inquisitive fingers.

Disregarding the more obvious locations, such as the wine rack and meat safe, or the vegetable storage units that were visited frequently, Jenny looked round the spacious rooms and after a while she spotted a cupboard in the far corner, one that she had never noticed before. That was hardly surprising as the huge basement was lit only by a single, low powered bulb at the opposite end of the room. She walked across and examined the small cabinet, wondering what its purpose was. Its dusty condition indicated that it was no longer relevant and, if there was room inside, this would make an ideal hiding place. She balanced the parcels on top of the cupboard and then opened the door. Years of damp and disuse had obviously warped the wood slightly but Jenny managed to prise the door open and looked inside. The cupboard, like Mother Hubbard's, was bare — or so she thought, until she noticed a small pile of envelopes lying on the shelf. She removed these and examined them, peering in the gloom, but with little success. She stowed the parcels away, forced the door closed and then returned upstairs to view her find in better light, and in warmer surroundings.

She noticed that all the envelopes were unopened, despite them being addressed to members of the family. The other common factor was that they all bore foreign stamps. One, which was addressed to her, was from Spain. She was about to open this when her mother-in-law entered the room bearing a tea tray.

'What have you got there?' Rachael asked as she set the tray down.

'I think it's the answer to a mystery. You remember being told off by Frances for not answering her letters? I think this is why you never got them.' Jenny handed three of the envelopes to Rachael. 'That looks like her handwriting and they're addressed to you.'

'Where did you find them?'

'They were in a cupboard at the far end of the cellar.'

Rachael was momentarily distracted. 'What were you doing down there?'

Jenny smiled. 'I was hiding Christmas presents.' She looked at an envelope. 'This one's addressed to all of us and was sent from Australia, and the other one is addressed to me and is from Spain.'

'How on earth did they get down there?'

'My guess would be that George hid them. You remember how things kept going missing when he started to behave strangely? Perhaps that cupboard is where he stashed things, for whatever reason we'll probably never know. Anyway, we'd better open them and see what they're about.'

Rachael attacked the Australian envelope while Jenny slit open the one from Spain. 'Oh, that's nice,' Rachael said, 'it's from Josh, thanking us for our help while he and Astrid were trying to cope with their bereavement, thank heavens it didn't require a reply. Who is yours from?'

Jenny looked up. 'It's from Carmen, our friend from the Spanish Civil War. She had to wait all this time to write because she wasn't sure it would be safe to do so but she's now decided to risk it.'

'Carmen, isn't she the woman who became involved with Josh and had his baby?'

Jenny smiled. 'That's right, although that baby is now an eighteen-year-old. I'll tell you one thing, if she's half as good-looking as her mother I'll bet she's a real heartbreaker.' She continued reading. 'Anyway, the good news is that they're both OK and she's hoping to hear back from us.' Jenny glanced at the date on the letter. 'My goodness, Carmen posted this almost fifteen months ago. I'd better get my skates on and reply immediately.'

'Yes, and I'll write to Frances and explain that I haven't lost the plot — but we think that George did.'

Although they made light of the discovery, it wasn't until a few years later that one of the letters had enormous consequences for one member of the Cowgill family, and to a lesser extent, all of the inhabitants of Byland Crescent.

* * *

Andrew Cowgill's parents and grandparents were extremely concerned by the fact that his period of National Service came at a time when British forces were actively engaged in both Cyprus, where there had been several fatalities during the unrest, and Egypt. There, the Suez Crisis had precipitated an Anglo-French invasion, but it transpired that the family's fears were groundless.

Much of Andrew's time was spent in and around the nearby Catterick Garrison, where he learned skills such as marching with a full kit on his back, assembling, firing and cleaning a variety of firearms, map reading, cross country running, more marching, boot polishing, laundry, food preparation, and yet more marching, preferably to the nearest hostelry licensed to serve alcoholic beverages.

Although these talents were essential to any soldier, they proved to be of little value to Andrew once his period of conscription ended. His closest proximity to a battle zone came when he witnessed a bar brawl between half a dozen other squaddies.

When their grandson had returned to civilian life, the Suez Crisis had been resolved. Now Sonny and Rachael were finally able to transform their plans, for what their son Mark referred to as 'an odyssey', into reality. That remark was as close as any member of the family dare come to frivolity on what was still a highly contentious subject, the fate of Billy, Mark's younger brother.

As Sonny was making preparations for their long absence, he reflected that they would be leaving both the business and their home in safe hands. Jenny and Mark would, he knew, take good care of Byland Crescent, while over in Bradford, Jessica and the team were continuing to produce excellent trading results. Figures for the latest financial year showed that Fisher Springs UK had achieved record profits, with all divisions making solid contributions.

Especially satisfying was the performance of their most recently acquired subsidiary. The profit returned by the insurance company, even after deduction of provision for unresolved claims, proved the wisdom of their investment. As Sonny remarked during the board meeting when the figures were presented, 'When I think of the thousands of pounds we've paid out in premiums with very little to show for the expenditure, I wish we'd made this decision years ago.'

'That's crying over spilt milk, Dad,' Mark replied.

Their finance director, Paul Sugden added, 'The good news is that if we have similar trading results in the next two years, unless we have to pay out on substantial claims, we'll have recouped the cost of buying the company in full and we'll also be in a position to repay the Australian loan should we wish to. That should bring a smile to their faces.'

* * *

Back in Byland Crescent, Andrew Cowgill faced the prospect of what to do with the rest of his life, a decision he had deferred until his conscription period ended. The problem he faced was which of two paths to take. He had the choice of either utilizing his language skills or indulging his love of all things mechanical, turning his talent in that field into his career. He certainly had no desire to follow in his father's footsteps.

As he was pondering this, Andrew's grandmother asked him a question that would determine which route to take — and in the process would change his life completely.

'I know you're a master of many languages, much like your second cousin, Josh, but how well do you understand Greek?'

Andrew blinked with surprise at Rachael's query. 'I learned a fair bit of Ancient Greek at school, Grandma, but that's a lot different to what's used today, or so I believe. I've certainly never spoken it, so my pronunciation of what little I do know could be way off the mark.'

'At least you know some, which is far more than either Grandpa or I do. How do you fancy getting the chance to improve it? As you know we're planning to visit Crete and your Uncle Billy's resting place, but the only way to get there is by flying to Athens, so we're intending to make it more of a holiday by spending time there and doing some sightseeing. Someone with even a basic knowledge of the language, enough to make themselves understood, might prove invaluable, so we wondered if you'd like to come with us for at least part of the trip. What do you think?'

'I'm not sure, Grandma, I'll have to talk it through with Mum and Dad first.'

'Do that. And perhaps you could visit other places on your way back, like Italy, Spain, or France for example?'

'Making it a sort of latter-day Grand Tour?'

Rachael laughed. 'Yes, I suppose so. What do you think? Would you like that?'

Andrew gave her a cheeky grin before adding, '*Ne, indaxi, Giagia.*'

Rachael frowned in puzzlement. 'What does that mean?'

'It's Greek for, "Yes, OK, Grandma."'

The longer Andrew thought about his grandparents' idea the more he came to realize that if he planned it right, this trip would give him a unique opportunity to hone up his language skills and might also present the solution to his dilemma over a chosen career. A few days later he sought a meeting with the two people whose support, both moral and financial, he needed — his parents.

'My idea is to go with Grandma and Grandpa as far as Crete, and then once they've got to where they need to be I can leave them to it. I think they might prefer to spend the last part of what I reckon is a pilgrimage on their own. Once I'm sure they're going to be OK I could go back to Athens, then I could go to Italy by boat, from somewhere like Patras. After that I could make my way slowly back via France and Spain. That way I can brush up on four different languages. What I have in mind is to spend a few months on this project and at the end of it I could look for a job as an interpreter or translator. I do know that there are a few publishers and news organizations always on the lookout for people with linguistic ability. The problem I have is that this is going to be a fairly expensive field trip.'

Although Jenny was saddened at the prospect of another prolonged absence from her son, she hid her disappointment well, merely saying, 'But you've only recently returned, Andrew.' She appealed to her husband for support. 'What do you think, Mark?'

'I know it'll be a wrench letting him off the leash, but let's face it we were younger than him when we went to Spain. Our parents didn't object, even though we were going off to fight in the Civil War. I can only imagine what went through their minds at the time, but they didn't stand in our way. Besides which,' Mark added, 'he doesn't do much when he's here, apart from bringing coal in and tinkering with his sister's transistor radio.'

Andrew grinned at the slur but looked at his mother, trying to gauge her reaction. He was relieved when she smiled. 'Go and talk it through with Grandma and Grandpa and I'll see if we've a bit of money spare for such extravagance.'

Mark turned away to hide a smile. It had only been a few days since he and Jenny had discussed finances. Apart from the considerable wealth his parents had accumulated over the years, Mark's shareholding in Fisher Springs UK, and his salary as a director, added to an inheritance from his grandmother, had resulted in a considerable amount of personal affluence. Having already made provision for Susan's educational needs they had decided to set aside another large sum for Andrew's continued vocational training in whatever field he chose to pursue. The timing of his son's request couldn't have been better.

Despite the decision having been made, there was much to organize before the trip went ahead. Travel documents, passports and other technicalities would take a considerable length of time to sort out, and during that process Jenny made a suggestion that prolonged the preparation process and added a further dimension to Andrew's travel plans. In doing so, Jenny was mindful of the correspondence she had conducted at intervals with an old friend and former colleague.

'I'm surprised you included Spain in your itinerary,' she told her son. 'Don't you think your command of Spanish is good enough yet?'

'I want to visit Spain because although my Spanish is pretty good there's always room for improvement, especially with things such as idioms. If I was able to spend some time there I could get to grips with colloquial Spanish and dialects. That would be most useful, especially as Spanish is the second most spoken language worldwide, after English. But I don't want to overdo it, Mum, because of the money. Unless you've won the pools and haven't told us,' Andrew replied. 'I'd dearly like to visit Barcelona as well as Madrid, but not for the language of course.'

'I wouldn't worry about the money,' Mark told him. 'We'll be able to fund your trip without having to go begging on street corners. But why did you say, "not for the language" when you mentioned Barcelona?'

'Because they don't speak Castilian Spanish there, they use Catalan.'

'So why Barcelona?'

'Because I'd love to see some of the work of Antoni Gaudi.'

'Who's he?' Jenny asked.

At the same time as Mark said, 'I've heard of him.'

'He was an architect, and some of his work is really famous.'

'Like the Scotsman, Charles Rennie Mackintosh?'

'That's right, Dad, and their lives more or less over-lapped, which is an odd coincidence. Gaudi's most famous work remains unfinished but it's still reckoned to be one of the most spectacular buildings of its kind. It's the cathedral, called La Sagrada Familia.'

'How come you know so much about architecture all of a sudden?' Jenny asked.

'It's all down to my language teacher. He's by way of being an enthusiast and I suppose it's rubbed off.'

'Well, I wasn't thinking of Madrid or Barcelona when I asked you about Spain,' Jenny informed him. 'I thought you might like to visit somewhere more remote, like Ibiza for example. We even know someone who might give you board and lodgings while you're there without you having to pay much for them. If you're keen, I'll write and enquire, shall I?'

'Is that your friend from the Civil War?'

'That's right, her name is Carmen Diaz, and she's a lovely person.'

'I wouldn't want to impose, Mum.'

'Carmen wouldn't view it that way. So, make the most of the opportunity.'

The response to Jenny's letter was an enthusiastic agreement and the only slight drawback was that as a result of this amendment to the original plan it was obvious that the travellers would not be able to set forth until the early summer of 1959.

CHAPTER THIRTY-TWO

Although the Fisher Springs UK results were greeted with delight both in England and Australia there was one member of the British board who had strong reservations. Surprisingly the director who had misgivings about the way things were heading was the person who presented those excellent figures — their finance director Paul Sugden.

There was little resemblance in the confident, competent, and articulate member of the senior executive group, to the diffident ex-soldier who had visited the company seeking work almost a decade or so earlier. Despite the authority his position and track record had given him, Paul refrained from voicing his doubts to his colleagues in the first instance, preferring instead to gather more evidence and then present his case for a second opinion. That meant seeking advice from his wife, which he did one evening as they were relaxing at home.

Home for Paul and Sally was now the large, semi-detached house in Baildon. Once they had put the children to bed, he began to expound his theory, knowing he was certain of both a fair judgement and a well-thought-out response.

'If the results are so good, what is it that worries you?' Sally asked after he explained the background to his concerns.

'Surely the time to become anxious is when the figures start to slide in the opposite direction.'

'It isn't the group's performance. My main worry is over the British economy. I know Harold Macmillan said, "you've never had it so good" and that might be technically correct as things stand at present but look at it another way. The economy has stagnated for many years, firstly because of the war and later due to the constrictions of rationing. Now it seems to be galloping ahead. My fear is that gallop might turn into a stampede and, if it became out of control, I dread to think of the consequences.'

'What evidence have you got to back up your theory?'

'From what I've been able to discover it seems that much of the expenditure people are indulging in is on borrowed capital, whether it be via bank overdrafts, this new-fangled hire purchase system, or mail order catalogues, paying over time. I'm not saying I blame them for this, because it's a natural reaction after the years of restriction, but I fear they might be going a bit wild and overdoing their freedom. My other worry is that this sort of attitude might be affecting businesses and their attitude to borrowing, as well as the man in the street.'

'What do you think will happen? How will this become a problem?'

'The worst-case scenario would be the sort of inflation and reckless speculation that gripped places like Germany and America during the nineteen twenties. That resulted in the Wall Street crash and thereafter the Great Depression. America hadn't really recovered from that a decade later when we were all plunged into war.'

'You really think that sort of thing could happen here?'

'I do, albeit on a much lesser scale. But even though our national economy is that much smaller, the effects could be just as far-reaching — certainly within Britain.'

Sally pondered his theory for a long time before passing judgement. In the end Paul was relieved by her response. 'If you're right, which I believe you might be, the only way the exchequer could act to bring the spending under control before it gets beyond redemption is by putting severe restrictions on all forms of credit. And that would only work if they were to apply it across the board. It would be ineffective to restrict company borrowing while allowing personal lending to go unchecked, so the overall result would be extremely severe.'

Paul hugged her, his gratitude evident. It was one thing to propound a theory but getting confirmation from another professional source that he was thinking on the right lines came as a huge relief.

'It's my duty to warn the board and suggest we pre-empt the issue by taking action beforehand, even if it's unilaterally. In doing so I'll present them with the statistical information I've shown you once I've been over it again to verify its accuracy. Even if, and when, I manage to convince my colleagues here in Britain I've also got to persuade our Australian directors to support our actions and that will be far from easy given that their economic situation is much different to ours. If I manage to do that, I might actually earn my inflated salary for once.'

Sally disputed this crazy notion. 'You earn every penny of your salary, Paul, so don't denigrate yourself by talking such nonsense, do you hear me?'

She only relaxed when she saw him smile.

* * *

There was one notable absentee from the next Fisher Springs UK board meeting. 'Dad presents his apologies,' Mark told them, 'but in view of the way the group is performing, he doesn't see any need to be here today. As you know, he and my mother are soon going on an extended vacation and they are busy preparing. Apparently,' Mark glanced at the boardroom clock, 'in a few minutes from now he'll be having his photograph taken for a passport. I told him to ensure the photographer was adequately insured because his photo will probably break the camera. He thought that was a great idea and said he'd offer the man coverage via our company.'

The other directors smiled and agreed that Sonny didn't need to be present. Of the quartet seated around the table only Paul was disappointed by Sonny's absence, for one specific reason. The task of persuading his colleagues to take on board his theory was likely to prove more difficult without the backing of the board's most senior member, one who had first-hand experience of having to work through a severe recession.

As Mark, David and Jessica were presenting their monthly reports, Paul thought quickly and by the time it was his turn he had worked out a strategy that would enable him to obtain Sonny's support for his proposal. Having presented the group figures and illustrated the continuing upward trend Paul added, 'There is one other matter I want the board to consider. I'm sorry your father isn't here today, Mark, because I would have valued his input. Perhaps you can convey my ideas to him and elicit a reaction based on his insight. He's the only one of us who can speak from personal experience about what I'm about to explain.'

Mark Cowgill nodded agreement although it was clear that he, like the others, was mystified by Paul's additional agenda item.

Because the board meeting was purportedly a routine one, none of the members had envisaged it lasting much longer than an hour and a half. In the event it was almost three hours later when they adjourned, and even then, despite intense discussion, no firm decision had been reached.

The consensus was that Paul's theory was too important for an initial, knee-jerk response, and that each of them should take away the statistical information he had provided and study the facts in the light of the warning he had flagged up. On one point they were all agreed, that once again Paul had exceeded his normal remit by bringing this potentially dangerous issue to their attention.

When Mark told his father of Paul's theory, Sonny knew that the subject matter was far too important to be left in abeyance, particularly as he was about to take a year's sabbatical. He phoned Jessica and suggested a further board meeting should be arranged for the following week, where every director would be present.

Although there was much discussion when they gathered round the boardroom table, there was little doubt that they were all supportive of the proposed measures and when it came to the vote the decision was unanimous. For the immediate future, until there was a further resolution reversing the policy, all capital expenditure was to be routed via Paul Sugden and any requisition order would require his counter signature before it could proceed. A memo to all staff members with purchasing power was to be drafted to this effect and sent out the following day. Apart from minor replacement items such as stationery, all budgets were to be trimmed and stocks would also be subjected to close scrutiny. Re-ordering, even for materials considered essential, should be limited to amounts necessary to fulfil extant orders. No new purchases would be allowed until, and unless, there was a matching sale.

Further measures would fall into line with this retrenchment policy. Bank overdrafts for all group companies would be trimmed until the accounts were in credit and no new borrowing would be permitted. This would be achievable in a shorter time scale via inter-company loans, with divisions that were cash-rich using their positive balances to fund the others.

'In reality,' Paul told them, as he distributed a fact sheet containing the relevant figures, 'as you can see from the amounts shown here these are relatively trivial amounts. The restrictions might inhibit expansion to some extent, but I regard that as of less concern than protecting the group's overall financial stability.'

'What about our customers?' Sonny asked. 'Shouldn't we be looking to ensure we don't end up with a load of bad debt? I remember that Simon Jones and Michael Haigh adopted a very tough vetting policy before the Great Depression hit us. That enabled us to avoid crippling losses when our customers went bust, which a lot of them did. Speaking as the sales director at the time, it was very frustrating, but in the long run it paid off.'

'That was the next point I was about to raise,' Paul told him. 'I've prepared a list of clients, identifying those that are the slowest payers. I was disturbed to see that a couple of them already appear to be struggling, as their payment schedules have lengthened markedly over the past eighteen months. One of them takes six months to settle outstanding invoices and then promptly re-orders.'

'That's a crafty dodge,' Sonny remarked.

'Why do you say that?' Jessica asked.

'By the sound of what Paul said, that customer is treating us as his bank. The advantage from his point of view is that he's able to borrow from us without having to pay interest charges.'

'How do you suggest we avoid similar practices being adopted by other customers?' David enquired. 'If things get as tight as Paul suggests, a few more could be tempted to go down the same route, and even some previously good payers might start dragging their heels.'

'There is a way,' Paul told them, 'but it's something I've been reluctant to suggest. If we revise our invoicing policy slightly, we could make it uneconomic for customers to delay paying us. At present all invoices are sent out with a thirty-day net payment clause. We could add to that a further section, incorporating a sliding scale of interest for accounts that remain unpaid after the thirty-day limit. The rate would increase on a monthly basis. If they haven't coughed up after the next period end, they'll finish up paying interest on interest.'

'Is that legal?' Jessica asked.

Paul grinned, a trifle ruefully. 'It certainly is. That's the standard practice used by banks and moneylenders.'

Having secured the agreement to his recommendations, Sugden was charged with implementing them. Sonny told

Jessica he would leave it to her to send the minutes of the board meeting to their Australian colleagues. 'Bear in mind I will be absent for a year, possibly longer.' His face was sombre as he added, 'The reason I can't be more definite is that it all depends on what we discover when we get to Crete.'

The other directors, mindful of the mission he and Rachael were about to undertake, wished him the best of luck, and Jessica tried to lighten the mood slightly by telling him she would endeavour to keep the ship afloat until he returned.

'I'm sure you'll manage,' Sonny told her, 'especially once Paul's measures begin to take effect.'

As they were journeying back to Scarborough, Sonny told Mark, 'I'm not sure how well our decision will be greeted in Australia. I think Luke Fisher for one might regard it as a retrograde step, but don't allow them to bully you into changing your mind. They've very little idea of how things are over here because they haven't been subject to the same restrictions. Luckily for us, Paul has highlighted the potential problem in time for us to take preventative measures.'

In the event, by the time the minutes of what would turn out to be a crucial board meeting reached Australia, Luke Fisher had far more urgent personal matters to contend with. The success or otherwise of either the British or Australian businesses were of absolutely no interest to Luke when set against the crisis facing him.

* * *

Jenny's correspondence with Carmen had increased rapidly once both parties were aware of each other's survival, safety and good health. At one point, Jenny had written of her son's decision to become an interpreter, which she told Carmen had amazed the rest of his family as they had all been convinced that he would have opted instead for a career in either engineering or the fledgling electronics industry.

Carmen's response surprised Jenny, for in her letter she confided in her English friend that her own daughter

Consuela had long wished to become involved in something of that nature.

'She is forever tinkering with anything that has moving parts, anything she can get her hands on. She's even built a radio set out of bits and pieces she's bought or scrounged. Unfortunately, such a career would be unthinkable for a young woman here in Spain, because the current regime frowns on anything that appears to be radical or liberated. Here, women, no matter how talented, are proscribed from science, industry and the arts, with very few exceptions. Unless they choose to take the veil as nuns, or to become secretaries or nurses, they are limited to the roles of wife, mother or in some rare cases midwives.'

Reading between the lines, Jenny guessed that was all Carmen dared to put in writing without risking the displeasure of the authorities. In Spain, censorship of mail, particularly letters sent overseas, was rumoured to take place, and although that rumour had no factual basis, caution was the better option.

In her latest missive, which reached Byland Crescent a month before Andrew and his grandparents left for Greece, Carmen wrote about how much she and Consuela were looking forward to his visit and went on to outline other problems that were concerning her greatly. Jenny explained some of these to Andrew, pointing out the great fear that must still be at the back of Carmen's mind, the dread that somehow, sooner or later, her part in the Republican cause during the Civil War would come to light. She secured his promise to behave correctly and to handle any encounters with locals diplomatically, bearing in mind with whom he was staying.

He promised to do so, adding, 'And if there's anything at all I can do to help your friend or her daughter I'll gladly do it.'

The only subject both women had avoided in their correspondence had been the Spanish Civil War and their role in it. There was certainly no mention made of the identity of La Trompetista, the charismatic leader of the small guerrilla group they had belonged to and the father of Carmen's daughter Consuela. Jenny was certainly not about to divulge her knowledge that his pseudonym hid the fact that he was Mark's cousin Josh. They had decided against telling Josh of Consuela's existence, now they hid Josh's true identity from the child's mother. For that very reason Jenny didn't inform Andrew of any of this, for fear that a careless word might cause distress to either Carmen or Consuela.

It was almost at the end of August 1958 when Mark, who had been given temporary permission to drive his father's cherished Bentley, the third such limousine Sonny had bought, took the travellers to York railway station on the first leg of their epic journey. As they pulled away from Byland Crescent, their departure was watched by Jenny and Susan, who waved them off enthusiastically.

For the next year, Jenny thought, there would only be three occupants in a house that had at times been filled with over a dozen members of the Cowgill family plus the servants. It would seem eerily silent for much of the time, until Susan switched her transistor radio on — full blast. The transistor, now popular in America, had been a gift from her Aunt Frances and Hank the Yank. Jenny shuddered at the thought of the songs of Elvis Presley and Bill Haley and the Comets, echoing throughout the house, and wondered how they'd cope. Perhaps it was as well George had accepted the retirement plan, he would certainly not have been amused.

The way of life had changed so much that it would be unrecognizable to Mark's grandfather, who had purchased the property nearly sixty years earlier.

CHAPTER THIRTY-THREE

It was mid-afternoon on a Sunday and Luke Fisher was sitting at home on the veranda, reading, his feet up, and a glass of lemonade at his side. His children and their cousins were playing quietly in the yard. The peace was disturbed as he heard his name being called and looked up to see Dottie cycling towards him as if the hounds of hell were following.

He jumped to his feet and ran down the few steps to meet her.

She screeched to a halt, her appearance dishevelled, tears streaming down her face. She dismounted and tossed the bike to the ground.

'Where's Bella?' he demanded, as the children gathered to discover the reason for the intrusion.

Gasping for breath, Dottie said, 'Oh, Luke, there's been a terrible accident. She was in collision with a tanker. You must go to the hospital immediately.'

By the time Dottie finished the sentence, Luke had run back to the house and snatched up his car keys, his speed that of a stampeding horse. 'Look after the kids,' he yelled.

The following week was, as Luke said later, the worst period in his life, even surpassing the grief, anger, and despair he had felt after his parents' tragic death.

When he reached the hospital, the specialist provided little in the way of comfort. 'Mr Fisher, your wife has a broken arm and damage to her knee ligaments. They should heal completely given time and with the aid of some physiotherapy, but that's a while down the road. That's the good news. Unfortunately, she has a fractured skull and severe internal injuries. She is on her way to theatre now. Excuse me.' With that, he turned and headed down the hallway.

Luke spent the next few hours pacing the corridors of the hospital. At last, the surgeon reappeared. Luke looked at his face for some indication as to Bella's condition.

'I'm sorry, Mr Fisher, we had to perform a hysterectomy. I'm afraid we were unable to save the baby.'

'Baby?' Luke sank to a chair. 'I didn't know.' For a moment he held his head in his hands before he looked up, his eyes filled with tears. 'But how is she?'

The surgeon patted Luke on the shoulder, an attempt at reassurance. 'We also had to remove her spleen and left kidney. Her head injury isn't as bad as was thought, but we'll keep her asleep for the next few days, give everything chance to settle down. Once she recovers from the procedures, she should be fine.'

'All I care about is Bella and making sure she's OK. Thanks for everything you've done, Doc.'

'No worries, I expect you'd like to see her. I wanted you to be aware of the exact situation before she wakes.'

It was six days before Bella was woken following the life-saving operation and Luke began to relax, albeit marginally. As he walked into her private room, Bella appeared to be asleep. Luke turned and closed the door as quietly as he could but when he turned round Bella was looking at him, a faint smile on her face.

'Don't look so worried, I'm OK.' Her voice was barely above a whisper, the effect, he guessed, of the painkillers and sedatives she had been fed both before and after her operation.

'You scared the hell out of me,' he told her as he kissed her gently on the forehead. She saw the tears in his eyes as he continued, 'I thought I'd lost you, and I couldn't bear the idea of life without you by my side.'

'I'm sorry I hadn't told you about the baby,' she said, a tear trickled down her cheek. 'And now we're not going to be able to have the big family we both hoped for.'

'I don't give a damn about that. All I'm concerned about is you. You're all that matters to me. As long as the kids we have are fine that'll be right enough for me. Let's face it, there must be plenty of couples who can't have children at all, so we're lucky.'

'How have they been? Do they understand why I'm not at home?'

'Not really, all they know is that they're staying with their aunt and uncle for a while. I told the nanny she could have a week off, in the circumstances. You'll need all the help you can get when you come home.'

As Bella continued to look at her husband, she suddenly noticed his unshaven appearance, rumpled clothing and wrinkled shirt. 'Have you been here all this time?'

'More or less, I've been outside your room or sitting watching you when they would let me in. Those chairs are damned uncomfortable and the food in the cafeteria is only fit for the garbage bin. I reckon some of the sandwiches are damned close to being antiques.'

Although Bella smiled at Luke's last remark, she was concerned. 'Now you know I'm on the mend I want you to promise you'll go home and get some rest. When you come back tomorrow, we'll see how I'm feeling and if I'm up to it, you can bring the kids to visit at the weekend.'

Luke smiled, albeit faintly. 'I ought to tell you that it already is the weekend. Today's Saturday, and you've been unconscious for a while.'

Bella yawned. 'It's no wonder I feel tired if they're pumping me full of drugs.'

'I'll come back tomorrow, but now you must get some rest. By the way, get used to hearing that phrase. You'll be told it often enough in the next few weeks.'

Luke bent over the bed and as he kissed her, whispered, 'I love you, Bella.'

As she drifted off to sleep, she murmured, 'Yes, you definitely need a shave — and a shower.'

The following day, Bella looked and sounded a little better, Luke thought, and judged it was time to broach a difficult subject. He was prompted to this by a letter he had read when he returned home. 'Do you feel up to telling me what happened, if you can remember? I've got Dottie's version and there was a constable here while you were unconscious, badgering me for information and asking when he could see you. He'll be back.'

Bella moistened her lips and began to tell Luke all she could recall. 'I was crossing that junction near home, the one with all the trees around it. Dottie was behind me. I was leading the way, but I didn't see the tanker until it was too late. He must have been going at a hell of a lick, because one minute he wasn't there, the next he was right on top of me.' Bella paused. 'The one thing I did see was the logo on the front of the truck. It was one of ours.'

'I know, Dottie told me.'

* * *

Over the following three months, Luke Fisher's involvement as head of one of the leading trading groups in Australia was reduced to a three-day working week. Luke had taken on board everything Bella's surgeon had advised him on the best way to ensure she suffered no ill effects from the accident. Luke was particularly conscious of the need for Bella to avoid any sort of exertion and not to lift heavy weights, even after her broken arm had healed and her knee had improved.

When Bella protested or complained that she was bored and had nothing to do, Luke told her firmly, 'I came too close to losing you for there to be any argument about this. You are the most precious thing in my life and I will not take the chance of anything bad happening to you. Apart from me, you've the children to think of, so you must be doubly careful for their sake.'

When he put it like that Bella complied, reluctantly.

In what little time he had in the office, Luke enlisted the help of his brother-in-law Elliott. Through him, Luke sought information regarding the driver of the tanker that had almost cost Bella her life. Unprepared to take the simplistic view of the accident adopted by the police, Luke asked Elliot to make discreet enquiries about the driver, his daily itinerary and to seek for any underlying cause of the collision rather than sheer recklessness.

'I know the police have arrested him because they worked out that he was speeding, but I want to know why it was that he felt he had to go so fast. And why was he working on a Sunday? If he had been set an unrealistic daily schedule it might be that the blame for what happened lies higher up the chain. Don't just check up on him, see what you can find out about other drivers, in particular if there have been many instances of them being given speeding tickets or being stopped by police.'

Luke thought for a moment then added an important amendment. 'On second thoughts, get Josh to do the investigative work. I've a couple of reasons for thinking that would be better. For one, people won't automatically link Josh to Bella as they would if it was her brother asking questions, and for another, Josh is ideally equipped for clandestine work.'

'How do you mean?' Elliot asked.

'Let's just say Josh has hidden talents.'

Elliot shrugged and walked away, puzzled by the cryptic statement.

The event that had prompted Luke's request was the letter he'd received from the driver of the tanker involved, while Bella was in hospital. In the letter, the driver made no excuses or attempt to shift the blame elsewhere, admitting his fault, and accepting full responsibility for the injuries caused. What Luke found strange was the fact that all their drivers had to pass a gruelling selection process and were sent on regular refresher courses. One of the key areas their tutors stressed with great emphasis was the highly dangerous nature of the cargo they were in charge of, and the potentially horrific consequences should their fuel tank be punctured or the fuel ignited through either accident, design or pure carelessness.

Although Bella protested that she was now able to undertake minor tasks, particularly as time elapsed, she found it well-nigh impossible to get Luke to agree.

'I've told you before, I'm not prepared to risk you harming yourself by trying to run before you can walk,' Luke told her. 'I want to be certain that you're fully recovered and then we'll see. But before then I'll need your doctor's approval, and that's why I've arranged for you to see him next week. After that, if he gives the go-ahead, you can take over some of the less taxing jobs, but if he says no, you'll have to be patient a while longer.'

Unusually for someone with such an impetuous nature, Bella accepted the restrictions, purely because it demonstrated, better than any words could, the depth of Luke's love for her. Apart from his concern over Bella, Luke had another major worry that had come to his attention during the period when he was spending more time surrounded by his family than previously. This was the noticeable decline in the health of Bella's father when every few days he walked along the road between the homesteads to visit his daughter. Since the death of his wife, Patrick Finnegan had become a shadow of the extroverted, fun loving and energetic spirit of earlier years. It showed in his thoughts, words and actions. The vibrant force that had seen him manage a multi-million pound, highly diverse trading empire, nursing it through any number of adversities and harsh trading conditions was gone, blown away by the tragedy of Louise's untimely death.

Now, but for the care and daily monitoring by Elliot and Dottie, plus the distraction provided by his lively grandchildren, Patrick's decline would have been even more rapid. Despite all the attention being lavished on him however, the signs of his decay were becoming all too apparent.

CHAPTER THIRTY-FOUR

Despite Rachael's optimism, Sonny had entertained serious doubts as to how effective their grandson's presence on their trip to Greece might prove. These reservations soon vanished once they reached Athens, their first port of call en route to Crete. Although he had played down his knowledge of the Greek language, Andrew's familiarity with words describing everyday objects and a rapidly growing collection of useful phrases quickly proved advantageous.

Tasks such as ordering food and drinks, arranging transport, and asking for directions, which would have totally baffled his grandparents, were accomplished with ease thanks to his growing mastery of the unfamiliar tongue. During the weeks of their sojourn in the Greek capital they visited every ancient site they could find, such as the Acropolis and Parthenon, plus the Ancient Agora, and the grave of the renowned, some would say notorious English poet, Lord Byron.

It was with some regret that the trio decided it was time to move on and once again Andrew's ability to speak and understand the language proved invaluable as he secured berths for them on a passenger ship sailing from the nearby port of Piraeus. They would make landfall in the north of Crete, in a port called Souda Bay, which, although they were at the time unaware of the fact, was the point where British troops, including Private William Cowgill, had disembarked some twenty years earlier.

Having secured lodgings in the nearby town of Chania, they spent several days wandering round the centre, where they saw ample evidence of previous invaders of the island, from the many Venetian and Turkish style buildings. Grimmer proof of a more recent hostile incursion came from the number of destroyed and bomb-damaged properties in and around the town centre. The Battle of Crete had been bitterly fought and the islanders' fierce resistance against a vastly superior, better equipped enemy had obviously come at a desperately high price.

Once Andrew had secured lodgings for his grandparents in a small taverna in the village of Vrisses, which he discovered was the closest point to the area they needed to visit, he bade them farewell, wishing them luck with this, the most vital and heart-rending leg of their travels. He was heading for Italy, he told them, on the first part of what he jokingly referred to as his Grand Tour. 'We'll have lots to tell Mum and Dad when we get back to England,' he told them on parting, 'and I think it'll be far more interesting than what's going on in England at present.'

'Don't be too sure of that,' Sonny cautioned him. 'Your parents thought much the same when they went off to fight in the Spanish Civil War. By the time they returned, one king had died, his successor had abdicated, another one had been crowned and we were about to declare war on Germany.'

Remembering that statement later, Sonny reflected on how prophetic his words had been, but in a way none of them would have wished for.

* * *

Once British Summer Time ended, the first indication that winter was only just on the horizon, and when Bonfire Night and the observance of Armistice Day were over, Mark and

Jenny Cowgill began discussing the forthcoming festive season. 'It's going to be a very quiet Christmas this year,' Jenny said, 'apart from you, me and Susan there will be nobody here.'

'I'm not so sure about the "quiet" bit,' Mark responded, 'not if Suzie keeps playing her transistor radio so loudly. Is it permanently set to maximum volume? If Andrew was here we could get him to turn it down. I get your meaning, though — I can't remember when the house was as empty as this. Even when we were away in Spain, the entire family, along with the Haighs and the Jones from Bradford, would gather here for the festivities. We'll just have to make the best of it, if only for Suzie's sake. At least she'll have our undivided attention. Let's hope we get some news from Mum and Dad before then, and who knows, even your son might think to drop us a line.'

'I don't see how that's fair,' Jenny protested. 'You only ever call him my son when he's done something wrong. I suppose you've forgotten your part in the process?'

'I do remember it, vaguely, but in case I've got it wrong perhaps you could remind me how it works.'

Jenny looked at him scornfully. 'That has to be the worst chat-up line of all time.'

Although Mark had been a little less than complimentary about their absent relatives' communication skills during the time they'd been away there had been some correspondence, even if it was neither regular nor laden down with facts. There had been two postcards to be precise, the first of these informing them that the trio had arrived in Athens, that they were safe and well and enjoying sightseeing. 'Two more old ruins among all the others,' Mark muttered on reading this.

'Don't be so rude about your Mum and Dad,' Jenny rebuked him. 'Look, Mum goes on to say that Andrew's Greek has proved extremely useful.'

'That makes a change, him being useful for anything.' Mark seemed to be set on teasing Jenny. It worked, but even as she was berating her husband Jenny failed to spot his hidden agenda, which was to prevent her pining and worrying about their son during his prolonged absence.

A later postcard sent them scurrying to the atlas in order to find the place it had been sent from. They failed to find the name of the town in the index, so Mark suggested they should check the page containing a map of Crete. After a moment he pointed to a location on the northern shore of the island. 'I reckon that must be the place. It's spelled Xania on the card and Chania on the map, but that might be down to the difference in language.'

Jenny turned the postcard over and read the message on the reverse. 'I think you're right, this says they've arrived in Crete and that the town is beautiful with a lot of old buildings and lovely views towards the mountains. Anyway, they're safe and well, which is what matters most.'

Despite Mark's derogatory comments about their son's failure to keep in touch, shortly before the end of November they received a postcard. This time they had no difficulty in identifying the location, even without his message. The picture on the front, the Colosseum in Rome, was too iconic to be mistaken. Andrew wrote that having seen his grandparents on their way to conduct the final part of their pilgrimage alone, he had moved on to Italy. 'Stating the obvious,' Mark muttered only to be rewarded by a baleful glare from Jenny.

'At least he's written, and he promises to send us a card from every stop on his way,' she replied tartly.

* * *

On reaching Vrisses, Sonny and Rachael encountered an unforeseen problem, that of finding someone with both a sufficiently good command of the English language and the knowledge of where to direct them. Although they were unaware of it at the time, the latter was compounded by a reluctance to divulge information. Recent wounds were still too raw for this subject to be broached without encountering a degree of suspicion, and in some cases overt hostility.

Eventually, after a couple of weeks' fruitless questioning, one man directed them to the proprietor of the village's only taxi, who they were told might be able to help. 'Should it be that Sifis does not knows, I am afraid you might have to be seeking for informations in some others places.'

Despite the serious nature of their quest, Sonny had difficulty disguising his amusement at the speaker's quaint phraseology. On reflection, he thought that the man's command of English, fractured though it might be, was certainly a good deal better than either his or Rachael's Greek.

The taxi driver had been reluctant to begin with. That was down to a misunderstanding. When the couple had approached him, the driver, taking in the man's erect bearing, deep blue eyes and greying-blond hair had initially mistaken them for Germans, and he would certainly not convey any German person to Xarani, or anywhere else in the Ximonia region. It would be like committing sacrilege — and probably make him an accessory to murder. Not only that, but his friends and fellow Cretans would despise him for what they would see as an act of treachery. However, when the man asked him the reason for his refusal the driver realized that he was British and his attitude changed instantly.

He apologized for the error, explaining that although he had no personal prejudice against German people, there was no way he would take foreigners to that area had they been other than British. 'They would not be safe, and they would not be welcome, for sure. However, as you are British peoples, this will not be problem to you. That is, how you say, a horse of a different colour, yes?' he added with a laugh.

It was then that the visitor surprised the taxi driver, in fact, shocked him. 'So you fought with the resistance, did you? That was a very brave thing to do.'

The driver stared suspiciously at him. 'Why do you think so?' he demanded.

'Your English is quite good, but the expression you used, that is very colloquial. I guess you might have learned it from a British agent. I was told that there were several of them operating in this area.' He didn't risk insulting the driver by adding that at times his phraseology was quaint.

'Were you a soldier?'

'I was, but I didn't serve in this area, or in the Second World War. My service took place during the earlier encounter.'

During their conversation, the driver had placed the luggage into the boot of his car and opened the rear door. The woman accepted the courtesy with a brief smile and a word of thanks before climbing into the back seat. As he closed the door, he reflected briefly that her expression soon changed back to one of sadness. The man, however, chose to sit alongside the driver in the front, gaining further approval from the Cretan.

The ancient taxi headed for the mountain road. Despite the assurances of the driver, his passengers were in considerable doubt if the vehicle would make it to their intended destination. They felt it was vital that they should reach the village because it was the nearest reference point they had to what they truly sought.

As they headed across the plain towards the towering mountains that they had been told housed their ultimate destination, their driver asked what the reason was for the English couple choosing to visit such a remote village as Xarani.

'We want to find the place where our son died,' the Englishwoman told him. 'He was killed during the retreat to Chora Sfakion in 1941.'

The driver automatically corrected her pronunciation of the tiny port from which the Allied troops had been evacuated following the Battle of Crete, but then asked, 'Is that all you know? That he died at a place nearby to Xarani?'

'We talked to some of his comrades and they told us that it was near the village that he died. He might be interred in a cemetery there. Alternatively, he might still be lying where he fell. All we know is that it was in the mountains close to Xarani.'

The driver frowned. 'It might have more difficulty than you think.' The driver crossed himself, the action causing him to let go of the steering wheel, to the mild alarm of his passengers. 'The problem would be knowning which graves is that of your son, because it is a sad thing to report that there would be heavy casualties in that regions. However, one way I can assure you of is this, for sure, there will be no bodies lying in the mountains. We would not be allowing any person after death, whether they had been friend or enemy, to remain lying unprotected, to be food for predators.'

Glancing in his rear-view mirror the driver saw the woman wince and hastily added, 'I can for sure state that nobody from our brave allies who lost their lives courageously defending Crete would ever be allowed to be remaining in unmarked places. If he died there, his body would have been recovered and placed to rest in the nearest graveyard along with those of our own peoples. I can also inform you, for sure, without dispute, that the burial would have taken place only after a service or blessing from the local priest. That is our tradition. This I can say for definite, because his sacrifice has the result of him becoming Cretan in the eyes of our villagers as if he was born on our island instead of yours.

'There is one way to which I might help with advice,' he continued, aware of how important identifying the exact place where their son had died was, and anxious to provide as much assistance as possible. 'Even if the position of his falling had been of too remote, the locals would in this instance have placed an *ikonokritos* there after they had covered the remains to protect them from the golden eagles, the vultures and the buzzards.'

'What is an *ikonokritos*?' Sonny asked.

'It is a small shrine, sometimes constructed of metals, sometimes of stones and into this the person's family or friends will place such small belongings for the deceased.' As he was speaking, the old car wheezed its way up the mountain side and round a bend on the road where the hillside plunged steeply towards the lower slopes. The driver pointed to the verge on their left. On the cliff edge they saw a small metal structure. 'There, *ikonokritos*,' he exclaimed. 'If those who were erecting the one in memorial to your son had been able to do this, they would have placed some small possessions of his inside the shrine and that would be helpful to identifying the exact locations.'

'That does seem a little more encouraging. All we were told was that it was somewhere in the mountains in this region, and we've already visited several other places, without success. However, Xarani is the last village on our list, so we have reserved a room at the *kafenion* there. The lady I spoke to on the telephone told me they do not as a rule take guests but would do so because we are English.'

'Perhaps when we reaches Xarani it would be of help for you to ask to speak with Kapitan Manolis. He was leader of *andartes* in that regions. If any person is knowning the whereabouts of the resting place of your son, he will be that man.'

'How will we find him?'

'You may ask anyone of the peoples, and if they remain still reluctant, you must inform them that Sifis the taxi advised you to request for him, and that Sifis would be unhappy if they fail to assist you. That should do the trick.'

There it was again, the unmistakeable English idiom. Sonny Cowgill smiled. He felt sure that before long he and Rachael would find out something about where and how Billy had died.

CHAPTER THIRTY-FIVE

Having received the all clear from the specialist handling Bella's case and seen the improvement at first hand, Luke decided that the time had come for him to return to work full-time. On the evening before he was due back in the office, Bella revealed her new plan to him. At first wary that she might be endangering herself in similar fashion to her cycling misadventure, by the time she finished telling him about it, the scheme had Luke's complete approval.

'It's actually in two parts,' Bella began. 'First of all, I still intend to keep fit, so I'm going to order some gymnastic equipment so I can do some exercise here at home. That has a double advantage because I'll be able to keep an eye on the ankle biters and I won't be at risk.'

'Bella, they're hardly ankle biters anymore. The youngest is five years old,' Luke shook his head, wondering what was coming next.

Bella shrugged and continued, 'The training's going to have to wait a few months though, until I'm certain I'm well enough to undergo a gruelling regime. The other part is something I can start on immediately, though. It stemmed from all this inactivity I've been forced to undergo while I've had a nursemaid and housekeeper taking care of my every need. I was tempted to keep it a secret and surprise you but having thought about it I realize I'll need your cooperation for it to work.'

Luke stared at her, his anxiety obvious. 'What is it you're thinking of this time?'

'I'm going to send away for a correspondence course. Once I enrol it will entail a lot of studying, some of it in the evenings and when I'm doing that I'll need you to mind the children. I won't be able to concentrate with the brood running riot.'

Luke grinned. 'I think I can manage that OK. What subject do you have in mind?'

'It came to me when I remembered something my father said a long time ago. He was talking about your mom and dad, and he told me that they used to work together, planning business strategy and so forth. I got to thinking that now all the ankle biters are at school, I'll be bored rigid, but I don't want to go back to my reporter's job. So, if you approve, I'm going to try and become proficient enough in business studies to be of some help at Fisher Springs.'

Luke reached across and hugged her. 'Darling, I think that's a wonderful idea.'

The revelation heightened Luke's optimism about his return to work. Her plans would, in his eyes as well as hers, strengthen even further the bond between them, making their partnership more complete than ever. Obviously, as Bella had pointed out, her active participation in the business would have to wait until she qualified. Nevertheless, the future was bright, a reflection of the lifetime collaboration his parents had enjoyed. James and Alice would, Luke knew, approve wholeheartedly of his choice of partner, and of the way the enterprise they had founded was progressing.

A stray thought caused Luke to smile. Bella's blunt, outspoken, no-nonsense habit of speaking her mind would, he guessed, ruffle a few feathers at Fisher Springs, and possibly elsewhere. That didn't worry him at all, because he knew her well enough to be certain that anything she said, or did, would be for his benefit and that of the company — and others would either have to like it or lump it.

* * *

During Luke's enforced absence, his role at Fisher Springs had been filled by Josh Jones, with assistance from Elliot Finnegan and the 'committee', as Josh categorized the panel of senior executives. This comprised principally the heads of each division within the group, thereby bringing to the table a wide range of skills, and an equally wide variety of priorities. Juggling the individual needs, while remaining impartial and focussing on the group's main objectives, presented Josh and Elliot with challenges such as they had never faced before. The need to ensure a healthy return from the group's activities had to be balanced with the provision of services that would benefit the community, and that was no easy task.

This might have proved daunting to many people, but Josh relished the opportunity to demonstrate that he was worthy of the faith that Luke Fisher had placed in him when he offered him a place on the board. In rising to that challenge Josh had drawn on his own ability, supplemented, perhaps subconsciously, by business practices and learning passed onto him by his stepfather, Simon Jones. During Luke's absence, Josh lost count of the number of times he had sought a solution to a problem by asking himself the question, 'How would Dad have handled this?'

Away from the office, Josh had one major concern, and this was only resolved a few days before Luke's return. Josh became increasingly aware that all was not well with Astrid. She was moody and liable to fly off the handle with little or no provocation, which was completely out of character. Her mood swings were so violent that one moment she would berate him for some perceived, usually trivial, domestic offence or oversight and then, before Josh had chance to do more than puzzle over her attitude or correct his misdemeanour, she would become loving, affectionate and cheerful.

He reached home one evening, fully expecting a virago to confront him with a sound dressing down for his late arrival. He had been detained by a task that he'd been performing at Luke's behest, conveyed via a message from Elliot. Josh had lost track of time, and entered the house on guard, ready to face a volley of abuse, or even some low flying kitchen utensils as punishment for a spoiled dinner.

As he was opening the front door, Josh wondered if Astrid was truly happy at their decision to make their home in Australia or if it would have been better for them to have remained in Europe, even possibly in England. Alternatively, he wondered if Astrid was bored, with little else to occupy her mind other than the fairly boring daily round of cleaning, cooking, washing, and ironing. Her only forays into town were shopping expeditions, apart from the rare occasions when Josh accompanied her or when they dined out.

He was more than a little surprised by the warmth of Astrid's greeting. Although she waved aside his apologies for his late homecoming, he was still wary, his caution heightened when she told him there was something they needed to discuss before they sat down for their evening meal.

She kept hold of his hand, leading him into the sitting room, where she positioned him in his favourite armchair. Instead of taking her usual place on the sofa, Astrid sat on Josh's knee, her arm around his neck, her slim fingers caressing him gently. 'I have an important question for you, Josh. I need an honest answer so that I can plan our future properly.'

Josh hardly dared to ask the question for fear of the reply. Did she want to return to Europe? 'What is it?' he asked, dreading the answer.

'How good are you at changing nappies?'

The question was so unexpected that it took a few seconds before the penny dropped. 'You're not, are you?' Even though Astrid nodded, Josh could hardly believe it.

'I certainly am. I knew something was wrong because my period was late, and because I was so grumpy, but I was still not sure. Then I began to feel sick, so I went to the doctor this morning, and that was when I knew without doubt. So, back to my original question,' Astrid grinned, teasing him, 'how good is your nappy changing?'

Josh's reply surprised her, and the explanation saddened them both. 'Actually, I have had quite a bit of practice.' His face clouded over as he continued, 'I used to babysit my sisters when Mum and Dad wanted an evening out. You remember me telling you about them, don't you?'

Astrid nodded, tears welling up as she recalled what her late mother-in-law had told her about the bombing raid that had killed Josh's half-sisters and left his stepfather crippled.

Instinctively, her heart touched by this memory, Astrid made a suggestion she felt was right and she hoped that Josh would approve of. 'If the baby I am carrying turns out to be a girl,' she suggested, 'how would you feel about us calling her Daisy Emily, in honour of your sisters?'

Josh's eyes misted over as he embraced her. 'That is a lovely idea, and perhaps, if you wouldn't object, if it's a boy we might name him Simon? What do you think?'

'I think I love you, Josh Jones, and that is also a lovely idea.'

CHAPTER THIRTY-SIX

Although Josh was delighted by Astrid's news, he curbed his desire to share this with anyone at work, being particularly reluctant for it to reach Luke Fisher, given the harrowing outcome of Bella's accident. It was only when Luke had answered Josh's question about Bella's health and recovery and had congratulated his deputy on the excellent work he had put in while he'd been away, that he enquired about Astrid.

Something in Josh's demeanour must have given the game away, because even as he was telling Luke that she was OK, Luke followed up the question by stating, 'My guess is that you've got some exciting news that you're hesitant about telling me in case I get upset. And if I'm correct, that means you've got a nerve-wracking few months ahead of you.'

After Josh acknowledged the accuracy of Luke's guess and been warmly congratulated, Luke went on to give him some sound advice that was experience based. 'Enjoy your free time while you can because you won't get any once the baby arrives. And when you've got three of them wreaking havoc, and waking you at all hours of the night, you'll begin to wonder what you did with the hours of the day that have now been lost to you. By the way, things don't improve as the kids get older, the problems just get different — and bigger.'

Eventually, their conversation turned to the enquiries Josh had made regarding the background to Bella's accident. 'I'm not going to defend the driver,' Josh began, 'because there's no way he isn't to blame for the collision. I managed to obtain a copy of the police report and they estimate he was going half as fast again as the speed limit on that road. They worked that out from the skid marks, the point of impact, and the position of the remnants of your wife's bicycle.'

'How did you manage to get hold of that report?' Luke asked, momentarily side-tracked.

'It's probably better that you don't know,' Josh told him with a wry smile. 'Anyway, the copy is there in amongst the other paperwork, but it would be advisable if you weren't to go showing it around to all and sundry.'

'Would you care to summarise the information you've gathered? I trust your judgement on this and I reckon you'll be a bit more impartial than I would by reading it. Apart from that I'm going to have plenty to do going through all those other reports you've left me. I never realized how much paper we generate in such a short space of time.'

'Like I said, the driver has to be held accountable, but I don't think it's entirely his fault.' Josh glanced at Luke and saw his expression darken. 'Sorry, I put that badly. I don't for one minute want to suggest that Bella was in any way to blame. What I discovered when I started nosing around was very disturbing, to put it mildly. Apparently, the head of the distribution section of the haulage division has implemented a different regime and put in place new delivery targets. He's done this totally off his own bat, without obtaining sanction from his superiors. That's probably because he knows they would never have agreed to it.

'What he's done is to increase the workload of all drivers and adding weekend deliveries. Along with their new itiner-aries, he's imposed penalties for any of them who fail to meet target. To be on the safe side I tested three of those routes using my own car. I drove at the maximum speed allowed by law and allowed sufficient minimum time to cover each drop-off en route. In all three cases my journey took almost two hours longer than the day's schedule demanded.'

'Wait a minute, Josh, did you say the section head had imposed penalties on the drivers for non-performance? How does that work?'

'He docked their salaries on a pro-rata basis, depending on how late they were.'

Josh glanced up and saw the look of horror on Luke's face.

'Can you prove all this?'

'I certainly can.' Josh's expression was grim as he continued, 'I got written evidence from a couple of men who resigned in protest, plus three more who are currently still working for us. Before they agreed to tell me anything, I had to guarantee their job security, because apparently this character has made all sorts of threats about instant dismissal, poor references, and the like.'

'In that case I want you to get rid of him — with no severance pay. If he objects, show him the evidence and then follow it up with a message. Tell him you've shown all this to me and that he's lucky, because the way I feel at the moment I'm tempted to stand him in the middle of the street and drive a tanker at him at full speed.'

* * *

That evening, Luke told Bella what Josh had discovered and the action he'd instructed should be taken. 'The man who ordered those drivers to achieve impossible targets is as much responsible for what happened to you as the driver — more so, perhaps. I'm not excusing the guy who was behind the wheel, but he was placed in a very difficult position. With a wife and two kids to support he couldn't afford to lose his job which was what the cretin in charge of the distribution network threatened.'

When he considered whether or not to tell her about the root cause of the accident, Luke had been persuaded to overcome his reluctance by the knowledge that he and Bella had never kept any secrets from one another. However, he had a back-up plan to divert her attention from a subject he knew would anger or upset her. After dealing with that topic, he opened the shiny new briefcase that had been Bella's Christmas present to him and removed a wad of folders. Bella eyed them with curiosity mixed with a little suspicion until Luke explained what they contained and his purpose in bringing them home.

'These are summaries and details of the group's recent activities, together with reports from Josh, Elliot, and the head of the UK operation, Jessica Binks. I thought that if you're serious about getting involved at Fisher Springs it would help if you became familiar with different aspects of the day-to-day running of the business and how we're progressing. The more you know beforehand the better equipped you'll be when the time comes to join the ranks. It might also prove useful in your studies if you can relate the theoretical questions to real life situations. One other benefit is that instead of waiting for answers to some of the questions you'll be faced with you can ask me — always providing I know the answers, that is.'

Bella was thrilled, more so by the knowledge that Luke had bought into her scheme so thoroughly. 'That's a great idea, Luke, and so thoughtful.' She eyed the pile of folders. 'Where do I start?'

'I reckon we should take half each, read them through, and make notes if necessary, then swap over and afterwards we can compare our findings. If you're happy with the idea we can make it a regular event, say once a month, what do you reckon?'

'Pass them over and let's get cracking, shall we?'

Later that evening, the wisdom of Luke's decision to begin Bella's involvement in the group's management struc-ture paid early dividends following her reaction to one report, and her interpretation of Luke's reading of it.

'I can't get to grips with what's happening in England,' he told her. 'This policy of drawing their horns in and tightening their credit control seems counter-productive to me.'

Bella looked up from her task of trying to get her head around the statistics provided by the farming division and concentrated instead on Luke's comment. 'Why do you say that? We don't know how things are in the UK. They were pretty grim when we visited England, and although they might have improved since then, for all we know they could be trying to imitate how your son and heir used to be, by trying to run before they can walk. Just because we're enjoying a boom here doesn't mean that everyone is doing as well. Apart from that, I don't think you can complain. After all, you can't have it both ways.'

'Luke frowned. 'What do you mean by that last remark?'

'It wasn't too long ago that you were foaming at the mouth over what you saw as their reckless, ill-thought-out extravagance. That was until Josh and I pointed out the error of your ways. As a result, from what I read in their report it seems as if their new divisions are now thriving and making significant contributions to their bottom line. Might I also point out that the insurance company you bought on the back of their innovative idea is also doing rather well. Having blown your top about them being spendthrift, I don't think you can complain about them now being overcautious. Incidentally, did you notice Jessica's comment about who instigated the policy over there?'

Luke smiled ruefully. 'You're dead right, as usual, Bella. I think the sooner you can start at Fisher Springs, the better. I'm beginning to wonder if your head for business isn't far superior to mine. I don't reckon I'll ever be a patch on my father, that's for sure.'

'Luke Fisher, don't you ever talk such complete rubbish again. Remember what we spoke about last week, when I reminded you of what my dad told me. Yes, your father must have been an exceptionally good businessman, but he had a lot of help, both from your mother and then later from my father as well. What you've done recently merely replicates his policy. You brought Josh and Elliot into the company, nurtured them and, once you saw their potential, promoted them, and gave them scope. It was you who recognized the latent talent in both men and I'd say that proves you've got an exceptional head for business.' Bella paused and then added, 'Sorry, I didn't give you chance to answer my question.'

'About who instigated the UK policy? No, I didn't notice.' Luke went to pick the file up but Bella stopped him.

'It was Paul Sugden, who, if you remember also came up with the insurance company idea. And who was it who gave Paul his chance with Fisher Springs? Oh, yes, I remember, it was me. Well actually, it was you, and that's yet another example of your excellent judgement.'

'I hope you're right, Bella.'

'I am right, Luke. I knew it from the start. I was only a kid but I saw the potential in you, not simply as a lover, but also as a brave, honest, decent and caring person. The fact that you're a good businessman is only a bonus.'

Bella paused and stood up, moving towards Luke as she lowered her voice to little more than a whisper. 'So, now that we've got that side of things cleared up, how about you display your talent as a lover. It is bedtime after all, and we haven't had chance to enjoy ourselves for far too long.'

Later, as they were dropping off to sleep, Luke murmured, 'One thing I do know for certain, I'm the luckiest bloke in the whole of Australia.'

CHAPTER THIRTY-SEVEN

Sonny and Rachael's first glimpse of the village that was their destination came as quite a surprise. Sifis slowed the taxi to little more than walking pace, which made Sonny concerned that the ancient vehicle's engine might be about to give up the ghost.

Sifis' opening words reassured him a little. 'I thought you should see where we are going better at a smaller pace.' He pointed towards the far distance, where, away to their right, they could just see a collection of small houses. 'That is Xarani.'

As they got nearer, Sonny stared at the group of small, whitewashed cottages that appeared to be on the verge of tumbling down the near-vertical slope of the mountain. 'They look to be in a dangerous position,' he said, voicing his thoughts subconsciously. 'It makes you wonder why the builders chose that particular location.'

The taxi driver chuckled. 'Those houses have been there for many centuries. Peoples from the village have been told from their parents, and earlier, that there was a settlement close to Xarani during the times of the Minoan civilisation, but the inhabitants and their dwellings were wiped away by a huge volcanic eruption and *seismos*.'

'*Seismos*, does that mean earthquake?' Rachael asked.

'That is correct. There is also much evidence of other occupations of the regions. I have knowledge of this from my cousin Andreas. He found a Roman coin of gold within these mountains bearing the head from the Emperor Constantine.'

Sifis crossed himself once more to the renewed alarm of his passengers, as they were now on a narrow mountain road that seemed to comprise one hairpin bend after another. Having regained control of the steering wheel he continued, 'Constantine was the son of St Helena, who discovered Christ's tomb.'

Sonny's mind went back almost fifty years to when he was a schoolboy and he recalled one of his lessons. 'I was taught a little bit about St Helena,' he told Sifis and Rachael. 'Apparently she was married to a general in the Roman army and they were garrisoned near York. That is an English city close to where we live,' he explained for Sifis's benefit, 'although the Romans called it Eboracum. There is a big open area in York which is named St Helen's Square in her honour.'

It was less than half an hour later when they reached their destination. As they neared the centre of the village, Sifis pulled the taxi to a halt outside what appeared to be a tiny eating establishment of the type Rachael and Sonny had learned were called *kafenions*.

'Here is where you have rooms to stay in,' Sifis explained. 'First, I will introduce you to Kyria Sofia, who owns the house. She is my cousin,' he explained.

Sonny turned to Rachael. 'Andrew told me that "Kyria" is a mark of respect for women, a bit like calling someone a lady at home. I think for men they say "Kyrie", which is like mister.'

Rachael nodded, determined not to disrespect anyone.

As Sifis was removing their suitcases from the boot of the taxi an amply built middle-aged lady came bustling from within the building, threading her way through the tables and chairs that covered what passed for a pavement. She greeted

Sifis with a volley of rapid-fire Greek, which seemed to surprise the driver, before she turned to Rachael and Sonny.

Sofia made a bow before greeting them. 'Welcome, welcome, it is an honour for me that you have chosen to stay in my house. Please take a seat and I will bring you refreshment from your journey while Sifis transports your cases.'

They obeyed the command, somewhat baffled and a trifle overwhelmed by the effusive greeting from their hostess. The explanation or at least part of it came a short while later when Sifis, having taken their luggage inside, emerged and returned to where they were seated.

'I must pay you for the taxi ride,' Sonny told him, reaching for his wallet.

'There is no payment to be made,' Sifis replied. 'I am sorry that I did not understand who you are until Sofia mentioned your name. I am honoured to have been of some service to you.'

Sonny attempted to insist, but Sifis waved his protests aside. 'It was only when Sofia told me that I truly understood your desire to visit Xarani. Now, I must tell you that a taxi ride is of small consequences compared to what I and many locals peoples here owe to your family.'

Seeing their deepening perplexity, Sifis continued, 'The story is not mine to tell, but Sofia explained to me that you will very shortly be joined by a man who is very anxious to meet with you. He wishes to express his gratitudes and will tell you all that occurred here. I must leave now, but before I go I should tell you that you will not be able to make payments here. Not for your rooms or your meals or your drinks. Also, when you wish for another taxi journey simply make request to Sofia and I will arrive pronto. It has been a pleasure to meet with you and I am proud to be of assistance.'

With a courtly bow, Sifis turned and jumped into the driver's seat and started the car engine, before waving farewell, leaving Sonny and Rachael staring at one another, completely bemused.

The taxi was barely out of sight, its exhaust fumes still lingering in the still air when their hostess reappeared with a tray. On it were three small cups of Greek coffee, accompanied by three glasses of water and a plate containing a mound of biscuits they had learned were called *paximathia*. As Sofia was placing these on the table, Rachael asked, 'Please tell us, Kyria Sofia, why are we being given such special treatment?'

'You will understand perhaps when my cousin Manolis arrives.' Sofia looked along the narrow street and exclaimed, 'Here he is now ready to meet you.'

The tall, darkhaired Cretan wore a beard, neatly trimmed as did many of his compatriots. Under the whiskers he was ruggedly good-looking, with dark, intelligent eyes that on occasion sparkled with humour and at other times reflected his grave, almost sombre expression. He bowed slightly as he introduced himself. Sonny didn't attempt to remember the surname, it being to his mind both too long and all but unpronounceable, but concentrated instead on the man's Christian name.

'Manolis?' Sonny asked. 'As in Kapitan Manolis?'

The islander bowed again in acknowledgement and gestured to a vacant chair. 'It is permitted?' he asked.

As Manolis sat down, Sonny noticed that he positioned himself in such a way that his legs avoided contact with the frame of the chair. This might have been out of politeness, so that he was facing both of them, but Sonny thought it was more likely a way of easing the discomfort caused by the frame. Cretan chairs design left a lot to be desired, and Sonny, no mean carpenter, had on occasion since their arrival in Greece wanted to attempt a modification.

'I must tell you that your visit to Xarani has been eagerly awaited or rather, should I say, wished for.'

'Why is that, Kyrie Manolis?' Rachael asked.

'It is because you bear a name that is much honoured here in Xarani. I believe you must be relatives of William Cowgill, am I correct in thinking this?'

Sonny nodded, completely confused by the question, while Rachael gave a small hiccup as she fought to avoid bursting into tears. After a moment or two she managed to say, 'William was our son.'

Manolis reached forward and placed one hand over Rachael's, the other gripping that of Sonny in a gesture of sympathy as he continued, 'I am uncertain how much or how little you know of the events that happened on the day your son died, but I will explain. That will give you a true understanding of why your son is so revered in our village.' He took a sip of his coffee as he gathered his thoughts.

'I and six of my fellow members of the *andartes* were guiding a troop of English soldiers who had been stranded after the withdrawal from Chora Sfakion. During the retreat the soldiers had lost most of their weapons. Your son was carrying a sub-machine gun but had only a few rounds of ammunition left. We had almost made it to safety and were about to begin our descent to the coast where a British submarine was patrolling ready to pick the men up. Unfortunately, at that moment we were seen by a German fighter pilot who was on patrol. He turned the aircraft and banked away and it was obvious when he returned that he was moving in for the kill.'

Manolis paused and took a drink of water, the emotions stirred by recounting what had happened clearly taking their toll. 'Had it not been for your son's courageous and selfless actions many, if not all, of the men on that mountain would have died that day. We lost three of the *andartes*, plus two British soldiers, but the others, I think in total twenty-three, survived. William might have been among that number, or he might have been slaughtered along with the rest of us, had he not chosen the brave path he did.'

Another sip of water quietened Manolis's obvious distress, and after a moment he continued his account. 'William managed to move away from the rest of the group and drew the pilot's attention by firing one or two shots towards the plane. The pilot focussed on where the threat was coming from and turned his venom on William, allowing the rest of us to reach cover. Although William was already wounded, he waited, holding off until the plane was at really close range and then, using up all his ammunition, he directed it towards

321

the plane's cockpit. The pilot returned this and at such close range William stood no chance. But he must have wounded or killed the pilot, because the plane plunged into the sea only a few hundred metres away.'

By the end of Kapitan Manolis's narrative both Sonny and Rachael were in tears.

'But how do you know this was our son? How can you be sure?' Rachael was in despair.

The Cretan reached inside his pocket and taking Rachael's hand, gently placed a leather bootlace with two metal discs attached onto her palm.

'His dog tags,' she gasped. Through her tears she looked at them. They were etched with a number, beneath which was stamped 'Cowgill W'.

'We knew him as Billy,' Manolis added, as Rachael passed them to Sonny.

Manolis's voice was gentle as he continued, 'I know that nothing I can say will ease the pain of your suffering, but I must tell you that we brought your son's body here to Xarani, where our priest conducted the funeral and burial service, which every man, woman and child in the village were proud to attend. William lies here, alongside those of his colleagues and mine who perished that day, for they were all comrades. If you wish, I will gladly accompany you to the graveyard, but if you would prefer to undertake that journey alone, I understand.'

After a while, Sonny managed to reply. 'Perhaps we could go with you in a little while, Kapitan Manolis, because I think we need some time to ourselves first. Perhaps tomorrow would be in order?'

'I am at your command, whenever you need me. One thing more I must tell you. During the years since your son's sacrifice there have been several children born in this village. Of the boys, three of them have been named Vasilis, which is the closest equivalent in Greek to William. I do not know how long you were planning to stay on Crete, but if you are here on January 1st then you must come to Xarani. That is the feast day of Agios Vasilis, and here in Xarani we use it to mark our respect for your son, to give thanks for his life and to honour his memory.'

Sonny and Rachael agreed to meet with Manolis the following morning, when he would take them to where Billy was buried.

After he left, they retired to the room their hostess had allocated. She opened the door, her anxiety plain. 'I hope this will be good for you,' she stammered, 'it is the best I have. We do not receive visitors here.'

Having assured Sofia that it would be fine, Sonny and Rachael looked around. The fixtures and fittings, although far from modern, were in good condition and the room looked spotlessly clean. A pair of French windows led to a small balcony with views across the village towards the sea. They stood for a while, staring out in the direction they knew was where their son had died.

'Are you alright, Rachael?' Sonny asked tentatively. He had almost been overcome by the details Kapitan Manolis had given them and dreaded to think how Rachael must be feeling. As so often before, her strength and willpower surprised him.

She turned and smiled, albeit a trifle sadly, but her reply was more than a little upbeat. 'I am, darling, because I am proud to have learned that we gave birth to a son who is a true hero. That thought sustains me even in this hour of darkness. My guilt over the parting with Billy will always remain, but the knowledge that there are so many men who would not be alive today but for his sacrifice will sustain me. And when we visit his grave, I shall ask for his pardon.'

* * *

Having met with Kapitan Manolis as agreed, the Cretan guided them to the seaward end of the village street, where, on a narrow, flat headland the church and graveyard were situated. As they approached the small, whitewashed building whose purpose was denoted by the cross affixed to the gable end, they noticed a group of men gathered by the gate.

'These men are my colleagues and they have come here to meet you and pay their respects. They are the members of the *andartes* who were with us that day. Here also is Papa Georgiou, our priest. It was he who conducted the service when we laid your son to rest.'

After shaking hands with the men as they were introduced in turn, Sonny and Rachael moved inside the graveyard, where Kapitan Manolis and Papa Georgiou guided them towards a grave in the centre of the plot. Alongside the grave stood an *ikonokritos* containing only a candle.

'We kept the identity tags safe in the hope someone would come, as you have,' Kapitan Manolis explained. 'But we had nothing to add on the hillside. That is why the *ikonokritos* is here, waiting.'

Rachael looked at the photograph in her hand, a young cricketer flushed with success. She reached forward, opened the front, and placed the photo inside. 'Forgive me, Billy,' she whispered.

She stepped back, and with Sonny beside her looked at the gravestone.

The inscription written in English simply gave the name William Cowgill, under which was a long, indecipherable text in Greek.

Seeing the priest and their guide standing a few yards away, obviously not wishing to intrude on their grief, Rachael beckoned for them to come forward. They did so, and the priest held their hands as he offered them some words of comfort and recited a short prayer, which Kapitan Manolis translated. 'Your son is at peace here because we chose the most fitting place for him to rest. It is in the heart of the graveyard, because we carry his memory in our hearts every day.'

'What is the inscription on the stone?' Sonny asked.

'We wanted the message to express our feelings and to obtain this and to ensure it was appropriate we waited and then consulted with one of the British agents after they came here to Crete to help us in our struggle against the Nazis. He listened to our story and then suggested that it was the most fitting tribute he could think of.

'It is a quotation I believe comes from the Gospel of St John the Evangelist. In English, it reads, "Greater love hath no man than this, that a man lay down his life for his friends."'

THE END

ACKNOWLEDGEMENTS

Thank you to the real Patrick Finnegan, whose generous charitable donation gave me the opportunity to take his, and his family's, names in vain.

My thanks especially to Val, for countless hours of hard work, proofreading, copy-editing, and making coffee, the list goes on!

And to Jasper and all the team at Joffe Books, Emma, Steph, Nina, and Hanna, for their faith in my work.

ALSO BY BILL KITSON

THE COWGILL FAMILY SAGA
Book 1: BROTHERS AND SISTERS OF BYLAND
CRESCENT
Book 2: STORM CLOUDS OVER BYLAND
CRESCENT
Book 3: COMING HOME TO BYLAND CRESCENT

Thank you for reading this book.

If you enjoyed it please leave feedback on Amazon or Goodreads, and if there is anything we missed or you have a question about, then please get in touch. We appreciate you choosing our book.

Founded in 2014 in Shoreditch, London, we at Joffe Books pride ourselves on our history of innovative publishing. We were thrilled to be shortlisted for Independent Publisher of the Year at the British Book Awards.

www.joffebooks.com

We're very grateful to eagle-eyed readers who take the time to contact us. Please send any errors you find to corrections@joffebooks.com. We'll get them fixed ASAP.